BY BRENDAN DUFFY

The Storm King

House of Echoes

The

STORM
KING

The

STORM
KING

A Novel

Brendan Duffy

BALLANTINE BOOKS
NEW YORK

Copyright © 2018 by Brendan Duffy
Map copyright © 2018 by David Lindroth Inc.

Published in the United States by Ballantine Books, an imprint of Random House, a division of Penguin Random House LLC, New York.

BALLANTINE and the HOUSE colophon are registered trademarks of Penguin Random House LLC.

Hardback ISBN 978-0-8041-7814-3
Ebook ISBN 978-0-8041-7815-0

Printed in the United States of America on acid-free paper

randomhousebooks.com

9 8 7 6 5 4 3 2 1

First Edition

Book design by Debbie Glasserman

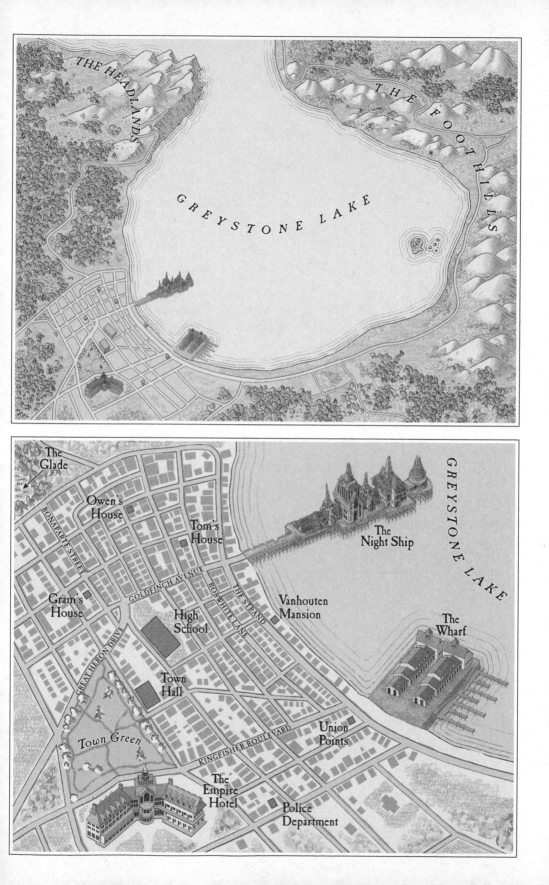

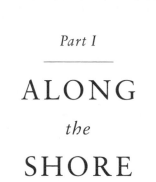

Part I

ALONG

the

SHORE

THE BOY WHO FELL

I

FOR NATE, SATURDAYS in the spring mean baseball.

His teammates think playing the outfield is ignominious, but he likes it. There's a meditative appeal to a morning spent watching for hard-struck balls as they spin and slow at the height of their parabolas.

He's not the most attentive of fielders, but Nate does all right at the plate. He's third on Greystone Lake's junior varsity team in RBIs, and when he takes warm-up swings the shouts from the bleachers are authentic.

His mother, father, and brother are among those cheering this last Saturday in April. It's just a scrimmage against North Hampstead, so Mom's attendance is unusual. She goes to the real games, but most weekends find her up with the sun and working in her vegetable garden. Nate's little brother, Gabe, would play in the grass as Mom fussed over her plants. Neither of them are in the garden today, because Mom strained her back, and her seedlings can survive a few days without weeding. Gabe doesn't mind, because he likes baseball.

For some time, he's been counting the days until he graduates from T-ball. Dad doesn't make it to all of Nate's games, either, but this is the kind of day that makes every cell in your body sing, and he can read the *Times* during lulls in the action as easily as he could at their kitchen table.

Nate's team wins thanks to a triple he hits in the final inning. Though the matchup isn't an important one, there are whoops and smiles all around. His coach gives Nate the game ball, and Nate feels proud that his family was there to watch him play well and win.

Mom calls him her baseball hero. What type of pie would her baseball hero like for dessert tonight? she wants to know. There's an organic market at the Wharf, and she'll make any kind he wants. She asks to see Nate's game ball, and that makes him feel proud, too.

His team plays on one of the high school's fields, near the center of Greystone Lake, and it's just a few minutes' drive from there to the Wharf in Dad's old black Passat. The Wharf itself is only a few minutes from the McHales' home on Great Heron Drive. The town along the shore is not a large one.

It's early in the year for tourists, but there's still a good crowd at the market. Visitors browse for honey, jams, and baked goods while the locals from the Lake and nearby towns buy produce trucked from afar and fish fresh from their home waters. The sky being bell clear and the breeze warm, Dad suggests they picnic in the headlands. This isn't something they do often, but it's an intoxicating day. The lake glitters in the sun, and from that height the town will look like a jewel set into the crown of mountains.

They buy baguettes, cured meats, cheeses, and sun-brewed iced teas. Gabe wheedles himself a bottle of artisanal root beer. Vendors sell cherries from California and strawberries from Arizona, but Nate is drawn to the first of the season's peaches from Florida. He touches them as carefully as he would an infant's head. Mom buys a basket of the fruit.

The Passat's trunk is full of baseball equipment and a pile of uncorrected papers from Dad's AP U.S. history class, so Dad places the bags of food in the back with Nate and Gabe while Mom rides up front with the peaches on her lap. Nate's game ball is still where she left it on her seat. To avoid sitting on it, she gently places the grass-stained ball in the basket with the peaches.

This is important.

Nate realizes later that it had all been important.

The headlands rise along Greystone Lake's western shore. Hiking paths are carved throughout the protected woodlands, with parking lots marking the major trailheads. Among the nooks of interest that dot the headlands, Nate's parents favor a particular meadow. In the deep of the old-growth forest, an open space slopes toward the water and offers an unmatched view of the lake and town.

To reach it, they drive beyond the great houses of the Strand, where the boulevard branches from the shore to the headlands. The road there climbs the hills in switchbacks above the lake; it's closed during the winter months when its blind turns are too treacherous to be passable.

But this Saturday in April, winter is a distant memory. The wind carries ripe forest smells into the car, and waterfowl patrol the shore below them.

Nate is watching one such flock when the Passat swerves and he's knocked hard against the window glass. He looks up to see a green Jeep with flashing lights looming beyond the windshield. His mother gasps, and the basket of peaches overturns in her lap. There's another car now, a shiny SUV straddling the center line like an elephant walking a tightrope. Dad accelerates to get the Passat out of its path. A curve is just ahead.

Nate sees Dad stomp the brakes, but their speed does not change. He hears Mom scream his father's name as she bends to pull at something at his feet. The peaches, Nate realizes. *No,* he thinks a moment later. *The baseball.* Dad cannot slow the car because it's wedged under the brake. Mom tries to pull it away, but it will not budge while Dad presses all of his strength into the pedal.

Gabe reaches across the space between them to grab Nate's hand. In the flurry of the moment, this surprises Nate as much as the knock against the window, because Gabe made it very clear on his last birthday, his sixth, that he expected everyone to stop treating him like a baby. Nate looks at his brother and sees that his mouth is wide open but no sound is coming from it.

He wants to tell Gabe not to worry, but then they're through the guardrail. The bright sky that had filled the windshield darkens into the empty slate of the lake. No more than a few seconds have passed since Nate had his head rapped against the glass, but that life is already over. He realizes this when Mom turns to look at him.

He often tries to recall the look in her eyes. What does a mother try to convey to her child when they have moments to live? Fear or regret? Sadness or pity? When Nate summons her expression in that instant, he tries to find love. But the only thing on her face is horror. They fall too quickly for it to be anything else.

In the movies Nate has seen, events like this are shown in slow-motion. This underscores the importance of the scene. In these fraught seconds, the slightest look and gesture is given momentous gravity. Consciousness extends as it senses the imminence of its conclusion.

But these moments don't stretch for Nate. The Passat falls like the ton and a half of metal that it is. One moment they are weightless and his mother is looking at him, and then the windshield explodes and the lake takes them.

NATE COMES BACK to himself on the rocks. There's a tortured sound around him. A raw and gasping cry like a person torn in half. It echoes across the water and up the cliffs as if it cannot find a place to rest. His chest feels as if it's crushed in the fist of a giant. To breathe is agony. He cannot feel his arm, and his baseball uniform is now more red than white. His first thought is that the lake's glittering surface was a lie, because he is cold to his marrow. There's a phantom memory of ice water locked in a vise around his throat.

His body is wracked with pain and seizing with chills. He wipes blood from his eyes and searches the stony water for his family, but they are gone.

Only then does he realize that the scream he hears is his own.

One

Nate had missed holidays and weddings and more birthdays than he could count. It took a funeral to bring him home.

A Greyhound got him to Syracuse, where he transferred to a local line that made the long haul to the North Country. Eight hours after leaving Port Authority's sticky fluorescence, he was again in the foothills of the Adirondacks.

A medical journal sat open on his lap, though he hadn't read a word for miles. Instead, he was on his phone, listening to one of his section's residents detail this morning's battles. White blood cell counts, biopsy data, and scan analyses. Numbers falling, rising, and static. Today, more skirmishes were being won than lost: the closest thing to victory anyone who fights cancer could hope for. But the failures ached.

He'd called for the path results of a bulky lymph node resection he'd performed on Nia Kapur, a mischievous nine-year-old with huge amber eyes and the best, snortiest laugh Nate had ever heard.

He'd worked with Nia and her parents since the beginning of his pediatric surgical oncology fellowship. But the results from her lymph node were not good. The data his resident delivered meant that his time with the Kapurs was drawing to its end.

"Dr. McHale?"

"Sorry, Gina, spotty reception up here." He cleared his throat. "Can you give that last part to me again?"

Nate listened to what he'd missed, thanked her for the update, and wished her luck in weathering the coming storm.

Churning ever closer, a hurricane tore along the coast.

Medea.

Someone at the National Weather Service had been steadily replacing retired hurricane names with classically inspired monikers—Antigone, Brutus, Circe—giving each storm gravitas and a suggestion of animus. Nate thought the time might soon come when storms were named after forgotten gods, their energies stoked by millennia of human neglect.

The timing of the storm was terrible. But in its own way, it was also perfect.

The bus shuddered around a curve, and Nate watched as the lines between land and sky fell into familiar contours. It was September, but the window was ice under his fingertips, the luminescence of the summer mountains already fracturing into color. The wild forest began to lose ground to tidy colonials with manicured lawns and sculpted flower beds. Through the trees, he caught the first flash of light gleaming against dark water.

It had been a long trip, but Nate was finally there.

He was one of the last riders remaining on the bus, and the only one to disembark at the town green.

At first, Greystone Lake looked much as he'd left it. The town hall's neoclassical dome was still painted the red of the autumn maples. The limestone façade of the Empire Hotel still shone like a great pearl through the dogwoods that lined the green. To the north were the headlands, to the east was the Wharf, and to the south were the foothills. This was Greystone Lake. This was home. And Nate knew its every corner as if it were part of his own body.

He extended the handle of his bag and made his way down to the Wharf. It had been fourteen years since he'd walked these streets, and he had to remind himself with each step that this wasn't a dream. The outline of each building, the arc of every curb and lamppost. Everything was familiar, but everything had changed. Nate had changed, too.

As he picked his way down Kingfisher Boulevard he understood why there were so many adages about this kind of homecoming. Each step was a new round of Spot the Difference. Fresh signage on familiar storefronts, obsolete pay phones replaced by sleek bike racks. Renovations, restorations, and new construction. Returning home after a long absence was a unique mélange of recognition and discovery.

A cluster of children, too young to be in school, were herded gently by their keepers along the edge of the town green. A gust kicked a drift of dried leaves at them, sending them into high-pitched squeals of mock terror. They were closer in age to Livvy, but right now Nia Kapur was the child at the forefront of Nate's mind. He'd have to call her parents. It was the kind of news he'd rather give in person, but it'd be days before he'd be back in the city, and little Nia might not have many days left.

He tried to think of exactly what he'd say, but they'd not yet invented the right words for this.

Nate got his first unfettered view of the lake once he neared the base of the hill. It glittered in the sunlight, though its serenity didn't fool Nate. There was a well-known saying in the little town along the shore: *The lake returns what it takes.* This applied to fishing nets as well as drowned bodies, jetsam as well as secrets.

While here, Nate planned to push this gem of lore to its limit.

In his pocket, his phone vibrated with a text message.

THE STORM KING   11

MEG: YOU HOME SWEET HOME?

A host of adjectives could describe the town along the shore, but "sweet" wasn't among them. *Just got here,* Nate typed back. *You in NJ yet?*

The bus was an atrocious way to travel here, but with a Category 3 edging past the Carolinas, stranding Meg without the car hadn't been an option. Two days ago, it had looked like the hurricane would pinwheel into the Atlantic, but high pressure had kinked the jet stream from its usual course. Medea would strike inland, and when it did it would be the worst storm the Northeast had seen in years.

He'd been updating Meg regularly with the notifications pinged to him by his weather apps: wind-speed stats, pics from obliterated beach towns, the inevitable comparisons to Katrina and Sandy. When it came to such things, he had an abundance of caution that his wife rarely shared. Nate believed he'd successfully convinced Meg to take Livvy out of the city to weather Medea at her parents' home in the suburbs, but he wouldn't relax until he got confirmation that they'd arrived safely. According to Google Earth, his in-laws' house was 134 feet above sea level and two miles from any river likely to flood.

Even without Medea, this trek to the northern hinterlands was poorly timed. Meg felt she was on the brink of making partner at her law firm. Livvy had another ear infection. Things were busier than usual at the hospital. The schedule of their lives was like a chess match in three dimensions, but right now the Lake was where Nate had to be.

He could have rented a car for the trip north, but there was something in the monotony of the bus that appealed to him. The jolt of its acceleration, the lurch of its brakes, and its faithful pauses at each waypoint of its rambling route. More than a drive, taking the bus felt like a journey. A necessary transit between the world he'd made and the world that had made him. He'd worked more than he'd meant to during the ride, but Nate knew those long hours had helped him adjust to the idea of returning home. Even under the best circumstances it would be jarring to see the lake's silver skin lap the shore, hear the wash of traffic along the wet asphalt of the Strand, and smell this tree-spiced wind.

His grandmother had called him three weeks ago, as soon as they'd found the body in the headlands. This was before any official identification had been made, but Nate hadn't needed to wait for dental records or DNA.

Grams's pub, Union Points, was across a cobblestone street from the Wharf. The establishment and the tidy brick building that housed it had been in Nate's family for more than a century. Generations of McHales had manned its taps and swept its floors. Nate no longer knew where he fit into his family's legacy in this town, but he still felt a swell of warmth at the sight of the place.

Other than a plastic tarp fixed where a plate glass window should have been, the old pub looked good. Inside, its black wood surfaces had been polished, and its exposed brick walls hung with stylish photographs of the town and the lake. The place was empty except for a trio of college guys at the counter and a boat crew occupying a booth in the back. A girl with shoulder-length black hair pressed at a flat-screen register behind the bar.

The bartender had a smile on her face, but when she turned to Nate, her body went rigid. Her open expression closed like a flower on the brink of night.

"She's in the back," the bartender finally said after an uncomfortable pause. She barely looked old enough to tend the bar. "Want me to get her?"

"Sure," Nate said.

In this town there was no point in wondering how a girl this young knew him by sight.

The college guys paid no attention as Nate settled in a few stools away, but the locals in the back got quiet. Their curiosity pulled on his shoulders, a familiar weight.

He heard Grams's sure stride before she burst through the kitchen doors. He Skyped with her every Sunday but hadn't seen her in person since her last visit to the city back in July. She'd been spindle tall and steely gray for as long as he'd known her, and she looked only a little more stooped than he remembered.

"My beautiful boy," she said.

Nate bent to kiss her on the cheek and she pulled him tight.

"I'd have met you at the green," she said.

"And abandon the place to this crowd?" His gesture encompassed the empty tables and half dozen patrons. "Can't trigger a riot in my first ten minutes home. Got to pace myself."

She cuffed him on the shoulder. "Be good, you devil."

"What happened to the window?" he asked.

"Oh." She glanced at the front of the bar. The plastic sheet tensed with the breeze like an inflating lung. "That last thunderstorm. Fella keeps bringing the wrong size pane. We'll need to plank it good and tight for the hurricane. You're so thin, boy." She poked him in the ribs. "I'll bring you something."

When she disappeared into the kitchen, Nate's phone buzzed with a new message. A pic of Livvy and her china doll grin ensconced in her grandmother's lap. She and Meg had reached the New Jersey hills. They were safe.

He tucked away his phone, and the girl behind the bar slid him a pint.

"Looks like you could use that." Perhaps it was an apology for her initial reaction. "This can't be an easy place to come back to." She was pretty, with her high cheekbones, green eyes, and porcelain skin.

He nodded. Something he liked about the city was how so few of its millions knew or cared about his business. The beer gave him an excuse not to look at her.

"I'm TJ," she said. She bit one edge of her red lips, and Nate couldn't tell if the flicker in her eyes was hospitality, curiosity, or something else entirely. He didn't want to find out.

"Nice to meet you, TJ," he said. He rubbed his eyes as if he were tired, displaying the flash of his wedding band. Focusing on the static undersides of his lids, he wished for the girl to dissolve into the floor-boards.

The girl remained, but Grams returned from the kitchen with a grilled cheese and a cup of tomato soup.

"Tommy know you're coming up today?" Grams asked as she settled in next to him. TJ moved on to the college guys, who seemed happy to have her.

"I emailed him and Johnny. I think we're going to meet up later."

"He came in for lunch with the chief. The station'll tell you where he is. Anyone else you want to catch up with?"

"Maybe." There were, in fact, a good many people he intended to renew acquaintance with. "I guess I'll see people at the—you know, at the funeral."

He took a deep pull from his pint. The lager was a local micro-brew. It tasted of the summer fields and youth, and in this moment these were painful things to be reminded of. The memories that kin-dled retracted the tendrils of his consciousness from Meg and Livvy. They pulled him away from Nia Kapur, the hospital, and everything else in his city life. But this was necessary. This was what he'd come here to do.

He sensed Grams's eyes on him.

"I know nothing good brought you here," Grams whispered. She kneaded his shoulder with a papery hand. "But it's so good to see you."

He let his forehead rest against her bony shoulder and shivered with the chill of wet skin on a summer night. She placed her hand on the thatch of his head and leaned into him like they were back to be-ing the only people in the world.

Nate reminded himself that this was Greystone Lake. This was death and loss and secrets and lies and rage. But it was also home. For the next few days, he must make himself belong here again. This was the barest minimum of his debt.

When Nate sat up, Grams's gray eyes brimmed with tears.

"Who loves you more than anyone, boy?"

...

AFTER EATING, NATE left the Union to take a look at the waterfront on his way to his grandmother's house on Bonaparte Street. Grams had offered to drive him, but the pub was beginning to gather a crowd, and Nate didn't mind stretching his legs.

Despite the approaching hurricane, small craft still cut across the undulating plain of the lake. A group of swimmers broke the waves along the far shore. Nate knew the devoted tried the waters no matter the weather or season. The Daybreakers, a loose confederation of eccentrics, took their exercise by swimming a lap of the lake's southern bulge whenever it wasn't iced over. Each day, often at dawn, they let themselves be erased by the frigid water. Even after so many years, thinking about this still made Nate light-headed.

He saw that a tourist storefront had sprouted between the pub and its back parking lot. GREYSTONE LAKE emblazoned golf shirts and sun visors, locally made ceramics and woodcarvings. Nate scanned the store's wares for a plush toy he could take home to Livvy or a knickknack for Meg's parents. He told himself he was shopping, but what he was really doing was stalling.

Seeing Grams had been good. Livvy adored her great-grandmother, and Nate loved watching them together, but he'd enjoyed having Grams to himself this time. For a little while, it had felt just like the old days. But spending time with Grams was the only easy thing he had to look forward to during this homecoming. He'd need to see Tom and Johnny next. Like Nate, they'd been there from the beginning, when things began to go wrong.

The shop offered towers of postcards: images of the lake in each season, time-lapses of the sky and shore. Some depicted the colorful wares of the weekend markets and the fall forests, but there were also black-and-whites from long-gone eras. During Prohibition, some resort towns withered while others blossomed. Thanks to its proximity to the St. Lawrence, Greystone Lake had flourished as a center for smuggling across the northern border. This was the Lake's time of legend, when wealth and crime and giant personalities wrought stories equal parts myth and history.

Nate was drawn to one such postcard. A staged photo of overall-clad men astride lumber freshly mounted above the waterline. The uninitiated might take this for a snapshot of the Wharf construction, but Nate knew otherwise. The stocky man in the center of the picture, dandy as a vaudevillian in seersucker and a straw hat, was a young Morton Strong. On the back, "1919" was printed right under a description: "The construction of the Greystone Lake Entertainments Pier, popularly known as the Night Ship."

The Night Ship.

Until the development of the Wharf area in the 1950s, the Night Ship had been the center of Greystone Lake's tourism industry. In its prime it featured restaurants, shops, and game rooms. It also included a nightclub, the Night Ship, from which the pier eventually took its name. During the sixties the tourist district consolidated around the Wharf, and the Night Ship found itself isolated in the residential part of Greystone Lake. It was bankrupted, condemned, and barricaded soon after. The town had tried to tear it down, but preservationists thwarted those plans.

As a child, Nate had been glad it hadn't been demolished. It was a ruin, but a spectacular one. While its boardwalks sagged and buckled, its graceful roofs and fairyland spires did not seem of this world. It was a relic of a more optimistic age—and like everything that old, it had a story all its own.

Nate focused on the lines of Morton Strong's face.

He tried to pull meaning from the pilings that struck up from the silver water, to discern intent in the arcs of steelwork in the background. He searched this moment of the Night Ship's birth for any hint that the pier would come to shadow his life as it had.

"Look what the lake dredged up."

Nate turned to see Tom in the shop's doorway.

"Deputy."

"Doc."

Nate's oldest friend offered his hand, and Nate used it to pull him into a bear hug.

"You look good." It was strange to see Tom in a uniform, but it suited him.

Tom laughed. "Look at you in here, browsing like a weekender. You want a ride to Bonaparte Street? I'll run you up."

"Can we use the lights?" Nate had been about to buy the post-card of the Night Ship. A strange impulse. Instead, he returned it and gave the tower a spin to conceal his interest.

Tom clapped him on the shoulder. "Even let you work the siren. You solo this weekend?"

"Livvy's got this ear thing again." Nate followed his friend back onto the street. "Long drive for a sick three-year-old. Plus, there's the hurricane."

"Believe me, I know. Been filling sandbags with the Kiwanis club all morning."

"Really? Sandbags?" The lake was tempestuous, but hardly the Atlantic.

"Gosh, you've really gone full-tourist, haven't you? A four-foot storm surge will swamp the embankment. You should know that!" Tom laughed. "A bunch of places got reamed by the last hurricane, so we're going all out on prep this time."

"Got to keep the place pretty."

"Pretty's what pays the bills around here. How does it look to you?"

"The Lake? Fantastic," Nate said, and it was the truth. The town's storefronts and waterfront were exquisitely maintained, just as they'd been in their youth. The grandeur of the Lake's vistas were also extraordinary. The peaks of the headlands. The rippling forests of the foothills. The way all of this beauty was doubled by the mirror of the lake.

It was a storybook town, but as in any fairy tale, things were not as perfect as they first appeared.

"Lots of improvements since you were last around. Johnny

opened up that place last year." Tom pointed to a tea shop down the block. Its windows were planked over in preparation for the coming onslaught, and its awning was being rolled up. "Desserts and pastries supplied by the Empire's kitchen. Oh, and Emma runs it. That's her right there. Want to say hello?"

Emma Aoki, who'd once been their classmate, was the woman closing the awning. Her head was tilted to the surge of clouds whipping in from the south. She'd always been slight, but now she looked made of paper. Nate was a block away, but in the push of the wind, he saw that her dress hung on her as if from a hanger. She frowned at the weather, and then her eyes crossed the distance between them. Something in her expression changed, but the frown remained. More than a decade gone, but she knew him at a glance.

"She looks busy," Nate said. He waved to her, and after a moment she raised her hand to match his own. "Maybe later."

They turned down a side street to where Tom's cruiser was parked.

"Actually, I'd like to catch up with everybody at some point. Do you keep in touch with them?" Nate asked.

"Mostly. Some more than others."

"And Emma? You see a lot of her?"

"Sometimes." He chucked Nate's bag into the trunk. "Oh, like, date? Nah."

Nate got into the passenger side and let the battered seat mold to his body. "She's very thin. Has she been sick?"

"We're not all your cancer patients, Doc. Not yet, anyway." The cruiser lurched onto the wide arc of the Strand, the street closest to the shore.

Tom himself seemed in good health. He looked like he kept in shape, but they'd reached the age where some men begin to fall apart. He had a touch more weight in the cheeks. A new groove in his brow. The angle between his chin and throat had begun to loosen to a curve. Nate wouldn't have called his friend's hairline receding, though he had more forehead than he used to.

"Emma's been having kind of a tough time, though," Tom said. "She's living in those apartments by the packing houses—they might be new since you left? Anyway, they had a sewage problem a week or so ago, and her place is on the ground floor."

"Shit."

"Exactly. I think she's staying with her parents."

Grams's street was named not for the French emperor but for a species of gull. If Greystone Lake were shaped like a boomerang lodged against the western shore of the lake's southern bulge, then Bonaparte Street was laced through the center of its length, with her house located halfway between the town's center and its northern-most edge. Imposing mansions built in the late 1800s glittered along the Strand, while more modest homes like hers sat farther inland. The center of town comprised the Wharf and tourist district. Fishermen, rundown work piers, and old packinghouses took up the bulk of the Lake's southern wing. The Night Ship was a dark blade struck deep into the waters close to the town's northern limit.

Clouds now shrouded the sky, and the lake trembled in the growing wind. Nate guessed this would be the last of the sun they'd see for days.

Tom pointed out some of the changes to the Lake's homes and businesses as they traveled the few blocks to Grams's place. Familiar houses had been painted in new colors. Yards had been landscaped. Fences had sprung up, and new expansions loomed just shy of property lines.

These were all signs of a prosperous town, and this was good. A living place had to change. Families come, families leave, yesterday's students become tomorrow's teachers. This was natural and right, but heading toward his grandmother's home, Nate found it wrenching. One day everything they did would be forgotten. One day everything they loved wouldn't matter to anyone.

They parked in front of Grams's little yellow house. Tom turned to him when Nate made no move to exit.

"Tommy, you know I've got to ask. I need to know what they know."

Tom cleared his throat.

"Grams said hikers found her."

Tom nodded. "During a cloudburst. Picked their way through the rocks, trying to get out of the downpour, and there she was."

"What do they know?"

"Dad's not letting me anywhere near it. But she—her body—there wasn't much left. Fourteen years, Nate."

A moment passed with nothing but the tick of the cruiser's cooling engine to mark it. Nate had already known the scant information Tom gave him, but such conversations had to begin somehow. Easy questions blaze the path for the harder ones that must follow. Nate touched the glass of his window. Cold as the lake at dawn.

"He wants to talk to you, you know," Tom said. "My dad."

Tom's father was Greystone Lake's chief of police, as he had been for twenty years.

"I've been thinking about her mother," Nate said. "Is it better to know for sure?" Since Livvy's birth, Nate wondered what he'd do if she ever disappeared. If she vanished and was never seen again. This fear was always with him. Even in his most euphoric moments, it waited like a rock under the waves. When Nate sang Livvy to sleep, he could never decide if closure was better than hope. "I keep thinking about what I'm supposed to say to her."

"Not to mention her dad."

Nate's response was a sound, the noise of an old scar torn raw.

"Grams *must* have told you."

Nate could only shake his head. The car's close air felt too thick to breathe.

"He's been out for years. Parole. I thought you knew. I'd have told you if—"

"It's fine. Doesn't matter." Nate said this as calmly as he could. He unbuckled himself and pulled at the door handle. He had to get out of the car.

He counted his breaths as Tom opened the trunk to pull out his bag.

"You don't have to talk to him." Tom's expression was the one he'd worn so often when they were younger. A veneer of geniality over panic. "No one'd expect you to. Jesus, I really thought you knew."

"It's fine," Nate said again. The breeze from the lake was brisk, and standing in it helped. "You just took me by surprise." He smiled and patted his friend on the shoulder.

Nate took his bag, and they made their way up a short stretch of slate flagstones to the front stoop. Nate pressed the handle, but the door didn't budge. He rammed his shoulder into it as if it might have warped in its frame. He'd opened this door a thousand times and never once found it locked.

"Hold up, Doc." Tom dug through his pocket and slid between Nate and the door.

"She gave you a key?"

"I'm very trustworthy. Got a badge and everything."

Tom unlocked the door, and Nate walked into the life he'd left behind.

Dried hydrangeas on a console beside a pile of unopened mail. The scent of lavender soap behind a smell of wood polish. The shuddering of the floor under his feet as the furnace thrummed.

He wandered the length of the foyer, looking around like a tourist in a museum. The colors of the place seemed to have faded. A wall he remembered as yellow was now cream, a forest green armchair toned down to olive. Though Nate was the same height he'd been when he graduated high school, everything seemed smaller. More delicate and somehow less real. As if the couch in the living room was more a concept of furniture than a place a person would actually sit.

A mosaic of photographs cluttered the far wall. At the center, an old black-and-white of his father, and the rest rippled from it. Shots of Nate's med school graduation, his wedding, Livvy with a grin as big as the world.

"She's beautiful," Tom said.

"Thanks, buddy." Tom had visited them in the city just before Livvy's birth, but their talk of additional get-togethers never panned out. It occurred to Nate that all his best friend had seen of Livvy came from holiday cards and the occasional texted photo.

They ascended the creaking stairs to Nate's boyhood bedroom. Inside was a narrow twin bed, rows of thin pine bookcases, a dresser, and a little desk. Horror movie posters covered the walls where books did not. This was nearly a replica of the bedroom he'd had at the house on Great Heron Drive before the accident, before he'd moved in with Grams. Nate had lived here on Bonaparte Street for just over two years, but of all the years of his life, these were the ones that had left the deepest marks.

"Just like you left it, huh?" Tom said. "Good to know that some things don't—"

Nate turned to his friend. He followed Tom's gaze to a shattered window by the bed. On the faded blue plaid comforter, he saw a chalk-white ball lipped in red stitching. A baseball.

A *baseball*.

Nate's world narrowed to the three-inch sphere.

Behind him, Tom said something. Nate could hardly hear him over the thunder of his pulse crashing inside his ears. He went to the window to peer through its diamond shards.

For an instant he felt one with the window's jagged edge.

Through that window, beyond the trees, Nate caught the glow of the lake. It occurred to him that the mountains around the town looked like jaws that could slam shut at any time, the lake itself an insatiable maw. For a vertiginous moment, he recognized nothing about this place along the moody plain of deep water.

But this was Greystone Lake. This was home.

Two

Nate held the baseball with the tips of his fingers, as if it might break if he squeezed too hard.

An object indistinguishable from this had once destroyed his world. Nate hadn't touched one in ages. Like everything else here, it felt smaller than he remembered.

"Kids," Tom said. "It's September. Everyone thinks they're a Yankee." He said this quickly. "I'll call Mace Hardware to fix the window."

Nate scoured the ball for the flat creases of a brake pedal pressing to the floor. He searched its pale skin for half-moon scars left by his mother's fingernails.

He looked at Tom. "Are we still meeting up with Johnny later?"

Nate's voice hit all the notes of a man without a worry, but he wanted to ask Tom again about her body. He wanted to hear everything there was to know about it. He wanted to carve every detail into his skin and carry it with him everywhere he went.

"Sure," Tom said, zipping up his coat. "Drinks at the Empire, around six?"

"Perfect."

"Got to put in some face time at the Wharf first," Tom said, checking his phone. "More windows to board, more doors to sandbag. It's an electrical one, too, like Hurricane Katrina. Gonna be a real show."

Nate followed him down the stairs. Rattling sounded from other rooms where branches rapped the windows. When Tom opened the front door, cold air flooded the hall like a cresting wave.

"It's real good to see you," Tom said. "Back here at the Lake."

"You, too. But we do have to talk later, Tommy." Nate lowered the wattage of his smile. "You, me, Johnny."

Tom offered his hand, which Nate accepted.

He watched his friend cross the lawn and get into his police car. Patience didn't come naturally to Nate, but it was a virtue he'd cultivated over the years.

First, do no harm.

Once the cruiser was out of sight, he realized that he still held the baseball. He'd clutched it so tightly that the braid of its stitching ran across his palm, as if he himself had been assembled.

He trekked back to his boyhood bedroom, going right for the closet. Brass-buttoned blazers, yellowed shirts, oversized flannels. His old raincoat, dark as funeral garb, hung right where he must have left it fourteen years ago. He poked through the clutter at the base of the closet to uncover a box filled with sweaters. He pulled aside the clothes to reveal a clutch of three baseballs.

The first of these had appeared on the front stoop his first day of junior year. He'd found the second in his locker a few weeks later. The third, just before the Halloween when it all started.

That last one had crashed through the same window as today's baseball.

Kids, Tom had said when he saw the broken window.

Nate added the new baseball to the others and covered them again with sweaters. Out of sight, at least.

Downstairs, he gravitated to the living room's shrine of photos.

He examined each one carefully, indulging the pain that flowed with the memories they conjured. Mom, Dad, Gabe. His treasured dead.

His eyes rested on the last of the series. Livvy in a Christmas dress, beaming like a cherub among a pile of presents. In three years she'd be the same age as Gabe. In four, she'd be older than him. Nate could hardly make sense of such math.

He swept up the broken glass in his bedroom, then hunted for a piece of cardboard to block the shattered window. He unearthed a cobweb-netted ladder from the garage so that he could check the gutters. Medea was forecast to drop as much as two feet of rain on the North Country over the next three days.

The gutters were utterly clogged. So far it had been only drizzling, but the aluminum troughs already brimmed with tannin-stained water. He reached into the downspout and pulled out handfuls of deteriorated leaves and twigs. As if he were disemboweling the carcass of a strange creature, each fistful came out in dripping clumps.

While he worked, Nate mentally composed how he'd deliver Nia's pathology results to the Kapurs. She needed more than surgery now. Chemo, radiation, and immunotherapy were the usual options, but these were beyond Nate's expertise. When he spoke to her parents, he'd give them a short list of good oncologists to take over her treatment. The facts of her condition were clear, but the tone in which he delivered them would be critical. Hope would be an essential element to any future course of treatment, but Nate wouldn't mislead them on medical realities. He had an obligation both to them and to the truth. There would be more conversations to come, but it was important that he get this first one just right.

He'd just moved to another corner of the roof when his phone buzzed. He shucked off his work gloves, letting them flutter to the lawn below. When he worked his phone from his pocket, his wife and daughter's faces grinned from its display. He slid his finger across the screen to answer.

"Sorry, I meant to call," he said.

"Where are you?" Meg asked.

"On the roof. There's about a decade's worth of leaves in these gutters."

"Bea didn't waste any time putting you to work, did she? Always liked the lady's style."

"Was the drive okay?"

"Some traffic on the bridge. A little more than ninety minutes door to door. Can't complain. You're the one with the eight-hour bus ride."

"Do you guys have enough groceries?" Disaster preparedness had become competitive sport, and the networks had been hyping Medea even before they knew she'd turn inland. Nate felt a clench of guilt to not be there with them.

"It's not like it's the apocalypse."

"It's *probably* not the apocalypse," Nate corrected her.

"We've got enough bread and eggs to survive an asteroid collision and simultaneous zombie invasion."

"That's what I like to hear. How is the monkey?"

"It's sad monkey faces all around, I'm afraid."

"Are the drops helping?"

"Who can tell? Dr. Klieg swears she'll grow out of these. Before she's thirty, hopefully. How are things there?"

"Fine," he said. "Good."

"Liar." Nate could almost see her brush a lock of long dark hair from her face. "You want to tell me about it?"

Nate's life with Meg felt so full that it was easy to forget how incomplete a sketch of his youth his wife must carry in her head. Nate imagined that a part of her enjoyed the fantasy that he'd blossomed into true personhood only upon meeting her. That everything before then had been practice, and, in a way, perhaps it had been.

He'd told Meg many stories about this town along the shore. But he hadn't told her everything.

"Wouldn't know where to start."

"Well, let me know when you figure it out. How's Bea?"

"Indomitable. I was thinking we could have her down for a week around Thanksgiving."

"Livvy would love a turkey day with Grams, wouldn't you?"

"Is she there?" He could picture them, snuggled under the yellow bedspread in his in-laws' guest room, tapping through a game on the iPad as stars from her night-light pinwheeled across the ceiling above them.

There was a burst of static as the phone changed hands.

"Daddy?"

Nate smiled at the rustle of his daughter's voice. "How are you feeling, monkey?"

"My head hurts." Livvy spoke too closely to the receiver, making everything she said sound like a secret.

"I'm so sorry. Momma's taking good care of you though, right?"

"Tell me a story. Tell me about the Night Ship. Momma says you're there. She says you're by the lake."

"I wish I was with you." From the top of the ladder, Nate needed only to swivel his head to see the Night Ship's towers stark as obsidian against the colorless water.

"Did you go there? Will you take me?"

"It's no place for little monkeys."

"I like ghosts."

Nate had once mentioned the Night Ship in his dramatically censored stories of Greystone Lake. It had latched onto Livvy's mind. She asked about it before bed and during baths. She drew pictures of it and constructed it from sheets and pillows.

"You're a very brave monkey. I'm not as brave as you are."

"Some ghosts are nice, I think."

Not in the Night Ship, he thought.

"Did I ever tell you about that time Ronald the Rhinoceros lost his horn, and his friend Bali the Blue Parrot had to help him find it?"

"Ronald can't lose his horn!" Livvy giggled. "They don't come off!"

"That's what he thought, too. But one morning he woke up and looked in the mirror to brush his teeth and couldn't find it anywhere."

Nate spun Livvy a story of cozy jungle adventure, but his thoughts wandered into the dark towers behind him. It had been fourteen years since he'd stepped into the Night Ship, but when he closed his eyes he could see its rusted arches of riveted steel, its moss-stained glass ceiling panels, its promenade tapering into impermeable darkness. He could smell its rot and hear the breath of water lapping against weathered pilings.

Livvy had her usual questions, but they soon faded into murmurs.

"She's finally out," Meg whispered into the phone. "Been trying to get her to nap since we got here, so thanks for the assist."

"How come that never works when I'm there in person?" He listened as Meg extricated herself from the bed without waking Livvy. "How're your parents?"

"In an uproar. They dug up three old radios. You know, just in case. And you can't turn a corner without colliding with a pallet of bottled water. Dad spent half the morning rearranging the brickwork off the patio. Don't ask me why."

"Well, at least they're having fun."

"Time of their lives."

"And you're hunkering down until it's over, right? No driving? No catastrophe tourism?"

"You know me, Doc."

"That's why I asked."

"You be careful, too. Don't let those ghosts get you."

Nate laughed, because Meg had meant it as a joke.

She told him about the vacation home of one of their acquaintances on the Outer Banks. Yesterday it had been a three-bedroom cottage, and today it was an array of splintered stilts. As Nate listened, he stole another glance at the Night Ship. The trees had begun to sway, and the lake was curdling with whitecaps. Thunder drummed in the distance. The mountains and forests around the town tossed and shook as if waking from a long slumber.

THE DAYBREAKER

THE COLD WATERS closed upon her like jaws, and she let them gnaw at her.

Like any beast, the lake had its moods. To strangers, it seemed calm during silver afternoons and welcoming in a summer gloaming, but to understand the lake was to know that its undercurrent was always the same. Below the skin of its waves, the deep water was hunger itself.

That's why she swam it with such ferocity. Each Daybreaker plied the numbing waters for a reason, and she swam them to be erased. She swam for the lake to devour the girl she'd once been.

Today the whole world felt ravenous. The waves struck rougher. The wind bit harder. The forests quaked under the roiling sky. A hurricane gathered beyond the horizon, and all elements bayed in anticipation.

Every storm recalls another, and this town along the shore had endured so many.

Ahead, the black bulk of the Night Ship speared the pallid water like a toppled colossus. The old pier was abandoned and battered and broken, but in some ways not diminished at all. Because a place like this was more than wood and steel and glass.

She usually gave the edifice of the pier a wide berth, but since the discovery of the body in the headlands, each day had become more uncertain.

Something was wrong.

Something was going to happen.

The lake returns what it takes, and after many years of quiet, the seeds of old sins had floated from its depths to bloom across the shore. As with much of the pain in this town, the Night Ship was the root of this latest trouble. Today, she kicked for where the waves hurled themselves against the pier's foundations.

Deep in the Night Ship's undercroft, a young prostitute had given birth to twin girls and was told to snap their necks the moment they were born. Or so the story goes.

During Prohibition, three bootlegger brothers were captured by Old Morton Strong and fed to his tropical fish one piece at a time. Or so the story goes.

A busybody socialite had once threatened ruin upon the night-club, and so Just June pushed her from the balcony of the Century Room. Or so the story goes.

The Night Ship had many stories.

Some of their endings were yet unknown, even to her.

The current made negotiating the pier's pilings dangerous. Swimming among the moss-wreathed pillars felt like diving through a sunken temple. She twisted onto her back to watch the black mass of the Night Ship shut out the sky.

Sometimes she pretended she could hear the screams of the dead ride the gusts that whistled through the pier's undergirding. She couldn't imagine their howls were any more terrible than their silence.

She didn't believe in ghosts, but that didn't mean she could not be haunted.

Once through the pilings, she slid back onto her belly. The Night Ship was no longer above her, but she was always in its shadow.

The first rumors of thunder rolled from behind the mountains.

A storm approached, and she knew it was made of more than wind and rain.

Three

When Nate finished speaking with Mrs. Kapur, he set aside his phone and massaged his eyes with his fingertips. These calls were never easy, and this one had been harder than most. He knew he'd done all he could for Nia, and now it was someone else's turn to try. But he bristled at his failure to fix her. Cancer was as senseless a scourge as there was. The war against it had good days and bad, and the bad ones felt very bad indeed.

He showered before heading to the Empire. It was good to stand under hot water. He was tense from the phone call, stiff from the bus ride, and filthy from the gutters. Once he was clean, he dressed in a trim blue suit.

It was dusk at the edge of night. Along the wet streets, the town's lamps blushed with the cold light of small moons. He carried an umbrella, though the wind made this difficult. Stray drops as big as marbles fell as he made his way to the hotel. He'd scrolled through hurricane updates before leaving Grams's house. A bridge in Virginia washed away. An island in the Chesapeake vanished in the storm surge. Thousands of flights canceled, and transit systems from Baltimore to Boston closed or scheduled to close.

The Lake's shopkeepers had taped or boarded over their storefronts' glass, and some were now assembling sandbag barriers around their entrances. Gusts from the lake whistled like blades as they cut among the trees and skimmed along gables.

The townspeople's preparations meant Nate could walk among them unrecognized. He wielded his umbrella like a mask.

The town green was deserted. Through shuffling foliage Nate saw the Empire Hotel, its silhouette gothic against the slate sky.

Nate had done a poor job of keeping up with Tom, and he'd fallen out of touch with Johnny back during their college years. As with a lot of childhood friendships, there was no single moment when it ended. It had simply faded from the foreground to the background before disappearing from the picture altogether.

Johnny had still invited Nate to his wedding, four years ago, and Nate had sent a gift but skipped the nuptials. Through Tom, he'd heard the reception was lovely, though apparently it was the divorce that had been truly spectacular. Since then, Johnny had inherited the Empire and become one of the Lake's most prominent citizens. His father, Mr. Vanhouten, died three years ago, having taken what the locals call the long walk off the short pier. In his case, the pier in question had been his own pool's diving board. While its chlorinated water had drowned him, it was safe to say it'd been the fifth of gin that did him in.

Above Nate, thick clouds buckled, swirls ribbed with black. The rain was still only a patter, but the wind was full of threats.

Gaslights flared in white and blue flame on either side of the Empire's ebony lacquer doors like spirits trapped in glass. A doorman clothed in black and gold opened the door, and two officers stood just inside the entrance.

The police presence wasn't the only change about the place. A streak of modern design had brought the Empire into the twenty-first century. The marble floor was as glossy as Nate remembered, but where walls once dripped with impasto paintings of the lake, now antiqued mirrors and panels of embossed leather stretched for the ceiling. Sculpted curves of indigo velvet had replaced the right angles of striped satin couches. Massive wrought iron lighting fixtures flared with blue glass hung where crystal chandeliers had once sparkled. The concierge desk was manned by young people in black suits while tourists and busboys crisscrossed the shining floors.

"Dr. McHale?" A young woman with a bun of taut blond hair offered Nate her hand. "Mr. Vanhouten is in the Colonnade."

Nate followed her through the lobby to the Empire's restaurant. On their way, he noticed caution tape cordoning off the Greenhouse, a glass enclosure popular for weddings that segued into the hotel's gardens. Beyond its entrance, workers tightened tarps over the ceiling and arranged plastic drop cloths around the parquet floor.

"What happened in there?" Nate asked his escort.

"Storm damage."

"And the hurricane hasn't even hit yet," Nate said.

A polite smile was the only response he got.

Unlike the lobby, the Colonnade was just as Nate remembered it: a two-tiered room with most of the tables arranged in a wide space at the bottom of a short flight of stairs. Booths lined the walls of the upper level. The glow of sconces and muted chandeliers brushed the cavernous place with ghostly light.

He spotted Tom first, hunched over a table. He'd changed out of his uniform and into a blue oxford shirt. There was a crease between his eyebrows, and he shook his head emphatically at something. His face smoothed and then cracked into a smile when he noticed Nate.

"Buddy!" Johnny worked his way out of the booth and rose to embrace Nate. He gripped Nate's upper arms for a moment as he looked him over. "You look fantastic, man. It's kind of irritating, actually."

"You, too." Nate patted him on the shoulder.

Johnny had grown his hair longer to compensate for its thinning.

He'd gained weight, too: The profile of his chest and belly had united into a single, avian curve. He wore a gray suit, oddly ill-fitted for someone so rich. The cutaway collar of his shirt was askew like the broken wings of a dead insect. He seemed to have a tough time getting himself back into the booth.

"Crazy how long it's been, huh?" Nate settled in next to Tom. "The hotel looks amazing."

Johnny waved over a waiter. A tumbler festooned with lime peels and crystallized ginger appeared. "Dark and Stormy," Johnny said with a crooked grin. "Seemed appropriate. And let's get a head start on the next round," he told the server.

Johnny's own glass was nothing but ice, but he raised it anyway. "Welcome home to our—" He glanced at Tom. "Does 'prodigal son' apply? 'Wayward brother'?"

"How about, 'to old friends'?" Tom said. Nate had obviously interrupted a tense conversation between the two of them. Behind his smile, Tom looked brittle.

"Works for me."

"And absent ones," Nate added.

The three of them clinked glasses.

A chime just like this had sounded innumerable times in myriad places through uncounted centuries. These drinks that friends share. Their toast done, Nate should have sensed the beginning of a companionable evening. Instead, he felt most keenly the things that separated them.

A thousand pieces of himself had been constructed around the scaffolding of this pair, but how well had these connections weathered the years? Perhaps not as well as Nate hoped. He tried to remember the last time they were all together, and if he'd marked it as a moment that mattered.

"How long are you in town?" Johnny asked.

"Sunday, unless Medea has other plans."

"Short visit, but you must be a busy guy."

"Aren't we all?"

"Yeah, Tom rescuing cats in trees. On a good day, I'm a glorified wedding planner."

"Cats are more the fire department's wheelhouse, actually," Tom said. He turned to Nate. "I didn't ask about your job before. You're still in your fellowship, right?"

"Yeah, couple years to go. It's a long slog." He hadn't yet taken more than a sip of his drink, but Nate beamed at the waiter as he arrived with a new round.

"Not just a doctor, but a surgeon. Not just a surgeon but a pediatric surgeon. Not just a pediatric surgeon, but a pediatric oncologic surgeon." Johnny shook his head and took a gulp from his tumbler. "Way to make the rest of us look like bums, man. Let me guess, you also operate exclusively on orphans and refugees."

"Nah, got to save some of the really selfless stuff for my retirement." Nate held up his cocktail. "This is delicious. And seriously, look at this place. This town. You guys." He widened his smile until it embraced all of them. "We've done okay, haven't we? It's so good to be here with you both."

"Wow," Johnny said. "So did the total cornball slushiness start when you became a dad, or is it just a side effect of the sleep deprivation?"

Nate's grin remained undimmed. Johnny rolled his eyes, though he did it with a smile. "All right, fine. Show me the munchkin already, I know it's killing you. Entire phone full of pics right there in your pocket and everything."

Christmas, Halloween, birthdays, beach vacations, bath time, gelato disasters—it was amazing how many photos a father acquires. Nate didn't foist them on his friends for long. It was good to show them the family he'd built so they could share in its success. But there was a line between pride and boasting he was careful not to cross. He needed things from these two, but not their envy.

"Oh, and I love the new lobby." Nate said, putting away his phone. "You've got terrific taste."

"I'll pass the compliment on to my ex, if I ever see her again. But she did have great taste, didn't she, Tom? The concierge she left me for had the most beautiful eyes. Who needs a Caribbean vacation when you can take a dip in eyes like his?"

"Business has been good, too," Tom said, ignoring Johnny. "Better than ever."

"Looks that way," Nate said. "You'd never know this was the off-season."

Johnny had already drained his new drink, but he stretched his neck searching for a last drop. The ice clattered against his teeth. These cocktails clearly hadn't been his first.

"When we were at the Wharf we saw Emma battening down the hatches at the tea shop," Tom said. "Nate was thinking we could all meet up before he heads home. Put the band back together and all that."

"I hear there's going to be a funeral," Johnny said. "Great time for a reunion." He went again for the bottom of his empty glass.

Tom exhaled at a volume just a decibel below a sigh.

"Yeah, I'm sure we'll see a lot of people there," Nate said. "But it'd be nice to spend time with them afterward. Not just people from our group, but everyone—Lindsay, the Sarahs—everybody from the old days. It's been too long since I've seen them, and I'd love to reconnect." He grinned as if nothing would please him more than to have every memory of this place and its people carved on marble and framed in gold.

Johnny peered at him from the hollows of his eyes.

"Selfless. Sappy. And now what's this? Nostalgic? What're you going to throw at me next, Nate?"

Nate didn't let his irritation show. Instead, he set doctor's eyes on Johnny. Bloodshot and slightly yellow sclera. Periorbital dark circles. A ring of sweat around his collar. Johnny had his mother's dark skin, but his was ashen. Nate's old friend wasn't in good health. The extra weight wasn't helping him, and neither was the alcohol. Nate wondered if Johnny drank the same way Mr. Vanhouten had.

"Johnny's in a mood," Tom told Nate.

"All these windows with a hurricane on the way?" Nate gestured to the wall of glass that opened the Colonnade to the gardens. "I don't blame him." He remained the personification of affability, but Nate didn't intend to drop the idea of a reunion with their class-mates. A gathering like this would be the easiest way to talk one-on-one with all their old acquaintances.

"You're more or less right, is the funny thing," Johnny said. "Four weddings to go this month and the Greenhouse looks post-apocalyptic. Maybe that's the nuptial theme we should be pitching. Bride's side is on the left and here's your gas mask. Fifty-fifty chance of being skewered by a support beam."

"I saw it was closed. What happened?"

"Storm damage," Johnny said. "That's what we're calling it, isn't it, Tommy?"

The waiter arrived with another drink for Johnny. Nate pried a wedge of crystallized ginger from his stirrer.

"A tree?" Nate asked. He only asked because Johnny seemed in-tent on talking about it. They'd have to get it out of the way before moving on.

"A big one," Tom said. "Might have been two hundred years old. Took out half the glass, but the steelwork is what's taking so long to fix."

"Must have been quite a storm," Nate said.

"Sure," Johnny said. "But, to be honest, I kinda hold the chain-saw responsible."

Tom shook his head. "Come *on.*"

Nate was about to ask another question, but an older man ap-proached the booth. Tom's father, Greystone Lake's chief of police.

"Officers will stay through the night and make rounds on the half hour," Chief Buck told Johnny.

"Chief! It's so good to see you." Nate rose to offer his hand.

The chief and Nate's dad had been inseparable in their youths. That friendship had continued up until that long-ago April drive in the headlands. Their wives had been good friends, and their sons as close as they had themselves been as children. Nate imagined they must have found a pleasing symmetry in this. He thought that for them to watch their sons play while their pretty wives laughed as the day closed on their good lives in their nice town must have been the very distillation of happiness.

"Nate." The man accepted Nate's hand but didn't return his smile.

"How are you? It's been ages. I'd love to catch up."

"How about tomorrow, before the funeral. Say nine o'clock at the station? I'll make sure they're expecting you." The man's face was as immobile as the mountains. He dropped Nate's hand and walked away from the booth.

The chief's coldness left Nate stunned. Every recollection he had of him was that of a fond uncle. When he sank back into the booth, Tom and Johnny were both staring at their cocktails.

"He told me to go to the police station." As if they hadn't heard for themselves.

"The body," Tom said. *Her* body. "There are questions."

Nate knew that this would happen. It was inevitable. Questions must be answered, statements given. For fourteen years, this town had satisfied itself with the fiction that its most beautiful daughter had run away. Another hapless urchin from a deficient home destined for the gutter. Nate had known better, and now the rest of the Lake had finally caught up. The discovery in the headlands had changed everything.

Nate turned to Tom.

"I told you. I'm being kept away from it," Tom said. "For obvious reasons."

"You have to know something."

"I don't. Truly."

Was this how they had this conversation? Nate wondered. He'd expected it to take longer to work their way toward this. He'd planned to reestablish rapport first, but maybe that had been foolish.

Perhaps that etiquette belonged to a more civilized time in a gentler place. After all, this was the Lake. He'd returned here to talk about only one thing, and that thing was murder.

The silence around their table stretched until it seemed sure to snap.

"That night," Nate leaned forward. "I know it was a long time ago. But—"

"You want to talk about graduation, Nate?" Johnny asked. His voice had the volume of a whisper but the intonation of a shout. "Here? Now? You think half the restaurant isn't watching us? Trying to read every word on our lips? I know you've been away for a long time, but give me a break."

Nate scanned the room. A few patrons at nearby tables glanced away from him. The bartenders along the wall dropped their heads to the glasses they polished.

"Besides, we have more to worry about than ancient history."

"Nate doesn't want to hear any more about the stupid Greenhouse," Tom said.

"You know that's just the tip of it, Tommy. How about the sewage backup at Emma's apartment?" Johnny asked. "You want to hear about that, Nate?"

"Tom told me." He didn't know where Johnny was going with this.

"How about the burst pipe in Adam Decker's law practice? No? What about Owen's wrecked car? And the Union's window?"

"Grams said that was storm damage." The shadow of a thought began to coalesce at the edge of Nate's mind. The shape it took wasn't one he liked.

"It happened during a thunderstorm, but *we* know that doesn't really mean anything, don't we? Not even nor'easters chuck bricks through windows. No more than they use chainsaws to fell trees or axes to chop through drywall to get at pipes."

"Johnny." Tom leaned across the table, getting right into Johnny's face. "Enough."

But now Nate had to know. Even if he didn't want to.

"Okay. You're saying the damage wasn't caused by a storm."

"Sound familiar?"

Storms not as the cause of damage, but an occasion for it. This was a phantom pulled directly from their own tumultuous youths.

"A window in my old bedroom at Grams's house was broken, too," Nate said. "A baseball."

Johnny's face glistened. "A baseball. Fantastic. And what, you thought that was a coincidence?"

Nate didn't think that, even if for a moment he'd pretended to. The rum churned in his stomach. He'd considered many contingencies for this difficult return home, but he hadn't prepared for this. He didn't know what it meant. It seemed impossible, this reprise of their adolescence. A prank in astonishingly poor taste, but he could tell his friends were serious.

"What's going on?" he asked them. "Talk to me, guys. What do I need to know?"

Johnny's mouth was pursed and tension was coiled across his forehead. Tom's jaw was clenched, but his eyes were vulnerable, haunted.

These were the faces of men with secrets. Nate knew because some early mornings, before he remembered who he was supposed to be, he saw the same signs in his own reflection. He'd journeyed here to the cursed territories of his childhood to settle the debts of those years. He'd come here to balance the equations of pain. But the past was a place Nate could only peer at from a distance. Because it frightened him, what he'd find. There were monsters there he couldn't face.

"Please."

He searched his friends' faces, and for a terrible moment he wasn't sure if he knew the people he found there.

It hadn't always been like this.

REVENANTS

I

NATE WATCHED FROM the shadows as the streets ran with clowns, witches, and pop stars.

On his left was Tom, his hockey mask dripping with gore. To his right, Johnny, in the blood-spattered scrubs of an escaped mental patient. But costumes were for kids, and Nate's childhood had ended back in April with a precipitous drop and a fatal stop. This Halloween, Nate trod the Lake disguised as nothing more than the boy he used to be.

"Do you hear the thunder?" Tom whispered.

"God, relax already," Johnny said. "They're almost gone."

A costumed pair trudged away from them. One seemed to be a very large boy in an outfit that looked like a pile of liquor boxes. He was dogged by a petite woman dressed in a tight jumpsuit and cat ears—the boy's mother, Nate assumed. The distance was too great for Nate to hear the details of the woman's tirade, but she was furious about something. She had to get on her tiptoes to hit the boy on the back of his head, and the sound of impact was dull in the clear, wet night.

Nate returned his gaze to the small brick house across the street, where there was still no sign of movement. Alone among its neighbors, this home had no pumpkin or cemetery, no cobweb-netted bushes or backlit ghouls. With every light burning and each curtain agape, the house was open to the world. Exposed.

The burly boy and his mother faded around a corner, though Nate still heard the woman's complaint over the murmuring of the trees.

"I don't see anybody else," Johnny said.

As the rain had thickened, the crowds of trick-or-treaters had thinned. The street was finally empty.

"All right," Nate said. "You know what to do." They had toothpaste, shaving cream, and eggs. "Go," he told them, and they went.

Johnny scampered across the lawn. From the movement of his arms, Nate could tell that he was already emptying a tube of toothpaste into his palm. Tom's motions with the shaving cream were less committed. He squirted a jet of it at the base of the Bennetts' driveway, then glanced to where Nate still stood in the bushes. Nate neither uttered a syllable nor moved his face a millimeter, but Tom got the message. He began emptying the can in methodical zigzags down the length of the drive.

Nate picked up three cartons of eggs and then stared again at the scene in front of him.

They'd hidden in the bushes for a long time, because something about the house bothered him. He didn't like the way it was both well lit and empty. He'd done his homework and knew that Mrs. Bennett and her younger children were out of town. That just left Lucy. Maybe she'd gone out with her new crowd. Maybe she'd left the lights ablaze to dissuade the very vandalism under way.

Johnny slopped tartar control gel across the window closest to the door.

Would she be sad when she saw her defaced home?

Would she be angry or disappointed or afraid?

Nate was soaked, but his fury kept him warm.

He launched the first egg from the street. It exploded against her bedroom window.

"Nice one," he saw Johnny mouth across the distance between them.

Nate had planned to peg each of the second-floor windows with eggs, then shatter the rest against the roof. He wanted the house to be sullied. He wanted its every surface and feature desecrated. Instead, he found himself launching volley after volley at Lucy's window. He still had one good arm, and his aim was dead-eyed.

She'd assaulted his own bedroom window the week before. The third of her cursed baseballs had left slivers of glass sparkling from his bed to his desk. The worst violation yet. The toothpaste, the shaving cream, and the eggs smeared, sprayed, and thrown across her property under the cover of this sopping Halloween night was his turn in an ongoing conversation in which words would never suffice.

Could eggs shatter glass? He wanted to string their viscous whites from every wall in her room. He wanted their stench to taint every thread of clothing she owned and infuse every dream she had with specters of sulfur and hellfire.

He pitched the eggs at her bedroom, and each one failed. Johnny moved to other rooms and Tom filled the mailbox with Barbasol, but Nate remained fixated on that single window. The shrapnel of shells and their evicted contents became a slick that ran from gable to gutter, but in the steady light the glass was uncracked. Magical thinking had shadowed Nate since April. As the cartons emptied, each impact's wet thump stung more than the last. If he broke this window, he'd feel better. If he broke this window, it would have all been a dream. If he broke this window, his family would be alive. Halfway through the last dozen eggs, a wave of emotion crested and threatened to pull him into grief, but he nursed this into a seed of incandescent rage. When Nate stared at the house, he expected to set it aflame with his anger.

Maybe this was how he'd missed the black Mustang creeping toward him down the empty street.

Someone tugged at his sleeve. The distraction sent one of his eggs wide and skittering across the eaves.

"Time to go, dude," Johnny said. Both he and Tom were next to him. Nate got the sense they'd been there for a while, trying to catch his attention. Time had become an inconstant variable in his universe. Sometimes entire days dissolved to night without him noticing. Then there were eras of glacial ponderousness when every week of junior year became its own lifetime.

Nate finally saw the car. Even if he hadn't recognized it as belonging to Adam Decker, Lucy's boyfriend, that its headlights were unlit was reason enough to be suspicious. Now he understood the house's blazing lights and empty windows. It'd been made to look like a target impossible to resist. An enticement.

A trap.

His friends were right. It was time to go. But as he dropped the last of the eggs, something else caught his attention.

An ember brightened on the far end of the shadowed driveway. A cigarette attached to a hand attached to an arm attached to a girl. She moved closer, and as she did her features took shape between the brightness of the house and the darkness of the street. Her hair hung in soaked mats around her jacket. It looked black in the shadows, but there was a gleam of auburn where the light struck her.

"Come *on*, Nate," Tom said. "We've got to *run*."

But Nate didn't run. Lucy must have been hidden in wait for him even longer than he'd watched the house for her. She now moved toward him. Her cigarette disappeared in a dance of sparks across the wet asphalt.

Wheels screamed, cutting through the susurrus of the rain as the Mustang came to life. Color blazed back into the world by way of its headlights.

Johnny's emphatic swearing drew Nate's gaze to two other figures approaching from the direction opposite the Mustang. Adam Decker's neolithic friends, Nate assumed. They gunned the engines of their absurd mopeds.

"Street's blocked!" Johnny said.

Nate returned his attention to Lucy. She'd halted her approach. He took a step toward her, just to see what she'd do. She didn't budge.

"Guys, we're dead," Tom said.

Lately, Nate wondered about this world of the Lake. How he could be *in* a place, *of* a place, and yet remain so distinct from it. At parties, his friends could chatter and bob their heads to music, but Nate was sure that his ears heard a different song than everyone else. He might stand in a circle or sit on a ragged basement couch, but he was not there. He was in the lake, far below the frigid waterline where only the fish could breathe.

"Cut through the Cohens' backyard," he said. "Head to the Strand. We'll meet at Johnny's."

"What about you?" Tom asked.

Nate had his share of unhealthy habits, but worry was not among them. A boy with nothing to lose had nothing to fear.

"Be right behind you."

"Dude, I mean—"

"Go," Nate said, walking toward the girl in the driveway.

It was a small house. The Bennetts' former home on the Strand had a three-car carriage house of roughly the same dimensions. It took Nate only a few steps until he was face-to-face with Lucy.

Same school, same grade, but Nate couldn't remember if he'd been this close to her since April. He felt sure that if they'd exchanged a single word since then he'd remember its every inflection. For months they'd orbited each other like binary stars. All motion was dictated by the other without them once coming into direct contact.

But that was ending now. A collision was ahead. A supernova.

Tom's and Johnny's footsteps cut across the road for the Cohens' lawn. They would have debated before fleeing, Nate knew. They were good friends, and good friends didn't abandon one another lightly. But there was a clock on this action, and its metronome was the roaring of engines.

Nate thought his friends would be safe. The teens on the mopeds and in the car weren't here for them. Events had escalated between him and Lucy since she'd left the first baseball for him back in August. Each felt they'd been wronged by the other, but Nate knew he had the stronger grievance. When you got down to it, what was his crime? All he'd done was live.

"Are you happy?" Lucy asked. It was shocking to hear her address him directly. Her voice was deeper than he remembered. It rasped like dried leaves caught underfoot.

She must have been hoping to ask him this. Maybe this question had been on her tongue since April. He could conclude only that it was rhetorical.

He wasn't given time to answer.

A hand gripped Nate's collarbone and spun him around. He was shoved over the rim of the driveway's masonry, and he tumbled onto the black slick of its surface. Three seniors loomed over him, but Adam Decker was the only one who mattered. He was a blond giant and a standout on the varsity football and lacrosse teams. A schoolyard legend for the worst reasons.

"Why're you down there, man?" Adam asked him. "You'll get all wet."

Nate tried to get to his feet, but the stockiest of the bunch pushed him back.

"The Boy Who Fell keeps on falling," Adam said.

A group of snakes was a pit, and a gang of rats was a plague, but what was the collective noun for bullies? A clod? A rash? Perhaps a remedial? Nate liked it, but the Latin root was problematic. *Remedialis,* as in "remedy."

"Doesn't the miracle boy speak? Or did he lose his voice in the crash, too?" the stocky one asked.

They were a disease, not a cure.

"You must like Halloween, huh, McHale?" Adam said. "Ghosts and zombies all over town?" The massive teen's eyes were gray-blue, like the lake on a winter day. "Maybe tonight you think your mommy, daddy, and baby brother will come back from the dead." He smiled, but his lake-water eyes did not waver.

Nate carefully got to his feet. Adam, Stocky, and the third guy, with skin like a plate of baked beans, boxed him against the garage door. Nate couldn't read the expression on Lucy's face. He wanted to throw her own question back at her. Wanted an honest answer in return.

"Whaddaya think, Luce?" Adam turned to Lucy. "Guys? You ever see someone fall off a cliff and still look so pretty?"

Nate was tall and lean, not yet entirely filled out, but he was on his feet.

He shifted his eyes to Lucy and grinned.

Her emerald irises widened. At first, Nate thought she was excited for the coming carnage. But then she bit her lower lip. And what did that crease between her eyes mean?

Adam stepped between them.

The blond boy moved like a train, but Nate was ready. He adjusted his stance, clenched his fists, and raised them. Then Adam's face twitched and blinked and then he dropped to the pavement with all the unraveling grace of a collapsing tree. When the bully fell, he revealed Johnny behind him. Nate's friend's teeth were bared and he had the thick limb of a fallen branch raised above his head like a club.

Beans stooped to help Adam while Stocky jolted Nate hard against the garage door. But then Tom surprised Stocky by shoving him, sending the older boy off-balance and stumbling over his feet.

Tom and Johnny. They'd come back for him.

Of course they had. They'd never leave him. Since April, Nate had given them more than enough chances and reasons to. If they were still side by side with him now, they would surely be with him forever.

"Don't think they're kidding around, man." Johnny brandished the tree limb like a bat.

Nate tried to remember what he'd done to earn such friends. On his bad days he wished they'd leave him alone—not for his sake, but for theirs. What better lives Tom, Johnny, and Grams would have now if Nate had never found his way out of that car.

Lucy backed away, but caught his eye one last time. *Are you happy?* Nate wanted to ask her. He wanted to scream it.

Adam staggered to his knees. He was unsteady and clutching the back of his head. When he pulled his hand away there was blood.

Nate had prepared himself for a fight, and that was what he intended to get. Adam's strength matched against Nate's fury. He wanted to find out what would be left when they clashed. He wanted to see what would be wrought.

"Please." Tom grabbed Nate's elbow.

The fire inside him flickered. If there was a fight now, Tom and Johnny would bleed along with him. This was why he'd sent them away. If only they'd left him, how much easier everything would be.

"Please."

Nate turned to Tom, and for a moment he had the urge to tell him about the abyss inside him. That hole at his center that he couldn't imagine filling with anything but agony. Maybe there were words that could convey this—a sound he could utter that wasn't a howl—but Nate didn't know them.

So he let himself be prodded into motion. One foot. The other. Then the three of them were running for the Cohens' lawn.

"I can't believe you hit him like that," Tom told Johnny.

"Me either," Johnny said. "Do you think he's pissed?"

The Mustang's wheels squealed behind them.

The deluge was made visible by the car's headlights, casting translucent veils over the night. The wet grass gleamed like a field of jewels spliced by the shadows of trees.

Nate glanced back to see the car gaining speed. He watched it tear across the lawn, kicking clumps of turf aloft to join the wind and rain. He wondered if Lucy was inside. He wondered if she was trying to scare them or kill them. Surely one murderer was enough for any family.

They weaved among trees before climbing over a post-and-rail fence at the property boundary. From the sound of car doors opening, Nate knew the chase wouldn't end there. The headlights projected the long shadows of their pursuers. Nate heard their feet slap against the wet ground.

They ran across another lawn and onto the shimmering expanse of the Strand.

Ahead was the barricade that cordoned the Night Ship from the rest of the town. Greystone Lake's children had a tradition of leaving offerings of glow sticks at its base, and on Halloween this shrine burned more brightly than at any other time of the year. Green light bathed the battered wood in an otherworldly sheen, and beyond this the Night Ship's towers stood sentinel against the purpling headlands.

Tom called for help. It was unseemly, though not insensible. But the grand homes here were set far back from the road. And it was Halloween, the best night of the year to ignore knocks at the door and screams in the dark.

There was only one place left to go. Nate didn't utter its name, and neither did the others. But there it was, just ahead. Its barricade burned in a miasma of green light and its spires were etched against the boiling sky.

Four

The Colonnade's lights wavered. A blast of thunder reverberated through the cushion of Nate's seat.

"There've been a bunch of pranks around town. The ones Johnny's talking about happened during a thunderstorm that hit about a week and a half ago," Tom said. "But there's no evidence they're connected."

Johnny snorted. "I have a seventy-five-thousand-dollar repair bill that tells me we have different definitions of 'prank.'"

Returning to the Lake, Nate knew he'd face uncomfortable alchemies of past and present. Waterlogged secrets and calcified lies risked being revealed. But he'd come here to confront these on his own terms. If what Johnny said was true, vandals once again roamed the Lake cloaked by rain and wind—a development as unexpected as it was unfathomable.

"Tell me about the thunderstorm," he said. The three of them leaned toward one another across the table, their words low but clear. Nate could feel the sear of gazes from around the restaurant, and he could only imagine how he and his friends looked to them now. Still plotting, these boys. Still secretive and strange and up to no good.

"It brought some gray days, but there was hardly any punch to it," Tom said. "Bit of wind, a little rain. Anyway, the vandals used chainsaws and bricks and tools. It's not like they cared if anyone blamed the weather for the damages."

Nate and his friends had started in much the same way. They'd singled out people who they felt had to be punished. Lucy had been the first of their victims, but not remotely the last.

"So they hit the Empire, and Owen, and—"

"Emma, Adam Decker, and Grams," Johnny finished.

Grams had told Nate that the window at the Union broke during the last storm. Not a lie, but a deliberate omission. He understood why. Even the thought of someone hurting her made something dangerous stir inside him.

"All people from the old days." A replay of their high school history, except this time Nate and his friends weren't the perpetrators but the victims. "And whoever they are, they only started causing trouble after her body was found?"

Tom went back to studying the umber gradations of his drink, but Johnny smiled.

"See, Tom. Our Storm King was always smart. That's what I've been saying. We're being targeted."

Johnny's use of his old nickname grated Nate to the bone.

"You're jumping to conclusions," Tom told Johnny. "The Lake's always had more than its share of property damage. This time you're on the receiving end of it, and you're taking it personally."

"Isn't connecting the dots in your job description, Deputy?"

"You can't believe it's coincidence, Tom." Nate couldn't afford the luxury of denial. "Someone's using the storms as cover. Five thousand people live in the Lake, but Johnny, Owen, Emma, Adam, and Grams are the ones they hit? What about the baseball through my bedroom window? How many people these days could know what that would mean to me?"

"Well, that circles around to the elephant in the room, doesn't it?" Johnny pointed to Nate. "All of this started because of you. You might as well have taken a wrecking ball to my ceiling and cut Owen's brake line yourself."

The accusation was reductive, but for Nate it triggered a line of thought. The Thunder Runs, as they'd called their youthful hijinks, hadn't been havoc for its own sake. Nate and his friends didn't attack the innocent: Their targets deserved their punishment. So if the current vandals were truly retracing their old paths, it made Nate wonder what they believed him guilty of. He had so many sins. But if they only began destroying things after the discovery of the body in the headlands—

"You can't blame Nate," Tom said. "He hasn't been back for years. He didn't do anything."

"We *all* did things," Johnny said. "*A lot* of things, to a lot of people. But it started with him, and we all know it."

Johnny was angry. That was something Nate understood.

"I'm sorry about the Greenhouse," he said. "Really. But I'm more worried about what these vandals know. They're obviously onto some of the shit we pulled, because how else could they be reenacting what we did back then? But if they know that much, they could know all kinds of things. The timing can't be a coincidence. Her body is found and then—"

Nate stopped in midsentence because it wasn't just anyone's body they were talking about. It was *Lucy's*. None of them had yet uttered her name, and Nate was suddenly aware of what a betrayal this was. Everything else had already been taken from her. Her name was the last thing she had left.

He was about to amend what he'd said when a tall blond man arrived at the table with a bottle of Hudson Valley bourbon and three tumblers.

"Looks like you're starting to run dry," the man said.

Owen Liffey had been a pudgy boy and even heavier teen, but he'd grown into a broad razor of a man. A tailored gray suit showed off this build as a pair of square silver glasses brought out his bone structure. The lank blond hair Nate remembered from their youth had been trimmed and artfully styled.

The transformation was stunning. It was marred only by a bandage over his right eyebrow.

"Wow. I can't believe it." Nate shook his head. "Sorry, that sounded really patronizing, didn't it? But you look great, you really do, O. Good for you. Dammit, that's an even worse thing to say, isn't it?"

Owen laughed and clasped Nate on the shoulder. "It's okay. I'm used to it."

"O's just being polite," Tom said. "He lost the weight years ago."

"The Empire has a certain rep to uphold." Johnny grabbed the bottle with one hand and patted his swollen belly with the other. "Can't have a bunch of fat asses running the place."

Nate remembered hearing that Owen's father had died a few years ago, and that his mother had suffered a serious stroke not long after.

"I'm the manager these days," Owen said. "Speaking of which, and apologies for mixing business and pleasure, but Lindsay Stone called back," he told Johnny. "She's fine with the raw bar changes, but she wants a gratis upgrade of the wines."

"Of course she does." Johnny uncapped the bourbon and sloshed a generous amount into the tumblers. "Lindsay's wedding reception was supposed to be in the Greenhouse this Saturday." An amber stain crept across the tablecloth. "The hurricane's been less of a hassle."

"I thought she was already married," Nate said.

Johnny shook his head. "Is this engagement three or four for our lovely Lindsay, Owen?"

"Three, I think. She came awfully close last time."

"Who's she marrying?"

"Some idiot," Johnny said. "Anyway, her dad lost the deposits the last couple times so I offered the house as an alternative space. I'd go the Vegas route if I had to do it again, but she loves the attention. The back lawn has enough space for two big tents, and as far as settings go, they can do a lot worse."

The Vanhouten mansion was a massive Georgian on the waterfront side of the Strand. No matter the season, its grounds were immaculately maintained by the same gardeners who handled the landscaping at the Empire. In the boys' youth, a person would never guess that the sprawling place housed only a teenager and an alcoholic.

"Still, it's going to suck. For me, at least. Have to host a day care too, just for Sarah Carlisle's kid, who looks like a thing that roams the forest eating campers. Of course, Lindsay's spitting blood about the funeral being the day before her wedding. Like some final revenge of Lucy's, she said."

Lindsay had always been difficult. Some people mellow with age; others ferment.

Owen's phone chimed, and he checked its screen. "Front desk. We'll catch up tomorrow, okay? At the funeral?"

A chord of dread thrummed within Nate. He'd hardly let himself think of the funeral, but he had a convincing, ready smile that kept him a favorite with the nurses and children on his ward. He shook Owen's hand.

"He was a late bloomer, wasn't he?" Nate said once Owen was out of earshot.

Johnny rolled his eyes.

"He used to want to be a veterinarian, right?"

"And Tom wanted to be an architect, and I wanted to live someplace where the temperature occasionally wanders above freezing," Johnny said. "O probably didn't count on being sole caregiver to his shrew of a mother, either. Not everybody gets what they want, Nate."

"The cut on his forehead. That's from—"

"Rolling down Snake Hill without brakes, crashing through the barrier on Finch, and slamming into an elm tree," Johnny said.

"He's lucky to be alive," Tom said. "His car was totaled."

"So how'd they do it?" Nate asked. "You're saying these vandals pulled off, what, five attacks during one storm?" Even at the height of their mischief, Nate and his friends had never attempted more than one Thunder Run a night. Burst pipes and backed-up sewage were complicated undertakings, while cutting someone's brake lines could easily have fatal consequences. He wondered what kind of people he was dealing with.

"We don't know how many there are," Tom said. "We asked the high school to keep their ears open for anything. The middle school, too."

Kids. Nate knew as well as anyone that vandalism was the province of the young.

"There'd have to be a whole pack of them to get us at once," Johnny said. "That or they're real overachievers."

"They didn't get Tommy," Nate said.

"Tom, you'd tell us if you secretly spent your free time leading a band of urchins on a terror campaign, wouldn't you, buddy?"

"They didn't get Lindsay, either," Tom said. "If Adam's on their list, you'd think she'd be there, too." The people who'd suffered damages were an odd combination of old friends and enemies. "Maybe there are a lot of vandals, but not enough to get all of us at once? Or maybe they don't want to mess with a cop, or, you know, Lindsay?"

A slow breaking roll of thunder shuddered from the ceiling.

"Sneaky and smart and totally amoral," Johnny mused as he poured himself more bourbon. "Dangerous combo, huh, Nate? The makings of a real monster, don't you think?"

Nate ignored the jab, because he'd just realized something that should have occurred to him half an hour ago. If these vandals were taking a page from his old playbook, then they'd wait until the next storm to carry out more destruction. And the next storm was happening right now.

He worked his arms into his jacket as he got up. Whoever was doing this, they'd already attacked Grams twice. Two broken windows—one at the Union and one at the house on Bonaparte Street.

It was just before nine o'clock, and Nate figured the pub would be safely occupied for hours. That left the house. He wasn't going to let his grandmother suffer anymore because of him.

"I have to get back to Bonaparte Street," Nate said. He retrieved his umbrella from the floor. "They might come back."

"Patrols are running all night monitoring wind damage," Tom said. "I asked them to keep a special eye out around places vandalized last time, and I added Grams's house to the list."

"What happened to 'no evidence,' Tom?" Johnny asked. His glass was somehow empty again. "How about 'jumping to conclusions'?"

"I'm the cautious one, remember?"

"What does that make the rest of us?" Johnny asked.

Tom started to edge his way out of the booth. "I'll drive you to Grams's," he told Nate.

"It's fine, I'll walk." It wasn't far. Besides, if these vandals were anything like Nate and his friends had been, they'd be on their feet, dipping in and out of darkness on the side streets of the battened-down town. If he was with them in the throes of the storm, Nate had a chance of catching them. Then he could find out what they wanted. Then he could find out what they knew.

"Maybe you haven't been keeping abreast of current events," Johnny said. "But it's pouring out."

Nate turned to him. "Don't you remember, Johnny?" He flipped up his jacket collar and smiled. "I like the rain."

REVENANTS

II

FEET SHATTERED THE puddles behind Nate as he and his friends sprinted for the Night Ship's barricade. Adam Decker and the others were close.

The town children's altar of green glow sticks gave the scene ahead an infernal quality, as if the barricade marked not only the division between the Strand and the pier, but the border between this world and another. This thought set a hook in Nate's mind, distracting him enough that he didn't notice the boy crouched in front of the shrine until he collided with him.

They tumbled over the sidewalk in a tangle of limbs and phosphorescent batons.

Tom yanked Nate back to his feet. With more difficulty, Johnny helped the other boy off the ground. In the unearthly light, Nate recognized the overweight boy they'd earlier seen being assailed by his mother. He wore a catastrophic rendition of a robot costume. His chest piece was a box studded with corks and stray keyboard pieces. His mask might have begun as a brown paper bag, but it had been pulped by the rain. Past its oatmeal clots Nate recognized the pudgy jowls of Owen Liffey, one of their classmates. The big guy got to his feet, ungainly as a newborn elephant.

Behind them, Adam yelled something indecipherable into the wind.

Nate scrambled over the planks of the barricade. He reached back to help Tom, but found Owen in his place. The sound of the seniors' rage must have spurred the heavy boy to run, and the Night Ship was the only place to go.

Tom and Johnny followed Owen over the barrier, and the four of them sprinted down the long, battered pier.

"They're not following," Johnny shouted after a minute.

"Would you?" Tom asked.

They slowed to a jog. They were halfway down the pier. The storm had obscured the moon, and what light the town cast broke across the waves. Nate felt a spike of vertigo as he crossed the lake's restless surface.

The reality of what they'd just done began to sink in.

Owen had been bringing up the rear. He was as out of shape as he looked. "What's going on?" he asked, doubling over from the exertion.

"Running for our lives, obviously," Johnny said.

"And you came *here*?"

Nate peered back down the taper of the pier. Shadows shifted in the radiance of the glow sticks. Adam and the others were still there, but appeared unwilling to cross the threshold. Nate hadn't hesitated. Before April, he'd been as afraid and fascinated by the Night Ship as any other kid in town. But now . . .

"We have to get out of the rain," he said.

"How?" Tom asked, though he surely knew the answer.

"It might be haunted, but at least it's dry," Johnny said.

Nate started toward the Night Ship.

As he neared the structure, his eyes began to pull apart the layers of darkness. The immense building ahead was a slick of black struck between the silken water and the bleak sky. He was amazed at how large the deserted structure really was. The pier it sat on extended so far into the lake that you couldn't appreciate its dimensions from the shore. It was a world in itself.

The boardwalk that ringed the enormous place was there for everyone to see, but all that Nate knew of the Night Ship's interior came from black-and-white photographs and the stories that were traded like contraband among the town's children. At the height of its popularity, dozens of shops and eateries had populated the pier. He knew that a central promenade lanced the interior of the building like a spine. Many of the establishments that flanked this airy corridor also opened outside onto the boardwalk, so that their patrons could enjoy the fresh air and unparalleled views of the water and mountains.

Nate put both his hands on the wooden doors to the Night Ship. They were battered, warped, and weather scarred, but they were also unlocked. They screamed when Nate pushed them open. Once inside, his eyes adjusted to the dark well enough to see the storm heaving through the ribs of the pier's ancient steelwork roof. Rain pounded what remained of the glass-paneled ceiling, and the air brimmed with the reek of stagnant water. As he took his first steps down the promenade, he imagined how it might have looked on a summer day eighty years ago. Light streaming onto polished wooden floors, men in linen suits and straw hats arm in arm with women draped in silk and lace.

The ruined pier was a gravestone for a dead world. A faded history filled with grace and style. But elegance wasn't the same as innocence.

During the day, the Night Ship had been a favorite spot for weekenders and the summer people, but things had been different after sundown. Just June and Morton Strong could have told you that, and their victims would have had a few things to say on the subject as well. Confections far stronger than sodas and ice cream had marked the last days of the Century Room.

"Well, I guess it's *drier*," Tom said. Though water dripped all around them, a surprising number of the glass ceiling panels were intact.

"Just as dark, though," Johnny said. He hugged his shoulders and began to shiver. His mental patient hadn't dressed for an all-weather escape.

"I have something," Owen said. Nate heard the rustling of foil, and a moment later there was a *pop* as a viridescent light kindled in Owen's hands. "I was going to leave it at the barricade." He handed the glow stick to Nate.

Owen was about five years too old for such nonsense, but Nate appreciated the light. He used it to lead them. The wide promenade stretched under riveted arches of steel supports. Creeping through it was like descending the throat of a leviathan. The drumming of water sounded from unseen corners, and the wash of the lake against the pilings below them ebbed and surged like shuddering breath. They passed entrances to shops and restaurants as they made their way down the warped hall. Their distressed signage was barely legible in the scant light. Café des Amis, Burton's Sodas, Bit o' Sweet Shop.

Then it appeared in front of them. The promenade ended at its doorstep. Nate could just make out its name and the image of a galleon with its sail full with wind, cutting for the horizon and a huge full moon. The Night Ship.

Every bad thing that had happened on this pier had taken place in there. If the building were a body, this nightclub was its heart.

Nate sensed his friends' unease as the light skirted the infamous bar's sign. He felt something himself, but it wasn't fear. His damaged arm had also begun to hurt, as it sometimes did during storms.

"Let's go in," he said.

"Uh-uh," Tom said. "No way."

"Nothing else has been mega-creepy yet, I guess," Johnny said.

"This is where all the people died?" Owen asked. He peered through the stained glass doors.

Nate tried one of the handles, then forced the door with his shoulder. Even then he was able to work it open little more than a foot before it caught on the warped flooring. Nate, Tom, and Johnny slipped through, and with some effort Owen joined them.

Shadows of tables and chairs littered the dark space in front of them. Nate could make out the hulk of a massive bar on the left side of the room. The rear of the nightclub was two stories of windows. Nate couldn't see the rain hitting the glass, but he could hear it.

"Just June used to live right here," Tom whispered as if they were in a church. "She and her sister May were twins. They called them the Night Ship Girls. Their mother was one of the prostitutes upstairs in the Century Room. When they were young, before everything happened, they lived in a little room under the dance floor, and at night they'd crawl through the walls, spying on the customers through peepholes."

It was easy to imagine hidden eyes peering at them through the cavernous dark.

"Just June made all the boys swoon, cost ya just a dollar to bring her to your room," Johnny sang.

A large cylinder shrouded in disintegrating velvet stood to the right of the nightclub's entrance. Its color was impossible to determine in the sickly light from the glow stick. When Nate examined it, he saw that it concealed a spiral staircase that led both upstairs and downstairs. Nate knew from the stories that the legendary Century Room, the club's VIP section, was above.

"They say June wasn't even in her teens when she started working as one of Morton Strong's enforcers," Tom continued. "Old Mort used to own the whole pier. Back then, this place had prostitutes, gambling—you name it. Strong was the North Country's answer to Al Capone. June was nine when she pulled her first fingernail from one of the Century Room's welchers."

"Strong, Strong, don't ever do him wrong. He'll set ya on the short pier, but the walk you'll take is long."

The Lake loved its stories. Nate knew this, because he'd become one of them. He was the Boy Who Fell. He was the one whose survival cleaved to no logic but the lake's own ineffable imperatives.

"Check it out," Johnny said. "Bring over the light."

Nate followed the sound of his friend's voice to the sprawling bar. He tripped over something, and the rattle of glass broke the silence of the place.

"Bottles everywhere, man," Johnny said. "Still stuff in them, too."

Nate gave Johnny the glow stick. A few dozen bottles remained on shelves where there had surely once been hundreds. There were more on the floor, some intact and others bristling with shards.

"It's weird that they left all this stuff here, isn't it?" Owen asked.

"Looks like they left in a hurry," Johnny said, lowering his voice by an octave. He put the light under his chin to cast his face in eldritch angles.

Shattered glassware was strewn across the floor, and some of the tables appeared to be half-set. Nate imagined the place packed with crowds: happy patrons one moment, a riotous stampede the next. He imagined them overturning furniture and tearing at one another to escape.

"I don't remember how it closed," Tom said. "Did it shut down after Just June got through with it?"

Nate shrugged. A place like this was built of myth and varnished in legend. Like all the Lake's stories, the truth hardly mattered. Here was a place so strange, girls might scurry as quiet as rats through passages hidden in the walls. Here was a place so vast, dancers might spin to the band never knowing that a room above them rang with screams. Nate sat on one of the stools. The bar's surface was scarred with marks as if scoured by countless fingernails.

Lucy's face floated to the surface of his mind. She wore that look she'd had when Adam was only inches from laying into Nate. The look of a person who'd unwrapped a coveted gift only to realize it was something they didn't at all want.

"Maybe the liquor's still good," Johnny said. "I'm freezing."

They were sopping, and it wasn't any warmer here than it was outside. He uncorked a bottle and sniffed it. "Brandy, I think." He pushed it over to Nate.

"Alcohol can go bad, you know," Owen said. "It can make you blind."

Nate tipped the bottle into his mouth and swallowed a sludge of peach and gasoline.

Lucy had been as angry at him as he was furious with her. But her rage had dissolved at the very moment it seemed sure to deliver its dividends.

"We saw you on the street before," Johnny told Owen. "Was that your mom with you? She's a piece of work. I saw her hit you."

"Oh," Owen said. He looked at the floor.

It puzzled Nate, this thing with Lucy. They were enemies. They had been since April, though her hatred had never made much sense to him. He'd already lost so much. But if he had to parse the chances that compounded upon other chances to lead to the accident, if he had to scrape past the death and pain that obscured the facts, it was difficult to remember why, for his part, he'd judged Lucy as guilty as he had.

"Your dad's one of the managers at the Empire, isn't he?" Johnny asked.

"Yeah. And Mom's an accountant there," Owen said.

"What'd you do to get her so pissed?"

"Breathing would piss her off." Owen lifted his eyes from the floor. "She hates how fat I am. No one wants to have a porker for a son. That's what she calls me. The Porker. She puts me on all kinds of diets."

"I guess trick-or-treating isn't exactly Weight Watchers approved."

"Yeah, she didn't like that at all."

Above, Nate could just make out the banisters of the Century Room. Legend had it that Morton Strong and Just June once threw a meddling do-gooder from its heights to the bar below. Maybe the planks upon which Nate's stool sat were the same ones that had shucked the woman's brain from her skull.

Morton Strong and Just June were the Lake's most infamous villains. They were the bad guys in the stories that most haunted the Night Ship. They were murderers, thieves, and extortionists, yet there was still something to admire in them. Because imagine shaking loose the restrictions of law and goodness and rightness. Imagine tearing loose of other people's expectations and other people's rules.

Imagine being free.

"So you were hiding from her?" Tom asked.

"I wasn't hiding."

"You were standing in the dark by yourself in the rain," Johnny said. "Or is that normal for you?"

"Give him a break, Johnny," Tom said.

The Lake's stories weren't the same as truth. The kind of lore that mythologized the Night Ship was the type that grows from teller to teller. Stakes are heightened and nuance is lost. Events are polarized until all that's left to see is black and white. Every story needed villains, but Morton Strong and Just June had once been people, and no single word could sum up the true nature of a person. Even if it could, you had to remember that people are always changing.

Kindness is Spackle. Tragedy, a chisel. The shape that's left is who you are.

This made Nate wonder what kind of people June and Strong had been before the Night Ship. It made him wonder what had turned them into the Lake's most celebrated monsters.

"Come on, tell me, O," Johnny said. "Why're you hiding? What does she do?"

Nate sometimes possessed searing focus; at other times his thoughts wandered landscapes of circuitous paths. His consciousness occupied more than one time and space, as if the accident in April had hammered more than his ribs and arm into shards, as if more than just his shoulder had been dislocated. Sometimes he had near-impossible insight, while other times he missed things that were right in front of him. Perhaps that's why he only now became aware of the change in the room's weather.

When he glanced at Johnny, he didn't recognize the look on his friend's face. This wasn't some trick of the alien lighting. His irrepressible friend was gone. Someone else was in his sodden clothes.

"Tell me what she does," Johnny said again. He put his hands on Owen's shoulders.

" 'What she does'?" Owen frowned.

"To hurt you," Johnny said.

"It's just she cares a lot about what people think, you know?" Owen said. "And—" He hesitated. "Forget it, you wouldn't get it, anyway." He turned back to study the floor, but Johnny used his palm to force Owen's gaze back upward.

"Oh, you think my dad likes toting around the only kinky-haired kid at the club? You think this black mark that stares back at him from every family photo warms his ice-blue blood?"

"Johnny—" Tommy said.

But Owen nodded. "I guess it's sort of like that." His head bobbed faster as he chewed it over. "Yeah, I mean, not exactly, obviously, but—you're right." In the odd light, his blush was orange. "Sorry. I shouldn't have said that you wouldn't—"

"It's fine, O. But since I do get it, you gotta tell me what she does."

"Everything's just so beautiful at the Empire, you know? So at home everything's got to be exactly right. She spends every weekend on her rose garden because she knows the neighbors are jealous of it. She takes her dogs to the groomer once a week." Once he'd started, it poured like water through a crumbling dam. "Everything in her life is perfect. Everything but me. The *Porker*. She likes it when I'm not around," Owen said. "Then she can pretend she's got the life she wants."

Nate waited for tears to pool Owen's eyes, but the boy's gaze was dry. The weight Owen carried in his face gave him a cherubic look, but in the strange light, it looked like a mask.

Owen's story was unpleasant, but that wasn't what hooked Nate's attention.

"Why, Johnny?" Nate asked.

Johnny talked about movies and video games. He lived for sneaked liquor, prurient humor, and basement parties that ended in a closet with a girl and a stopwatch. He didn't assail acquaintances with soul-baring questions. It wasn't who he was. Something was wrong, and it had nothing to do with Owen or his mother.

Johnny's face clouded with something. Doubt. Fear. Whatever it was, Nate didn't think it would last. The thing about secrets is that most of them want to be told.

"Show me." Sometimes Nate understood things he couldn't possibly know. He'd never claim the ability to read a person's mind, but sometimes he thought he could feel its texture.

Johnny didn't say anything, but when he grabbed the hem of his soaked scrubs there was already something like relief in his eyes. He pulled his shirt over his head and stood bare-chested before them. He hugged his shoulders in the cold and looked at the floor before turning around.

Tom gasped.

Though Johnny stood in the full illumination of the glow stick, Nate first thought a shadow had fallen across him. Three black stripes divided his back. The space between them was mottled, its true colors impossible to discern in the tinted light.

"I came home Tuesday and found Dad in the kitchen," Johnny said. He kept his back to them, but turned his head to speak. "He'd pulled everything from the fridge onto the floor, and he was rooting through it, looking for something. The mustard, he said. What did I do with the goddamned mustard? I don't even eat mustard, but that doesn't stop him. He starts ripping into me. The usual stuff: I don't respect his things, I'm an ungrateful cockroach. The worst thing that ever happened to him. Possibly second only to my whore of a mother. I know—no one ever accused him of originality. I try to walk out, but he doesn't like that, either. He pulls me back, and I shove him away. I shouldn't have done that. He's wasted, obviously, and falls right over. He gets lo mein on his suit. He throws me against the counter. I try to run and he hits me with a kitchen chair." Johnny started to slip his shirt back on. "I slammed into the wall headfirst. The chair broke, but a new one appeared a couple days later. The wall was patched up, too. Maya cleaned up the mess, like she always does."

"*Johnny.*" Tom's hands were clasped over his ears as if what had been said could be unheard. As if forgetting could make it untrue. "You know you can sleep over whenever you want, right? With Nate, too," he said, looking over at Nate.

Nate's own arm and side had been similarly bruised after the accident. Even from the depths of tranquilized shock, he'd registered the extraordinary color on his side where three of his ribs had broken. Every touch met with a dagger of agony and an alien firmness. Looking through red eyes at his skinny body, at the bandaged incisions under the plastic sheath over his arm and the expanding nebula of subdermal hematomas, Nate understood truly and completely that he'd one day die. That no matter the infinities of his mind, this meat and bone was all that tethered him to this earth.

And look at how tenuous that connection was: a hair's breadth from being undone by a baseball and the promise of a peach pie. And he'd been the lucky one. The lake returns what it takes, but he was the only one given back in time for it to matter.

Johnny's shirt was back on, but Nate could still see the ruin of his back. He could imagine his friend being chased by a man twice his weight. A man who was supposed to love him. He felt the breath knocked from Johnny when he crashed against the wall. That surge of pain as his stunned body took its inventory of the damage. He watched the childhood drain from Johnny as he lay on the kitchen tile, replaced with something cold and numb and knowing.

It'd be easy to despair at how unjust the universe was, but that wasn't Nate's way. He'd spent energy taunting Lucy and being baited by her, but he now understood that this had been childish. They were both victims. Their pain had been mighty, but their wrath had been misdirected.

There were true monsters here at the Lake. Lucy wasn't one of them, and they didn't infest the halls of the Night Ship. Beasts like Mr. Vanhouten and Owen's mom were the real enemy. They infected this town—and like any disease, they had to be treated. Like the pain they caused, they had to be burned away.

"We'll get him, Johnny," Nate said.

The others turned to him.

"Your mom, too, Owen." He felt his mouth crease into a smile.

"What do you mean?" Tom asked.

Nate decided that neither he nor his friends would ever be victims again. He grinned because he understood that while misery was an affliction, wrath was a tool. While anguish was weakness, fury was power.

He smiled because at last he knew what to do with his unquenchable rage.

Five

Medea was coming.

Nate could feel this in the wind and see it in the webs of electricity flaring within the soaring topography of the sky. No storm of his youth came close to what Medea was about to inflict upon the Lake.

In its deep place, a part of Nate twitched in its sleep.

He wasn't far from the Empire's entrance when a small figure detached itself from the shadows of a side street. Against the gray of the pavement, it was a silhouette of pure darkness. The way it was slumped made Nate take notice. *A kid,* he thought. Suspicion pricked across his neck. This wariness wasn't just from the knowledge that vandals once again haunted these streets. Looking at the shrouded person, dressed in black, standing in the rain, an old thorn caught in a tangle of memories. There was a lacuna in Nate's mind, right in the center of the worst day of his life. He was rarely reminded of this absence, but this was one of those times.

He slowed his pace. As he did, whoever it was stopped to stare at him. Something was wrong. What Nate had first taken for a long raincoat was actually a mismatched collection of shirts and sweaters. The clothes were strange, nearly rags, and it was difficult to see where one layer ended and another began.

Then the person slid back the hood. An old woman.

"You," the woman said. Her voice was hushed in astonishment. Then she crooked a single finger at him. "*You!*" She was a wizened thing, and her face stretched into a furious grimace. The mass of wiry white hair that her hood had concealed shot from her head in all directions.

"I'm sorry?" Nate heard himself saying.

"After everything, you come back here? You ruined it!" she screamed. "You ruined everything!"

Nate was familiar with the insanity of strangers. His ER rotation had been a master class in everyday madness, and his trips via the subway were refresher courses. This woman had martyr's eyes, blazing with righteousness and resignation. He gave her a wide berth, his hands raised in surrender.

The woman's face changed as he moved. Lucidity took grip. For a moment it seemed as if *she* suddenly had become afraid of *him*. Then she donned her hood and bolted. She cut across the road with surprising speed, her footsteps breaking the shining palette of the street.

Nate looked around, but the sidewalks were bereft of witnesses. The woman was gone, the shadows on the other side of the street absent even a hint of movement. He might as well have imagined her.

He hurried to put the encounter behind him.

As he made his way to the house on Bonaparte Street, he was caught between the need to rush there to protect it and the desire to submerge himself in the rhythms of the storm and let it guide him to the vandals who'd fallen upon the Lake.

Walking these rain-scoured streets gave Nate the sense of homecoming he'd been missing. This was an all-sensory revelation: the wetness of his cuffs clinging to his socks, the scuff of his steps through puddles, the thousand shades of dark that marked the squalling night.

The only thing that wasn't right was that he was alone. Again, he'd left his friends behind.

Despite his umbrella, Nate was soaked to the knees by the time he got to Grams's house. The home looked the way it was supposed to. The lights in the living room were on, and his grandmother's car was in the driveway.

The door was locked again, and he had to ring the bell.

"I meant to give you a key," Grams said as she opened the door. She looked him over. "Don't tell me you walked, boy. I thought you'd get a ride with Tommy. I'd have picked you up."

"I didn't think you'd be back so early." When he'd lived here, Grams rarely returned from the Union before two in the morning. He shucked off his shoes and peeled away his sopping socks.

"I let the managers lock up on weeknights."

"Good. You're not going to be young forever, you know."

Grams snorted. "I don't suppose you actually ate anything. Got some fish and chips warming in the oven. That a suit you're wearing? Is the Academy Awards in town? Mailman must have lost my invitation again."

As Grams went into the kitchen, Nate climbed to his bedroom. He changed from his suit into jeans and a sweater. Back downstairs, he flicked on the outdoor lights and surveyed the front lawn from the panels of the door. Raindrops glistened across the grass, and branches shuddered in the wind.

In the kitchen, an aluminum pan filled with breaded fish and French fries was at the center of the table between two place settings. Bottles of ketchup and tartar sauce were close by.

Nate sat at his old place.

This was how they'd eaten in his last years of high school. Grams would come home around six, and they'd share something from the

Union's kitchen before she headed back to the pub in time for the drinkers' shift.

Grams asked how things had gone at the Empire, and Nate told her how great it had been to see Tom and Johnny. How he hadn't realized how much he'd missed them. Maybe he'll come back to town again soon, he said. Maybe he'll bring the whole family.

It's what she wanted to hear.

"You should have told me about the window at the Union," Nate said once they'd finished eating.

"Now why'd Tommy go and bother you with that?" She started to gather the dishes. "I didn't want you to worry. It was only a window. Just had it boarded up snug and tight to keep the inside dry. Nothing to fuss about."

"A window here was broken, too."

"What? Where?"

Nate could believe that she hadn't noticed it. If she had, it would have been cleaned up. Grams started for the stairs, but he was quick to spare her the climb.

"My bedroom. I swept up the glass and boarded it with cardboard. Tommy's having someone fix it tomorrow."

"We have the funeral tomorrow."

"And the hurricane. Don't want to go into it already down a window. The funeral's not until late morning?"

"Eleven o'clock."

"I don't know when the worst of Medea is going to hit."

Grams flicked on the kitchen's little television. The screen came alive with data and scrolling weather advisories. Medea was the only news.

The meteorologists had honed the hurricane's projected path. Its trajectory would take the eye north of the city but south of the Lake. The coast would see the worst of it, but the storm had a diameter of over five hundred miles, so the Lake would get more than a glancing blow.

Nate tried not to let himself be lulled by the footage of shattered boardwalks and inundated towns. Surf churned where islands had been. Rain-glazed lenses filmed abandoned shore communities. This time tomorrow these places might not exist at all. When this was over, they might be only names on an obsolete map.

The universe didn't care. It never had.

Shootings, wars, diseases, bombings. You had to work not to be dulled by the ceaseless repetition of tragedy. Because Nate knew it wasn't enough to witness the pain of others. To make it matter, he had to *feel* it.

"Poor people," Grams said. On the screen, sheathes of roofs cut through the ocean like breaching whales. "We're so lucky, boy."

Lucky that they didn't live on the shore. Lucky that they didn't want for food or shelter or so many other things. Lucky because of all the people they loved who'd been taken, they were still here.

"We are, Grams." No matter what had happened, this was undeniably true.

Nate was grateful for the family he had and the life he lived. But he'd lost too much to ever feel safe.

Medea couldn't be fought any more than reality itself. But this wasn't true for everything. Drunks who ran families off cliffs, bullies who tortured the weak, vandals who attacked grandmothers.

They could be resisted. They could be stopped.

They could be punished.

November 30

I thought this journal was just another one of Dr. Karp's stupid ideas, but I've got to get this down somewhere.

It started at the boutique. Or maybe way before then. Halloween? April?

I don't know. It's hard to track it all back to one thing. Karp says perspective can only be achieved by treading a path of time along an incline of self-awareness. Seriously, that's what the guy said. Like he's trying out slogans for crappy inspirational posters. Headshrinkery aside, I get that it can be hard to get a handle on things, especially while you're still drowning in them.

Anyway, the boutique. I shouldn't have even looked through its windows, and going inside the place was totally insane.

Textbook self-destructive behavior, Karp will tell me if he ever reads this. Indicative of self-hatred. Serious comorbidity with depression. Dangerously habit forming. Total cliché.

Whatever it is, it happened. But let the record show that I didn't do it for me. I did it for Mom.

Christmas is only a month away, and we're a mess. The babies are so young that they barely even realize Dad's gone, that Mom's tired, that our food's down to supermarket generics. Christmas is supposed to be magic for kids, but they don't even know this, and maybe that's the saddest part.

This time last year, I had a long wish list of fancy gifts, but I'm not one of those girls anymore. I don't need to compete with everyone else, which is good, because I can't.

No present's worth Mom picking up another shift at the hospital. She works too hard already. For Christmas I wanted there to be at least one nice thing for her under the tree.

Me, Lindsay, and the Sarahs loved this boutique. Everything here's delicate and expensive and made to be admired. I used to fit right in—you could have hung a price tag from my pinky finger and propped me in the corner. But that was before I learned that something fragile is just about begging to be crushed, and anything beautiful is asking to be defaced.

Everything in the shop still looks like it'd be at home in a Manhattan art gallery except Mrs. Sackett, who'd fit in better in some moldy Egyptian exhibit. The old bag's on the phone when I come in, and I'm happy to slink right past her.

I try on a pair of huge sunglasses, pouting in the mirror like an actress. Part of me wishes Lindsay and the others would sashay in, all chittering like we all used to. They'd freeze when they saw me, and the silence in the little store would grow and fester and bloat until it became a physical thing.

My eyes are on my reflection, but my attention's on my left hand as it drifts to a display of bracelets. My fingers creep along the smooth band of a silver cuff studded with amethyst. They slide through the cool metal, and just like that it's sitting on my wrist, perched like a crown on my winter skin.

I play with the sunglasses awhile longer before moving to the pashminas, then get ready to stalk past Mrs. Sackett. The woman used to be one of Mom's friends back in the days when they returned her calls.

I should have smiled at Mrs. Sackett, but my smile's broken. I check in the mirror sometimes and it's all edges. About as heartwarming as a chainsaw.

Would have been wasted anyway.

Sackett clears her throat. Lifts and injections have left the creature's face a weird combo of puffed and taut, but she can still squint her eyes. Now they're slitted with disgust and, I'm pretty sure, satisfaction. Those bracelets are hard to resist, aren't they? she asks me.

Of course she'd been watching. Hoping for me to screw up.

Our family's disgrace is the kind where no one's worse to us than the people we used to think of as friends. A criminal, just like her father, Sackett will tell the vultures at the club.

Oh my gosh! Totally spaced, Mrs. Sackett! I tell her in the

most convincing little girl voice I've got. That I'd stumbled home just before dawn and already smoked half a pack probably doesn't help. I pull off the bracelet and put it on the counter.

Sackett the Hatchet. Lindsay came up with the nickname, and it fits the lady way better than the tops she wears.

What an airhead! the Hatchet says with a smile as fake as her tan. And then: Cash or credit?

Obviously, I'd planned to plea ditziness and return the bracelet. But of course the Hatchet's not going to let me leave her store before milking this for every possible drop of drama. This is around when I realize how idiotic it was for me to come here. Even before the trial and settlement, I knew the woman was a beast. And now her boutique is the forbidden territory of a lost life. Might as well be marked with caution tape and hung with blinking red signs. Trespassers will be prosecuted.

Well? the Hatchet asks me again.

I'm not rich and popular anymore. Sometimes I think the only thing left of that girl is her pride. But the card I'd been an authorized user for was shredded months ago, and I doubt I've got more than ten dollars in my pocket.

I ask her how much it is.

Three fifty-nine ninety-nine, she tells me.

Crazy, right?

Not including tax, she can't help adding. Surgeries have dulled the Hatchet's expressions, but the glee in her eye is like neon.

I check and find out that my wallet holds all of seven singles.

If you can't pay for it, I'm afraid I'll have to call the police, she says. She lifts the phone's receiver to her ear.

It really was an accident, I tell her.

We should probably leave that to the authorities, she says. I'm sure the security footage will help, she tells me.

Getting picked up for shoplifting won't be the worst thing to happen to me—not even close—still, something about this really hits me. Like being carted to the police station will prove how far I've fallen and trash any hope of recovery.

I've got to admit, begging for mercy occurs to me. I could throw myself to the floor and grovel like a dog. But that'd give this town exactly what it wants. They want me on my knees just to kick me in the face.

I think about escape. Adam's right outside, idling in his stupid car. Things have been rough between us since Halloween, but he might actually like the idea of being a getaway guy. But this is a dumb fantasy.

I picture Mom picking me up at the station. Everyone would know, but they already know worse things about us. Our family burned to the ground months ago, so one more match won't make a difference.

So I'm doomed. But if the Hatchet's going to take me down, I'm going to make it hurt.

Fine, I tell her, go ahead and call the cops you plastic, coyote-faced—

And I never get a chance to finish what I'm sure would have been a world-class burn, because right then, out of nowhere, someone says: I'll cover it, Mrs. Sackett.

I turn and see Nate McHale in the doorway.

The Hatchet stares at Nate, turns to me, then back to Nate, like having both of us in her little store at the same time contradicts some basic law of physics.

It's not easy to avoid someone in a place as small as the Lake. Especially when you share three classes with the guy. Still, I've been doing a decent job of it since Halloween.

This journal's supposed to be whatever I want it to be, right? Worries and nightmares and dreams and all that teenaged shit. Well, ruining that Halloween for Nate was a primary short-term goal. Call me petty. It'd be the closest thing to a compliment I've gotten in weeks.

By Halloween, Nate and I had been playing for months. A

sport without rules. After breaking his bedroom window with another baseball, I knew Nate couldn't resist some old-school Halloween mischief. So I made the house too juicy to resist and hid behind a tree with a cellphone.

Shaving cream sprayed, toothpaste squirted, eggs launched. I guess it was too wet to bother with the TP. I know he's doing all this to hurt me, but watching it happen, I don't feel a thing. That little brick house is where I sleep, but it isn't my home. Home is broken. Pieces of it are scattered between here and Ogdensburg.

That's where Mom and the twins were on Halloween, visiting Dad. They still go every other week, but I wonder how long that'll keep up. I've gone a couple times.

I remember them floating Nate's kid brother up to the surface. Red polo shirt and khaki shorts. Bobbing there, facedown like a doll. Dad wasn't in cuffs then, but he would be soon. You don't run the chief of police's best friend and his family off a cliff and get away with it. Not with a belly of Bloody Marys and a BAC twice the state limit. If Mom hadn't been home with the babies, she'd have been driving. If I'd gotten a B+ in English instead of an A, Dad might not have taken me out for brunch in the first place.

I was ten feet from Nate when he told the police about the baseball stuck under the car's brake. He said it was all his fault—his words! It came up in the trial, but the poor orphan boy was all anyone cared about.

Anyway, Nate's deep into his eggs when I dial Adam's cell. I only let it ring twice before hanging up. That's the signal. I guess I light a cigarette, too. Nate's sure to see it, but I've got to make my entrance sometime, so I do.

Tom and Johnny run, but Nate stays.

The two of us, alone. It's been a long time coming.

Are you happy? I ask him. Is this everything you wanted? Did the eggs and toothpaste and shaving cream make you feel like a man in control? Did that money you got from my family fill the cracks in your broken arm and the holes in your family tree? Do you feel better, knowing that you're the Lake's golden son, and I'm its most hated daughter? I don't actually say all of this, but I wish I had.

There's a funny look on his face, but before he can say anything, Adam and the others rush him. Alpha male crap.

Adam's about to knock his head off when Nate smiles. I know this doesn't sound like anything, but right then it feels like the most outrageous thing he can do. The light from the garage catches the blue in his eyes and makes his skin gleam. He's smiling, but past that there's a look way too old for his face.

Those eyes. That face. The sadness behind it. Nate's always been cute, but that's when I realize he's beautiful.

I'm not even sure what happened next. Tom and Johnny appear out of nowhere, then Adam's on the ground with his head bleeding. There's running and shouting and then we're piled into Adam's car gunning for the boys.

We lurch over the curb, all shouting to get them, but I can tell from the sound of my own voice that I don't mean it. That's when I understand I don't want this anymore.

Me taunting Nate. Nate hounding me.

Our old world is wreckage. There's no way back.

The boys have darted into the trees because they're not idiots and they don't know what we're going to do. Neither do I. I can point Adam in a direction, but who knows how far he'll take it. Will he run over the boys? Will he crush them between the Mustang's fender and the trunk of a tree?

Am I happy?

Next thing I know, Adam's shaking me and I see we're stopped in front of a fence. Nate's only a flicker in the headlights. Adam asks if he should chase them down, and I hesitate. Such a stupid mistake.

Adam has a predator's nose for weakness, and next to me I

can almost hear him sniffing. He makes a face at me, pushes open the door, and runs after the boys.

So yeah, things haven't been great between me and Adam since then.

But, back to the boutique. Once the Hatchet sees Nate in the door and pulls herself together enough to pop her eyes back into her head, she says hello and asks if she can help him with anything.

Nate tells her he's here to pick up a shipment of glassware for his grandmother.

It's crazy to hear him in a regular, everyday conversation. Talking about glassware. The collar of his jacket's up, and his face is pink from the cold. His dark hair's been pulled into waves by the wind.

He says the right things in exactly the right way, but this close to him I see that nothing touches his eyes. Something about him reminds me of a ventriloquist's dummy. That calm face isn't the real him, is what I think I mean. Neither is the polite voice, because how could it be? How can he make any sound but a scream?

In the back of that ambulance in April I saw a boy broken in every way a person can be broken, so who is this?

The Hatchet knows the shipment he's talking about, and she leaves the counter to get it. She says a couple other things that make it sound like she's flirting with him, which is just too disgusting and wrong for words.

As Nate turns to follow the Hatchet, he makes eye contact with me. Peering into his arctic eyes I can still barely wrap my head around the fact that he's here. That he's sort of helping me. That he's almost smiling at me.

With Hatchet distracted, there's nothing to stop me from walking right through the door. I mean, am I supposed to just wait around to get arrested? But leaving won't help. Greystone

Lake's too small a town. A cop car will probably get to the house before I do.

I never noticed it before the accident, but this town's a place hardly anyone escapes from.

Nate comes back with a box that clinks like a New Year's party at midnight.

Mrs. Sackett tells Nate she'll send the invoice to the Union. She tells him to have a good day and to say hello to his grand-mother for her.

I remember the rest word for word, just like I remember ev-ery quirk of his voice and every twitch in his lips.

"I'll also take that bracelet," Nate says. He puts the box down so he can reach into his pocket.

"Oh, you don't have to bother with that," the Hatchet says. She glances at me, a blush somehow permeating her foundation, bronzer, and spray-on tan.

"It sounded pretty important." His smile is like the noon sun, but his eyes are as cold as the lake. He picks the bracelet up from the counter and weighs it in one hand. I try not to stare, but I can't help it.

"It's the perfect Christmas gift for my grandmother." He takes a credit card out of his wallet.

"For Bea?" the Hatchet asks. "She might have simpler tastes."

"Most people don't know what they want until they get it." He glows with something I've never seen before. Something you can't measure or map. Its own kind of magic. "If you could wrap it in something festive, that'd be great."

The Hatchet might say no to anyone else, but Nate McHale isn't anyone else. Dad saw to that.

The woman rings up the purchase and Nate signs the receipt like it's an attendance sheet. Boom, four hundred dollars. I should be grateful, but it's also sort of infuriating.

Nate gathers his things, and I can't decide what to do next. If I walk out of the boutique with him, he'll expect me to say something. To thank him. But hanging back with the Hatchet is dangerous. If she changes her mind about calling the police, there's nothing I can do to stop her.

Nate thanks the Hatchet like a gentleman straight out of Austen and turns to leave without another word. I find myself following him.

"Young lady," the Hatchet calls from the counter. The door shuts behind Nate, and I can already feel my mouth tighten into a look of pure murder. The plaster of her face is winched into as stern a look as it can make. "Come here again, and I'll call the police."

I can't get out of the shop fast enough. It takes everything I've got not to slam the door, throw my fists at the sky, and scream out the boiling rage inside me.

Nate's standing to the side of the door, his hand fishing in his coat pocket. I realize then that he doesn't expect me to say a thing to him. My thanks would mean no more than my apologies.

He pulls a red stocking hat over his ears and looks up at the clouds. For a second his eyes mirror the colorless sky, and I understand that this boy is no longer of this world.

"I guess you're going to try to give me that bracelet." I'd felt a powerful need to say something, and this is what came out.

"You'd hate that, wouldn't you?" These are the first words he's said to me since April. He doesn't even look at me.

He stoops to lift the crate of glassware from the ground. He's stronger than he looks.

I try and fail to think of something else to say to him. I'm alone with Nate McHale, off my game and in his debt, but for some reason this is a moment I don't want to end.

On my sleepless nights and lonely walks I've thought of a

million things to say to him. Things to ask. Things to tell. Things to demand. Now every one of them flies away. Maybe this is what this journal was meant for.

My words and my fury were there a second ago. I don't know where they've gone. He walks away. I watch him turn the corner, and he's gone.

But I'm not alone. A gaze burns into the side of my head. I look across the dreary street and see Adam watching me through the open window of his black Mustang.

I pull my face back into a scowl and try to rediscover the person I've been. Furious and forbidding and casually cruel. I jut my chin to Adam. Anything but anger or its close relations might as well be weakness.

I check the traffic before crossing the street and that's when the engine roars. I'm sure the surprise was all over my face. Adam lurches the car from its spot and tears across the lanes, cutting a turn only inches from me. The tires spin on the asphalt as he floors it. The smell of burning fills the air as the Mustang speeds away.

What I'm trying to say is that it's been bad, these last couple months. Really, really bad. But seeing Adam peel away like that made me realize that things can still get worse.

REVENANTS

III

WHILE CLEANING HIS breakfast dishes, Nate looked through the window into another gray morning. Ashen skies lanced by withered trees. Lawns of dead grass spotted with rotting leaves. The desolation of December without the consolation of snow.

Behind him, he heard the answering machine kick in. He must have missed the phone ringing. He picked up the handset midway through the machine's recitation of their number.

"Dude, you got to get to your computer," Johnny said.

"What is it?" Nate kneaded his bad arm. It'd been hurting all weekend. Low barometric pressure was no good for it, and the skies had been heavy for days.

"This'll change your life."

He started up the stairs as call-waiting pinged in his ear. "I've got another call."

"It's probably just Tom."

Nate knew it then. The pain in his arm sang with the weather, and something new was in the wind. "What's going on?" He jogged to his computer.

"Picture's worth a thousand words. You gotta check your email."

"Working on it. How about you give me a hint?"

"Ugh. You want spoilers? Come on, man."

"The modem's dialing in."

"Yeah, I figured you didn't have a dying dolphin in your room. Is there anything on the planet more annoying than that sound?"

"One thing springs to mind."

"You in yet?"

"Email's loading."

"How about now?"

"Dude, shut *up*. Okay, I'm in."

Nate had gotten thirty messages since checking his inbox that morning.

"Do you see it?" Johnny asked.

Nearly all of the messages had the same title: *FWD: Guess whos back on the market?*

"Open it," Johnny said. "And get ready to pick your tongue off the floor."

A series of photos were attached to the end of a long chain of forwarded messages. He clicked on the first one.

It was the nude chest of a girl. The image captured her from her waist to her chin. Her right arm was crossed over her left breast, but the other one was entirely exposed. Her breasts were smaller than the kind you'd expect to find on the Internet. The image was more artistic than erotic. Not the usual kind of pornography at all.

"Okay . . ." Nate said. He scanned the names of the email's other recipients and recognized most of them from school.

"Keep going," Johnny said.

The next photo was cropped to show a single nipple and the bottom half of the girl's profile.

"You still with me, buddy?" Johnny asked.

The last image was from behind. Just the swell of her hips and a tease of breast were visible here, but the profile was as unmistakable as was the flash of auburn hair that cascaded around her shoulders.

"Maybe it's Photoshopped," Nate said.

"No way, man. This is the genuine article. Lucy Bennett's gone viral."

Nate scrolled down to the original message and saw that the pictures had come directly from Adam Decker. Along with the images, the blond bully had sent his friends this message: *Thats right guys, I'm a free man again so you got some real competition now. Think I can do better than this last piece? Game on.* The email had been sent the night before.

"Adam did this?" Nate said. He was irritated to hear surprise in his voice. Nothing should shock him anymore. He'd been paying careful attention to Adam Decker since Halloween, and he knew what the hulking teen was capable of. He'd learned that being a real bully required a skill set beyond physical strength and the willingness to use it. It demanded relentless cruelty and the belief that no line existed that couldn't be crossed.

"Yeah," Johnny said, "and his friends forwarded it to more people, who forwarded it to even more. Like twenty people sent it to me."

Call-waiting sounded again in Nate's ear.

"Couldn't have happened to a nicer girl, huh?" Excitement thrummed through Johnny's voice. It was like Romans cheering in the Coliseum as people exactly like them were cut to pieces on the bloody sand below.

"I've got another call."

"Come on, don't hang up," Johnny said. "I mean, I get why she'd be upset, but she looks kind of amazing. I think she has some pretty freaking great—"

Nate switched calls.

"Did you see it?" Tom asked.

"Yeah."

"I was hoping to catch you first. Getting pictures of her by email—especially pictures like *those*. I didn't know how you'd take it."

"Me? I'm fine, but—"

"What?"

"Adam. He did this to his own girlfriend."

"Kinda doubt the winter formal's in the cards for them now, don't you?"

"Hasn't she been through enough?" Before Halloween, Nate had taken his own shots at Lucy. He understood now that she hadn't deserved them, which was one reason why he'd tried to make up for it yesterday at the boutique. He'd stopped Mrs. Sackett from calling the police on Lucy. They were even now.

"Well, not compared to you. Compared to you she's barely—"

"Stop," Nate said. "Don't compare her to *me*. Try comparing her to every other person in this town. Every other person *you've ever met*. Who else has a dad in prison? Who else lost all their friends and all their money? Does anyone else feel totally alone all the time, and just when she felt so sure things couldn't possibly get any worse?"

"Okay, yeah," Tom said. "It's a really crappy thing. You're right. It sucks for her. I wouldn't wish it on anyone."

"People like Adam, they'll hurt anyone they can get away with hurting just because they can. And he did it to his own girlfriend. That makes it betrayal." It was one thing for the universe to conspire against you, but for people to do it to each other—to those who trusted them? "He can't get away with it."

NATE STARED AT his bedroom ceiling as a reel of destruction played through his head. He imagined Adam Decker being chased down the Strand by crop threshers with whirling blades, tied by a line to a motorboat that whipped him across the lake's freezing surface like a skipped stone, encircled by townspeople on the beach below the cliffs as they pitched its smooth rocks at him one by one.

Nate had left his email open, and the ping of a new message pulled him from the furnace of his mind. The email was from Tom: *Got an idea. Room 214, HS. 3:00.* He'd also sent the email to Johnny.

It was Sunday, but Nate bet some of the school's entrances would be unlocked. Opening night for a student production of *Our Town* was only a few days away, and he suspected the auditorium would be filled with the sounds of hammering and the smells of fresh paint.

He doubted whatever Tom had come up with would sate his own appetite for ruin, but it might be a start. When he pulled on his coat, his mind danced with razors and ropes and flames.

Greystone Lake's high school was an imperious neoclassical building that loomed over its neighbors. Nate was a block away when Johnny and Owen crossed the street in front of him.

"Nate, the Vengeful King himself," Johnny shouted when he saw him. "O was over, so I brought him."

Nate nodded to Owen. The big guy wasn't really one of them, but he'd demonstrated he could be trusted.

After Johnny had showed them his bruised back on Halloween, Nate promised that they'd punish Mr. Vanhouten. That storm had been perfect cover for his plan. When they'd crept out of the Night Ship, the Lake's streets had been empty except for the roar of wet leaves by the legion. Rain had scared their faces as they'd approached the Wharf, where Johnny's father docked his beautiful sailboat, the *Pharaoh*.

They'd cut the *Pharaoh* loose from its moorings, and the wind had done the rest. Its bottomed-out hull had been discovered all the way out on Blind Down Island two days later. The lake returns what it takes. The boat was a small loss for Mr. Vanhouten, but Johnny had been flying high ever since.

Though Mr. Vanhouten blamed the storm and the dock supervisor, Johnny knew the truth. He'd enjoyed the intoxication of revenge without the hangover of consequences. Destroying the sailboat had been good for Nate, too, though in a more complicated way. The fury inside him had to go somewhere. So many things in the world deserved it.

Owen had accompanied them back on Halloween, and they'd hung out with him a few times since. Nate had intended to punish Mrs. Liffey, Owen's mother, during the next big storm, but this morning's email had sent Adam Decker to the top of his list.

"Any clue what Tommy's cooking?" Johnny asked. "Not like him to start trouble."

Nate had himself been pleased by Tom's enthusiasm. This morning, it seemed like his friend hadn't understood why Nate wanted to protect Lucy from Adam. Nate wasn't sure that even he fully understood it.

"You think this has to do with Adam sending those pictures of Lucy Bennett?" Owen asked. "Because I thought we didn't like Lucy either?"

"Adam's our enemy, O," Johnny said. "Remember Halloween?"

Room 214 was in the school's science wing. Each classroom had hexagonal tables with sinks and designated taps for Bunsen burners. Hazard signs were hung next to the doors with safety rules for the labs.

Nate entered the lab first and was confounded by the sight of Tom crouched in a corner. Then he saw Adam and Adam's friend with the face like baked beans perched on a lab table and understood. The wider of Adam's two minions appeared from behind to hustle the other boys into the lab.

Stocky slammed the lab's door behind him.

When the door shut, the pressure in the room changed. The buzz of the ventilation system seemed to amplify.

"Hey, Nate," Adam said. "How's your day going?" His laid-back smile didn't touch his unblinking eyes. Both he and Beans tapped lacrosse sticks against the lab bench to the rhythm of a song only they seemed to hear.

"We don't want trouble," Nate said. Trouble was, of course, exactly what he'd come here for. This just wasn't the kind he'd expected.

"Well you got it anyway, McHale."

Nate and his friends outnumbered the seniors, but the older boys had lacrosse sticks and weight-room bodies.

"Funny how things work out," Adam continued. "I was just thinking about how we were overdue to pay you back for Halloween when we happen to run into your buddy here." He pointed to Tom.

"They wanted my email password," Tom said. "I didn't know why." He looked miserable. A line of blood slipped the rim of his lip.

"Lucy was the one who had it out for me," Nate said. "The whole planet got your breakup email. So what's your deal?"

"My boy remembers that knock on the head you gave him," Beans said.

"I needed stitches. You've had stitches, McHale. No fun at all," Adam said. "Besides. That slut *is* the reason we're here. I saw you yesterday, outside that old bat's store. I saw you and her." He snorted and shook his head. "Guess she played me, huh? Still, I've got a rep for not leaving the ladies disappointed, so here we are."

Tom turned to Nate with questions scrawled in block letters across his face, but Nate had no answers. There was indeed something between him and Lucy, but it wasn't any kind of romance as he imagined it. But Adam's certainty—unsound though it was—was all that mattered in this moment. The bottom line was that Adam had emailed those pictures of Lucy because of Nate.

"You're just as dumb as you look, aren't you?" Nate said.

Johnny groaned and Beans shook his head.

"Smart guy with a smart mouth," Adam said. "The Lake's survivor has a death wish. You're an honors student, right, McHale? Is that *irony*?"

"Just you and me, Adam. Let my friends go."

Adam shook his head. "You're not the one who got me these stitches—respect the effort, though."

They wanted a fight and nothing would dissuade them. The younger boys must have seemed like easy prey, but Nate knew something Adam and his friends didn't. He wasn't sure when he'd first grasped it, but he understood now that both boys in the backseat of that Passat had died on that bright April day. Whoever had woken on those rocks with his shattered arm and broken ribs was someone else. Out of synch, out of place. Maybe even out of his mind.

"This is just the beginning, McHale."

"Yeah," Beans said. "Got a whole semester of payback left before we graduate."

"Probably longer in your case," Nate said.

Adam and Stocky laughed as Beans's face turned purple.

"You want to say that again?" Beans reached for the menace of Adam's voice but came up short.

"Stupid *and* deaf?" Nate said. "Gosh."

Beans had a fistful of Nate's shirt in an instant.

"See, I've got you figured out now, McHale," Adam said. "Should've known back on Halloween. That dip into the lake did a number on you, didn't it?" He laughed.

"Your concern for my mental health is real touching."

"You *want* to get seriously messed up. You *want* us to break every bone in your body. So the question is, how do you actually hurt someone who likes the pain?"

For the first time since entering the lab, Nate felt the itch of something like concern. Adam suddenly didn't sound so stupid.

"You listening?" Adam asked. "I asked how you really hurt someone who gets off on pain?" Adam swung his lacrosse stick hard into Tom's stomach. Tom gasped and fell to the tiles.

Nate took a step toward Tom, but stopped himself because he knew that's what Adam wanted him to do. The more Nate showed that he cared, the more his friends would be made to suffer.

Beans chose this moment to jab the netting of his lacrosse stick into Nate's belly, then torqued it to crack the grip against the side of Nate's face. The momentum of the blow sent Nate swaying. Points of light swam across his vision. Beans brought the stick down on the flat of Nate's back, sending him to his knees.

"You guys are so tough, beating on younger kids," Owen said.

"Shut it, fat boy," Adam said.

Nate's vision cleared and he tried to catch his breath. As he crouched on the floor, a shadow fell around him. Someone kicked him in the ribs.

"That's all you got, McHale?" Beans asked. "And after all that big talk."

Nate rocketed off the balls of his feet, slamming the crown of his head into Beans's face and nose. There was a porcelain snap. Beans dropped his lacrosse stick and covered his face with his hands, but Nate didn't give him time to recover. He head-butted the older boy again, and this time the result was a wet crunch. Beans howled as he careened into a glass-encased shelving unit.

Then everything seemed to happen at once. Friends and enemies collided into wordless sounds and animal struggles.

Johnny locked in a violent dance with Stocky.

Owen moving toward Beans.

Tom staggering up from where he'd fallen.

Beans vomiting onto the floor.

Distracted by the surge of action and disoriented from the knocks to his head, Nate had missed what was right in front of him.

Adam clocked him with his lacrosse stick, sending him hard against a table. Nate fell into an array of test tubes and beakers, knocking them onto the floor, where they disintegrated into a cloud of singing fragments.

The big teen caught him again with a strong cross-check to the other side of his face. Nate quickly detected a strategy in Adam's strikes. He'd bring the stick hard on Nate's left side in order to move him to the right. He'd knocked him on the head in order to bring Nate's face within the range of a savage kick. Nate realized he was being herded to the corner of the lab with the emergency shower, where there'd be no chance of escape.

Stick to ribs. Knee to stomach. Fist to kidney. Nate knew he had to do something while he still could.

He fought past the pain and leapt for a lab stool to throw at Adam. For a moment, the lacrosse stick got entangled in the stool's legs. This caused Adam's assault to stutter, and Nate seized his chance to lunge for a second stool, which he whipped at Adam's head, swinging for the horizon.

He threw his whole weight into the blow, and the force of its impact knocked him to the floor. Adam joined him a moment later. Eyes rolling to white, blood at his temple, knocked out cold.

Nate couldn't have sparred with Adam for more than a minute, but in that time the lab had transformed. Broken glass glittered across the floor alongside pieces of cracked molecular models and fragments from shattered shelving units. Stocky slipped in a pile of Beans's vomit and crashed into the bottles of chemicals that had spilled from the busted cabinet.

The warnings around the room were right: A laboratory was a hazardous place.

Nate looked over in time to see Tom fumble with a fire extinguisher, and a cloud of vapor engulfed Stocky and Beans. *Nice one, Tommy,* was Nate's last thought before he felt the floor lurch beneath where he lay. He unspooled onto the firmness of the tiles.

As the room dimmed, he caught a glimpse of a shadow watching from the doorway. But before he could articulate a thought, the world went black.

December 1

Mom,

I'm proud of you and I love you, and that's why I have to go.

I thought I could handle everything with Dad and what happened with my friends, but that was before I knew that wasn't the end. Things aren't going to get better for me. I get that now. Everyone here wants me to fail, and I'm just going to drag you and the twins down with me.

I know this sounds dramatic, but I swear I've thought it through. I know you haven't touched my college fund. College isn't what I need right now. Use it for yourself, Tara, and James. You deserve a break, and I want to give it to you. That's one thing I can do right.

Don't worry about me. Once I leave this place and these people, I know things will get better. I just need a fresh start. Or maybe I don't know exactly what I need, but I know I need some time to myself to figure it out. It'll only get worse if I put this off, Mom. I know you'll say that it'll all be fine, and that's one of the things I love about you, but try to see my side of this.

This isn't goodbye. Not at all, okay?

I love you and Tara and James, and I love Dad, too. Tell them for me? Tell them every day so there's no chance they'll forget. I'm sorry to leave like this, but I know it's the best thing. You can be mad at me, but I promise that you won't ever be as angry at me as I am at myself. I hope you forgive me. I swear that this isn't goodbye.

Love,
Lucy

Six

Nate hadn't worn his old black raincoat in fourteen years, but a bespoke suit couldn't have fit better.

As he dressed in it, he felt like a druid preparing for something sacred. And in a way he was. No task was more important than protecting the ones you loved.

He'd waited for Grams to turn in before venturing out. When he took the stairs down he avoided the third and sixth steps from the bottom. He extinguished the kitchen lights behind him and exited through the back door into the weeping night.

Outside, he let his eyes adjust to the dark.

The town was battened down. No cars, no voices. The only sounds were from the rain and the wash of leaves in the branches above him.

After the accident, Nate had sometimes spent nights listening to these trees as they were tossed by the breeze that swept in from the lake. The leaves murmured like a stadium of people. He'd lie between two knotted roots, close his eyes, and try to pry meanings from the sound. *Was that Gabe's whisper? Was that Mom's laugh?* But if there were messages to be heard, they weren't meant for his ears.

Sometimes their sound lulled him to sleep, and he dreamed.

In these dreams Nate ran along an endless loop of a hallway somewhere in the depths of the Night Ship. The floors were lined with wooden planks, as were the walls and ceiling. He ran but also fell, as if the corridor sometimes became as vertical as a mineshaft. The hall was empty, but Nate wasn't alone. There was someone else, a shadow always just out of sight—either ahead or behind Nate, he wasn't sure. In this chase, Nate couldn't tell if he was the hunter or the prey.

The dream always ended the same way. His feet began to slap against water as the lake slowly filled the space. At first, the flood was easy to run through, but soon the planks pulled away from one another to let more of the lake in. The water was so cold that it burned his skin. The pressure of its weight crushed his rib cage and squeezed his lungs to bursting.

He'd wake up gasping, his shirt drenched with sweat, Grams shaking his shoulder. From the way she pursed her lips, he'd know he'd been screaming.

"You're okay," she'd whisper. He never knew if she was asking or telling.

Nate hadn't had that dream in years, but sweat pricked across his forehead thinking about it.

The backyard was littered with leaves and broken twigs. The rain had picked up, and the wind had gotten stronger. The tops of trees rocked against the opaque sky.

Lucy's funeral is tomorrow, Nate thought as thunder throbbed somewhere behind the mountains.

Tomorrow, Lucy will be laid to rest.

We are burying Lucy tomorrow.

No matter how he framed it, this was a fact he couldn't grab hold of.

Everything in the backyard looked as it should, so he moved on to the front. Wrought iron lamps lit the street. The halos they cast hung in the rain like orbs of static.

The neighborhood was empty, the town was asleep. Even after so many years, this lit a fuse in Nate's chest. It was the perfect kind of night. If these vandals were like Nate and his friends had been, he wouldn't have long to wait.

He sat on a rim of masonry behind a stringy hydrangea, where he could watch the street without being easily seen.

The minutes ticked away, then hours. In the dark Nate thought about Meg and Livvy and how they'd both be warm in their beds as the night wailed outside. He thought about little Nia Kapur. Most of all, he thought of Lucy, and how what remained of her was on a tray, waiting to be put out of sight forever.

Finally, movements out of time with the storm tugged Nate's gaze down the street. Two figures walked toward him, avoiding the puddles of illumination from the streetlights. One was tall and the other was short. Both wore dark, hooded coats similar to the one Nate had wrapped himself in. They carried something awkwardly between them.

Nate shielded the light of his phone with his raincoat. He pulled up Tom's number so it'd be right there when he needed it. He eased himself off the masonry and onto his haunches.

The duo stopped at the base of the driveway. Nate could now see that the object between them was a bucket. The larger of the two also carried a stepladder.

There was a time when Nate might have torn through the bushes to seize the vandals. A black specter like a shard from the storming night itself. He would frighten, then capture. Because terror lays bare a person's secrets as surely as a scalpel reveals bone. He'd envelop them like a nightmare thing and tear loose what they knew and thought and dreamt.

What did they want? What did they know?

He'd turn the full eye of his rage onto them and—

No.

Nate pictured Meg's smile and imagined Livvy's laugh. Finger by finger, he forced his hands from the fists they'd locked themselves into. He raised his face to the rain and remembered who he was supposed to be.

He had to be patient. To do the damage Johnny had credited them with, these vandals would need to exceed this mismatched pair. He had to be sure none of their friends lagged in the shadows.

They stood at the edge of the driveway for several long moments before trudging onto the lawn. It seemed to Nate that they'd been evaluating the house rather than waiting for accomplices. As they crossed the soggy grass, Bonaparte Street remained desolate of anything but scattered branches and storm-blown leaves.

Soon the vandals were close enough that Nate could see the material of their sturdy coats billow around their skinny teenaged bodies. He wouldn't have trouble handling either of them.

His plan was to tackle the smaller of the two and be rough enough to frighten the tall one away. The violence was regrettable, but necessary. Then Nate would call Tom. Tom would be the policeman he was, and the kid would tell them who else was involved. They'd pick up the ringleader. Whoever they were, Nate had a constellation of questions for them.

The taller of the two turned his attention to the ladder as the short one stooped toward the bucket.

Four strides was all it took to get right behind the gangly one. Nate extended his leg and grabbed a fistful of the boy's jacket. The kid was all limbs. Nate yanked him backward and the teen tripped against Nate's foot. He gasped when he hit the wet grass, the wind knocked from him.

Neither had said a word, but the boy's wheeze got the smaller one's notice. The little figure was half turned toward them when Nate pushed him with all his strength.

The kid hardly weighed anything. Nate could have picked him up and thrown him across the street. The little guy squealed when Nate knelt on his chest.

Nate should have called Tom then. He meant to. But his adrenaline was thrumming and he was seized with the need to see this kid's face. He had to see the face of this child who thought he could get away with vandalizing Grams's home and pub. If these vandals knew about the Storm King and his Thunder Runs, then they had to know that Nate McHale's enemies didn't go unpunished.

He pulled aside the kid's hood, and a shocked young face stared back at him. Nate couldn't see much in the glow of the streetlight— soft blond hair quickly becoming soaked, babyish cheeks without a blemish—but it was enough to be sure he had no idea who this child was, and that the figure he'd taken for a small boy was actually a girl.

But that didn't change anything.

"Who are you?" he demanded.

She was speechless, astonished from being tossed onto the ground and subdued. She broke his gaze, her attention seized by something to Nate's right.

The tall one.

He turned just in time to see the top of the stepladder whipping toward his head, then there was a crash of light and he saw nothing at all.

THE BOY WHO FELL

II

THEY PILE BLANKETS on Nate, but these do not warm him.

He doesn't remember when the boats pulled alongside the rocks, but they're here. People in brown come first, then people in blue. The ones in blue have the blankets. Theirs are the hands on his back and along his arm. He doesn't want them to touch his arm, but one of them makes noises into his ear. He knows her, he thinks. Someone's mother.

He lets her see his arm and her eyes widen. *Don't look,* she tells him. *Don't look.*

They have many questions. He has only one. *Where are they?* he asks. The people in blue say many things, but none of these are answers.

He's wet and he's cold. The blankets catch the sun like the lake. Smooth stones are at his feet. He doesn't know where his shoes are.

Two policemen stand nearby. Nate knows them but cannot think of their names. They stare up the face of rock. They whisper, but Nate can hear them.

Impossible, one of them says. *Two hundred feet,* he says. *At least. Into shallow water.* Two men in black wet suits are on one of the boats. They fall backward into the lake. It's not a loud sound, but the splash makes Nate jump. Someone's mother whispers to him, and he tries not to pull his arm away from her.

Another boat is coming now. More men in brown. Nate knows the one on the bow. He knows him well. The chief doesn't wait for the boat to stop, but jumps into the water to his knees. He runs for Nate, but it's hard to run through the lake. Its waters are hungry.

He puts his hand on Nate's head. It hurts, but not badly. The chief starts to say something but he stops. His face goes white, and Nate knows he's seen his arm. The woman in blue doesn't let Nate hide it.

Nate asks his question and watches the chief's pale face crumble. The man falls to his knees on the rocks. A new gravity takes grip of Nate. It is so powerful that he feels a breach open within him as if he has shattered under its pressure. Not another break in his ribs or in his ruined arm, but a crack at his foundation. Something is lost, and he is diminished. The sun fades. He doesn't feel less cold, but he stops shaking. He knows that from now on he will be less than what he was.

Beyond the people in brown and blue, there's a dark figure watching him from the shallows where the lake breaks against boulders. A smudge of black in a plane of light. He wonders if he's the only one who can see it. The moment he thinks this, it disappears under the surface. It's gone, but he still feels it watching him. He thinks it's been watching him the whole time.

One of the men in wet suits breaks through the mirror of the lake. *Three,* he calls out. Someone asks a question. *No,* he says. *Crushed like a can of Coke.* The chief on his knees in front of Nate whirls around to shout something at the man in the water. His voice is strangled with pain.

The man in the wet suit looks across the water to Nate. He has quieted himself, but Nate can still read the word on his lips.

Impossible.

REVENANTS

IV

NATE SAT WITH Johnny in the back of an ambulance, stinging from disinfectants. His friend told him that the fight in the lab had been broken up by Mr. Granger, the high school's principal, soon after Tom began using the fire extinguisher.

"How long was I out before Granger showed up?" Nate asked. An EMT cleaned a cut along his eyebrow. He'd also bruised two ribs and dislocated his thumb. The head injury had probably caused him to pass out in the lab.

"I didn't see you go down," Johnny said. The EMT picking glass out of Johnny's elbow told him again to stay still. "I only saw you and Adam on the floor when Granger ran in. God, the look on his face." He laughed and then winced, holding his side. "Bet he thought you were dead. Adam, too, probably. Bye-bye, pension."

They faced the school, but Nate had the sense of people milling just out of sight. The high school wasn't far from the commercial streets, and anything that required the EMS squads from three towns would be quite an event.

"How did Granger know to go to the lab?" Nate asked.

"Some janitor heard the racket and tipped him off."

"Lucky he was here on a Sunday. Lucky someone heard us at all."

"Yeah, lucky for *them*. You realize you took out two of them within, like, sixty seconds of each other?"

Nate remembered flashes of color and sound with no more specificity than a dream. Strangely, he recalled the actual bout of unconsciousness better. Sleep was a slide into the folds of self, but this was like a switch being thrown. First he was, and then he was not. Not underpinned by thought and light, the fading was one of annihilation. Nate remembered the shadow by the door and knew that it hadn't been the school's principal. He could trace the outline of its chasm of true dark within a field of black.

"Tom and Owen got knocked around a little, but not as bad as us," Johnny said.

A rap came from the side of the ambulance, and a tall man peered inside. "How're the patients?" Chief Buck asked the EMTs. They gave him a rundown as he looked Nate over from gashed forehead to splinted thumb.

"We're fine, Chief," Nate said.

"Got off easy, then. Those boys being so much bigger." The chief gave a good impression of avuncular levity, but Nate saw the fear in his eyes.

Sometimes, speaking with the chief reminded Nate too much of his dad and that lost life. He imagined the chief must feel the same way.

"I'm fine. Really."

"Concussions are serious business." The chief had been there in April, too. He'd seen the bodies of his best friends and their younger son pulled from the lake. He'd held Nate's hand in the back of an ambulance as it screamed through the center of town.

The lights, sirens, and medical prodding had already brought Nate perilously close to the memories of that day in April. He knew this feeling would only strengthen once his grandmother arrived. He imagined Grams threading the crowd of gawkers to search the backs of the ambulances for him. He knew exactly what shade of fear would color her face when she found him. This time it would be an expression put there not by chance stacked upon chance, but by basic cruelty.

Pain rippled from his hurt thumb as he clenched his hands.

Mr. Granger appeared and pulled the chief aside.

"We still have to get Adam back, you know," Nate told Johnny once the chief left.

"But we sent him to the hospital."

"That was self-defense. Now he has to be punished. For this, and for what he did to Lucy." Nate knew this with complete certainty. He kneaded the scar tissue and knitted bone of his bad arm. It ached, and he knew that the weather was going to worsen.

The equations of pain were askew, and they must be balanced.

THE STORM NATE'S arm foretold finally arrived.

A blip of a thunderstorm, but it was enough to clear the streets and keep people inside. When he and his friends set out into the rain, the town was cowed under the howling night.

The bruise around Nate's left eye had blackened along the orbital ridge. Under its brace, his thumb had turned a cadaverous yellow. His ribs were as multihued as mold blossoming on a slice of wet bread. He was sore everywhere.

Grams hadn't let him go to school that morning. "You look like you've been through the wars," she'd told him.

"I'm hurt, but I want everyone to know I'm okay. Otherwise, they'll talk." He didn't want a repeat of the whispering that had followed the accident last spring. After that, he was the Boy Who Fell. He was precious—and a precious thing is a thing held apart. "I can't deal with that again."

Grams nodded and looked away. For an agonizing moment, Nate

thought she was going to cry. They could both be stubborn, but he relented. He let her take care of him through the day but convinced her to go to the Union for the night shift, and even got her to agree to him sleeping over at Johnny's house despite it being a weeknight. He swore he'd take it easy.

But these were lies he told to protect her. Nate didn't plan to have a relaxed evening any more than he intended to sleep over at the Vanhoutens'.

Johnny had given each of them sturdy black raincoats from the *Pharaoh*. They were just about the only things salvaged from the sailboat they'd wrecked. The black rubbery skin of the coat dangled heavily just below Nate's knees. They saw only one car on their way to the Deckers' house, and its headlights glanced off their coats as if they were just pieces of the dark. They were invisible in the night.

The Deckers' home sat in the foothills, far beyond the Wharf. This was a remote and wooded section of town, no neighbors within sight. It was a sprawling clapboard farmhouse with a look of neglect about it. Battered shutters along the ground floor were missing slats, their vacancies gaping like mouths. There were no streetlights here, and the black would have been impenetrable if not for a single light by the front door.

Johnny called this adventure a Thunder Run. He and Owen were enthusiastic about punishing Adam for what he'd done. Tom, less so.

"We could press charges," he'd said when they'd rendezvoused at the Night Ship. "It's assault. They'd get in trouble."

"Adam's dad is on the town council. You think as chief of police, your dad wants to file charges?" Johnny had asked.

"Boys will be boys. That's what they'll say. Besides, we hurt them more than they hurt us," Nate said. "People are going to think they already got what they deserved."

"Exactly, Nate, we already hurt them, so—"

"That's what *they'll* say. I don't agree."

"But, I mean, when does this end? If we get back at him and then—"

"The Storm King has spoken, Tommy." Johnny clapped Nate on the shoulder. This was the first time the appellation had been uttered. This was their first full stride into whatever country waited beyond the frontier of the ordinary.

The others all turned to Nate. "So what's the plan?" Tom asked.

The house looked empty, but Nate knew by now that such appearances could be deceiving. He jogged to the front door and rang the bell before anyone could stop him. When he rang it again and there still wasn't a twitch from the home, he turned back to his friends. They couldn't see his smile, but it was there.

"Nobody home."

"They could be back any second," Tom said.

Nate set out for the silhouette of a detached garage. He probed its windows with his flashlight. As he did, a rattle descended from the sky. It began at the tops of the trees and then fell to the roofs of the house and garage, filling the night with the percussion of a million drums. Hail. The pellets themselves were a quarter of an inch across, and they covered the ground in no time.

The garage door was unlocked, and Nate was the last one inside. He flicked on the lights and watched the hail skitter across the gravel driveway and bounce into the air like popping corn. He thought he saw a whirl of movement in the dark beyond the scant range of the light. An eddy of shadow in an ocean of black.

"Earth to Nate?" Johnny said. "I said his car's here and there's lots of stuff to play with." Johnny pulled an ax from where it hung on the wall. He kicked one of several red jugs, and it thudded dully. Adam's black Mustang glowered at them under fluorescent lighting.

"But we want to make it seem like an accident, right?" Tom said. "Like with the *Pharaoh*?"

Nate wasn't sure. No one searches for culprits or assignations of blame when weather is involved. In addition to cover, storms supplied plausible explanations for all kinds of damage. Under the guise of a storm, they could take something from Adam. But at the same time, Nate wanted to make him afraid. He wanted to make sure the bully would think twice before hurting anyone ever again.

"We could clog his exhaust pipe," Johnny said.

"What'll that do? Like wreck the engine?" Tom asked. "Or send fumes into the car? I mean, we don't want to kill him . . . right?"

"We could use the gas on the garage," Owen said. He pointed to the red jugs. "People would blame the lightning?"

"They can run tests to know the difference," Tom said. "They'll know it was set on purpose."

"But if you want to send a message to Adam, to stop hurting people or whatever, then send a message," Owen pressed, echoing Nate's own thoughts. "If it looks like an accident, how'll he know he's being punished?"

Nate remembered what he'd decided on Halloween, that pain had to be *burned away*. "Let's see what else we've got," Nate said. He liked the idea of setting the garage on fire, but Tom would need convincing. His friend was right about them being able to run tests for accelerants. Nate just had to figure out if this mattered to him.

Johnny and Tom followed him to the rear of the garage while Owen stuck by the door.

"Gotta say, I kind of think O has a point," Johnny said once they were on the far side of the garage.

"Arson?" Tom said. "I was just thinking we were going about this all wrong."

"So you're chickening out." Johnny shook his head. "Shocker."

"What if we go through Adam's computer and—"

"Owen said you'd do this," Johnny said.

"Get into his email and—wait. You were talking about me with *Owen*?"

Nate couldn't see Owen from where they stood, but Tom wasn't exactly whispering.

"He told me you didn't get it," Johnny said.

"Get what?"

"The *point*. When we were alone we let people get away with hurting us, but now that we're not alone we can finally hurt them back. Nate knows what I mean."

In the fluorescent light, Tom's face flushed yellow.

"You were never alone, Johnny," Nate said.

"Right." Johnny looked away and snorted. "It's a nonstop twenty-four-seven-share-a-thon with you."

"How many times have you slept over at Tom's house when you've had a problem with your dad?" Nate said.

"Forget it, Nate. None of that really matters," Tom said. "Not when you've finally found someone who *gets* you." He stalked away from them. Tendrils of sediment filtered from the ceiling as the garage door slammed shut behind him.

"I didn't mean to hurt his feelings," Johnny said.

"Really."

"But you know he doesn't get it. I'm *glad* he doesn't. But you do. I saw it in your eyes on Halloween when we trashed Lucy's house," Johnny said. "You're hurt, but the pain makes you strong. And I think you like it."

In the distance, Nate heard Tom shout something, but he couldn't make out what he was saying.

"Someone'll hear him." Johnny shook his head and started for the door. Nate followed, but Tom burst back into the garage before they'd gone more than a few steps. Panic had thrown his eyes and mouth wide open. The night behind him wasn't as dark as it had been.

Outside, the grass blazed. A sheet of flame masked the house and clawed at the sky.

Nate and the others rushed toward it. The fire that glistened along the house's siding was a liquid thing. It ebbed and surged with the rhythm of the wind and a pulse of its own. It didn't seem real.

Owen stood in front of the inferno. His wide silhouette seemed to contract against the curtains of flame. The two red gasoline containers lay on their sides near his feet.

Tom pushed the larger boy, shouting something Nate couldn't make out.

"We gotta get out of here," Johnny said. Rain lashed his face.

Nate tried to remember if he'd seen any extinguishers in the garage, but it was already too late. The fire had found the roof. He was surprised that the house was going up so easily. Surely the siding had been wet, but perhaps none of that mattered when gasoline was involved. It was important to remember how many things he didn't yet know.

Ahead of them, Tom shoved Owen again. But the big guy didn't seem capable of doing anything but stare dumbly at the flames.

The house, being in the foothills, would be visible to the whole town, and it wasn't late enough to hope everyone was asleep. Nate pulled Tom away from Owen.

"We have to go." He had to shout to be heard over the deepening stir of the inferno. The heat of it was like a slap to the face.

"But the fire." Tom pointed wildly.

"It's too late." Nate knew they had to get away. They had to get away *now*. Even so, he found himself drawn to the crackle and blaze of the burning house. The ramshackle home with its broken shutters and stained siding had been ugly and had only uglier days ahead of it. Cloaked in the spikes and whorls of glorious flame, the place had been given a last chance to be beautiful.

In a sudden gust, the wind peeled burning shingles from the roof. He and Tom covered their faces as the flaming wedges showered them. Nate heard a gasp of ignition and saw the grass at his feet come alive with indigo flame. Owen must have spilled the gasoline as he doused the sides of the Deckers' house. It had pooled into a teardrop on the lawn and Nate stood in its center.

The fire was strange. It rippled like water and lit the stalks of grass from the bottom up, crisped like upside-down birthday candles. Its midnight flame undulated like the lake on a spring day as seen from a great but rapidly dwindling height. Its smell was not very different from the barbecues he and his family once enjoyed along the shore. The scent of it thick around him, Nate could see his father at the grill. One of his hands tended the burgers and the other was on Nate's shoulder. Nearby, his mother ran the beach behind Gabe as he tried to tease flips from a kite. She shouted instructions to him, but they both laughed too hard to get it right.

Then Nate was on the wet lawn, fallen hail digging into his back, the taste of charcoal and grass in his mouth. Tom had pushed him down and away. He rolled Nate from the puddle of flame as Johnny swatted at his legs. There was shouting, but Nate couldn't find words in the noise. There were tears in his eyes, but they weren't from the pain.

"Say something!" Tom screamed.

"We have to go," Nate whispered. Johnny and Tom pulled him to his feet. His ankles hurt. In the amber glow, he saw his jeans were charred and his socks were black.

"I didn't mean to," Owen said. He sounded as bewildered as the rest of them must have looked. "I thought I'd burn part of the wall, you know, like a lightning strike."

Tom helped Nate to the road as Johnny pulled Owen away from the burning house.

"Psycho, totally insane, pyromaniac—" Tom hissed into Nate's ear as he helped him walk.

"Wait." Nate bent to roll up the cuffs of his jeans. They were stiff and still searingly hot. His hands came away from them black.

"They're ruined," Tom said. "You're going to have to throw them away. Somewhere no one can find them. It's evidence. Jesus, there's evidence everywhere. We're going to reek of smoke. I didn't hear any fire alarms go off, but they can see those flames anywhere in town. We probably only have a couple minutes until—"

Nate rolled his cuffs and let Tom talk. His sneakers were ruined, too. Plastic oozed from them like oil paint. He'd gotten burned only in a narrow band between his shoes and jeans, but it was agony.

"I'm sorry, guys," Owen said. "Jesus. I'm so sorry."

"Can you walk?" Johnny asked Nate.

They jogged a route to avoid the main thoroughfares. The fire-house siren sounded as they neared the residential streets. A police car, lights whirling, sped through an intersection a few blocks away.

"Oh, God," Tom said. "What if my dad gets called in? I told him we'd be at Johnny's house. Should we go there in case he checks up on us? Or Nate, should we go to your house instead? We could tell Grams there was a change of plans."

"We stink of smoke, Tom," Johnny said.

"We can't go to anyone's house," Nate said. He turned back to the foothills where flames teased the sky. "We have to stick with the plan. We have to go back to the Night Ship."

One day he would understand that when you flee one thing, you're running into the arms of something else.

WHEN THEY WERE out of the rain and finally able to rest, the Night Ship felt like home. They'd set up a makeshift camp there soon after Halloween. Nate rolled onto one of the foam sleeping bag pads. His singed ankles were screaming.

"We're not getting in trouble covering for you, Owen," Tom was saying. "This isn't an all-for-one, one-for-all kind of situation."

Johnny sat next to Nate. "Can I see your legs?" he asked.

Nate had hoped to postpone the moment he had to examine the burns in good light, but he propped himself on his elbows as Johnny got a lantern. Johnny turned the light onto Nate's shins and hissed. They'd been boiled red, utterly smooth where the hair had been scorched. Blisters spilled from raw skin like clusters of insect eggs. It was appalling, but Nate had survived worse.

"How bad does it hurt?" Johnny asked. His face was tightened into a knot.

"Not bad." Nate was actually only a little uncomfortable at the moment. Adrenaline, maybe. Pain only came when his socks or jeans brushed against his burned skin.

"I'm so sorry, man," Johnny said. "You're supposed to run a burn under water, or something, aren't you?" He stood up and went to his backpack, shunting aside clothes and bags of chips. "Maybe this'll help." He produced a bottle of water and a T-shirt.

"Okay," Nate said. The damp T-shirt felt like razor blades against his skin, but the chill of the water smoothed away some of the discomfort. "Thanks. That does feel better."

"If we run out of water, we can always get some from the lake."

"No, no, no. Not from the lake."

"Okay, okay. No worries, buddy. You're the Storm King," Johnny said. "Not a problem."

"Tom, I'm sorry!" Owen said. "I thought you guys weren't going to end up doing anything, and he had to be punished, just like Nate said. I didn't mean for the whole place to go up."

"Calm down," Nate said. Johnny helped him to his feet. "Both of you."

"But we wouldn't even be in this—" Tom began.

"It's done, Tom. It happened. Now we have to figure out what to do about it."

"They could still think it was lightning," Johnny said.

"Did you leave those empty gasoline jugs on the lawn?" Nate asked.

Johnny's face froze in horror, and Tom banged his forehead against the bar counter.

"They would've figured it out anyway." Nate limped closer to the bar. "Like Tom said, they can tell if a fire's accidental or not."

"Why don't we just tell them the truth?" Tom said. "If the gas jugs are still there, then so are the fingerprints. Well, one of our fingerprints, anyway," he said, turning to Owen.

"We need to stick together," Nate said.

"I don't know, man." Johnny held his head in his hands. "I wish we'd just stayed home."

"It would have been fine if Owen hadn't gone full pyro and *burned a house down*," Tom said.

"*Enough,* Tom," Nate said. "I'm the one who wanted to go after Adam." He had to remind them why they were here. "Even if he gets expelled for the fight, it wouldn't make up for what he did to us, or what he did to Lucy. Think about how much trust it took for her to send him those pictures. What kind of a monster takes that gift and turns it into a weapon? He has to suffer for that."

Tom took a step backward, and Owen's eyes bulged. Johnny's hands slid over his mouth. Nate was confused by their reactions until he realized that his friends weren't staring at him. He turned to see Lucy Bennett standing in the nightclub's entryway. Her wet hair was slicked around her face in ropes.

She walked into the Night Ship. She looked up at the ceiling and through the two-story windows. "I was there," she said.

"What?" Johnny's voice creaked like a rusted gate.

"At the Deckers'," Lucy said. "When Owen poured gasoline on the wall. When the fire went up around Nate. I was worried about your legs," she told Nate.

"I'm fine," Nate said. He tried to absorb the fact that she was here and speaking to him, and already knew their secrets.

"You just had to take one step to get out of the fire, but you didn't."

Nate didn't know what to say.

The light from the lantern cast shadows under her cheekbones. Her wet hair made her look somehow new. "I was going to run away," she said. "I was so close. When he sent out that email and— I just couldn't face anyone today. I had to think, so I started walking. But the storm . . . there's something about a storm, isn't there? Something safe. Do you know what I mean?"

Nate knew. He found peace in the storms, because that was when the world pulled aside its mask to show its true face. Life was a mael-strom from which any respite was an illusion. The fury inside Nate was at home where the horizon blistered with lightning and the world shook with thunder. In a place like that everything made sense.

"I guess I'd been heading for Adam's all along. Maybe I wanted to do something to him, too. But you beat me there. I could hardly see you in your black coats, but that's why you wear them, isn't it?" Nate realized that he was the only one she was talking to.

"I almost ran to you when the grass caught on fire around you. I kept thinking you were going to move, but you didn't. It was so strange, Nate." Her eyes pooled with light as she looked at him. "You had your hands in front of you like you were reaching for some-thing. And you looked so sad." She turned to the others. "Then you all ran. The garage was open and the lights were on. It was all wrong." She shook her head. "I know where they keep the gas. I put one of the jugs back in there, and then threw the other one in the woods. Had to make it look like someone *tried* to cover it up."

Johnny looked confused. "But why—"

"I wiped down everything I could," she said. "The jugs, the door to the garage, the light switch. I made sure the door locked behind me."

There are moments when you realize that everything you know about a person barely amounts to the most superficial of impres-sions. Nate discovered that this dripping girl whom he'd spent hun-dreds of hours contemplating was a wondrous stranger. What else might be there, just under her lovely skin?

"I don't get it," Tom said. He put both his hands on his head and began walking in a circle. "I don't get what's happening."

"What's happening is that Lucy made an obvious case of arson look a little less deliberate," Nate said. "Remember, only the Deck-ers' prints are in the garage."

"You're saying that—"

"The police might blame them." Nate turned to Lucy. "They wouldn't be the first people to burn down their own house and do a crappy job of hiding it. If nothing else, it's enough to confuse every-thing."

"Mr. Decker's been having money problems," Lucy said. "His stores haven't been doing well. They might even lose their farm in Gracefield. I overheard a phone call a couple weeks ago."

"Motive," Tom said, nodding. "A nice way to get insurance money. And a storm's a good time to set a fire. All kinds of things can happen in a storm."

"You might have saved us." Nate didn't know if Mr. Decker would really get blamed for setting fire to his own home. He didn't know if he wanted that to happen in the first place. But maybe Lucy had muddied the waters enough to shift any blame away from them. "Thank you."

"We're even now," Lucy said. She was right in front of him. "I heard you. I know you did it for me."

Thunder detonated above them. It shook the pier like a quake. Lucy rested her cold palm against his wet face. When she touched him, Nate understood something he'd overlooked in all the months since April. He and Lucy were two halves of the same disaster. They were as conjoined as lightning and thunder.

It was strange to be surprised by something that felt so inevita-ble.

From the beginning, this was the collision they had been hurtling toward.

She kissed him. On the broken dance floor of the Night Ship, in front of his friends and all the pier's ghosts. The kiss was only a brush of lips against lips. Less a kiss than a promise. Nate felt this in the voltage that sang through him when the tip of her tongue grazed his mouth and in the way her hand tightened on his bicep.

It was a promise in the way that all beginnings were a promise. Nate found that it was easy to forget himself in the ecstasy of this beginning. In its rush, he could forget that a person was comprised of all of the things that had happened to them, and that life's equa-tions of pain must find a balance. He could forget how the universe stacked chance upon chance in a way that can turn the smallest of things into the most momentous of events. He could forget that he was hunted by shadows, and that even on its brightest day life was really a storm.

With her lips on his, Nate found that he could even forget that time proved all promises to be lies.

Seven

"But why were you outside to begin with?" Meg asked.

Nate was in the emergency room at the little hospital in Gracefield, one town over from Greystone Lake. They'd checked him over and stitched the cut on the crown of his head. He believed he had only a minor concussion, but the emergency room doctor insisted on a CT scan.

"I was checking for storm damage," Nate told her. This was essentially true.

"And some kid clocked you?"

"I didn't get a good look at him. I think he was a kid."

"You're lucky Bea heard the commotion. Is she still there?"

"She went to get me some dry clothes." Nate didn't know how long he'd been unconscious on the lawn, but it'd been time enough to get soaked through. His phone hadn't been spared. An ominous discoloration spread across its screen. "I'm really completely fine."

"A man doesn't call his wife from the ER at three in the morning to let her know he's fine. He calls to let her know he isn't *dead*. You understand the difference, right?"

Despite Meg's suggestion to the contrary, Nate knew from experience that she would have been more upset if he'd waited until morning to tell her he'd been hurt.

Soon after they'd begun dating, back when Nate still had a habit of getting into a particular kind of trouble, a minor incident had landed him in the ER. When he'd showed up at Meg's apartment the next night and startled her with a split lip and two fingers in splints, she'd been furious that she was only then learning of his injuries.

Nate had never seen even a hint of her anger before this. *You should have told me the second you had a free hand to dial,* she'd shouted at him, *I could have helped!* He realized that Meg wasn't upset for being kept in the dark, but because she'd imagined him suffering for a day without her even knowing. This had been a concept long lost to him: that pain could be diminished by being shared. It made him wonder for the first time if this thing between them could be love. A gentler genus of love than what he'd known before, though a species not without its teeth. He felt the sting of its bite now, in this ER at three A.M., in this cold plastic chair not far from his hometown, where lies so often felt like mercy.

"I'm telling you—"

"Yes, that you're fine. Other than the concussion. Other than the bruise to your brain that you got when a random hoodlum smashed you over the head with a stepladder. I don't suppose you asked him why he was carrying a stepladder around in the dead of night in the middle of a hurricane?"

"I'm alive. I'm not going to die. I'll get a second opinion on the CT scan as soon as I get home, just to be safe."

"I wish you'd never gone back there."

"That makes two of us." His first real lie to her. They were quiet together for a few moments. "But I really *am* fine."

"I'm actually glad now that you didn't drive there. But taking a bus back is ridiculous. Can't you fly from Albany or something? Or are you even supposed to fly with a concussion? God, then there's this damn hurricane."

"I'll figure it out, love. You need your sleep now. Solo monkey duty and all."

"Don't worry your sweet little head about all this complicated medical business, dear," Meg said in her grumbling facsimile of Nate's voice.

"Exactly right, dear." Even woken from a dead sleep by an emergency call, she could make him smile.

"Be more careful, please?" Meg said after some silence.

"Believe me, if I see another stepladder, I'm running in the opposite direction."

"I'm serious, Nate."

And he knew she was.

"Come back here the fastest, safest way you can, as soon as you can."

"I will, love. I promise I will."

They said their goodbyes, and when Nate hung up, the waiting room seemed colder and emptier than it had been.

He was tired but actually did feel mostly fine. The stitches on his scalp felt tight, but he hardly had a headache. He was cold, though. The hospital was refrigerated, and his clothes were still wet.

While he waited for Grams and the CT technician, Nate tried to sear the details of the vandals he'd tussled with into his memory. He'd caught only the edge of the boy's profile, but he thought he'd have a decent shot at identifying the girl. The light hadn't been great, but he guessed her age somewhere between thirteen and fifteen. That put her between eighth grade and sophomore year.

In Nate's day, Greystone Lake's school district had hovered at around a hundred students a grade. The classes were probably larger now, but it still wouldn't take him long to go through a yearbook.

He could find this girl. Once he did, he'd have them all. He'd know everything they knew.

Outside, sirens crescendoed, and Nate guessed he wouldn't be alone in these fluorescent halls for much longer.

His phone startled him with a sound like that of a live cat being skinned. He'd hoped it would survive getting wet, but this looked increasingly unlikely. It wouldn't even display the name of the incoming caller.

"Hello?"

"Nate, thank Christ you have your phone on. You've got to get to the hospital."

"Tom?"

An ambulance shrieked to a stop outside the emergency entrance, its revolving lights blazing through the automatic doors.

"Dad just called. There's been an accident."

"I'm already here. I'm fine, though."

Police and paramedics were clustered like a fist around a stretcher they ran through the doors.

"There was an explosion at the Union. I don't know much, but—"

Nate missed everything else Tom said. He repeated the words he'd heard to himself. He rearranged them and tried all kinds of punctuation, but couldn't find a way to make them mean anything else. The smell of smoke entered the room with the emergency squad.

He would have recognized the form on the stretcher anywhere, but he still searched it for proof of identity.

The scuffed shoes, the singed strips of a cardigan.

Her familiar hands, charred and blistered.

His grandmother's blackened face under the fogged plastic of an oxygen mask.

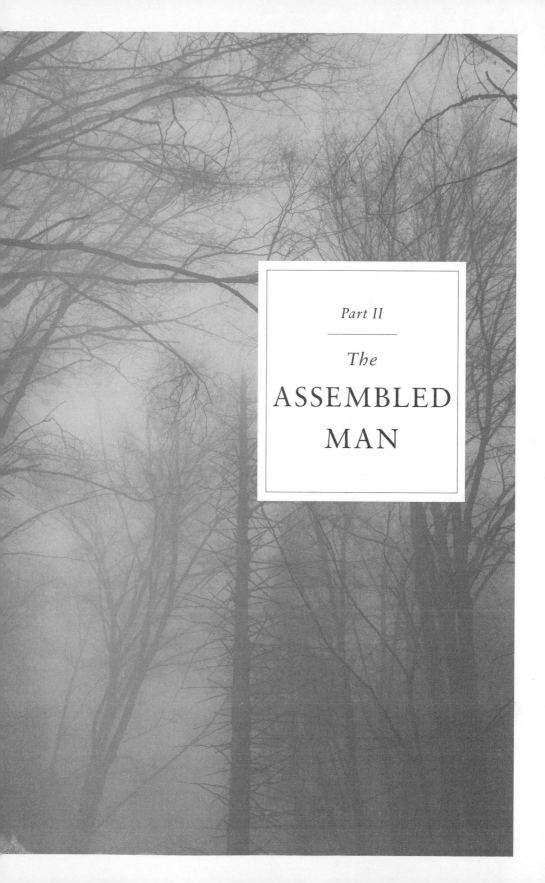

Part II

The

ASSEMBLED
MAN

Eight

Ten percent of Grams's body had second- and third-degree burns. She had a fractured spine and two cracked ribs. She'd been unconscious when they found her and had yet to wake up.

From interrogating police and paramedics, Nate constructed a skeleton of what had happened.

His best guess was that Grams had been on her way to Bonaparte Street to get him dry clothes when she drove by the Union and noticed that its lights were on. The pub should have been locked up hours ago. She'd had the foresight to call the police before entering the place to investigate.

Perhaps things in the bar and eating areas of the pub looked as they were supposed to, but she'd been drawn to the kitchen. When she opened its swinging doors, she'd breathed fresh life into an oxygen-starved fire that smoldered there. This triggered a flare-up powerful enough to knock her across the room. An officer, responding to her call, saw the explosion and pulled her free of the blazing pub.

Nate had seen her chart. They were keeping her fluids up and were worried about her lungs. Her face was blistered, her hands and arms ravaged, and she'd fractured two vertebrae. Nate couldn't shake the smell that had accompanied her arrival at the hospital. Melting plastic and burned food. He'd washed his face a dozen times, but couldn't flush it from his nostrils.

He'd been the doctor-grandson and fired questions at the staff, grilled the paramedics, and double-checked the IVs and infusions and doses. He'd woken acquaintances with burn experience in the middle of the night for their advice. He wanted her airlifted to a burn center, but she was too unstable to move, and flying in this weather had its own risks.

The crisis had given Nate focus and direction. Lucy, the troubles of the Lake, and the ghosts of his youth were pushed to the rim of his concerns. But now that the active phase of the disaster was over, he was deep into the desolate territories of waiting. Here, the reasons he'd returned home cast their shadows over everything, each doubt and question and regret intensifying in shifting umbras and penumbras.

It was dawn, and he'd spent the last hour with his head in his hands.

Nate had been tested by water, but on that long-ago night when they'd burned Adam Decker's house, the fire had but tasted him. It had been a kind of baptism, that dip into flame: the true beginning to their Thunder Runs, when Lucy joined them and together they reigned over the shore like bloodied angels. A world of new possibilities opened to him that night. Beautiful and terrible.

Someone tapped his shoulder. Tom in police-issue rain gear.

"What took you so long?" Nate asked. Tom had called him hours ago.

"It's crazy out there." Tom collapsed into the chair next to Nate. His eyes were sunken and bloodshot. His stubble made him look twice his age. His shoes and trousers were splattered with mud. "The hurricane. The vandals. How is she?"

"Not good, Tommy. She shouldn't be alive at all." It was amazing that she'd survived, but the spine injury alone could lay her up long enough for her to develop pneumonia, and that wasn't her biggest problem. Even under the best circumstances, a full recovery was hard to imagine. Nate wanted to break his fists against the wall, thinking of how unfair a way this was to close out a good and gentle life.

"But she's going to be okay?" Tom asked.

Nate felt as if he was on the threshold of a precipitous descent. A furious and familiar creature waited for him on the other side of the drop. Its eyes burned like ice, its smile was a blade, and it was now so close that Nate could feel its cold breath lick across his face.

"McHales are hard to kill," Tom said, looking at him uncertainly. It was a risky thing to say.

"Some of us." Despair was as useless an emotion as there was. But it had a dangerous cousin. As Nate sat up in his chair he felt himself slide a little closer to it.

"They're finished now, you know," Tom said.

The vandals, Tom meant. Nate was certain they'd set the fire at the Union. Maybe they hadn't meant for anyone to get hurt, but their intentions were irrelevant. "Yes." The creature inside him tried to affix its serrated smile to Nate's face, but he still held it at bay. "Finished."

"This is a felony."

Nate nodded, though the letter of the law had never held much interest for him. He'd long followed his own commandments.

"Unless it really was an accident," Tom said. "We'll run tests to find out."

Nate wished he could believe bad wiring or some flaw in the installation of a gas line was to blame. The universe was senseless in its violence, and another curse from it would be easier to accept than the fact that it was all his fault. But he was sure that the fire had been set deliberately, and that the old pub had been targeted because of his connection to it. He also knew that Grams never would have been outside at that time of night in the first place if not for him.

"What happened to you?" Tom asked, pointing to Nate's chest. Nate looked down at a bloodstain on his T-shirt. It took him a moment to remember how it got there.

"Some of those kids were about to do something to Grams's house. One of them knocked me out with a stepladder. Joke's on me, I guess. Should've been more worried about the pub." The CT technician still wanted pictures of Nate's brain, but he'd been waving him away.

"You saw them? Can you make an ID?"

"One of them, maybe. A girl."

"I'll get the yearbooks from the high school and middle school. If we find her, then . . ." Tom trailed off.

Nate followed his friend's gaze to his own hands. Droplets of blood trembled from the white promontories of his knuckles. He didn't need to examine his hands to know that his nails had sliced into his palms. For years his hands had been marred with such half-moon scabs.

He wiped the blood onto his jeans. There were ruined anyway. Next to him, Tom's face was an amalgam of alarm and dread. They'd been here before, the two of them, in this place between action and reaction. In this space between victimhood and vigilantism. And not a single good thing had come from it.

Before Tom could say anything, a torrent of swearing permeated the emergency room's glass doors. They slid open, and Johnny hobbled through, heavily supported by Owen.

Tom stole another look at Nate's bloodied hands before hurrying to meet the pair struggling through the entrance. Johnny slung his free arm around Tom's shoulder when Tom reached him. "What happened?"

"Little shits broke into my house and slicked oil or something all over my stairs."

"How bad are you hurt?" Tom asked. "How far'd you fall?"

"Half a flight maybe. I don't know. Marble looks good but it's a real bitch once you get down to it."

"Why didn't you call an ambulance?" Nate stooped to examine Johnny's injured leg. The bloodstain on his pants had prepared Nate for something awful, and the splintered stalk of bone lancing through rent flesh didn't disappoint. Compound fracture of the tibia.

"They're so loud."

"Holy God," Tom said, seeing the state of Johnny's leg.

"You're lucky you didn't break your neck," Owen said.

"Yeah, the second I saw my leg tricked out like a George Romero prop, I thanked God for how amazingly lucky I am."

"They'll need to operate," Nate said. "How are you even able to speak in complete sentences right now?"

"There might have been some self-medicating going on," Owen said.

"Go and narc on me, Owen. Christ."

"You need to get that treated, like right now." A sleepy-looking orderly was ambling toward them with a wheelchair, and Nate motioned for him to hurry up. "And make sure to tell them whatever meds you took."

Chief Buck came through the automatic doors. His rain gear was slicked with water, and his expression was as dark as the sky.

"You, too, Johnny?" He grimaced at the wound, then glanced at Tom. They stared at each other for a moment, and Nate watched something pass between them. The chief wrapped his arms around his son and Tom hugged him back.

"I'm so sorry about Loki," the chief said.

"Loki?" Nate asked.

"Tom's black lab, you asshole." Johnny's voice was saturated with disgust. "Poor dead Loki."

"Your dog died? I didn't know you had a dog."

"You don't know *anything*. And he didn't die, he was *murdered*. The bastards drugged him or something and put him behind the back wheel of Tom's cruiser."

"So you—"

"I—ran over him. After I called you, to tell you about Grams, I was on my way here. And then, when I pulled out of the garage—I—" Tom's voice wavered as he kept his eyes fixed on some imaginary point. "The second I felt the car lurch, I just *knew*. He was my—" He swallowed and closed his eyes. "He was a good dog."

Nate realized that Tom's eyes were red and his clothes were covered in mud because he'd been burying his beloved pet.

"I was heading over to help him when I fell down the stairs," Johnny said. "It probably shocks you to learn I'm not usually up and about at five in the morning."

"I wish you'd told me, Tom. I'm so sorry."

Tom shrugged and looked away.

The orderly and a nurse eased Johnny into the wheelchair and pushed him toward triage.

Tom and Owen trailed Johnny then settled into chairs across from where Nate had been seated. He was about to join them, but the chief's grip on his arm stopped him.

"How's Bea?"

"Not good, Chief."

"Is she awake?"

"No. If she does wake up she'll wish she hadn't." A tsunami of agony awaited Grams if she returned to him.

"I'm going to see her. Don't go anywhere." Chief Buck exchanged words with the nurse at the intake desk and disappeared through a set of doors.

"Did they hit you last night, Owen?" Nate asked as he dropped into his chair.

"Not this time."

"They got me instead," Tom said. "I was an idiot for thinking they'd leave me alone." He spoke without heat, as if his front door had been egged and not his dog murdered. But his eyes were wide and gleaming with tears.

Medea's carnage played mutely from the waiting room's television. Roiling mud where a highway had been, parking lots filled with submerged cars, Coast Guard rescues from foundering ships. All of the footage, blurred and choppy and water-slicked.

These were scenes from the lives of the unlucky. Edited, packaged, and broadcast to places where electricity still ran in lines through the walls instead of in bolts that splintered the sky. Viewers, from the comfort of their couches, were the fortunate ones. But luck doesn't last forever. In the carousel of disaster, Nate knew that everyone gets their turn.

"It'll be okay," Owen told Nate. He'd leaned across the space that separated them. "No matter what happens, it'll all be okay." It was a platitude people used as a placeholder for something better, but Owen delivered the words with conviction.

"I don't think so, O," Nate said. "Not this time."

"When my mom had her stroke, I didn't know how to handle it." Owen shook his head. "Dad was gone by then, and I had to deal with all of it. The doctors, the bills, the rehab. Everything. It seemed totally impossible. Because it was new, and horrible, and changes everything in your life. But people do stuff like this all the time. People who aren't as tough and smart and well-off. Because we've got to, you know?"

"Yeah." The big guy was trying to help, and Nate couldn't fault him for that.

"And the thing is—the thing to remember—is no matter what happens, you get used to it. You can survive it," Owen said. "I mean, if I can do it, believe me, you can." He hazarded a smile.

Nate just managed to raise his mouth to a less-grim line when the chief returned from the ICU.

In the years Nate had known him, he'd only seen the man's stoicism slip a few times, and this was one of them. Grams looked as bad as her condition suggested, and the chief had known her since his own youth. Of course he was shaken. She was his best friend's mother. But by the time he got to Nate, he'd regained his composure.

"She's a tough lady, your grandma," he said. "But you've been up all night. Must need some air. Let's go for a ride. May as well get that talk out of the way."

The man strode for the automatic doors, and Nate understood that this wasn't a request.

"See you later, Nate," Owen said. "Be careful out there."

"I'll let you know if anything with Grams changes." Tom's face was a complicated mosaic of grief and sympathy. But there was something else there, too. Something in the tautness of his mouth and the intensity of his friend's eyes that Nate couldn't place. It could have been some iteration of Tom's dread at the sight of his bloody hands. Nate wasn't sure. When he raised a hand in farewell, Tom matched it with his own.

Dawn should have come, but there was little sign of the sun. Clouds gouged the sky from one end of the horizon to the other. Rain lashed at the streets as wind ripped at the trees.

The chief had parked under the ER's overhang, so they avoided the worst of the rain. The interior of the car was cold, and under his raincoat Nate's clothes were still damp from Grams's lawn. Next to him, the chief's face was stone.

The air in the car was faintly scented with plastic and soap. Within it, Nate couldn't smell the rain or mud or shredded foliage. He could feel the wind only so much as Medea rocked the cruiser. The car was a tiny pocket of the raging world where temperature and breeze could be adjusted at the turn of a dial. This should have brought comfort, but it didn't.

In one of the Lake's stories, Nate felt he'd be entering the middle section. This was the crucial stage where agendas were unveiled and true characters revealed. The action here could break in any number of ways. Nothing was assured, because in the Lake the good guys didn't always triumph. Few of its stories had heroes to begin with.

These were fraught chapters, but it was in these pages that Nate believed he had a shot at learning what he wanted so badly to discover.

Chief Buck hadn't uttered a syllable since putting the car into drive. The rasp of wipers pawing at the windshield was the only sound in the tight space.

While their conversation would surely be about Lucy, its shape depended upon what the chief knew, or believed he knew. But Nate found the chief's silence suggestive. His years of dealing with sick children and their terrified parents had taught him that it usually took only a small thing to put a person more at ease. A crooked smile. A stupid joke. A question that had nothing at all to do with whatever catastrophe that had fallen from a clear sky to expose the cardboard underpinnings of their lives. So it was clear to him that the chief didn't want him at ease.

They were driving down the flooding streets toward a performance, and Nate guessed it starred everyone's least favorite half of the Good Cop/Bad Cop routine.

The chief wanted Nate off-balance. He saw Nate as being out of his element, exhausted, and dulled with shock, and he intended to make the most of it. Nate expected traps to be set and trip wires to be strung. And it was true that the story of their long-ago high school graduation was a perilous narrative, overgrown with long-thorned brambles and pockets of pitch-black. Traversing it with a hostile escort at his heels was dangerous. It was a history easy to become ensnared in. It was a story that bit back.

But Nate didn't let himself worry.

He'd been known to pull off a solid Bad Cop himself.

GRADUATION

I

"TELL ME HOW it all ended," Lucy said. Her hand was in Nate's hair, resting flush against his scalp. "Tell me about the last day."

His stubble bristled against her belly as he smiled. He'd told Lucy many stories about the Night Ship, but something about this one particularly thrilled her.

"In 1964 the pier was gearing up for its—"

"*Stop!*" Lucy tightened her hand into a fist, pulling the waves of his hair into taut bands. "You know that's not how I like our stories."

Nate laughed into the curve of her ribs, then rolled off her and pulled on his jeans. It was mid-June, but the planks of the Night Ship were cold in the early morning. In the dawn, the lake glowed like the sun.

"Just June," he said. He peered around the cavernous dark space of the dance floor as if uttering her name might conjure the woman herself. Like all legends, the details varied from telling to telling, but the bones remained the same. "How does that old rhyme go?" he asked. Like the best ghost stories, the Night Ship's tales weren't merely told, they were performed.

"Just June made all the boys swoon, cost you just a dollar to bring her to your room," Lucy sang. It was a children's verse, but on her lips it sounded like an invitation.

"They say Just June grew up in the Night Ship, that she and her twin sister were the daughters of one of Morton Strong's prostitutes," Nate continued. "Since the father could have been anyone, she was known only by her first name. 'June what?' her clients would ask. 'Just June,' she'd answer." Nate threw open the door to the boardwalk. He was usually more careful in daylight, but it was so early that not even the Daybreakers were out yet. He turned to look at Lucy, lying on her side in a puddle of clothes. The cool breeze on his bare chest, the sun of a new day, and the sight of her made him feel like he could live forever.

"And by 'clients' you mean . . ." Lucy affected a confused look. Nate lay back down next to her and ran his finger from her neck to her navel.

"Johns, tricks, transactional lovers. It's the world's oldest profession, but it's a tough thing to make a career of. Terrible retirement package. June was smart and fierce, and for a while was Strong's right hand, but she was mostly one of his whores. She'd pounded the sheets since her early teens by some accounts, and that kind of life takes its toll. Into her middle age, what'd been a flood of customers had slowed to a trickle. New, bright-eyed young things arrived to work the beds of the Century Room every season, and June couldn't compete. No longer the bombshell with all the right moves and the body to pull them off, June was all but used up. Soon the only clients she could get were the strange ones, the ones with the weird fetishes and kinks."

"I wonder what qualified as kinky back then?" Lucy asked. Her fingernail clicked along the zipper of Nate's jeans. "I'll have to do some research."

"And she didn't just have herself to worry about. Her twin sister was a few matches short of a box. May was her name. June and May, the prettiest months of the year. They were the Night Ship Girls. Strong could have used May as a prostitute, too, but maybe he had a scrap of humanity after all. She was paid a slave wage to scrub the kitchen and mop the floors. June was devoted to her sister. May was June's heart. And they both relied on June's usefulness to Strong. But June was no longer the draw she'd once been, and this hadn't gone unnoticed by old Morton. The club had a reputation to uphold; the girls who worked there had to have a certain je ne sais quoi, and Just June had begun to look more and more out of place. 'End of the summer,' Strong told June one Memorial Day. Come September, she'd have to find some other place to sell what little she had left to offer. You can imagine how that must have felt for her. The Night Ship was all she'd ever known. She was afraid. And she was angry."

"Hell hath no fury," Lucy said. She was living proof of the phrase. The year and a half since Adam Decker's house burned had marked a run of terrible luck for the enemies of Lucy Bennett.

"And it wasn't just Morton Strong she was angry with." Nate leapt back to his feet. "She loathed the younger girls who'd replaced her. Her clients filled her with disgust. In fact, she'd begun to hate just about everyone who had anything to do with the Night Ship. They all had to pay. But she was no dummy, our June. She was sweetness itself when Strong told her that her days were numbered."

"They never see the sweet ones coming, do they, McHale?" Lucy rolled onto her stomach and kicked her feet into the air. It was a classic pose, but like everything else, Lucy found a way to make it her own. She pulled her journal out from under her crumpled tank top, but Nate knew her attention was still on the story. They were almost to her favorite part.

"So she plays nice, our June, right up until the big Fourth of July celebration. Independence Day is the centerpiece of every resort town's summer, and the Lake goes all out. Fireworks are shot off from Blind Down Island. Sailboats festooned with lights bob on the water. Bands play in the bars and along the streets. Packs of children run along the shore trailing a wake of sparklers. The Lake is rocking, and no place rocks it harder than the Night Ship." Nate moved to the scarred dance floor. "Men in linen suits dance with women draped in silk." He shuffled his feet to the tune of an imagined song. If Nate tried, he could see others in their finery moving to the same rhythm. "The air's thick with cigar smoke and the euphoria of a summer night. Elaborate centerpieces blazing with candles and sparklers erupt from every table. Punch overflows from two hundred glasses. The Night Ship is *the* place to be. And you know how things can feel on a night like that. The right place, the right time. The right music, the right clothes. The right girl." Nate turned to Lucy. "Everything so perfect, you can't imagine a future less golden than the present."

Lucy smiled and looked down at her journal. She was as fearless a person as Nate had ever known, and he loved that he could still make her feel shy.

"But it wasn't to be for the folks at the Night Ship that Independence Day. The backdoor operations in the Century Room were put on hold for big celebrations like this. No reason to flaunt their indiscretions in front of the town's leading citizens. So the prostitutes worked as waitresses and played the role of eye candy. But Just June was relegated to the kitchens," Nate said. "A final insult."

"In more ways than one."

"The Night Ship throws the best parties. But the best parties have the worst hangovers. Around midnight, some of the patrons begin to get queasy. Too hot, they figure. Too much smoke. Too much booze."

"What was in that punch, anyway?" Lucy said. She wrote something in her notebook. She was always scribbling in it. In the fall, she'd be studying journalism at NYU while Nate would be just a subway ride away at Columbia.

"Indeed. The punch at the Night Ship was notoriously strong, but this year, Just June put her own twist on it. A one-of-a-kind blend of nail polish, antifreeze, rat poison, and who knows what else. At first only a few guests get sick, but within the packed hall, it soon becomes clear that something's deeply wrong." He jumped onto a table.

"Fear ripples through the crowd. First a woman screams, then a man pushes. An animal panic takes grip. Consider that this is a crowd wasted on punch and poison, with half of them in high heels. Remember it happens at the end of a pier in a stifling nightclub decorated with elaborate sparkler displays."

"Mayhem." Lucy smiled.

"People rush for the exits in the front and the back. The ones who go for the back get stuck among the seats arranged there for the fireworks. In the crush, some are pushed off the boardwalk into the water. Others jump into the lake by their own choice, hoping to swim for shore. Those who make for the promenade have better luck, but they also have more incentive. Some of those sparkler displays had been knocked over in the flight for the doors and set tablecloths and women's dresses ablaze. The curtains soon follow." Nate pointed to a charred wall on the far end of the club. The stubs of burned drapes still hung there like shorn hair. "The Lake's children used to leave sparklers at the barricade, you know. Before they started leaving glow sticks. Anyway, at some point the massive aquarium by the restrooms shatters. This contributes to the chaos, though it also douses a few of the burning women."

"A party no one's ever going to forget."

"Between the fire, the poison, the drownings, and the stampede, over a dozen people die that night, with many more seriously injured. Morton Strong is among the partygoers who make it out of the Night Ship, but he indulged in a bit too much holiday cheer. Most of the poisoned revelers survived, but June's punch destroys his insides. He doesn't live through the night."

"So Just June gets the revenge she wanted," Lucy said.

"No one's coming back here after that. The lawsuits bankrupted the entire pier. That was the party that sank the Night Ship. But, in Shakespearean fashion, June's revenge is achieved only at tremen-

dous personal cost. Though she gave her twin, May, the strictest instructions on how to remain safe throughout the night, May's a sweet
soul who could never turn her back on someone who needed help.
When she sees a woman running, dressed in flaming lace, she has to
help her. While trying to smother the burning woman's dress, May is
caught in the push for the exits and is trampled to death by the
crowd. June finds her on the boardwalk amid thrashing tropical fish
from the broken aquarium, soaked to the bone, broken from a hundred stomping feet. June comes undone. She brought down the Night
Ship as much for May as she did for herself. Vengeance for a lifetime
of indignities. But now she's responsible for the death of the one
person who matters to her. May was her heart. And no one can live
without their heart. June's alone now, with only one route out of the
trouble she's made for herself."

"The long walk," Lucy said.

This part of the story always sent a shiver through Nate. Beyond
the windows, the lake lapped the headlands like innocence itself.

"She tied herself to one of the boardwalk's wrought iron benches,
then shoved it through a broken railing and into the cold water below," Nate said. "Something that heavy might have kept her body
hidden for a good long while, but the lake—"

"The lake returns what it takes," Lucy said. Her green eyes flickered toward him. The old adage couldn't be uttered without recall-
ing the accident of two years ago when Nate had been inexplicably
returned by that same cold water.

Those words signaled the end of many of the lake's stories. For
Nate, they marked the beginning of a second life.

"I liked the part you added about the flaming lace," Lucy said,
shutting her journal. "Sometimes imagining the clothes on the riot-
ers is my favorite part."

"And here I thought it was the body count." Thinking of the lake
had turned Nate's thoughts toward his family. These days, there was
little anger attached to the memory. He'd found ways to exorcise
such rage. There was still a sense of absence: an ache he felt sure

would never leave him. But this was survivable, especially on a morning like this. In the dawn, there was a sense of something perfect and unbroken about the universe. As if everything was connected through some golden design in which nothing was ever truly lost. In which no one was ever really gone.

"You still with me, McHale?" Lucy asked. She wrapped her arms around him from behind. His skin slid against hers as he turned to face her. Though the lake was still empty, there was something audacious about her nudity.

"Always." He rested his forehead against her crown of auburn hair. "But we should go. Your mom'll be up soon."

"You realize we're not fooling her, right?" Lucy said. She walked to her clothes and shimmied her underwear up her thighs. "We're not fooling anyone. I see the way Grams looks at me. She knows I'm the filthy slut tarnishing her beautiful golden grandson."

Gold doesn't tarnish, Nate thought. He turned his T-shirt right side out. "It's not about fooling her. Grams knows I sneak out to be with you, but it'd be more unseemly to do it in the open. What would people say? If anything, lying to Grams and your mom is the best demonstration of our respect for them."

"Golden boy with a silver tongue." She shook her hair free of her top. "One day, you'll get someone into real trouble."

Nate rolled up the foam mat they'd been lying on and tossed it behind the bar. It settled among the sleeping bags, coolers, lanterns, and alcohol they stored here. They'd never seen a stranger in the year and a half that they'd been coming here, but they were still careful.

When Lucy was ready, they headed for the spiral staircase that led to the Century Room. These stairs also descended to a dark maze of low-ceilinged rooms constructed for God only knew what purpose. The stories about the Night Ship spoke of hidden passages in the walls and under the floors, though Nate had never succeeded in finding these. However, there was a large, intricate trapdoor in the undercroft that doubled as a boat launch. Nate and Tom agreed that this had probably been constructed for bootleggers during Prohibition. Concealed behind an array of pilings, this was the perfect way to get to the abandoned pier undetected.

Nate had left the launch door open, and their black canoe bobbed serenely where he'd tied it. In the shadow of the pier, the lake was obsidian. He held Lucy's hand as she stepped into the boat. Once seated, she picked up a paddle and propped it by the bow where it would be ready for him.

Nate was the only one who ever rowed. He liked squiring Lucy across the waters, as he knew she liked being squired. In the quiet of the lake, there was just the two of them.

Nate's own step into the boat coincided with a swell that sent the vessel rocking. They didn't come close to capsizing, but the oar tipped into the water. It floated just a foot from the hull, but Nate hesitated to reach for it.

"I got it, McHale," Lucy said. Nate had dated Lucy for months before she'd managed to coax him into a boat of any kind. He still didn't like the lake.

She retrieved the paddle, and he managed not to shudder at the slick cold on its rubber skin. Another reason he liked the exertion of rowing solo was that it left less time for him to dwell on the lake and how they so precariously rode its icy skin above its unfathomable dark. He pulled a chain to raise the launch door and turned the latch to lock it.

"It's supposed to rain, you know," Lucy said. As Nate pulled them free of the Night Ship's shadow, her eyes lit like shards of sea glass. "They sent out an email about bringing umbrellas to graduation."

"I saw it," Nate said. "Occasional cloudbursts." He knew where she was going with this. As he paddled, he looked at the web of scars on his bad arm. He tried to see past the healed flesh to the places where his bones had been pinned together in a patchwork that somehow held. Today, he detected only the faintest of aches. Before a storm—the kind of storm he looked forward to—his arm howled like sonar. The pain pulsed with the beat of his heart and the rhythm of thunder.

"I hope it doesn't mess up the party at Jim's house."

"A little rain won't stop the party. You might say some parties only really get started once the weather kicks in." He smiled at her, but she shook her head.

"You told me the Thunder Runs would end once school was over."

"School will be over. Tomorrow," Nate said. They'd had this conversation before. When they began, Lucy had been as fired up by their storm-borne justice as the rest of them, but she'd gradually lost the taste for it. While she might suggest the occasional target, she hadn't been on a Thunder Run with them in many months.

"Swear to me that this is the last one."

"What happened to my bloodthirsty girl?"

"She grew up," Lucy said. "And moved on. See that you do the same, or she might just move on without you." Her eyes twinkled when she said this, but Nate knew the threat was not entirely unserious.

"It's the last one. I promise. Then we're done with the Thunder Runs and the Night Ship."

"Cross your heart?"

Nate looked out over the lake's mirrored surface. The sun had risen enough to dim the glory of the dawn. Blue had not yet filled the void, and the water Nate pulled them through was as colorless as the sky. "The reign of the Storm King is ended," Nate said. "His foes lie vanquished, and peace dwells now in his realm along the shore." He smiled, though saying this made him sadder than he'd have guessed. But nothing lasted forever. Soon they'd be in the city, where their lives would accelerate into a future they could scarcely imagine. To move on, some things had to be left behind. Lucy was right: The Storm King and his Thunder Runs had served their purpose. Now it was time to grow up.

He must have sighed, because Lucy was still watching him.

"What am I going to do with you, McHale?"

"If you run out of ideas, I can do some research," he said. She smiled at that. He rowed in silence for a while. The lake was beginning to come to life. A fishing boat with its rails lined with yawning tourists cut through the water on their way to the lake's northern bulge. Closer to shore, the heads of Daybreakers bobbed as they began their morning rituals.

"You have a plan?" Lucy eventually asked him. A rhetorical question. The Storm King always had a plan. "Nothing too reckless, right?"

"*Moi?*"

"It's just that it would be a shame to spend your first night as a high school graduate in jail." It was their usual repartee, but as before, Nate detected an undercurrent of gravity. "And nothing too complicated."

After the early misstep of burning the Deckers' house, they'd stuck to acts that could be plausibly blamed on storm damage or other natural occurrences. The most elaborate of these targeted a coach on the soccer team who'd been giving Tom grief. When an early blizzard struck over a weekend when the man and his family were out of town, Nate knew just what to do. Temperatures had plummeted, and the boys spent the night hosing down trees on the man's property. As the layers of water froze, one of the trees finally shattered under its weight. It collapsed against windows and walls, and completely cut off the driveway. It'd taken them a brutal four hours in polar cold to accomplish this, but the gleaming wreckage they'd left behind had made it worthwhile.

"I'm not planning an ice storm or a fire or flood or anything like that," he said. "Actually, I'm planning a gift."

"A gift?" Lucy asked.

"For you." He grinned at her as he pulled them the last lengths to the Vanhoutens' dock. "This last one will be just for you."

Nine

The chief maneuvered the cruiser to avoid the crest of another toppled tree. The ribs of its branches bristled like the skeleton of an alien creature.

Nate finally broke the silence within the car. "Has there been much damage?" The sun should have crowned the mountains, but the day was monochrome. The lake and its forests bled together in gradations of gray, the bleakest of watercolors.

"Some flooding. Downed trees. Parts of the foothills lost power."

"Maybe they'll reschedule the funeral." Surely a murderer wouldn't bring up his own victim's funeral.

"Fourteen years. Don't think they want to wait any longer."

It seemed absurd for anyone to venture out into this weather. But for Lucy's funeral, the backdrop was fitting. The town's cemeteries were inland, but Nate imagined a gravesite prayer along the shore. Clinging black suit pants coated with mud to the knees. Dark umbrellas inverted and whisked away to join the clouds. A wall of the lake's colorless water surging for the assembled. To wipe them away. To wipe them clean.

"Tom told me Mr. Bennett will be there," Nate said. As hard as it was to believe, Mr. Bennett had hardly entered Nate's mind in years. This was one reason why learning that the man had been released from prison had been such a shock. "Have you seen him since he got out?"

"The Lake's too small to avoid someone like that."

"Grams must have seen him, too." Nate hated the idea of her running into him in the hardware store or at the grocery.

"Your Grams is a good woman. That man paid for what he did. That's what she told me when he made parole."

"Do you believe that?"

"More interested in what you believe, Nate."

"I'm not angry at him anymore, if that's what you mean. I'm not going to cause trouble. But I don't plan to shake his hand, either."

"That family's been through a lot."

"There's a club for that. I'm on the board."

"Money was always a struggle for them," the chief continued. "Mrs. B did her best, but she wasn't the same after Lucy disappeared."

Three weeks ago, the chief would have said "run away" and not "disappeared." The discovery of her body in the headlands had changed everything. In the span of a single wet afternoon, one of the Lake's most treasured stories had taken another twist. The details of its ending were yet to be determined.

"I gave her boy odds and ends to do at the station. He was grateful, too. It takes character to take charity and be truly grateful, don't you think?" Nate detected a hint of insinuation there.

"I'll keep my distance, just the same."

"The man's burying his daughter today. Death rips people apart, but it can bring them together, too."

A laugh erupted from Nate. Trapped within the confines of the car, it was a terrible sound. A father, husband, healer, and upstanding member of society didn't make a noise like this. This choking gasp of scorn came from the darkest and deepest place inside him.

"Something funny?"

"My grandmother might not live out the day. We're about to bury my high school girlfriend. And you want me to make nice with the man who killed my family? Yeah, that strikes me as just about hysterical."

The chief took his eyes off the road long enough to look Nate over. "It really does, doesn't it?"

They traveled in silence the rest of the way to the Greystone Lake police station.

The wipers couldn't match the deluge that fell from the seething sky. From the side window, Nate saw that the sewers were already overflowing. Torn leaves and branches accumulated along the curbs like detritus on a beach.

The chief pulled into his reserved space. This was as close to the station's entrance as one could get, but every part of Nate not protected by his black raincoat was freshly soaked by the time he got inside.

The little station had been renovated since he was last here. There was wood laminate where there'd been linoleum. Light fixtures had been upgraded from fluorescents to the slightly warmer shade of LEDs. There were artificial plants, and an open plan had replaced rows of high-walled cubes.

Nate followed the chief through the reception and down a hallway. Apart from a single officer at the front desk, the place looked abandoned.

"In here," the chief said.

It was an interrogation room.

"Sit," the chief told him. "Be right with you." The man closed the door, leaving Nate momentarily alone.

Nate didn't like the small room. The chair was uncomfortable, and its seat was too low. The air was stale and the walls too close.

This was all by design, of course. No one seated here was supposed to feel at ease. It irritated him how well it worked.

He wanted to talk to Meg. He needed to hear Livvy's tiny voice. He needed them to help hold together this version of himself he'd constructed. But his phone's display barely deigned to light.

When Chief Buck returned, he sat in the chair across from Nate and placed a cardboard storage box on the table between them.

"Do you have any objections to us recording this interview?" the chief asked.

Nate shook his head.

Chief Buck nodded to the mirrored glass and declared the date, time, and subject for the record. "Fourteen years ago, we interviewed you several times in connection to Lucy Bennett's death."

"In connection to her running away, actually."

"At the time we believed she'd run away because—"

"Of the note she left her mother," Nate finished. The note had shown up a few days after Lucy went missing. It'd been found under the Bennetts' dining room table. One might suppose it'd been there all along and simply gone unnoticed in the chaos of Lucy's disappearance. The letter itself had been vague and desperate and just what you'd expect from a teenage runaway. If you were inclined to believe Lucy was the kind of girl who'd flee her life, its few sentences would have confirmed the suspicion.

"Obviously, finding her body has forced us to reexamine the circumstances of her disappearance."

"How do you explain the note?" Nate asked. Officially, the search for Lucy continued for weeks, but any urgency to the investigation had been sapped by the discovery of that letter. Nate wondered how much the chief now blamed himself for that.

"A ploy on the part of her killer, perhaps. A prank by children. A lot of people were in and out of the Bennetts' house that week."

"Surely you had the handwriting authenticated."

"Why don't you let me ask the questions, Nate." The chief

rubbed his eyes for some long moments. When he stopped and looked at Nate again, his face seemed freshly sharpened. He pulled six black notebooks out of the cardboard box and dropped them onto the table with a thud.

"These are Lucy Bennett's notebooks. She wrote everything down. Everything."

"They never found those," Nate said, shaking his head. He and the others had worried about Lucy's journals in the days following her disappearance. She was constantly scribbling in them. She never let even Nate read them. *Everything* might very well have been written in their pages. But she must have hidden them, because the journals never came up during the investigation, and Nate had searched for them himself.

"We only recently discovered them."

"Really." Nate didn't believe it. They *looked* like the same kind of Moleskine notebooks Lucy used, but those were sold everywhere. The sheaves of cream-colored pages wedged between their black covers were worn, staggered like an old deck of cards. They clearly hadn't been picked up at a bookstore yesterday, but Nate was sure this effect could be faked. The chief had anywhere from weeks to years to prepare for this conversation and ample time to construct useful props.

"They contain detailed accounts of your relationship with her and the crimes you committed at the time."

"'Crimes'?"

"Vandalism. Breaking and entering. Destruction of property. Criminal mischief. Arson."

Nate laughed, and this time it was the laugh that he sometimes paired with his ready smile. Pure delight. Because only a great actor could be a good liar.

"It's all in here, Dr. McHale." The chief patted the stack of journals.

"If those are her journals and anything like that's in there, they're probably just notes for her novel. You know she wanted to be a writer."

"The events in her account match the dates of fires and floods and other incidents of vandalism around town," the chief said.

Having their Thunder Runs come to light was undesirable, but not catastrophic. They'd been minors, and the statute of limitations had run out for nearly all of their transgressions. The burning of Adam Decker's house could cause them trouble, but this seemed unlikely.

"Nate?"

"Sorry, just trying to figure out what Lucy might have been working on. I mean, I guess if you're talking about serious damage, like arson, it'd all have been public knowledge. If something in the Lake catches on fire, everyone's going to know by the next day, way before they read it in the paper. Hell, in a town like this, someone gets into a fender bender while grabbing their morning coffee at the Smart-Mart, everybody's talking about it by lunch time."

"She's not just mentioning incidents; she's describing how they occurred and explaining why you perpetrated them. You targeted specific people due to personal vendettas and committed some serious property damage as revenge."

"Vendettas? Come on, Chief. Like I said, Lucy wanted to be a writer. Maybe these were exercises for her." Nate pretended to think it over. "It sort of reminds me of those found-footage movies, you know? Lucy loved those. Remember *The Blair Witch Project*? I realize the whole genre's pretty played out now, but there were a couple months when people thought that movie was real. Lucy loved that kind of thrill. That something that should be totally unbelievable could be rendered in a form that made it convincing. It just requires a little suspension of disbelief. Because the thing is, people want to believe the unbelievable. Putting it together like a book, making it look like a real-life journal of a real-life teenage girl using actual people and genuine events. It's an interesting angle, if you think about it. The author as protagonist adds to the mystique."

The chief's face was as blank as an untouched page. "What?"

"It's pretty meta, especially for back then."

"You're saying these notebooks are some kind of creative writing project?"

"Lucy was very private about her writing. I'm sure people told you that. But what's the alternative? That I ran around town wreaking mayhem? A one-man natural disaster?" He made it sound offhand. A throwaway line.

"Not alone, as you know. You carried this vandalism out with the help of your associates, John Vanhouten, Owen Liffey, and Thomas Buck."

Nate thought he'd put on a good act of being unflustered, but when the chief listed his friends' names he realized how much tension he'd been carrying in his shoulders. The chief had misstepped and in such an obvious way that it was almost disappointing.

"You all have a lot to answer for."

"So do you," Nate said. For his whole life, he'd held an image of Tom's dad as the archetype of the perfect cop. Objective, just, tough, smart, relentless. But only human after all.

"Are those really Lucy's journals?" Nate now thought they probably were. The idea of this tugged at him like a fish hooked on a line, though not for the reasons the chief might guess. Nate wanted to turn their pages and trace their words and navigate the channels of Lucy's mind as inscribed by ink onto paper. If they were real, these pages were the most tangible things that survived of her.

"I said they were, didn't I?"

"You did." Nate massaged his temple. He was tired, but he'd only just begun.

The chief's silence and the set of his mouth suggested that he knew something had changed in the dynamics of their interview, but couldn't yet tell what.

"I've got to change my clothes," Nate said, getting up from the chair. There were a couple ways to play this, but this feint seemed like the best tactic. This would divert them from the path the chief had chartered and take them into fresh territory, where all sorts of interesting things might be revealed.

"We're not done here."

"Yeah, we are. I haven't been read my rights so I'm not under arrest. I can leave whenever I want. This interview isn't even really being recorded, is it?" He turned to the room's one-way mirror and knew there was no one behind it.

"I have more questions for you." The chief grabbed his arm to restrain him, and this was a mistake.

The man's rough grip propelled Nate to the edge of very dangerous country. For a moment, he faltered. For a moment, he forgot the person he'd assembled for the world to see. He tore the man's arm away from him with a speed and strength that sent the startled police chief heavily back into his seat.

"No. *I* have a question for you." There was a hint of the Storm King in Nate's voice. A threat of thunder beyond the mountains. He leaned against the table, looming over the seated lawman. He was angry, and he'd forgotten how good this felt. "What else did you hide?"

The chief looked as confused by Nate's question as he'd been surprised by his strength.

"You've had those journals for fourteen years, haven't you? You found them right away, but never introduced them into evidence because they'd incriminate us. They'd incriminate Tom."

The ease with which the chief had uttered his son's name had made obvious to Nate what a charade this interview was. The chief said it without a granule of hesitation, without a mote of contrition. And if that wasn't enough, Nate couldn't imagine a scenario in which it would be regulation for a law enforcement official to get this deep into a murder investigation in which his own son might have played a role. No, this was an off-the-books interview. A performance indeed, with the interrogation room as a private stage.

The older man's face folded itself into something carefully expressionless.

"What else is there?" Nate asked again. If the chief had been keeping the journals secret, he might be hiding anything.

"It's an active investigation. I'm not about to tell you details just because—"

"What did her body tell you?"

"Nate, I said I'm not—"

"Cause of death. Trace evidence. The scene."

"Stop it!" The chief's face cracked, and he was suddenly shouting.

It'd taken less to provoke him than Nate had expected. A furnace of stress churned under those layers of granite.

"Know your place, son. A girl's dead, and I'm the chief of police. And don't forget that I know what you are." He rapped on the stack of journals.

"Even if there's any truth in there, it happened half a lifetime ago. I'm not that kid anymore."

"You better not be. Because this kid"—he patted the journals again—"is poison."

"Come on, Chief." For a weak moment, Nate wanted the man to like him again, to be the uncle and father figure he'd once been. "You can't think I'd actually hurt anyone."

Now it was the chief's turn to laugh. "I guess a good liar can even fool himself. You wouldn't hurt anyone? Damn, Nate. We both know that's not true. What about Tommy and Johnny and Bea and how you abandoned them once you got what you needed out of them?"

"I didn't abandon them. Our lives went different ways. It happens to everyone. I tried to stay in touch."

"What, an email twice a year? And Bea must be so grateful to see her only kin in this world every other Christmas."

Nate saw Grams more often than that, but he knew this was a game he'd lose just by playing. Time for a new strategy. He could push the chief on the increasingly inexplicable runaway note, or edge the conversation toward the Lake's current crime wave, but leaving the man to stew felt like the best option.

Time and pressure. That's how gems are made.

"Well, I'll leave you to it, Chief," Nate said. "Sounds like you've got a murderer to catch."

"The people in town think I'm looking at him right now."

"Oh, I know." Nate started to put on his coat. "The Lake loves its stories. The Night Ship Girls. Just June and Morton Strong and the Century Room. *The Boy Who Fell.*" He spat the words like they were acid on his tongue. "Everything here becomes a *story*. It makes it *seem* like life makes sense, but it doesn't. It never has."

"You're a cynic."

"Cancer doesn't care if you're a saint or a serial killer. The kids I treat don't get it because they smoked for fifty years or never wore sunscreen. They're innocents. There's no purpose or meaning or justice. There isn't an iota of sense to their suffering. There's no more reason to it than a car going off a cliff because a kid wanted a peach pie instead of cherry. Because he played baseball instead of running track. Because he hit a triple instead of striking out."

They stared at each other, and for a moment it seemed like the chief had run out of things to say.

Nate started for the door.

"I didn't bring you here just to talk about Lucy," the chief said. He pulled a photo out of a manila folder and slid it along the table.

The photo was of a kid. It looked like a yearbook picture. What did the chief expect him to do with this? How could Nate know anything about her?

Yet he did. Seeing her with a shy smile in full color and direct light had thrown him off, but now he recognized the curve of her lips and the delicate arch of her nose.

"She was there," Nate said. "Last night. With some tall kid. The guy who hit me over the head. They were going to deface Grams's house or something. You have to bring her in. You've got to question her."

"That's not going to happen."

"*Why?* This is the same group of kids who greased Johnny's

stairs. The same ones who killed Tom's dog and blew up the Union with Grams *inside it*!"

"Because she's dead, Nate." The chief turned the photo so he could look at it himself. "Her body washed up on the shore this morning."

GRADUATION

II

BANNERS CELEBRATING THE end of the year were hung all around the high school. The jubilation in the halls was unrestrained. Other seniors were clustered in front of Nate's locker, and they grinned as they let him through. Michelle Duchannes kissed him on the cheek, and Parker Lang thumped him on the arm.

Nate himself felt nearly delirious with joy. Exams were over. High school was over. After so long, after so much, his real life was finally about to begin.

Johnny leaned against the locker to Nate's right. He was the only one in sight not visibly beaming.

"How did physics go?" Nate asked as he flicked through his locker's combination.

"Sixty-three."

"*Sixty-three!*" Nate slammed the locker shut as soon as he opened it. Johnny had needed at least an eighty-five to bring his average up enough to pass. "We studied so hard."

"Kritzler had it out for me from the beginning."

"Did you talk to him? Is there homework you can make up or an extra project or—"

"He's not budging. I tried everything."

"I'm so sorry, man. But one course in summer school won't be that bad. I bet it'll only be a few hours a week."

"My dad, Nate. *Christ*, my dad." Johnny hit his head against the bank of lockers.

"They'll still let you walk, right?"

"Yeah. They'll just hand me a blank envelope."

"Maybe he doesn't need to know."

"But Tufts will know! And he had to pull every string there was to get me in there."

"There's always another string." Nate opened his locker again. All that remained were a few books from AP biology that he hadn't gotten around to returning and the photos that decorated the inside of his door. Lucy had made a big blue and white Columbia pennant and hung it just above his locker. "If he got you in, he can keep you in. It's going to suck telling him, but I can be there with you if you want."

"What happened?" Tom approached them, holding hands with Emma Aoki. Owen loomed behind them like a walking refrigerator.

Nate let Johnny update the others while he carefully peeled the photos from his door. Nate and Lucy as homecoming king and queen. He, Tom, Johnny, and Owen fishing off the Vanhoutens' deck. They were good memories, but the best ones he had from the last year weren't the kind you recorded for posterity.

Emma tutted and patted Johnny on the shoulder. "Me and Laurie are going to get bagels then help Jim set up for tonight," she told Tom. "Want to come?"

There was an officially sanctioned graduation celebration after tonight's ceremony, but the real party would follow that at Jim Tatum's house at the edge of the headlands.

"I'm eating with the guys, but maybe I'll swing by Jim's after," Tom said. "Call if he needs me to pick up anything."

Emma clutched Tom by the back of his head and kissed him before sauntering down the hall.

"Thunder Run tonight?" The hallway was loud, but Owen whispered anyway.

The question and the pain in Nate's arm made him smile. The meteorologists forecasted the rain to begin midafternoon, but Nate guessed they'd see the first drops closer to dusk. He was rarely wrong.

"Yep. Going to finish out on a high note," Nate said.

"We gotta get Kritzler, Nate," Johnny said. "He ruined me."

"We already planted those termite nests in his walls."

"I don't think he even noticed. Wouldn't they have tented his house or something?"

"The longer it takes him to find them, the more damage they'll have done. A debt past due accrues interest."

"But Nate—"

Silken hands wrapped themselves around Nate's eyes. He slid around in their grasp to hoist their owner up and onto his hips. Lucy clutched the sides of his face as her thighs gripped his waist. He kissed her as he spun them around in the center of the hall.

"Love," he said as he slowed their pirouette.

She kissed him once on the forehead before letting him lower her to her feet. He paid no attention to the group of underclassmen girls staring at them with their hands clasped over their chests. He pretended not to hear Johnny sigh next to him.

"So who are we getting tonight?" Owen asked.

"Lindsay." Nate grinned at Lucy.

In the wake of Adam Decker's forwarding of her private photos, none of their peers had been more vicious to Lucy than Lindsay Stone. The two had been best friends before the trial and hostile afterward, but the release of those photos had marked an escalation to open warfare across the battlefield of high school politics. Their relationship had lately cooled to a détente, but Nate selecting Lindsay as the Thunder Run's final target was symbolic. This was his graduation present to Lucy.

"*Again?*" Johnny rolled his eyes. "But we have to get Kritzler next, come on."

"Nate's done with the Thunder Runs after this." Lucy addressed the others, but her gaze was fixed on Nate. "The Night Ship, too."

He nodded to confirm.

Johnny slumped against the walls of lockers.

"One more wouldn't be that big of a deal though, would it?" Tom said. "We could play it really safe. Nothing risky. Like maybe we could—"

"Are you *deaf,* Tom?" Lucy asked. "He said he was done."

Tom took a step backward, stung by her venom.

"I'm getting my nails done," she told Nate in a gentler tone. "Then I'm going to see if Jim needs any help."

"A manicure?" Nate asked. Lucy had never shown any interest in such things. Nate had only seen her in a dress maybe a half dozen times in the last two years.

"And a pedicure."

"Whoa, really?" He was genuinely surprised. Money was always tight for the Bennetts, and it wasn't like Lucy to splurge.

Nate's compensation had been feeble compared to what he'd lost, but his misfortunes had netted him more assets than he could imagine spending. Whatever black arts his financial adviser employed ensured that these resources grew quarter by quarter. He would have bought anything for Lucy. He would have paid the rent on the Bennetts' house if it gave her one less thing to worry about. But she rarely accepted his gifts. She was proud and tough, and Nate admired her for it.

"Our new lives start today, McHale." She dug a finger into his sternum. "Remember that."

He thought about it constantly. In three months, they'd be living in Manhattan. On weekends they'd go to plays and visit museums and walk in those famous parks. They'd meet Tom for dinner a couple times a week. Next year, they'd move in together. They'd get a one-bedroom somewhere between Columbia and NYU. There'd be artwork on the walls and someday a dog. Eventually there'd be a ring and a pair of children. One day they'd have everything they ever dreamed of, and their journey to that perfect place started today.

He kissed her hungrily, feeling the bones of her face against his palms. He ran hot and she ran cold, and he kissed her until they reached perfect equilibrium. Before he pulled away, he landed a peck on the crown of her fiery hair.

She smiled at him before she walked away, and it lit a blaze deep inside him.

When he turned back to his friends, they avoided his gaze.

"So, we're grabbing pizza, now, yes?"

"I guess." Tom still seemed hurt by what Lucy had said.

"I bet I could eat a whole pie right now," Nate continued. He grabbed his books, carefully folded the Columbia pennant into his bag, and closed his locker for the last time. He hammered a fist against it by way of farewell.

His friends accompanied him to the room where he was supposed to return the books. They walked down the center of the hall, and people parted to let them pass. He nodded to everyone and returned the pats and playful punches he received.

He dropped off his books, accepted a manly half hug from Mr. Davidson, and slid through the school's front entrance into the bright sunshine.

Summer was brief and erratic in this corner of the North Country, but today was a furnace, the humidity making the air thick enough to sip.

"I'm not built for this weather," Nate said as he pulled off his T-shirt. The June sun on his skin made him feel immortal.

"It's going to be a lot hotter in the city," Johnny said. Nate knew Johnny didn't like the idea of them going different places next year. But Johnny was tight with Owen, and Owen was going to a branch of UMass not far from Tufts. It'd take some getting used to, but they'd be okay.

"Can't you keep your clothes on for five minutes?" Tom muttered.

"You know, we could still do another Thunder Run," Johnny said. "Lucy wouldn't have to know."

Nate stopped dead in his tracks. He was in the most buoyant of moods, but he hated to repeat himself. "Was I not clear?" He turned the full glare of his blue gaze on Johnny.

Johnny looked away and somehow became even further slumped.

"You guys can still get Kritzler, though," Nate said as they started walking again. He'd given Johnny the stick, and now it was time for the carrot. "You don't need me."

Johnny made a sound somewhere between a moan and a wheeze.

Nate hooked his arm around Johnny's neck as they walked. The trees lining the street brimmed with blossoms. The aromas of flowers and mowed grass layered the clean mountain air. He was sorry his friend couldn't share in the euphoria of the day. The future and all of its spoils lay spread before them.

"It won't be the same."

And Nate's heart thrilled at the thought, because Johnny was right. After today, nothing would ever be the same again.

Ten

Her name was Maura Jeffers, and she was dead.

She'd been fifteen and a sophomore at the high school.

Jeffers was the last name of a thrift shop owner Nate and his friends had done a Thunder Run against in the old days. The man had gotten handsy with Lucy, so they'd painted the windows and walls of his shop with sugar water. In no time, the place had been infested with insects. In case people weren't already suspicious of secondhand clothes, a front window clogged with carpenter ants gave them pause. The town along the shore was a small one, so odds were good that the groper and this girl were somehow related.

The chief handed Nate a flimsy cup filled with coffee.

"I assume you take it black," the chief said.

He didn't, but Nate smiled anyway. He even managed to conceal the fact that he was being scalded by the sleeveless cup.

The chief had made Nate give an official statement about his scuffle with the kids on Grams's lawn. Nate had been honest, except for the preamble of standing sentinel over the house for hours in the rain. The story he offered stated that the vandals had woken him as they prepared their mischief and so he managed to stop them before they did any damage.

Chief Buck had significantly dialed down the heat of their interview. Whether this was because the man had softened or because he'd simply decided to change tack, Nate wasn't sure. He intended to be cautious until he figured this out. The chief had moved their conversation from the interrogation room to the relative comfort of his personal office.

"Didn't this place used to be bigger?" Nate asked.

"Added a closet during the remodel." He pointed to a door on the side of room.

Nate sipped the coffee. A bouquet somewhere between pond water and petroleum.

"How is it? Probably not up to city standards."

"It's perfect. How did the Jeffers girl die?" Nate knew she'd been found along the shore, but that didn't mean she'd drowned.

"Medical examiner hasn't looked at the body yet."

"You must have an idea."

Chief Buck ran a finger around the rim of his coffee mug. The phone at the front desk trilled through the silence. Though it was early, the line had been ringing virtually nonstop. Medea had Greystone Lake's finest stretched thin.

"She was strangled."

Nate winced. The idea of strangulation bothered him nearly as much as the idea of drowning. "I guess I was hoping it could be explained away as an accident."

"The ME will make the official call, but we're treating it as homicide."

"Strangulation's an intimate way to kill someone," Nate said. It was something he'd read, but it seemed true.

He imagined wrapping his hands around a slender young neck and tightening his grip until something essential snapped under the pressure. Crushing the trachea would feel like squeezing a stalk of celery to pulp. He'd have to be face-to-face with the girl, staring into her wide eyes as delicate capillaries exploded like fireworks under the strain. He'd have to be utterly unmoved by the desperation on her dying face. *No,* Nate thought.

I'd have to like it.

The chief raised his eyebrows.

"Maybe you should let me handle the profiling." He picked Nate's statement off his desk. "What about the boy she was with? You say you didn't get a good look at him."

"He was tall. Taller than me, but all arms and legs. At least it seemed that way. They were both wearing baggy raincoats." In his official statement, Nate had downplayed the physical elements of his confrontation with the teens.

"Boys grow like weeds. Remember when you shot up that one winter?"

Nate grinned. This could have been the casual remembrance it appeared to be, but was more likely just another halftime substitution for Bad Cop. Either way, a smile was the smart response.

The chief looked at Nate and chewed the side of his cheek. "You think you could identify him?"

"From a picture? I don't know. Maybe in person."

The chief pulled a photo from the folder and slid it across his desk.

Like the portrait of the Jeffers girl, it looked like a yearbook photo. The boy in the image had an aquiline nose that seemed familiar. His smile had a mischievous twist to it, and his cheeks were ripe with baby fat. It was hard to imagine a teen as skinny as the one Nate had tussled with owning such a cherubic face. Nate tried to imagine the boy in profile.

"I don't know," Nate said.

"Mother says he's grown about a foot since it was taken. She's bringing over something more recent. Maybe that'll ring a bell."

"Are you saying he's also—?"

"Only *missing* for now." The chief said this casually, as if adolescents were objects routinely mislaid.

Nate's memories from last night were disjointed. Not surprising, considering the blow to the head. Still, he sifted through every image and sensation he'd retained. His hands had been wet as he pulled back the raincoat's hood to reveal the girl's face. Then he'd turned away from the girl and seen the stepladder swinging toward him and—

"Let's get back to Lucy." The chief held up one of the Moleskine notebooks. The abrupt transition confirmed that this wasn't just a cozy chat. "Considering recent developments, would you like to make any addendums to the statements you made fourteen years ago? Fresh impressions are the most reliable, but time can shake some details loose."

The chief was offering him a purportedly no-strings-attached chance to revise the record.

Nate sighed. "It's been such a long time. And how many times did you talk to all of us back then?" A subtle reminder that Nate was hardly the only suspect. "I keep thinking, if only that note hadn't shown up. If we hadn't thought she'd run away, maybe we'd have found her body sooner and had more evidence to work with." In point of fact, the chief still hadn't given him the slightest clue about what Lucy's remains had revealed, but Nate hoped he was getting closer.

"In Lucy's case, homicide was always on the table, even with that note left behind," the chief said. "And don't forget that she still might have run away, just like the note said. Maybe she just didn't make it very far." He took a sip from his mug and looked at Nate over its rim.

"But now we know someone hid her body in the foothills," Chief Buck continued. "Now we know it was murder, so we're taking a fresh look at statements, witnesses, everything."

"You must have learned something from her body," Nate said, trying again. This is what he most burned to know.

"Fourteen years is a long time. Fourteen years, Nate." This was nearly verbatim what Tom had told him the day before. It was suspiciously similar. And something about this warned Nate away, nudging him to change the topic.

"So do you want to talk more about Lucy, or about this Jeffers girl? And this other kid." He pointed at the boy's photo. "What's his name?"

"Peter Corso. Pete." The chief squinted at Nate. "But they're connected, aren't they? Lucy, Maura, and Pete. The names in these old notebooks are the same that are showing up at the top of the damage reports from two weeks ago and last night. You might be surprised how many overlaps there are. You saw Maura and Pete about to deface Bea's house, so they're likely with the group causing the trouble now. Whatever you boys did years ago is happening again, only this time it's happening to you."

In a way, Nate was proud of him.

"Have you talked to Tom about this theory?" The chief was clearly convinced of the journals' accuracy, but there was zero chance of Nate conceding this.

"Tom." The chief's eyes clouded and he leaned back in his chair. He was quiet for several long moments. "Some things become hard to talk about. You'll understand when your little one gets older."

Unlike everything else, these lines didn't seem like a tactic or stratagem on the part of the chief.

"He doesn't know," Nate realized. "You didn't tell him you've had her notebooks this whole time." Tom would have warned Nate if he'd known.

"He wouldn't understand. And I didn't want to—" he broke off.

Nate followed Chief Buck's gaze to the framed photograph hanging on the wall, a picture of Tom at maybe age seven or eight, towheaded, gap-toothed, and holding a fishing rod.

"He wouldn't understand that you deliberately withheld evidence? Or that you did it because you thought you were protecting him?"

The chief looked weary, and Nate didn't think it was an act, either. They'd unwittingly put him in an impossible spot, and the man had been treading water there for a very long time.

"He's my *son,* Nate." The chief held his gaze, then touched the topmost of the Moleskine notebooks. "I love Tom more than anything. More than my life. And the truth is, I wish I'd never found these things. They have him as a cruel and needy and weak boy. And reading them it's hard—" He paused, trying to find the right words. "It's hard for me not to question everything I thought I knew about him. Sometime I look at him and have to wonder who he is. Who he *really* is."

"Lucy didn't like Tom," Nate said. "They never got along, so I'm not surprised she made him look bad. You can't trust a single thing that's written in there. It's fiction. Besides, you know who Tom really is. How can a teenage girl's scribblings change that?"

The chief looked at him with a new expression, one that lifted Nate's own spirits. Because the look on the man's face was hope. Distrust was hard and suspicion was tough, but hope was something Nate could work with.

Chief Buck's private line rang three times before he answered it.

"Be right there," he told the person on the other end. He returned the receiver to its cradle. "They need me out front." He got up and walked toward the door. "Stay here."

Nate pulled out his phone. The display failed to light up, though it didn't seem to be completely inert. Somehow its digital assistant still worked and was able to tell Nate it was almost eight A.M. Its stilted voice sounded as if it was being filtered through Auto-Tune then broadcast from a distant star system.

Lucy's funeral would be starting in a few hours, but with the chief out of sight, Grams returned to the forefront of Nate's mind.

Through the office's glass partition, Nate saw the hall was empty. He walked around to the computer, and was unsurprised to find it password protected. From the chief's landline, he dialed nine for an outside line then 4-1-1 for directory assistance.

He was quickly connected to the hospital in Gracefield, where they said that Grams's condition was unchanged. He asked again about transport to a burn center, and he was again told that the weather was too poor to move anyone anywhere.

Nate ended the call, feeling worse than before he'd made it. He thought he was finally close to learning something useful from the chief, but Grams needed him, too. Without a car, he didn't even know how he'd return to her side. He realized he was lucky the chief hadn't called his earlier bluff about walking out of the interrogation room. One of the perils of being a good liar was the threat of out-smarting yourself along with everyone else.

The rancid coffee had left him restless.

With an eye on the hallway, he started paging through the papers on the desk and checking its drawers. Most of them were locked, and the ones that weren't held nothing of interest. No matter what the chief claimed, the discovery of Lucy's body must have revealed *something*. But of course, he wouldn't have left Nate alone in his office if there'd been anything here worth finding.

Nate had been avoiding them, but when he ran out of places to snoop, he turned to the pile of battered Moleskine notebooks. He picked up the one on top, handling it as he might an egg from which any manner of creature might hatch.

He opened it to the bookmarked page and immediately con-firmed that it was filled with Lucy's handwriting. His gaze was natu-rally drawn to his own name penned in her slanting script.

> *. . . regret telling Nate about Sarah Hernandez laughing at me because of that newspaper column. He thinks he's being protec-tive, but he takes things too far. Always too far. I wish he could see his own face when it goes blank with anger.*

Nate shut the journal and dropped it back with the others. He hadn't talked to Lucy in fourteen years, and now this had become the last thing she'd said about him.

He scanned the room, desperate to distract himself from her words.

That's when he noticed something that shouldn't have been there. A security keypad was attached to the handle of the closet that the chief said had been added as part of the station's renovations. An odd precaution for a coat closet, even in a police station.

The chief had already been gone for a few minutes, but the hall beyond the office was still empty. Nate quickly went through the desk drawers again, searching for any scrap of paper that might contain the pass code. Employing a sophisticated security system while storing the key to its deactivation nearby was a classic mistake. He checked the bottoms, tops, and sides of the drawers. When he didn't find anything, he checked under the desk's blotter, the monthly calendar, and the computer's tower and keyboard.

Nate turned back to the keypad. There was no way to tell how many digits it wanted from him. On the upside, it looked willing to give him an unlimited number of attempts.

Using significant dates as a password was another error people regularly made. He pulled the monthly calendar from under the desk blotter and scoured its pages. He plugged in the four digits that represented Mrs. Buck's birthday, their anniversary, and Tom's birthday with no luck.

He'd really been counting on Tom's birthday. His friend's checkered smile grinned at him from the photo framed on the wall.

I love Tom more than anything, the chief had said.

Nate again plugged Tom's birthday and month into the keypad but this time followed them with all four digits of the year he'd been born—the same year of Nate's own birth.

The lock disengaged with a click, and Nate pulled the door open to reveal a space larger that he'd expected. A walk-in storage area about eight feet deep.

In a crime thriller or police procedural, he would have flicked the light switch to be confronted with a mosaic of horrors. Crime scene photos. Stern mugs shots of suspects. Collages of video footage stills and blood splatter diagrams and grisly autopsy photos.

Instead, all that greeted Nate were clothes. Winter gear, hunting jackets, and extra uniforms hung from flanking rods. Above these, a miscellany of hats and sweaters were stacked to the ceiling. Male shoes of every variety lined the floor space two by two.

Nate swore to himself as he walked in, shucking apparel aside so his hands could verify what his eyes saw. He was sure he'd find something here, but the only thing he'd learned was that closet space was at a premium in the Buck household.

He was on his way out of the little room, thinking about what to do next, when he knocked a pair of galoshes out of their military alignment with the other sets of footwear. He stooped to nudge them back into order when he saw a squat filing cabinet pushed against the wall behind the coats.

Finally. Nate swept the clothes out of the way. This was what he'd returned home to discover. Finally, he would have every scrap of information the police had gathered. But when he got a closer look at what he'd found, his excitement sank.

His own name typed in all-caps Courier stared back at him from the cabinet's drawer.

GRADUATION

—

III

TOM MARVELED AT how easy it was to roll the car into position.

Even packed with three girls' luggage, it took only a stretch of the muscles to bring Lindsay Stone's brand-new silver Jetta to the edge of her patio.

Tom had worried that this Thunder Run relied too much on luck and timing, but, as usual, Nate had been right about everything.

The friends had spent the evening with the rest of their class on a boat the high school had chartered for its newest graduates. The school administration hoped a wholesome night cruise around the lake would curtail the anticipated debauchery, but bags of vodka-soaked gummi bears made their appearance even before the first brassy strains of "Pomp and Circumstance."

As Nate predicted, Lindsay Stone hadn't abstained from these revelries. She'd been tottering by the time they disembarked. Johnny had the nimble fingers of a Dickensian street urchin, which he used to snatch the car key from Lindsay's purse, but the truth was he probably could have asked her for the fob and she'd have handed it to him with no memory of the event. Still, Nate had praised Johnny up and down as they got into position for the Thunder Run.

After the boat docked, they donned their black raincoats and leapt from shadow to shadow until they got to the Stones' colossal Tudor on the Strand. In silence, they watched the looming house from a hedgerow across the street.

Lindsay's car had remained parked here because it was already crammed to capacity with luggage. She and the Sarahs planned to spend the rest of June and all of July on a road trip across the country. This sounded like fun to Tom, but Nate thought it terribly cliché.

"How much will they actually see, hopping from one five-star hotel to the next?"

"Obviously they're not doing it right, but that doesn't mean it isn't worth doing," Tom told him. "I'd like to see the desert, and the mountains. Real mountains."

"We should do it," Nate said, after thinking about it. "Maybe next summer. When we get to California we could drive up the Pacific coast. That'd be cool."

It *would* be cool.

Tom and the others hid in the shrubbery for half an hour before Sarah Carlisle pulled up to the Stones' mansion and punctuated the night with three blasts of her Audi's horn.

Lindsay soon appeared, still wobbly but more casually dressed. After a tense moment with a slippery flagstone, she was in the car and off to Jim Tatum's house, where the rest of their class was assembling.

They waited another five minutes. When the Stones' residence remained dark and the Strand stayed empty, they crept along the perimeter of exterior lights to the car park in the back.

Nate handed Johnny the key fob and smiled. Lindsay wasn't at the top of Johnny's list, but she was on it. The key was a gift from the Storm King.

Johnny unlocked the door, and Tom cringed at the accompanying tone and flare of lights. The engine was started, the gear set to neutral, but Nate insisted that they push and not drive the car down the grassy embankment. He didn't want to risk the uneven tire treads on wet ground that might come with putting the car into drive.

Had she *really* left the car on with the key in the ignition, Lindsay would wonder. Was the wind from the lake matched with the incline of the driveway *really* enough to propel the Jetta such a distance? These were the kinds of questions that plagued the target of a Thunder Run.

"The speed at the end here is important, gentlemen," Nate said. "Don't let up until she goes over. I don't want her to get stuck on the edge."

Tom was steaming inside his black raincoat. There'd been a brief downpour, but he hadn't felt a drop since they'd been on the water. Still, they couldn't risk being seen. Especially now that these adventures were finally coming to an end.

Nate counted off, and they leaned into the car.

Of course, Nate was right, and they needed to coax every spark of momentum from the Jetta. The car still caught on the lip of the pool for a moment before plunging nose-first into the deep end. Water erupted in fantastic quantities, surging across the patio and drenching them to their knees. The rear of the car swayed uncertainly before settling, its taillights glaring just above the churning water. It remained in that position, vertical in the pool like a piece of modern art. Tom glanced at Nate and was relieved to see his friend found this hilarious.

"Away! Away!" Nate whispered to them. A Thunder Run quickly exited was a Thunder Run well done.

They slid among the trees, through lawns, and over fences until they reached Johnny's BMW, parked several streets away. Even then, they didn't utter a word until their raincoats were out of sight in the trunk and they were all safely inside. The Storm King had rules no one dared break.

"That was good, guys," Nate said. It was important that he be the first to speak. "You killed it, Johnny, from beginning to end. A thing of beauty. Now we know what a summer's worth of sunk plans look like. Might have even cracked the bottom of the pool."

"We're lucky Dr. Stone didn't buy his daughter a Hummer for graduation," Johnny said as he fastened his seatbelt.

Tom was relieved to hear some lightness in Johnny's voice. He'd been in a wretched mood for most of the day, and Tom couldn't blame him. A high schooler finding out he wasn't graduating hours before the ceremony: Now that was cliché. Nate had been great to him, though. Promising that he'd help Johnny break the news to Mr. Vanhouten. Swearing to help Johnny get through the summer session.

Of course, what Johnny really wanted was to nail Mr. Kritzler with a Thunder Run instead of hassling Lindsay for the thousandth time. But Lucy always got her way.

Owen was the only one who hadn't had anything to drink, so he was in the driver's seat. They might have an unofficial get-out-of-jail-free card with the local constabulary, but the Storm King didn't believe in recklessness—at least not gratuitous recklessness. Johnny was in the passenger seat, which left Tom and Nate in the back.

"We're lucky the Stones don't have a fence around their pool," Owen said.

"Yeah," Tom said. "Lucky."

Tom always felt rotten after a Thunder Run. Hollowed out, somehow. The ramp-up was always exhilarating while Nate psyched them up for it. *They need to be punished*, he'd tell them. *We are agents of karmic retribution setting a lopsided universe into balance.* It somehow made sense when Nate said these things. But afterward, Tom felt unsettled. Guilty. He couldn't take the same pleasure in destruction that the others seemed to. Afterward, he couldn't help thinking that in trying to reconcile the equations of pain they somehow edged them further out of balance.

"I'm sure it was insured, Tommy," Nate said. He wrapped his arm around Tom's neck, too tight.

Tom winced and waited for the pressure to ease. Nate was always too rough when he'd been drinking.

"To Jim Tatum's house!" Nate told Owen.

Owen pulled away from the curb, and Tom watched familiar houses hum past his window. Greystone Lake reeled by like a long camera pan of a memorized film.

He tried to absorb the fact that this era of his life was over. That high school was finally over. Did he feel different, he wondered. Had the world changed?

Nate had eased his grip, and his arm was draped loosely around Tom's neck as he looked through his own window.

Sometimes Tom knew exactly what Nate was thinking, and other times he could not begin to fathom his friend's mind. He imagined Nate's interior landscape as an awful and wondrous alien place.

Long lines of cars presaged the festivities at Jim Tatum's house. Though nearly everything in the Lake was within walking distance, the Tatum residence was on a big chunk of land at the northern edge of the town, abutting the protected forests of the headlands. It was a familiar venue for their class's festivities, and the location was perfect for an all-out rager.

The Lake had secrets, but the party that traditionally followed the school's officially sanctioned graduation events wasn't one of them. Everyone knew about it, including Tom's dad and the rest of the police force. But they'd once been teenagers, too. They'd once been as fortunate, and vital, and proud, and knew in some part of themselves that the most foolish thing young gods could do was not milk this incandescent age for its every drop. If you weren't in these fleeting years, you longed for them.

The authorities usually looked the other way as long as things didn't get too out of hand. Which was good, Tom thought, as he surveyed the stretch of parked cars. Because you didn't need to be Sherlock Holmes to know what was afoot.

Owen and Johnny exited the car, and Tom opened his door. Nate was still motionless, staring out his window.

"We're here, Nate."

When Nate turned to him it took only a fraction of a second for a smile to regain his face, but Tom still caught a glimpse of blank distance in his eyes. Tom didn't know where Nate went in moments like this, but he knew he went there alone.

Where do you go? Tom always wanted to ask him. Where do you go while you're right next to me?

"Let's get something to drink, boys!" Nate said. As he burst from the car, no trace remained of the depths to which he'd drifted. Once on the wet street he was thunder and light and joy.

The rain from earlier should have cut the humidity, but the air felt tropical.

The Tatums had a stately colonial, but the party was set far back from the house, through the woods in a clearing just shy of the headlands. The forest was dark, but music led them to the others like a beacon. Soon the flicker of a bonfire and the twinkle of lanterns cut through the stockade of trees.

Nate led them onward, and their gathered classmates let out a roar when they saw him. Tom felt proud standing next to him. His friend. His best friend. His oldest friend in the world. The eyes of their whole class were upon them as they cut through the undergrowth and Nate put his arm around Tom's shoulders. He pulled Tom's face to his own until they were only inches apart and looked straight into his soul as if to say:

This. This is what life *is.*

Eleven

Nate hesitated at the sight of his own name, but his hands did not.

They yanked the filing cabinet drawer open hard enough to jostle its contents. Its hanging folders swayed and fell, exposing an 8 × 10 of his teenage self leering sideways at him.

His senior portrait. His hair had been longer then, casual without being careless. Little about that boy had been careless. He was not quite smirking, but there was an undeniably satisfied look on his face.

There were other small cabinets pushed up close against the closet's wall. Drawers for Tom, Johnny, and Owen were in the same cabinet as his own. Adam Decker and his circle of friends had their own. A third contained Lindsay, Emma, and even the Sarahs. Friends, enemies, predators, prey, and others not so easily categorized.

Nate had been so starved for information and so eager to discover something—anything—about Lucy's murder that this trove overwhelmed him. He opened one drawer after another, pulling at files and paging through reports, but the first one he studied in depth was Adam's.

Adam and his accomplices had been expelled from Greystone Lake High after the violent confrontation in the chemistry lab. When their house burned down, the Deckers moved full-time to their farm in Gracefield, where Adam had finished his senior year. Nate wasn't sure what had happened to his minions, but Adam had been recruited by a solid New England college for lacrosse. His player profile photo was in his file. A Piscean-eyed Nordic giant in shoulder pads.

The material within Adam's drawer seemed scant compared with what was in Nate's section. In addition to official reports and photos and photocopies of evidence, Adam's file contained what looked like pages ripped straight from the chief's own notes. Written in caps on a piece of yellow legal paper: INCONSISTENT ACCOUNT. ATM CAM FOOTAGE CONFLICTS WITH TIMELINE FROM SWORN STATEMENT. Copies of withdrawal slips and gas pump receipts were stapled to this note.

In the days immediately following Lucy's disappearance, Nate had coerced Tom into prying, wheedling, and outright spying on the police investigation, but this information about Adam Decker was news to him. Decker had lied to the police, which meant he was hiding something.

Nate felt the thing inside him writhe.

He was supposed to be a man who built things up, not one who ripped them apart. He was supposed to make people better, not bring them pain. Despite the good life he'd constructed around this idea of himself, that wildfire of a teenager still burned inside him.

There was far too much here for Nate to absorb, and the chief was overdue to return. He toyed with the idea of letting himself be discovered inside this forbidden space. This would at least compel the chief to address the roomful of research he'd collected. Because it meant something, this closet and its concealed knowledge.

It meant that the chief never believed Lucy had run away. It meant he knew that her body had been out there, waiting, all this time.

Forcing a confrontation was tempting. Surprising the man could shake loose all kinds of interesting things. But Nate decided that the smarter move was to get Tom on board and access this place after hours. That way, they'd be able to pore through everything at their leisure.

Nate made up his mind to leave the closet just as he'd found it, but he couldn't resist another look at his own drawer. He couldn't understand why there was so much more in here than in any of the others he'd opened.

He straightened the hanging folders he'd accidentally dislodged. Among them was one enigmatically titled EVENTS. A quick thumb through its manila subdivisions revealed the damage reports, repair estimates, and newspaper clippings of a number of their Thunder Runs. The chief must have gone through Lucy's journals and researched each and every episode of vandalism she'd mentioned.

Nate knew he was out of time, but another folder caught his eye: PSYCH. As with the aftermath of his family's car accident, the weeks that followed Lucy's disappearance were blurred and nettle-edged. But a bad fight that July had briefly landed Nate back with his old therapist. There'd been talk of charges being filed, but as is often the case in such small towns, the incident was smoothed over in the end.

Copies of his therapist's notes from those sessions were filed here. The documents weren't anything approaching an official psych evaluation. They were casual, handwritten pages complete with doodles. This was a clear violation of Nate's patient privileges, but the chief could have outright stolen them for all he knew. It didn't matter now. What mattered were the words scrawled across these pages. Phrases like "dissociative tendencies," "highly manipulative and narcissistic," and "weak conscience/no conscience?" Boxed and underlined at the bottom of the page was a question: "ASPD?"

Nate knew from his psychiatry rotation that this stood for anti-social personality disorder. It was the umbrella under which psycho-paths and sociopaths were placed.

The chief had known Nate as long as anyone in the world. Was this what the man believed he was?

Nate was unsteady when he turned to leave the grim little room. And this was regrettable, because it was then that he most needed his strength.

A last filing cabinet was separated from all the others. It was closest to the door, which is why he hadn't noticed it at first. This one was Lucy's. Its contents were the reason Nate had come to Greystone Lake, and he didn't even need to open its drawers to find what he wanted. The chief must have been studying her files recently because a manila folder lay open on top of the cabinet. Her senior portrait glowed from it. It was startling to see her so youthful after all these years, though it was the only age she'd ever be. Nate pushed aside a pair of pressed uniforms and took an involuntary step toward her files, pulled like a flower to the sun.

She'd been so beautiful. He picked up the 8 × 10.

Behind it, there was a more recent photograph.

Despite his medical training and common sense, Nate had some-how convinced himself that those hikers in the headlands had dis-covered her body. But Lucy's body was long gone. Her long limbs had wasted and contracted into a stick figure's parody. Her skull grinned a shocking smile. Her once-white shirt had yellowed and shrunk to only a gesture of modesty. Her lustrous hair had been re-duced to something spare and dry and bristling. It wasn't a body, because after fourteen years, how could it be? She was a skeleton.

Nate's stomach lurched, but this was why he was here. He had to find out what they knew. Skeletal remains gave the medical examiner less to work with, but they still might have been able to re-create something of Lucy's final moments. He didn't need to fumble through the drawers to find the postmortem report, because it was right there, too.

Fracture of hyoid bone.

His eyes speared sentences as he paged for the ME's concluding remarks.

Colles' fractures of left and right wrists.
White underwear, partially torn, blood-stained with positive prostate-specific antigen (PSA) reaction in fabric analysis.

He had to force himself to breathe.

Remarks: Decedent's remains were presented to this office as a homicide victim. Hyoid bone fracture suggests strangulation as cause of death. Hyoid fracture is indicative of manual strangulation, though decedent's skeletal remains provide insufficient evidence to determine this conclusively. PSA-positive result indicates presence of semen in decedent's clothing. Paired with dual Colles' fractures of the wrist, this suggests violent forced intercourse. It is unknown whether intercourse occurred antemortem or postmortem. DNA from samples are too degraded for further analysis. GLPD were notified of these findings immediately upon conclusion of examination.

Nate's vision went bleary and it took every mote of self-control he possessed to make it back into the office before vomiting into the chief's trash can.

"What in the—?"

Nate turned away from the bin to see the chief standing in the doorway. The man glanced at the open door to his closet, and his face swelled with fury. "How did—the hell do you think you're do-ing! Interfering with an active investigation? Going through confi-dential documents! I could charge you."

"He raped her." Nate coughed the last thing left in his stomach into the trash can. "He raped her then he killed her."

The chief stooped to bring his face closer to Nate's. His eyes held a mixture of horror and hunger.

"Who? Who killed her, son?"

"*Who?*" Nate's shock turned to fury at the speed of lightning. He sprang from the floor, wrapped his hands around the chief's neck, lifted him off the ground, and slammed the man against the office's glass partition. Cracks exploded across the pane as shadows streaked the edges of Nate's vision. "Why don't you know? After fourteen years *why don't you know?*"

The man became loose in his grip. He clutched the chief's jaw with one hand while the other grabbed the side of his head. One pulse of movement would shatter his C3 vertebrae to sever the brain's connection to the diaphragm. Nate ran his hand to the base of the chief's jaw and left a trail of blood along the bristles of his cheek.

The sight of blood returned Nate to himself. He released the man and stared at his own hands. He'd again clutched his fists tight enough to slice his palms. The blood was his own.

"You didn't do it." The chief coughed the words out as he slid down the wall to the floor. His shoulders went slack, and Nate couldn't tell if this was in defeat or in relief. "You didn't kill her."

Nate collapsed to the carpet across from the older man.

He raped her then he killed her.

Nate's shouting had gotten the attention of the uniformed offi-cer who'd been manning the front desk.

"You all right, boss?" the officer asked. He hadn't drawn his gun, but his hand was on his holster. His gaze did not waver from Nate.

I never should have come back here.

"It's fine," the chief muttered hoarsely. "It's over."

Nate leaned against the desk. Every part of him shook.

He raped her then he killed her.

Someone else approached the office door. A man not in a uni-form.

Chief Buck staggered to his feet, looked into the hall, and waved the new arrival away. There was something frantic in the chief's gestures that set off an alarm in Nate's head.

He got to his feet.

The man was still huge, and wider than Nate remembered him. He seemed to take up the entire hallway. He was powerfully built, but softer around the midsection than he'd once been. An athlete gone to seed. The pate of his head caught the layout of the overhead lights.

Nate's trembling stopped, and he felt his body center itself into perfect balance. Before his vision dissolved into black and red, he became aware of his own unstoppable charge at Adam Decker.

GRADUATION

——

IV

THIS. THIS IS WHAT LIFE IS.

That was the message Nate's electric eyes telegraphed to Tom's as they trampled through canary grass to the welcoming roar of their classmates.

Like many good things, Tom's euphoria was ephemeral. It lasted only as long as it took for him to notice Lucy, all but elbowing her way through the crowd. She rushed Nate as if he were the last life-boat on a foundering ship. Nate pulled her tight while he still had an arm around Tom. For a moment it was as if the three of them were wrapped in a single embrace. But not even Nate was strong enough to hold both Tom and Lucy at once.

"I'll get drinks." Tom snaked out from Nate's hold.

Lucy lobbed a smirk at him as Nate closed his hug of her with the arm Tom had vacated.

While he, Nate, Johnny, and Owen had gotten pizza after school, Lucy had metamorphosed into something else. In addition to the manicure and pedicure, she'd gotten her hair cut and styled. She'd worn a sundress and heels under her graduation gown. She hadn't bothered with such delicate things since the days before her friendship with Lindsay and the Sarahs collapsed. If anything, her recent style tended toward grunge. But this was the New Lucy. Since the ceremony, she'd changed into short-shorts, a white tank top, and a jade kimono wrap that matched her eyes. *Things are about to change* was the message Tom gleaned from the plunge of her neckline and the careful auburn waves that bounced at her shoulder. She even wore a trio of white calla lilies in her hair.

There wasn't a line at the keg. He pumped it a dozen times before it released its beer in a flaccid trickle.

Red and orange paper lanterns were strung from branch to branch along the edges of the glade. A shoulders-high bonfire crackled at one end of the clearing while speakers pumped from the other. Jim must have rented a generator for the lights and sound system, but if there was ever an event for which to go all out, this was it. Their class had shared good times together. If this was to be their last, it should also be their best.

Once he'd filled two cups, Tom returned to find his friend listening intently to Jim Tatum. Someone had given Nate a joint, which he casually rested in the hand wrapped around Lucy. He held it for her as she took a hit. Jim must have reached the punch line because Nate leaned back and laughed. A rich, deep, genuine sound that made Tom smile.

Tom handed Nate his cup and was about to clink his own drink against his when—

"You're a doll," Lucy said as she plucked the beer from his hand. She gave him a sidelong glance and blew a flute of smoke from the corner of her mouth.

Tom felt a flare of anger, though he knew this was wasted energy. Lucy could get away with just about anything. Maybe he'd get another beer or maybe he wouldn't. Maybe he'd hang out with Johnny and Owen, or maybe he'd just walk home. If he did, Nate would eventually notice he was gone. Eventually, he'd wonder where his best friend had disappeared to on the greatest night of their lives.

Tom had almost decided to stalk away when Nate took note of the beer in his own hand. It was strange how the pieces of him so often seemed to be in different places. Nate glanced at the beer, looked at Tom, and raised the glass to him. As he began to tell Jim a story of his own, Nate removed his arm from Lucy and held the joint out to Tom.

Tom shook his head, but Nate ignored this. His conversation with Jim didn't falter, but Tom sensed the full focus of Nate's attention on the fingers of the hand that grasped the joint held out in offering. Long moments crawled past when Tom did not move and Nate did not budge. If Nate had the patience to wait, Tom would accede. They both knew this.

When he couldn't take it any longer, Tom snatched the spliff fast enough to send a flash of sparks to the grass.

He loved Nate like a brother, but sometimes he thought he might hate him, too.

He took a hit. A reckless hit. Sucking in as much as he could as deep as it would go. And then he took another. And another. Tom wrecked the joint, burning it down to a crisp of paper without wasting a speck of it. Then he flicked it to the ground. He spun around to go back to the keg. Tom didn't see if Nate had noticed, but he caught Lucy's gaze as he left.

She grinned at him, and it was the kind of look that could mean anything.

Someone was handing out pills, and Tom gobbled three or maybe four on his way to the keg. He never did this. Was four too many? Must have been, because everyone around him gasped. They were either blue or yellow.

Maybe it was the pills or the pot, or the strange sensations of beginnings and endings that collided inside him, but for Tom the next hours passed like a series of slides oversaturated with sound and color.

He talked to Sarah Carlisle. He stood near Lindsay Stone. Tom was conscious of Johnny and Owen together, as they often were. One moment they were by the keg and the next they were on the periphery, watching the people at the center of the glade and talking about what, Tom could not imagine.

He, Nate, and Johnny had been as one for nearly their whole lives. But fault lines had formed between them over the past year and a half. Lucy and Owen's additions had changed things, and the ever-shifting hierarchies of high school had pulled others into various ranks within their circle. The three of them were still best friends, but some best friends were better than others. Would Johnny miss him next year? Would Nate really meet up with him a few times a week once they were in the city? Tom didn't know. The constants in his universe were about to become variables.

Like the cars of a racing train as it begins to slow, Tom's syncopated senses gradually blurred back into a stream of linear experience. He was standing on a stump at the edge of the clearing and his arms were out as if he'd been giving a speech, and indeed he seemed to have the full attention of the three underclassmen girls who stared up at him.

He jumped to the ground, just managing to stick the landing. His shoes were gone. Winston Chu, wearing an eye patch for some reason, thrust a bottle at Tom's chest. He dutifully took a chug before passing it back. It tasted like sunscreen.

The fire was bigger than it had been.

Put it out, Tom almost cried. *They'll see it. They'll know.* Then he remembered he wasn't in the Night Ship. This was the other world he lived in, the one with simpler secrets.

Nate sometimes called Tom the Creature of Catastrophic Futures. He was so worried about the ramifications of the present that it was as if he didn't live there at all. The Storm King had tried to teach Tom about the thrill of the moment. But for Tom this always came with a hangover of regret.

And no matter how he pretended otherwise, Tom knew that

Nate was in no way a native of the Now. Tom could tell this from the look in his friend's eyes when he drifted.

But Tom tried his best to appreciate the treasures of the present as he absorbed the sights, sounds, and smells of the clearing. He watched his class, his friends, writhe and jump and laugh. For a few moments he stood outside of the current they were all caught in. *It's never going to be like this again.* And Tom didn't know if this made him happy or sad, grateful or wistful. It was so many things.

There were three kegs, and bottles of whiskey, vodka, and some flavored liquors being passed around. Pot was smoked along the periphery, and every few minutes a group of three or four would return from the woods pawing at their noses. The substances and their combinations addled them in movement and voices and dance, as though each dwelled within their own pocket universes governed by different laws of physics.

Of course, Nate was at the center of the dancing tangle. In the crowd he seemed to give off a light that rivaled the bonfire. His shirt was off, and most of the other guys had followed his example.

Lucy was in Nate's arms, and they were the gravity well around which the others orbited. Whether they were a sun or a black hole depended on the day. Today, Tom thought they might be something else. A neutron star of irresistible luminescence.

Girls ran their painted fingers across Nate's back as he twirled Lucy past them. Michelle Duchannes and Sarah Hernandez cut in for a moment to sandwich Nate between them. Grinding up against him, Michelle was unable to stop herself from touching his chest.

"There you are!" Emma appeared out of the crowd and threw her arm around Tom's neck. She kissed him wetly on the lips. "Let's dance."

"I don't really—"

She grabbed his arm and yanked him closer to the center of the gathering.

"Aren't you hot in that?" she asked. She ran her hands over his flanks.

Tom realized he'd sweated through his shirt. Emma pulled at its hem, and it was so wet it took them both to peel it off.

"I'm hot, too. You know what? I don't even care." She tugged her top over her toned stomach.

"Are you sure you really—"

She whipped off her tank top to reveal a lacy black bra. She twirled the shirt above her head as if she were a cowboy. When a bunch of baseball players from the class below them whooped from the sidelines, she chucked it at them.

Tom wrapped his arms around the small of her back and drew Emma to him. Her mouth tasted of cinnamon. It was okay, Tom realized. Dancing with beautiful Emma Aoki, next to a bonfire, half-naked in the forest on a summer night with people he'd loved his whole life. It wasn't bad at all.

"Buddy!" Nate cried, and wrapped him in a sweaty hug. "Where've you been? Are you having an okay time?" He peered at Tom with grave intensity, as if this was the most important question in the world.

There was an uncertainty in Nate's balance and a wayward energy in his eyes. The pills and who knows what else had been making the rounds.

"Shots!" Nate shouted. "We haven't even had a drink together yet." He called for whiskey, and bottles traveled toward them across a sea of waving arms.

"I think you've drunk enough, McHale," Lucy said, materializing between them. Her smile was less smug than it had been.

"I have to have a drink with Tom."

"Let's take it easy, huh? I'll get you some water."

Nate laughed at this. The Storm King did as he wanted.

"What happened to your shirt?" he asked Emma.

"I threw it away!" she said. Everyone within earshot ranked this among the funniest things they'd ever heard. Everyone except Lucy.

Nate handed Tom and Emma bottles that had come their way.

"He's had too much," Lucy told Tom.

Too much.

Too much booze or drugs? Too much misery or joy? Nate himself was *too much*. That was why he was so fiercely loved.

"He needs to slow down," Lucy said.

Tom stared at her. Was she asking him to help manage Nate? Was his friend really in that rough a state? If so, Tom must have been even worse off, because he couldn't do anything but laugh at her. Snorted at her like she was a dim child who'd managed to say something so stupid that it exceeded all previous standards of idiocy.

Lucy's eyes hardened to emeralds.

While he, Nate, and Emma clinked the necks of one another's bottles, Tom watched Lucy storm into the crowd.

It was clear Nate had no idea that Lucy had stalked off. Nate said something to Emma, and they both laughed. The three of them took another pull from their bottles and jumped to the music and were so happy. They were all so happy.

This is what life *is.*

The tides of the night swept Nate and Emma away, and Tom found himself near Johnny and Owen.

"Holy shit, Tommy," Johnny said when he saw him. He'd stripped to the waist, but Owen was still fully clothed. Owen gleamed with sweat, but he never took off his shirt.

"You guys having a good time?" Tom asked. Or that's what he tried to say. His tongue and lips disputed the order of syllables.

"Park it, dude," Johnny said. "I'll get you some water."

Tom collapsed into the grass and stared through the frame of trees that held the ball of sky. Sparks from the bonfire blazed and faded against the swirl of the galaxy. It was strange, Tom thought, how we are so small and yet so bright.

"The Thunder Runs don't have to end," Owen said.

Tom realized that the big guy had lain next to him. When Tom looked at him, the lenses of Owen's glasses danced with reflected flames.

"Nate said that himself," Owen said. "Back at school it sounded like you were up for getting Kritzler for Johnny. Are you still?"

"No."

Tom was surprised at how easily this answer had come. The Creature of Catastrophic Futures would have equivocated. He would have worried and waffled and hedged. But Tom resolved to do what *he* wanted for once. Maybe he didn't have to always worry about what other people thought. Maybe he was allowed to be selfish.

Maybe this was the true gift of the Storm King.

It was a few moments before Owen tried again. "Johnny said he won't do it without you. He's really pissed about everything, you know. He's mad at Nate, too, even if he won't say it. He's sort of abandoning us here."

"You realize some people manage to be friends without committing felonies," Tom said. "Nate's not abandoning anyone, and neither am I."

"It's not fair," Owen said. "People still need to be punished, just like Nate always says. *That* hasn't changed."

"But we have. We've changed." Tom stretched his hands to the universe as clouds began to clot the ether.

"If you think about it," Owen said, "we usually went after people Lucy had it out for. Or Nate. What about the rest of us? Aren't we allowed to get revenge, too?"

Nate had put together numerous Thunder Runs for Tom and Johnny. They'd hit Owen's mom on at least three separate occasions. Besides, Tom didn't want revenge on anyone. At this moment, everything in his life resonated in perfect harmony.

Johnny returned with a bottle of water and handed it to Tom. Tom thanked him, but Johnny had already fixed a scowl on the elated multitudes.

Tom wished he could grant Johnny a measure of his own joy. He didn't want his friend feeling so low on such a great night.

"Sorry you're upset, Johnny," he said.

"I feel better already."

"I told Tom we were thinking about keeping up the Thunder Runs," Owen said.

"I'm positive Lucy convinced Nate to go after Lindsay instead of Kritzler," Johnny said. "She's been pulling the strings behind the Thunder Runs the whole time. She may as well be keeping him on a leash. You *know* she's the reason he's ducking out in the first place."

"Get back at Kritzler if you want, but it isn't going to make you feel better," Tom said. This was the new Tom: a creature who said what he thought and felt not a moment of trepidation about it. "Your dad's your problem." This had always been the case. No matter who Johnny was mad at, it was always his dad.

"And what am I supposed to do about *that,* Tommy?" Johnny's voice was loaded with anger, but this bounced off Tom like rain off a leaf. "Especially now that I'll probably be stuck here with him forever." He jumped to his feet and headed for the tree line.

Something had happened, Tom realized. Something had happened and he didn't care. Something had happened and he didn't care and this felt *good.*

"Just think about it," Owen told Tom before following Johnny to the edge of the glade.

Tom lay back down on the grass. The bass from the music beat through the ground like the pulse of the earth itself. He searched for the stars, but clouds had taken them away.

After a while—he did not know how long—he sat up again.

The party was still going, but the crowds had thinned. There were fewer people dancing than there'd been. The center group had scattered into smaller cliques along the edges of the bonfire. The music had quieted slightly, its rhythm slowed.

Tom stood, and this was harder than he'd expected. He made his way to everyone else carefully, as if his feet were not quite his own.

He found Nate drinking beer near one of the kegs with Parker Lang and some of the other guys. His face lit up when he saw Tom.

"I thought you'd left!" He tapped the keg with his foot. "It's pretty much kicked, but I might be able to get some out."

Tom waved his hand. He'd drunk enough.

"I think Johnny and Owen took off," Nate said. "Not sure any-one else here can drive, either. We might have to hoof it back."

"Okay." From the way the world tilted, Tom realized that going home was actually an excellent idea.

"Emma was looking for you. Haven't seen Lucy for a while, ei-ther," Nate continued. "She wouldn't have left without telling me."

It seemed like a very long time ago, but Tom remembered Lucy being angry about something. He remembered her stalking away, but Nate was right: She wouldn't have left without telling him.

The fire had burned down enough to let shadows take root within the glade. Some of the Chinese lanterns had fallen, and it was hard to pull figures from the darkness thick along the perimeter of trees.

That's when he saw it. And every day that followed, he tortured himself by wondering how different things might be if he hadn't.

Just as stray underclassmen snuck into the graduation celebra-tion, it wasn't unusual for older kids to make an appearance as well. A party was a party, no matter whose it was. It was among a pocket of these college kids that Tom saw Lucy.

He squinted to make sure. He shaded his eyes from the glare of the bonfire. Even in the feeble light, her jade kimono wrap was un-mistakable.

Tom tuned himself to the activities of the college group, and heard a peal of laughter tear across the glade. Lucy had been hoisted into the air by one of the men. He held her above his head like a fig-ure skater might lift his partner.

If only he'd managed to restrain his reaction in that moment, Tom thought. If he had, maybe Nate wouldn't have turned to follow his gaze to the fringe of trees.

"Nate!" Tom rapped on his friend's back, hoping to distract him. The Creature of Catastrophic Futures had returned, and ahead of him every string of fate screamed of doom, doom, doom.

The man with Lucy in his arms was Adam Decker. His blond hair was freshly cropped, and his shoulders were astoundingly wide.

Tom couldn't imagine what Lucy thought she was doing. Why was she with the one person who was guaranteed to make Nate flip his switch? Why did she have to ruin *everything*?

"Nate." He tugged at Nate's elbow. "Nate." He couldn't think of anything else to say, and he later hated himself for that, too.

Tom watched Nate's face go slack at the sight of Lucy with Adam.

"Adam's saying hello. And Lucy's just being polite." Tom darted between Nate and the scene unfolding at the edge of the clearing. Another squeal of delighted giggling came from Lucy. "I'll tell her it's time to go. That'll give her the out she needs."

Nate's eyes faded to some middle distance.

Come back. Please, come back.

Tom put his hands on Nate's chest and found it dripping wet. It had begun to rain again. It was a downpour.

Nate shoved Tom aside and began to make his way toward Adam Decker. Nate was strong and tall, but fresh off a season of Division I lacrosse, Adam Decker was like something made in a lab. He saw Nate coming and returned Lucy daintily to her feet. He prepared to meet Nate with a glowing smile and comic book biceps.

He came here for Nate, Tom realized. After a year and a half, the blond giant had returned to teach Nate the lesson he'd failed to impart in that chemistry lab. This was a patient predator, one from whom no forgetfulness could be hoped or leniency begged. Tom could imagine Adam choosing this place and time so that he was at his best while Nate, after hours of partying, was at his weakest. Adam wanted to give Nate more than a beating: He wanted to humiliate him in front of everyone. And Lucy had given him exactly the chance he'd been hoping for.

Lucy looked from Nate to Tom, and Tom couldn't read the expression on her face. Was she happy to have Nate fight for her? Was she pleased that he'd left Tom's side to rush to hers? Was she trying to prod Nate into being more attentive, or demonstrate to Tom who Nate most valued? There was a lesson here, but for whom was it intended?

The scent of blood was in the air. Something was ending. Tom felt it, and so did everyone else.

The masses coalesced on the pair as they braced for collision. Nate was the Boy Who Fell, and his fight against Adam was immortalized in the saga the town along the shore told of itself. Front-row seats to its sequel were first come, first served.

When Nate tripped on his way to meet him, the hulking athlete's grin widened. Tom understood that his friend was headed to slaughter. Nate had somehow gotten far ahead, but if Tom hurried, he could still save him. He could throw himself between the combatants. He'd get hurt, but he didn't care.

But people were in his way. They'd poured from the woods and were closing in from the edges of the clearing. Tom ran, but he wasn't fast enough.

"Move!" he yelled, but no one paid attention.

There was a flurry of movement ahead, and the crowd gasped as one.

Tom knocked people aside to see. He shoved them and elbowed them and pulled them apart. He imagined Nate already on the ground in the mud, staring hopelessly at the sledges of Adam's fists. Blood running with the rain down his face.

A scream built in Tom's throat.

He slipped in the mud, and tore through the forest of legs ahead of him.

The crowd recoiled at something Tom couldn't see. An animal desperation threatened to swallow him whole.

I can save you.

He clawed his way past the last people who separated him from his friend. Nate was somehow still standing, though wildly unsteady.

He shuffled from foot to foot as if the ground beneath him bucked like a wild creature.

Tom gained an unobstructed view just in time to see Adam throw a hook at Nate. Somehow Nate managed to avoid it by leaning backward. This looked like sheer luck to Tom. His friend was so muddled that he barely kept his balance. Adam tried an uppercut, but the same thing happened.

How had he missed?

Adam began to look uncertain, and Tom realized that the crowd hadn't been reacting to the hits Nate had taken, but the ones he'd somehow dodged.

Nate staggered in a semicircle, and Tom saw his face for the first time. He no longer looked drunk at all. His lips were curled between smirk and snarl, and his eyes glittered like the lake at dawn.

Adam whipped a haymaker at Nate.

Tom watched as Nate ducked the mast of Adam's arm and thrust his left palm upward into the lacrosse player's face. Not missing a step, he landed a brutal jab to his opponent's midsection. Adam was thrown off-balance, his hands reflexively going to his nose. Blood caught the firelight.

Tom didn't dare breathe. Adrenaline surged with the other chemicals he'd filled himself with, and rules of the world were suspended.

He watched the predator realize that he was the prey.

Nate darted to Adam's favored side so quickly that Tom could not follow the motion. With a sweep kick, Nate knocked the man's legs out from under him. Adam landed on his back in the mud, his face glossed in blood, grimacing in pain.

Impossible.

Tom had forgotten that while Nate was strong, his power didn't come from his muscles. He'd overlooked the fact that while Nate was fast, his speed didn't come from his reflexes.

The blond giant was mass and calculation and patience, but

Nate was wrath itself. Adam had come to fight Nate McHale, but this was the Storm King.

Nate had once told Tom that he felt safest when the world quaked in a tempest, because that was when the true face of things was revealed. That's where all illusions of munificence faded away, and the stone heart of the universe was laid bare.

This was the transformation Tom witnessed in Nate. As he whirled and pivoted and punched, his friend shed before him any guise of boyhood he'd clung to. Beneath these things Nate had pretended to be, he was not just a storm, he was an apocalypse.

A kick to the ribs. An elbow to the sternum. Nate broke Adam against the muddy ground and took him apart piece by piece.

The Creature of Catastrophic Futures forgot himself and released the scream he held inside him. It wasn't a cry of horror but a flare thrown into the burning night, because even he found beauty in this violence.

Finally, every last rule and regret and obligation was stripped away under the raw truth of blood and dirt and storm. Here was something magnificent to feed that atavistic place that hungered for righteous carnage.

When Tom and the others in the glade shouted into the storm they howled the screams of the free.

Twelve

When Nate returned to himself, he was sprawled across rough tiles of carpet and handcuffed to a desk.

Tom sat on the floor across from him, his back braced against a wall. He looked exhausted in his filthy uniform. His eyes were red, and his hair was slick across his forehead.

"He's back," Tom said.

"Are you all right?" The chief came around Nate's side of the desk. The man's voice rasped like it'd been scoured. "I called a doctor."

"I'm fine," Nate said.

"Tom said you'd be." Chief Buck leaned against the wall. His face was gray yet flushed. "You have a temper on you, son." He rubbed his neck. "Hell of a thing to see."

"I'm sorry about—back there," Nate said. He was almost certain he'd picked the chief up by his throat. "That wasn't me. I don't know where that came from. I guess I was upset. It's been rough, the last day. I lost myself for a minute. After seeing those things, I just . . . I didn't know where to put it all."

The contents of the chief's files were burned in his mind: those high school yearbook photos of the children they'd been, the files pregnant with the bare facts, stark and unyielding in blue ink and Times New Roman. The pure shock of Lucy's remains. He knew how decomposition worked. But to actually see it.

He raped her then he killed her.

Adam Decker had been at the station. Nate had rushed him before his world dissolved into blood and shadow. But his old enemy had to be long gone by now. Nate's stomach clenched at the idea of his escape, and it was a battle to keep his face free of anything but puzzlement and regret.

"What things?" Tom asked his dad.

"Maura Jeffers." The chief's eyes didn't waver from Nate's. "Another dead girl, and with Lucy's funeral in just a couple hours. Brought back all that old pain, didn't it?" he asked Nate.

The chief knew perfectly well that the news about Maura Jeffers wasn't what had set Nate off. The man must still want to keep the files in the closet a secret from Tom.

Interesting.

"She was so young," Nate said, deciding to play along. "It's so senseless."

The chief nodded to him. "Talked to Father Stephen. Church lost power, and the burial will be pushed to next week, but the Bennetts want to go ahead with the funeral. Might not be much of a crowd, but they want it done with. Can't blame them, can you?"

"No, sir."

"Hodges and Antonetti are on the Wharf, keeping the tourists away," the chief told Tom. "It's blocked off, but they caught a few taking pictures. One gust and they'd be in the drink and mush against the pilings. And I just got a call that a transformer went down at Goldfinch and Bobwhite."

"I'll cordon the block." Tom stood and stretched his back.

Nate wondered how long his friend had been watching him. He wondered how long he'd drifted.

"I got it. You get this one home and dressed. And take a shower," the chief told Nate. He patted Tom on the shoulder and handed him a small key on his way out of the room.

Tom watched his father leave, then turned back to Nate. Nate was sure the key the chief had passed to Tom was to his handcuffs, but his friend made no move to release him.

"How's Grams?" Nate asked.

"The same. The doc thinks that might be a good thing, considering."

"And Johnny?"

"He needs surgery."

"I should be there, too."

Tom shook his head. "The road to Gracefield's closed. Downed trees everywhere, and they won't start clearing them until this blows over. I barely made it back."

Nate digested this. He had competing obligations, but the requirements of the living had to outweigh the demands of the dead. He'd never forgive himself if Grams woke up and he wasn't by her side. "You told me you'd stay with her."

"I planned to. But some downstate weekender caused a major incident at the station." Tom sat back down across from Nate.

"Was it bad?"

"I've seen worse. Only caught the aftermath, though. You'd exhausted yourself by the time I got here. You've been out for almost an hour." The lights overhead flickered. "We're on generators now."

Nate thought of Grams and the impediments the universe had built between them. "What is it, ten, fifteen miles to Gracefield? You could drive me as far as you can then I can walk the rest of the way. Or maybe I could ride a bike. Would a bike fit in your cruiser?"

It could have been the loss of his dog, a night of scant sleep, or the general stress of the day, but Tom looked different. His impassive expression was a hand-me-down from his father.

"You can't walk to another town through a hurricane. There'll be downed wires everywhere. The road's closed for a reason."

"Maybe I could follow the road, but walk inside the tree line."

Tom stared at him. "Yesterday, you were a husband, father, and surgeon, and now you're concussed and cuffed to a desk on the floor of a police station. How about you take a second to figure out how that happened."

"What am I supposed to *do*, Tom?" He tugged at the cuffs and winced at the pain.

"We have to go to the funeral."

Nate thought he might be able to convince Tom to help him get to Gracefield later. First he had to get out of these cuffs.

"Fine, Tommy. You're right. I can't get to the hospital in this weather. That was crazy. I just—I just can't stop thinking of Grams. I can't get her face out of my head. You didn't see her when they brought her in. You can't imagine how—" Nate let his voice catch in his throat, hung his head, and swallowed hard.

When he turned back to Tom his friend's face had softened, but not as much as Nate would have liked. "So we have a funeral to go to. Are you going to unlock these? Or is this desk my plus one?"

Tom seemed to wrestle with something, but he didn't struggle with it for very long. The key remained in his palm.

"Why'd Dad let you go?"

"I'm handcuffed to a desk."

"Why aren't you in a cell? Assault of a peace officer. Three counts, by the way. Destruction of government property. Then there's Adam Decker."

Nate remembered Adam Decker's bloated face and how his own vision had melted into black streaked with red. He couldn't see his hands bound behind him, but the knuckles of his right fist felt peeled, the joints stiff to the wrist in an all-too-familiar way.

Ten years without a brawl or bar fight. A decade without committing even a misdemeanor. People counted on him now. And they needed *him*. They needed Nate, not the Storm King. The Storm King brought holy ruin upon his enemies, but he never could protect the ones he loved.

"Like your dad said, hearing about that girl dying and then seeing Adam was too much. He got it. Why don't you?"

"Two hours ago, my dad would've loved to charge you with something."

"Which would have been awfully useful to know, Tommy." If Tom knew how hard the chief was going to come down on Nate, then why hadn't he warned him?

"You thought he was bringing you here to chat about the Yankees' batting order?" Tom dismissed him with a wave of his hand.

The gesture was theatrical. Overly practiced. A chime of doubt sounded from the back of Nate's mind. The chief had been keeping secrets, but Tom had secrets of his own. Nate sensed this with acute certainty. He was suddenly very conscious of his own helplessness.

"So why would he let you go as soon as he gets you where he wants you?"

"I guess he got whatever he was looking for." Nate shrugged as best he could and summoned the most guileless smile he had access to. "It's not like he told *me* what he wanted." It seemed like a good time to change the subject. "What was Adam doing here, anyway?"

"Reporting damage. Someone broke into his house last night, stopped up all the sinks on the first floor, and ran the faucets full blast until the morning. His cellphone was a casualty, the storm took out the landline, and he's just a block away." Tom frowned at him. "You punched him pretty hard."

"He should be used to it."

"This is the part where a well-adjusted member of society expresses remorse."

"Is he still here?"

"No. He's married with two kids now, you know. He's also a lawyer. Claims he won't press charges as long as you stay away from him."

"That's good."

"Neither is my dad or the two officers."

Nate wasn't sure what to say to that.

"You could have killed him, you know. My dad."

"No way." Nate scoffed and shook his head, but he remembered the feel of the man's life in his hands. The sinew of the masseter. The ridges of each cervical vertebra. An iota more force and—

"When's the last time it happened?" Tom asked. "You losing control? I saw it in your eyes when you woke up. Just like back in high school. You drifted. Your eyes went blank and someone else was there."

"There's no one here but me, Tom." He realized that his jaw hurt, too.

"You shouldn't have let Dad see that side of you. You shouldn't have come back here at all, Nate. This place is dangerous for you."

There was a menagerie of suffering in the cages of Nate's soul, and this town held all the keys. But pain could be more than a curse. Sometimes it could be a blade.

"I can be dangerous, too, though, can't I, Tommy?" Nate felt the grin on his face twist into something less innocuous.

Tom weighed the key in his palm, then finally unlocked the cuffs. Nate rubbed the blood back into his wrists. He pushed himself off the carpet and onto his feet.

"I'm driving you home."

"You're the boss."

They were in a back room Nate hadn't seen on his way in. He followed Tom down a short hallway past the chief's office. The office's glass partition was shattered, and there were holes in the dry-wall.

"We'll invoice you for the damages," Tom said.

"That seems fair."

The lights flickered overhead as they walked past the front desk. The uniform stationed there flinched at the sight of Nate. The young man held a bag of ice against his forehead. He pulled it aside long enough for Nate to see a contusion ripening there.

Outside, the world looked like the surface of an inhospitable planet. The trees were tilted at impossible angles, and the streets coursed with water. The wind was a roar that stripped away all other sounds. It was the height of morning, but might as well have been dusk. Above, the lead sky surged and boiled like rapids over rocks.

Tom's cruiser was parked close to the station's entrance, but Medea made them feel every inch.

A person wasn't supposed to enjoy being wracked by the wind and rain, but Nate found that he did. The gale tearing at his hair, rain slapping at his face, and thunder shuddering his bones woke him up and made him feel alive.

Once in the car, he struggled to shut the door against the torrents of the storm. "Nuts to have a funeral in this," Nate said.

"Says the guy I just talked out of walking to Gracefield."

Tom took the roads slowly, never going over ten miles an hour. Branches crunched under the tires, and the cruiser rocked in the swells of the gale. Trees lay vanquished across lawns with their root systems exposed for all to see. The sections of town that had lost power had the feel of utter abandonment.

"When's it going to let up?" Nate asked.

"Supposed to be a lull around noon, then it'll pick up again. Should be mostly faded by tomorrow, but the flooding'll go on for days."

As brutal as the hurricane was, Bonaparte Street was several blocks inland, and Medea's winds were blunted by trees and other structures. Nate imagined that things must be far more ferocious along the waterfront.

He'd weathered dozens of storms in the glorious ruin of the Night Ship, but nothing close to a hurricane. He pictured the wreckage of the promenade churning in the tumult of the gale. He could almost hear the storm howl through the hundred broken panes of the glass ceiling and feel the pulse of the lake's assault on the pilings like compressions to an inert heart.

Some trees on Bonaparte Street had been lost, but apart from fallen branches scattered across the lawn, Grams's house looked un-damaged.

"I've got to get ready, too," Tom said. "I'll text you on my way back."

"My phone's dead. It got wet."

"Let's say an hour. No need to be early."

Nate remained in the car, watching the dark house. Rain drummed against the roof, and leaves clotted the windshield wipers. "Is there anything else I need to know, Tommy?"

"Like?"

"Like anything. Your dad, Lucy—anything."

"*Christ*. I'm sorry I didn't remind you you're a suspect in an un-solved murder. Guess I figured you'd remember something like that."

"I'm not accusing you. What I'm saying is that I haven't been here in fourteen years, and you have. You know more than I do. I'm trying to remember things I haven't thought of in ages."

Tom made a scraping sound that might have been a kind of laugh. "Not all of us could run away, Nate. Even if we wanted to."

"Come on. I'm not trying to start a fight. You're the last person I want to fight with." He put a hand on Tom's shoulder. He waited for his friend's frame to relax. He waited for the conciliatory smile that heralded an apology. *I'm sorry, Nate,* Tom would say. *Today's been insane. Fighting with you is the last thing I want, too.*

But this didn't happen. Nate saw that he needed to escalate.

So he withdrew his hand, turned back to the window, and sighed. This exhalation wasn't calibrated to convey the frustration of the put-upon, but to communicate the despair of the defeated.

"I don't think Grams is going to make it, Tommy." He stared through the streaming glass at the unlit house. He allowed a silence to burgeon between them. "I don't know what I'm going to do." He waited until the quiet rang in his ears. As loud as it was, he knew it would be ten times more deafening for Tom. Then he pulled the han-dle and left the car. He shut the door behind him and sank his feet into the saturated lawn.

He was nearly to the front door when the cruiser peeled away from the curb like the flag had dropped on a drag race. Nate watched Tom scorch down the street, running over broken branches and leaving a mist of water in his wake. Guilt, pity, obligation—whatever mash of buttons Nate had pressed, at least one of them had done the trick. In their youth, time and pressure had proven the trick to getting Tom to do anything. This was how Nate would discover whatever his friend was keeping from him.

Nate had his grandmother's house keys, but the front door was unlocked. Grams must have neglected to secure it in her rush to get him to the hospital, but the Lake had become a battleground and her home had been left open for hours. When he stepped into the house Nate was both wary and ready.

Once inside, he bolted the front door behind him, then walked the perimeter of each room on the main floor. The house still had electricity, so he flicked each light switch he came upon, establishing some semblance of the daylight that should have filled the place at this hour. He verified that every window was intact and locked, and that the back door was as secured as the front.

Nate got a flashlight from the kitchen, then traipsed down the narrow stairs to the basement. The air was damp and faintly redolent of laundry. It was an old house, and the cellar was pocked with strange nooks and odd crawl spaces. He illuminated every cranny and opened every closed cabinet.

He was looking for anything: unsecured entrances, cracked windows, loosened pipes, ticking bombs, lurking intruders. These kids weren't going to take anything else from Grams. They weren't going to catch Nate unprepared ever again.

When he was satisfied with the state of the basement, he repeated the process on the main floor, second floor, and attic. The handyman Tom had called must have taken advantage of the unlocked front door, because the broken window in Nate's room had been replaced. When he decided that everything else looked in order, Nate took a shower.

The hot water felt good on his muscles. He was sore all over, as if he'd pushed himself far too hard in the gym after many months of indolence. Rage was power, but it came with costs. Missing hours and scarred hands. Aching joints and ground teeth. Broken trust and splintered friendships.

But this morning's blackout was the first one he'd had in over a decade. Tom was right: This town was a dangerous place for Nate. Maybe he should have stayed away. But now blood had again been spilled. Another girl was dead, and Grams might soon join her. Nate hadn't hurt either of them, but that didn't mean he was innocent. He'd returned to the Lake with debts to pay, and these had mounted in the short time he'd been back. He could flee this place as he had so many years ago, but he owed it to Lucy and Grams to do more than that. The Jeffers girl, too, even if he didn't yet understand how she fit with everything else. He had the sense, too, that abandoning the Lake fourteen years ago hadn't solved any problems so much as it had delayed them. Today's troubles were connected to the tempest of his youth. Accounts had to be settled, equations balanced. He had to unwind the secrets of the Lake once and for all. Like a visit to hell itself, the way out was the way through.

Particulates of dried blood collected around his feet while he tenderly cleaned the area around his stitched scalp. An ache resonated from below the scarred portion of his arm. The pain sang of a storm.

Before shaving, he wiped the condensation from the mirror and was surprised by how normal he looked. He searched his eyes for traces of the other, but the only person he saw was himself.

He was dressed and ready with time to spare before Tom returned.

Cold drafts from the chaos outside brought a sense of movement to the rooms of the empty house. The scrape of branches against the siding and creaks from the old roof filled the place with sounds. The windows groaned in the onslaught.

Nate had quickly examined Grams's room, as he had the rest of the house, but he returned there now. The bedroom was Spartan. A simple wooden bed frame and a chest of drawers. A narrow desk with a chair.

There was a black chest under one of the windows. Gram called this her memory chest. She stored ancient photo albums and other artifacts of the past within it. When he was young, Grams would sit with Nate and Gabe atop its stained wood and show them photos of their father as a boy, their grandfather when he was in the army, even their great-grandparents on vacation. They'd stopped looking at these after the accident, or at least they'd stopped looking at them together.

Nate unfastened the clasps of the chest, and its hinges squealed when he forced it open. Mismatched albums were piled in stacks. Nate immediately recognized a copy of his and Meg's wedding album and Livvy's baby book. A sprig of golden hair bound in white satin was fastened inside the front cover of the lace-lined book, and Nate slid his finger over it, its strands too fine to discern.

He still hadn't told Meg about Grams. He'd justified this with the fact that his phone was dead. But even with a landline within reach, he hesitated. He didn't know how to explain to his wife that within a day of arriving home, he'd been knocked unconscious, Grams had been put into critical condition, and the Union had exploded.

Anyone would have had a mountain of questions, but Meg was an excellent lawyer and nothing but the truth would have satisfied her. Nate didn't even know where the truth began.

One perfect April morning he had hit a triple in the last inning.

Johnny pulled up his shirt, and beneath it was a mosaic of pain.

Adam lifted Lucy into the air like she weighed no more than a promise.

He didn't know where the beginning was because he couldn't guess what the ending would be. As long as he was in the thick of it, the shape of the story would remain a mystery.

Gabe's baby book was beneath Livvy's, and this was a volume he couldn't bear to open. He moved it aside to find a collection of faded black paper bound by red ribbon. These held mounted, washed-out photographs of his grandmother and grandfather in their younger days. Arm in arm on a beach. Standing proudly outside the Union. Posing in front of a Christmas tree.

Nate closed the album and was about to return it to its place when an envelope fell from its pages. It was a strange color—a shade of red so dark that it could be mistaken for black.

It was addressed in spikes and loops of calligraphy to Mr. & Mrs. Richard McHale of 217 Bonaparte Street. He pulled out the thick stock within the envelope.

Declare Independence at the Night Ship

July 4th, 1964

Above these words was an engraved image of a galleon with its sails ripe with wind and its course set for a full moon of impossible size.

It was an invitation to an event at the Night Ship. Not just any event: This was the Independence Day celebration where, legend had it, Just June had poisoned the revelers and triggered a panic. This had been the party that sank the Night Ship.

The blast of a car horn permeated the rumbling of the storm. Through the window, Nate saw the bleary contours of Tom's cruiser.

He turned back to the envelope in his hands. Independence Day 1964 was perhaps the most notorious night in the Lake's history. He had no idea that his grandparents had been invited. Grams had never once mentioned it.

Another blare of sound came from the car parked outside.

Nate stuck the envelope into his raincoat pocket, descended the stairs, grabbed his umbrella, and girded himself to face the hurricane.

"Hi," he said as he got into the cruiser. The clean, ferocious scent of Medea followed him into the car.

"Hi," Tom parroted back.

They took Bonaparte Street at a crawl. Nate couldn't see the Night Ship, but he could sense it. His internal compass had reverted to an old setting in which the ruined pier was magnetic north.

Nate tried and failed to imagine his grandparents at the Night Ship's final celebration. The ancient pier had played such an outsized role in his formative years that it was easy for him to forget that it had long been an intimate part of the Lake's life. It had a deep, everyday history beyond its oft-told legends. This was a good reminder to Nate that the Lake's stories weren't the same as the truth, that he didn't know everything, and that he never would.

Next to him, Tom was silent. The wipers pawed uselessly at the windshield. They were the only sound in the car until they reached an intersection that they hydroplaned across. Tom loosed a torrent of swearwords as they spun helplessly across the lanes and then over the curb.

"You okay?" Tom asked once they'd come to a stop.

"Yeah."

Tom threw them into reverse and took the street again, more slowly this time.

"You're not dressed," Nate said. Under his raingear, Tom wore a clean deputy's uniform but not a suit. For the first time, Nate noticed a sweet smell inside the close air of the car.

"The whole county is literally a disaster area. This saves me the trouble of changing."

"You've been drinking." Nate knew bourbon when he smelled it. "It's ten-fifty in the morning." The Tom Buck he knew did not get sloshed before noon.

"I've been up since three. So it's more like midafternoon."

"Aren't you on duty?"

"Please give me a lecture on duty, Nate."

"Do you want me to drive?"

"You live in Manhattan."

"Slow down."

"I'm going eight miles an—"

"I want to see the Union. Stop here."

Tom stopped in the middle of the street. This might have been a problem any other day, but this morning theirs was the only vehicle in sight.

Nate lowered his window to see beyond the streaming glass. He jutted his umbrella into the assault of wind for some cover from the rain.

The fire at the Union had been set only a few hours ago, but a century might have passed from the look of the place. The three-story building was gutted. An accountant and a dentist leased the upper floors, and the windows of their offices gaped like unblinking eyes; their fragments glittered along the flooded street. Streaks of charred brickwork stretched past the two upper floors to the roof. Through the maw of vacant windows, fallen beams impaled the old pub like crossed blades.

Nate's great-great-grandfather had built this place over a century ago. His fingers had mixed the mortar between its bricks, and his hands had helped plane the supports that held up its ceilings. Nate's great-grandfather had polished the black bar every night for forty years. When his grandfather's polio-warped legs gave way, he'd roll from one end of the place to the other on a wheeled stool, leaving grooves in the floor that seared through decades of varnish. Nate's own father had swept clean those floors each night of every summer of his youth.

Meg and Livvy had never seen this place, and now they never would. It was gone, and the people who'd spent their lives here were now more absent than they'd been before.

In the bleak weather, the only color came from the bright lines of caution tape strung around the building's perimeter. Even the rain couldn't keep the scorched smell from the air.

Nate stared through the empty front windows and imagined his grandmother lifted by the force of the blast from the kitchen and tossed across the room. If he went inside, he wondered if he'd be able to trace the arc of her transit through fire and smoke.

"You can't go in," Tom said. "It's a crime scene."

Nate glanced at Tom then back to the remains of the pub. He let his gaze loiter more for Tom than for himself. Stress poured from his friend as palpably as the whiskey fumes. Micro-expressions quaked across Tom's face like wires trembling under tension. Nate was sure it wouldn't take much more for them to snap.

He closed his umbrella and rolled up the window.

Tom put the cruiser back into drive without another word.

The church was only a few blocks away. The stone edifice of its bell tower blended with the ashen palette of the sky. A spindly maple swayed on its lawn. There were perhaps two dozen cars in the lot, but the building looked as lifeless as everything else in the besieged town.

They parked and sat, watching the rain shatter against the windshield.

"Are you mad at me, Tom?"

"What would be the point?"

"Your dad said I abandoned you," Nate said. "You and Johnny. When it all happened, I had to get out of here. I'm sorry I didn't see you as much as I promised I would once we were down in the city. Every reminder of this place was—" He shook his head, making sure that his brow was furrowed with sincerity and that his eyes welled with feeling. "If you felt abandoned, I'm sorry. There's no way to make up for it now, but I'm so sorry. You're a good friend. The best friend I've ever had. Hurting you is the last thing I'd want to do."

He watched his friend's hands bloom white on the steering wheel. It took a few moments before Tom met his gaze.

"Why don't you just shut the hell up for once in your life?" Tom said as he opened his door. A mist of spittle clouded the air between them.

Nate had expected anger, but the vehemence in Tom's voice was more than he could have hoped for.

Tom left in a fury of movement, slamming the door behind him so hard that it rocked Nate in his seat. He watched through the windshield as Tom raised his hood against the storm and stalked to the church's side door.

The maple rooted on the church's lawn continued to rock. Its sway counted the seconds, and its trunk creaked in the onslaught. When the storm returned to full force, Nate suspected that what was now bent would then break.

June 19

*Sometimes I don't know if I can do it anymore and be everything
he wants me to be all the time.*

*Some days the two of us are the best thing I can imagine, but
other times it's like being buried alive. They're piling dirt on me
shovel by shovel, covering who I'm supposed to be. We keep talking about how things'll be great when we're in the city, like it's a
perfect future just waiting for us. But what if things aren't perfect? Because we're going to be the same people there. Even Tom
the Spineless Wonder will be there, sulking and filling the place
like a thundercloud. Nate's always so sure of everything, and I
don't know if that's a good thing or a bad thing.*

*Sometimes I think I love Nate. Some days I'm almost sure of
it. Other times I wonder if I only love the way people treat me
because I'm with him. The Lake's own son. The Boy Who Fell.
He's special, and being with him makes me special, too. So am I
using him, or is he using me? Is that what love is—two people
using each other?*

*There's no escape, though, and I don't think that's how love's
supposed to work. Always watched. Always judged. It's not just
Nate. Whenever I'm away from him, the Lake's eyes are on me. Is
she worthy of our perfect boy? Does a murderer's daughter deserve our golden son? Would it be that much worse in Ogdensburg with Dad?*

*Maybe I'll miss this old pier. The one place I can be by my-
self, away from those eyes.*

*At least no one in the city knows my story. There, I can be
anyone. I wouldn't have to fight for every inch. I could leave
Nate, and no one would care because in the normal world this
happens all the time. No one would skewer me with dirty looks
from across the street or tell the twins what a legendary bitch
their sister is. I think I could be kind if I wanted to be. I think I
could be just about anything if I could just be free.*

Tonight, I forgot for a second that I wasn't free. I could blame the alcohol and all the other stuff, but that'd be a lie. Yeah, Adam's done me worse than just about anyone in this town ever did, but he also liked me and not because he was afraid of me or because of who I'm dating. He liked me for me, back when I had nothing but myself to offer. And yeah, maybe I did want to remind Nate that I'm more than just some item on his checklist for a perfect life. That my needs and wants aren't always going to be the same as his. I guess it was stupid, flirting with Adam right where Nate could see us. A real bimbo move, trying to make a guy jealous like that, but everyone else is allowed to make mistakes, so why not me? It shouldn't have gotten out of hand the way it did.

Nate didn't look at me while he hacked away at Adam, but he did when he was finished. And Christ, his face. That way he smiles like a wolf. All teeth. I've seen that look before, but he's never used it on me. Not ever. It's different when those ice-cold eyes are on you. So I ran. Because I know Nate isn't really there when he's like this. He's something else, and whatever that thing is, it scares me. I think it scares everyone. Sometimes in bed I wonder—

Christ. No peace for me tonight. Not even in the Night Ship. Someone's coming.

GRADUATION

—

V

FOR NATE, EVERY song was an excuse to hold Lucy close and not let go. If he flung her spiraling outward it was only to clutch her tighter when she returned to him.

"Too bad you only dance when you're drunk, McHale," Lucy said into his shoulder.

Maybe it was the music, or the pot, or the pills, but the edges of the party blurred and faded until she was the only thing he saw in color.

This night was theirs, as would be every night to follow.

The glade was a torrent of everything. The music got louder, and the movements of the crowd became faster. The amazement of chemicals conflated Nate's senses in unexpected ways. The bass beat from the speakers smelled like pine. Seeing Tom's grin felt like a bath of indigo.

People appeared and vanished. Lucy was in his arms and then she was gone. He jumped to the rhythm with Tom and Emma, their movements out of tandem and perfectly in synch. Nate was a note in the song and together they were a chord and with the others in the glade they became a symphony.

The night declined, and the party diminished with it. The pace slowed, the fervor cooled, and their pack fractured. Nate found himself by the remains of a keg with Jim Tatum, Parker Lang, and Winston Chu. The beer tasted pleasantly of cigarettes.

The smoke from the bonfire brought a wistful ache to his eyes. This was the climax of their childhood, and it was ending all around him.

Tom reappeared, and Nate's energy returned at the sight of him. His friend. The best friend anyone could hope to have.

He looked unsteady, his Tom. The whole world was unsteady.

It became even more so when Nate saw Lucy being hoisted into the air by the large man on the edge of the clearing.

Nate was not jealous about such things. Seeing her lifted by the waist by most people wouldn't have triggered more than a wry smile. But Adam Decker wasn't just anyone.

There was a sensation of falling. Not falling down, but falling away, or falling into. The abyss appeared beneath him, and it took him whole.

The world turned black and red, and he had the sense of movement and electricity. The unquenchable fire bloomed within him, and Nate ceded himself to it. Adam Decker's vacant shark eyes grew and then diminished. There was wetness on Nate's skin. Ripples from impacts hummed from his fists and feet.

He came back to himself with his hands raised over his head, the glade a riot of rain and mud and smoke. A deluge of sound filled the space. He was soaked, and when he unclenched his fists they were tacky with blood. He felt his face, and it was not his own. Its lips were stretched into the most savage smile.

A figure was curled on the ground, a fallen giant of a man. A single hand raised in submission.

Nate became aware of the crowd around him. They were his

friends, but with their voices blaring he couldn't recognize them. They were howls and screams.

The fury had left him exhausted, but he became deeply conscious of a single fact.

Something is wrong.

Nate turned to scour the gathered and the palisade of trees.

Where was she?

She'd been here a moment ago. But had it only been a moment?

He stepped over Adam's crumpled form on his way to the tree line. Had she run away? he wondered. Had she run away *from him*?

Behind him, the screams of the crowd faded. A moment broken. An era ended.

Nate crashed into the undergrowth. Branches snapped, and brambles scraped his bare chest. "Lucy!" he called into the trees. Away from the party, the forest was strange. Faint smoke brushed with firelight lanced the air between the trees in spectral geometry.

Where had she gone and why had she gone there without him? He called for her again.

Arrhythmic footfalls broke through the brushwood behind him.

"You did it," Tom said. He was breathless. "You really did it."

"Did you see where she went?"

"You destroyed him."

"Lucy!" Nate screamed into the trees.

"Forget her."

He couldn't see Tom's face, but his friend's voice was thick, as if he was crying.

"Where is she, Tom? Help me find her."

"How'd you do it?"

Nate tried to remember why he'd fought Adam, but the tethers of logic had come undone. Its ropes unspooled around him, the universe unanchored and free to stack chance upon chance.

"What *are* you, Nate?"

"Help me, Tommy. *Please.*" Desperation crept up his throat like an ice lattice. He didn't know where it had come from. *Something is wrong.* He felt it in the ache of his arm and heard it in the skirl of wind through the branches.

Tom grabbed Nate's face and mashed his lips into his. Nate was somewhere else. Wondering where Lucy was and why she'd gone there. When he realized what was happening, he carefully pulled his mouth away from Tom's.

Tom opened his eyes and startled as if seeing Nate for the first time.

"Oh, shit." His face fell like a collapsing building. "I didn't mean to."

"It's okay," Nate said.

But Tom swore again and crushed his face into his hands as if to wring it dry. His temper overtook him like a squall. He slammed his head into the trunk of a tree. A wrenching sound poured from his chest, something raw and stripped of everything but anguish.

"Cut it out, Tom." Nate tried to pull his friend away from the tree. "You'll hurt yourself."

"Don't touch me!" Tom screamed as he wheeled on him.

Nate raised his hands in surrender. He didn't know what to do, but he had to find Lucy.

"Just don't." A look of utter exhaustion bleached Tom's features. Then he broke into a full sprint into the watchful trees.

"Tommy!" Nate tried to chase him, but the nighttime woods were too dense. He heard his friend tearing through the brush but couldn't see him.

Nate picked his way through the trees, calling Tom's name and then Lucy's into its pillars. But the forest was dark and thick, and deep enough to hide anyone who didn't want to be found.

HE REMEMBERED WALKING. He remembered the chafe of sore feet against wet shoes.

There was a place in the fever of the night when time had no meaning and events had no lucidity, and that's where he was. Where were his friends? Why was he alone? Where was he going? Dream logic supplanted the rules of the world. He thought of something or someone—the Night Ship, Lucy, Tom—and there it was. Maybe they'd been there all along.

He was jostled by choppy water near the shore, watching a mass of people on the stony beach. The lake was all around, trapping him as a star is imprisoned in the void. Its cold water erased everything it touched. He was erased. A boy wrapped in a Mylar blanket was on the beach ahead of him. The boy was huddled alongside police and EMS workers. Nate knew the boy: He felt sure of it. The boy needed help—he needed so much.

For a moment it seemed like the boy finally noticed him. It seemed like Nate might be able to shout to him, but the lake shook him like a boat caught in another's wake. Soon he couldn't see the boy, he couldn't see the beach, he couldn't even see the—

"Nate. Nate! Wake up, boy."

It took every ounce of will he possessed to open his right eye.

He was not in the lake or on the Night Ship or in the forest in some far-flung part of the headlands. He was in his bed.

"The chief's here," Grams told him. "Wants to talk to you."

Nate sat up, and the room lurched dangerously. An alien heat resided in his brain. His eyes remained blurry no matter how many times he blinked. His fingers felt rusted at the joints.

"Might want a quick washup first."

Grams flipped on the lights as she went back into the hall. He felt his pupils strain to contract as a shadow of sense snapped back into him. Greystone Lake's chief of police was downstairs, and Nate was a mess. In the bathroom he hurriedly washed mud and blood from his hands. He shook twigs and leaves out of his hair and slapped some of the pallor from his face.

The chief could be here for a multitude of reasons, but at four in the morning, none of them could be good.

Nate still looked rough when he was finished. His eyes were an atrocity of blood vessels, and there was a nascent bruise on his temple, but his smile was gold and gold doesn't tarnish.

He slipped into an undershirt, pulled on jeans, and trotted downstairs. His grandmother, wrapped in her robe, stood with the chief in the foyer. No one looked their best.

"Hey, Chief."

"Sorry to wake you. Lucy didn't come home."

"She didn't?"

"Mrs. Bennett called the station, and they radioed me. Normally wouldn't draw up a search so soon, but I know you're all close. Thought you and Tommy might have some ideas."

A shriek tore from the kitchen. The kettle. Grams scurried past Nate, leaving him with the chief.

"You've been drinking, I think." The chief squinted at him.

"A little," Nate admitted. His face wasn't built for sheepishness, but he did his best.

"You boys were safe, though."

"The safest."

"Your Grams is brewing me a bit of coffee. Tommy's in the car. How about you two put your heads together about where she might have gotten to."

After wedging sneakers onto his feet, Nate made his way to the cruiser parked in front. The shadow of Tom's profile was in the backseat.

"Hey."

"Hey," Tom said. He wore a polo shirt and khakis, like they were heading to school. Like it wasn't predawn and they weren't blitzed into another plane of existence. He didn't look at Nate.

"I feel about nine-tenths dead right now." Nate slid in next to Tom.

Tom didn't answer.

"I figure there's, like, an eighty percent chance this is a hallucination."

Still nothing.

"I never found Lucy," Nate said. "Wouldn't be surprised if half our year's passed out somewhere. She could be staying at Emma's."

"Dad tried there already."

"She didn't seem messed up enough to get lost and end up somewhere really random, but I'm not the best judge."

Tom turned to look out the window.

"She's probably just asleep somewhere. Kinda jealous, actually."

All he got from Tom was a sound of movement that might have been a shrug.

"Tommy, that whole thing—in the forest. Don't worry about it. Crazy night, huh?" He patted his friend on the leg. "You're making it weird, and it doesn't have to be. I don't feel weird."

Tom was silent for a few long moments before speaking. "I think I'm still drunk."

"Well, yeah, of course. You were annihilated. Me, too. Still am. Mixing pills with everything else was a crappy idea. Lesson learned."

It was dark in the car, but Tom seemed to nod. "Yeah."

Nate was pleased to lay the issue of that kiss—if that's what it was—to rest. He hadn't thought much about it, but when he did the strongest feeling he could detect was one of mild surprise. But the Creature of Catastrophic Futures was no doubt parsing and replaying and lamenting those two seconds in the forest and imagining the devastation wrought by its repercussions. It was good to put it in the open so they could brush it aside.

"So, for Lucy, I say we get your dad to check out the Wharf and boathouse while he drops us off at Johnny's."

"Johnny's?"

"Yeah, we tell the chief we'll check there, look in the gazebo, the pool house, the dock, whatever, but we'll really take one of the Vanhoutens' canoes to the Night Ship."

His eyes had adjusted to the dark enough to see Tom shake his head.

"I can't go there. Not tonight. I just can't."

"Lucy'll stumble home once it's light out, but if the chief's got it into his head to turn the town upside down, then we've got to clean out the Night Ship. Our stuff's still there, and they'll know we've taken over the place. Who knows, maybe she even crashed there for the night. Either way, we've got to play it safe. You'd think it'd be normal to wait until morning to start a search. I don't know how the chief thinks he's doing us a favor."

"Dad will flip if he finds out we're in the Night Ship."

"That's why we have to check it out first. If she's there, we'll wake her up, paddle her to the Vanhoutens, and tell the chief she was in their gazebo the whole time. No harm done. If not, we'll pull our things out of the Night Ship in case anyone decides to look there before she turns up."

"We're done with that place, Nate. You promised. You promised Lucy, too."

The chief exited the house and made his way toward them across the lawn.

"*Christ*," Nate hissed. The chief was close enough that he couldn't risk speaking at full volume. He hadn't expected pushback on this. "Fine. I'll go by myself. Just stay in the gazebo and do nothing. *Perfect*."

Chief Buck pulled open the door and settled into the driver's seat. The smells of coffee and the wet night entered the car with him.

"Ideas, boys?"

Nate answered and the chief replied. The conversation unwound in the inevitable ways and concluded in the only manner it could have: with Nate getting what he wanted. Tom would go along with him, just as he always did.

The chief dropped them in front of the Vanhoutens' home on his way to the Wharf.

Nate thought the mansion was asleep, but when he reached the rear he saw that the conservatory was lit. This was a glass-domed enclosure that jutted from the back of the house and opened onto the veranda. They gave it a wide berth, but Nate saw Mr. Vanhouten at the room's center, seated at a table staring at a near-empty bottle. The man had a profile that would look at home printed on currency, but he was trapped in the snow globe of the conservatory, braced against the table as if waiting for the shaking to begin.

The house and grounds were quiet as they picked through the gardens. Nate doubted Mr. Vanhouten would notice a 747 landing in his backyard, but they were still careful. A bruise of light gathered above the eastern mountains.

The Vanhoutens kept a variety of watercraft by their dock. Without a word, Nate and Tom hoisted a canoe from its rack and lowered it into the onyx water.

"What if Dad finishes at the Wharf and gets back to Johnny's before we do?"

"If you have to worry out loud, do it quietly. My head feels like a marching band's trying to escape it."

The lake was choppy, and Nate didn't like the idea of paddling across it in the dark. He prepared himself and stepped into the craft. Tom rocked the canoe as he got in, and Nate closed his eyes to help dispel a wave of nausea. Even on land, his vision had a drunken gradient to it. Half of his synapses skated the rings of Saturn. Was going to the Night Ship the right thing to do? Would it help them find Lucy? Did Lucy *need* finding?

A siren song of pain played in the pieces of his bad arm. It was this more than anything that called him across the water.

When they reached the Night Ship, they lowered the boat launch and secured the canoe. The undercroft was damp with humidity. The chief had given them a flashlight, though Nate could have found his way through this tangle of halls half asleep and without benefit of a single lumen. They ascended the spiral staircase to the main floor of the nightclub.

One of the camp lanterns shined in a corner, blazing the wall's rippling crimson paint and bristling the shadows of chairs and tables across the dance floor. Whatever intuition had led Nate to the Night Ship was on target. Someone had been here and not long ago.

"Lucy!" His voice reverberated from the walls and echoed down the hall of the Century Room above. *See, see, see, see* . . .

The sleeping bags and foam pads were where he'd left them the morning before. The only thing out of place was a tumbler of clear liquid on the scarred bar. He took a tentative sip and spat it out when his stomach rebelled at the taste of it. Vodka. Lucy's drink. He called for her again.

Behind him, Tom wandered in a circle around the dance floor.

"Are you going to help, or what?" Nate asked him.

"I'll check the Century Room."

Nate gave Tom the flashlight and took the lantern for himself. Sunlight stained the eastern clouds, but the interior of the old night-club remained stubbornly unlit.

This floor had a limited number of places to look, but Nate checked them all. Though they'd spent many a cloudy afternoon searching, they'd never found the hidden passages the old stories spoke of. They rarely went into the sprawling, filthy kitchen, but he inspected its cupboards and empty freezers. He told himself that in a haze of alcohol, Lucy might have passed out anywhere, but this didn't explain where he was searching for her. An exhausted girl doesn't climb onto a counter to wedge herself into a cabinet.

A sensation wormed through his gut. It was a feeling but it was also a memory. *Something is wrong.*

"Tom!" he called into the chasm of the pier.

His friend's response was muffled by distance and the vagaries of the Night Ship. The sound arrived as if filtered through time or a membrane of pure cold water.

Nate noticed that a door to the boardwalk was open. He followed a sliver of light into the morning. Low clouds blurred into gold against the forested mountains.

The weathered wood of the old pier looked like ancient skin, its planks bulging and puckered with a century of wear. Whole sections of the boardwalk railing had fallen away, leaving nothing but a single step between these planks and a drop into the lake's insatiable gorge.

The plain of water was empty and dark. Skeins of mist caught the blue dawn. Its surface was usually like that of a mirror, reflecting without revealing. But in this moment of strange light, the lake became transparent.

Nate probed its ripples with the beam of his flashlight. It sliced through the clean water as easily as if it were glass. The light caught a whirl of jade encased in the crystal of the water.

When he saw it, Nate's absent neurons were recalled from the outer planets with a speed that broke all natural laws. His attention coalesced into a single unwavering focus.

A knot of sublime green was wrapped around the pier's pilings just below the waterline.

No was all Nate could think. *No.*

"Nate?" Tom's voice and a patter of running feet.

He was dimly aware of shouting. His own shouting. The sun cracked the line of mountains and the secrets of the lake were laid bare.

Lucy's kimono wrap.

The water's talons raked him as he dove into the throat of the lake. The frigid water hit him like a blow to the chest. But he tore through it, swimming below the dark wedge of the Night Ship, groping where the light failed. The warble of his yell thrummed around him.

He swam and searched and struggled in the black. He ran out of breath. He ran out of everything. But this didn't stop his wordless scream.

The lake took his cry as easily as it had taken everything else.

Thirteen

Her jade kimono wrap and an unceasing ache in his core ensured that Nate never fully accepted the goodbye note attributed to Lucy. For myriad reasons, he couldn't believe that she'd run away.

Even after the search wound down, Nate circled the shore for weeks. He walked the headlands, paced the stony beaches, and paddled the boundaries of Blind Down Island and the unnamed outcroppings that dotted the colorless waters. The lake returns what it takes, but of Lucy there was no sign.

Each fruitless day wound him tighter. He dissected and analyzed his every memory of graduation. He played these forward and backward and in every conceivable sequence looking for something that made sense. He looped and repeated and obsessed upon every frame of that night until the memories themselves were buried under the thousand revisions and transcription errors of remembering. In the end, all he knew was that his fight with Adam had scared Lucy. Scared her enough to run from the glade to the Night Ship.

And then—

He didn't know.

Nate tried to get the police and his friends to help, to investigate, to *care,* but after that note appeared they and the rest of the Lake bolted for the easy answer that it offered. Dismissing Lucy as a runaway was preferable to the alternative. They should have known better: Greystone Lake was as beautiful as any town, but the Night Ship and its history should have reminded them of how terrible the truth could be.

As that summer ripened, paranoia blossomed in Nate. It was as if everyone else in town had reached some unspoken agreement to turn the page on this chapter of the Lake's story. He recognized that he was becoming increasingly obsessed. He saw the way people looked at him. If Lucy had indeed run away, then he surely bore some responsibility. If something worse had happened to her, then he was the most obvious culprit. His shaving and showering became erratic. Meals were forgotten and sleep became a stranger. Grams's expressions lunged from disquiet to pure alarm in a way he hadn't seen since the months that followed the car accident. Even Tom began to avoid him.

Week by week, strands of anger knotted like a cocoon around him. One morning, one of the Daybreakers said the wrong thing to him while he patrolled the shore. His vision went black streaked with red, and then he was bound to a hospital bed. The man who'd crossed him was also in the hospital, though not in its psych wing.

When he returned to himself, they sent him back to his old therapist, who gave him daily sessions and prescribed a course of medication. He was a few weeks shy of eighteen, a minor with curtailed rights under the close supervision of medical professionals, the police, and everyone else around him. The pills dulled him into a state that he could barely muster the energy to abhor, but they gave him the distance to think. From this vantage, Nate understood that he'd never find Lucy, yet would see her in the Lake's every buckled curbstone and hear her in each gust that skimmed its pewter waters. Lucy was gone, but Nate was alive. He would continue to live, but only if he left this place.

So he told his psychiatrist and Grams what they wanted to hear. He went through the five stages of grief at a plausible pace. He took his pills like a model patient. He made a tearful apology to the dawn swimmer he'd sent to the ER—a performance convincing enough that the man dropped his crutches and braced his casted arm around Nate to pull him into a cathartic hug. Weeping into the guy's shoulder, Nate watched the glances of relief exchanged between Grams and his doctor as they stood nearby.

With a promise to continue therapy in New York, Nate made it to Columbia a few weeks into the fall term. A challenging double major in biochemistry and English required a great deal of his time and rigor—a laudable use of his talents and energies, his doctors all agreed. However, his extracurricular regimen wasn't the kind a therapist or anyone else would have approved of. While he buried himself in coursework during the week, he used the weekends to vent heat from the furnace that seethed inside him. Thunder Runs had once served this purpose, but abandoning them was the last promise Nate had made Lucy. There were other ways.

The city was gentler than its myths led him to expect. He'd hoped for muggers on every street corner and tempers with a hair trigger. The world had softened, but he had not. Some Saturdays he'd work his way through blocks of bars before finding someone too drunk to shrug off his provocations.

Brawling exorcised his rage, because the person Nate most sought to punish was himself. He didn't know what had happened to Lucy, but he was certain that he bore a measure of responsibility for it. If he hadn't scared her the night of graduation. If he hadn't punctuated their time together with such extremes of fury and love. If he'd never dated her in the first place. Any one of a thousand untraveled pasts would have led to a present where Lucy was safe.

Each black eye and split lip helped him pay for this. With the number of injuries he sported in class, his professors must have thought him singularly clumsy.

As with the loss of his family, the wound of Lucy's absence didn't heal, but nerve by nerve it numbed. One winter, he met Meg, a 2L at the law school. There'd been other women, but not like her. Like Lucy, Meg was sharp and tough, and Nate could have filled a book trying to describe how kind, gentle, and funny she was. But those were just words. The heart of his love for her was a sensation that hummed from his center and did not falter.

Nate's passion for Lucy had been real and intense and hungry, but with the distance of time, he began to understand that this was not the kind of love that tended to endure. It had been an unsustainable passion.

Like Nate's rage, it couldn't burn forever.

He assembled a new man. One who could live within the rules of this world. A man his parents and grandmother would be proud of. A man who deserved the love of someone like Meg. Nate hadn't thought those askew equations inside him could ever be balanced, but somehow, variable by variable, they were. Or at least they seemed to be. Anger. Pain. Revenge. Guilt. These belonged to another life. These belonged to another Nate.

He finished his bachelor's degree early and went right into medical school. There were years of happiness. There was professional success. There was Livvy.

Then they found Lucy's remains in the headlands.

Nate opened the side door to the church, and a pulse of wind extinguished a cluster of nearby candles.

The church was neo-Gothic with high and narrow stained glass windows, lifeless in the gray day. The building had lost electricity, and promontories of candles assembled around the altar and along the aisles were its only illumination. Islands of light in drifts of shadow.

The congregation was larger than Nate would have guessed from the number of cars outside. Over half the church's pews were occupied with figures cloaked in black.

Nate spotted Tom seated in one of the rearmost pews.

There was some anonymity in the darkness of the place, but

Nate still attracted attention as he walked the side aisle. As faces turned to him, some became strangely lurid in the candlelight. He avoided eye contact, but he recognized former teachers, old friends, and members of Lucy's extended family. By the time he reached the back of the church, the crowd's muttering competed with the drumming of rain against the roof and windows.

Nate sat next to Tom, shook out his dripping umbrella, and removed his streaming coat. There was movement in the vestibule behind him. He got his first glimpse of the black box where what remained of Lucy would forevermore reside.

Seeing the casket, Nate's thoughts flew to Grams. She was going to die, he realized. They would put what was left of her in a box just like this one. If not today then tomorrow or next week or next year. One by one the universe would pick them all off. Because the one certainty in life is that no one survives it.

While he contemplated the casket, Nate became aware of eyes searing into the side of his head. A trio of mismatched teenagers stared at him from across the aisle. There was a short chubby kid, a wan towheaded boy, and a pierced goth girl. A punch line waiting to happen.

They stared at Nate with their greasy faces. He recognized the way their eyes burned with the unalloyed revulsion of children. One glance and he knew them just as they knew him.

"That's them." Nate nudged Tom. "The vandals." If the vandals' mayhem had been somehow triggered by the discovery of Lucy's remains, then it made sense that they'd be at her funeral.

"Evidence?"

"Look at them."

"Profiling."

Nate glared at the pew of teenagers. These were the children who'd landed Grams at the threshold of death.

He stared back at them, his gaze scorching and venom pouring from the points of his smile. He bore down on each of them until they looked away. It didn't take long.

"If it's them, they might know what happened to Maura Jeffers last night. Pete Corso, too. They're all in the same crew." No matter Tom's awful morning, he was still a police officer in a town where a child was dead and another was missing. Nate thought he could use this as a lever to reveal answers to the questions that mattered to him.

"Maura was the girl who washed up on the shore," Nate added, when Tom didn't respond. "And Pete's the boy who's missing."

"Yeah, I know who they are, Nate."

"So *do* something, Deputy."

Tom took out his phone and pretended to check his messages while he took photos of the teenagers.

The girl wore a large flower in her hair, incongruous with her vampire styling. A dahlia, either orange or red—it was hard to tell in the candlelight. Both boys had similar blooms slipped through the buttonholes of their shirts.

"What's with the flowers?"

"Lucy had flowers in her hair the last time anyone saw her."

"They were white. Calla lilies."

"The stories the kids tell make it a dahlia. They leave them at the barricade now," Tom said.

"What?"

"The way we used to leave glow sticks. Now they leave flowers, too."

Nate loathed the idea that she'd become one of their stories.

"She hated dahlias." This wasn't true, but he said it anyway.

The power outage had turned the church's organ into so many inert pipes, so the cantor struck up a hymn a capella. The congregation rose.

The family began their procession. With linked arms, Mr. and Mrs. Bennett led the way.

Nate had last seen Mr. Bennett in court, during his criminal trial. He'd seemed tall and powerful back then. Now he was shrunken and gray and overweight. A man with too-long hair, wearing a too-tight suit jacket. He gave no outward sign of being a destroyer of worlds.

The years had left their marks on Mrs. Bennett as well. Nate remembered her being as slim as a dancer, but she'd become stout. Her once fiery hair was mostly extinguished by strands of white.

Though it was impossible to imagine them any older than they'd been, Nate's own parents would be about the same age as the Bennetts. He wondered if his mom would have let herself go gray or if his father might have developed a prosperous paunch. Nate didn't have to wonder what his little brother would look like. He caught a glimpse of Gabe every time he saw his own reflection.

Nate savored the pain that came with working at these scabs, but he wasn't able to indulge them for long.

The girl captured his attention as soon as he got a good look at her. When she'd poured him a pint at the Union yesterday, she told him her name was TJ. Tara Jane Bennett. Lucy's younger sister. The last time Nate saw her she'd just finished kindergarten. Back then, she'd had the same auburn hair as Lucy. With that hair, Nate might have recognized her, but she'd dyed it black. Now that he understood who she was, looking at her was like seeing Lucy through a tinted window into an alternate dimension.

Compared to forgiving Mr. Bennett for killing her son, daughter-in-law, and grandson, it would have been a small thing for Grams to offer a job to Tara. Why no one had thought to tell Nate that the girl worked there was a separate question. Another secret to add to the tally.

Tara's brother, James, walked next to her. He still carried his mother's coloring; the light from the scattered candles flared across his hair. The twins had been five when Lucy disappeared, which put them at around nineteen now. James was by far the tallest of the quartet making their way down the aisle. In the flickering light, his face was all planes and shadows.

As James passed, he turned to the trio of mismatched teens. The young man exchanged a nod with them, and things began to make sense.

James's older sister's body discovered. Knowledge of her friends and enemies, one of whom was probably her murderer. Violence, destruction, rage. This was a ballad of revenge—a tune Nate knew by heart.

"It's him," Nate whispered to Tom. "James Bennett. He's the one behind the attacks. The fire at the Union. Loki. Everything."

He was pleased to see a slash of anger cross his friend's features.

"Dad gave him a job at the station one summer while he was in high school. He still comes around every once in a while if we need another set of hands."

Nate had been in the chief's office for fewer than thirty minutes before discovering secrets about that long-ago graduation night. What might James have found over the course of an entire summer?

"Do you know him?"

"Not really. I think he works at one of the places on the Wharf now."

By now James had reached the front of the church. He waited for his sister to take her seat.

A phalanx of black-clad men rolled Lucy's casket down the aisle. Its sides were polished to incredible reflection. Looking at it was like gazing into one of the lake's death-still inlets. The candlelight glossed its surface, making it strangely luminescent in the dark space. A single handprint marred its side.

Nate had long been a creature of focus. If he knew one thing, it was what he wanted. But the Lake had robbed him of this certainty. He had to see Grams through her injuries. He had to return to New York to be a good husband to his wife and a good father to his daughter. He had to make sure these vandals meant him, his family, and his friends no further harm. He had to uncover what these teens thought they knew. He had to find out who killed Lucy.

But there was no way he could do all of this at once.

As her casket passed, Nate's reflection stared back from its stygian wood. He forced himself to be present for this. Every single piece of him. He was here, and so were her lovelorn bones, and nothing else mattered. They were separated by layers of lacquer, inches of seasoned oak, and too many mistakes to count.

The pallbearers arranged the casket in front of the altar. The cantor finished the hymn, and the congregation sat. The priest spoke. Readings were given. There was no eulogy, and for this Nate was grateful. Funerals like this aren't for the dead; they're for the living. The half-stifled sobs from around the church made that much clear. Stray cousins and distant acquaintances mourned this chip taken from their own illusions of immortality. Their grief was lavish, but every tear they shed was spent on themselves.

For Nate, no words spoken by these people about Lucy could have been sufficient. He also couldn't see past the fact that Lucy's murderer was statistically likely to be among these mourners. These teary-eyed friends, family, and neighbors.

Though Adam Decker wasn't in the pews. At six-five he'd be impossible to miss. The file in the chief's closet said that Adam's alibi for that night hadn't held up to scrutiny. If he'd been lying about that, he could be lying about anything.

He raped her then he killed her.

The cantor broke into the recessional hymn "Amazing Grace," which everyone knew. Voices rose and swelled together in the flickering church.

Tears filled Nate's eyes as he realized that the funeral was ending. It was over.

He tried not to blink, but this didn't keep his eyes from running. Her lips on a cold night. Her hair tickling his bare chest. A descent into the freezing lake, and the burn in his lungs as he clawed farther and farther from the light.

The congregation filed out. There was a grip on his forearm. Tom. Nate looked at his friend through his swimming eyes and was so glad not to be here alone. He'd contemplated staging a confrontation with one of the vandals, but now a quick exit was necessary. People stared at him as he and Tom worked their way down the side aisle. Lucy's burial would take place later in the week on account of Medea.

He put on his coat and wiped at his eyes as Tom pulled him toward the door. The winds burst through the entryway, dousing ranges of candles. Someone clutched his shoulder from behind.

"I didn't know if you'd come," Mr. Bennett said. His voice was splintered like weather-beaten wood.

Nate couldn't speak or breathe. He could only stare.

"I heard about your grandmother. I'm so sorry. She's a good woman. A tough woman. If anyone can see their way through it, then it's her."

Here was the personification of so much of Nate's pain, and he couldn't think of anything to say to him. He felt as if he was floating three feet above his own body.

"I was hoping you'd be here. I thought, if one good thing can come from all this"—he gestured to the cavern of the church—"then it'd be to see you again."

Nate forced himself to inhale.

"I need to offer amends to those I've hurt. And no one's been more hurt than you."

"'Amends.'"

"There's nothing I can do to replace what I took from you. I know that. I don't expect your forgiveness. I don't deserve it. I just wanted to tell you to your face that I'm sorry. I'm so incredibly sorry for taking your mother and father and brother away from you."

Nate felt Tom's gaze drill into the back of his head. Nate understood that he was supposed to say something here. He knew that much, but anything more than that escaped him.

"I keep thinking about how different things would be if I'd made other choices—better choices, back then," Mr. Bennett said. "For Lucy, for Bea, for my family. For you."

Nate's thoughts used to travel that same line. If only he'd asked for a cherry pie instead of a peach pie. If only he'd struck out at the plate instead of hitting a triple. But the older he got, the more difficult it became to imagine the phantom futures that had been closed to him. That April day made Nate who he was.

Who would he be if not himself?

"I have to go," Nate said.

"Of course, I know you're a busy man. A big surgeon in the city. Good for you, Nate. We're all very proud of you."

The smile on the man's face was desperately sincere. That's what made it so shattering. "I'm so sorry. I really am. I'll be sorry for the rest of my life."

Nate nodded and felt his way through the side door. Outside, leaves and debris skimmed the surface of the street as if rushing toward something with incredible urgency. There was no sky or lake or town in this rain. He didn't open his umbrella or close his coat. He let Medea whip him.

Nate followed Tom to the cruiser. When he got inside he was just short of hyperventilating. They sat there, watching their breath fog the windows and letting the wind rock them from side to side.

Focus, Nate told himself. He tried to collect his thoughts and feelings and reorder them in a way that resembled the man he was supposed to be.

"I want to talk to Adam Decker," Nate said.

Tom turned to him. "You're joking."

"I found something back at the station," Nate said. "Behind the locked door in your dad's office."

"His closet?"

"He has filing cabinets hidden in there. Photographs, notes, transcripts. All relating to Lucy's disappearance. He has her journals, too. He's had them the whole time. He knows about the Thunder Runs. I denied everything, obviously. But she could have written anything in there. Anything. Everything."

Tom blinked at him as if he'd just awoken in a place where he didn't remember falling asleep. "You're saying my dad knows what we did back then?"

"Yes." Chief Buck had violated both law and oath to conceal this from his son as much as anyone. But the chief had had fourteen years to get to the bottom of this. Now it was Nate's turn.

"He's known the whole time?"

"Right."

"But—but," Tom sputtered. In an instant, he melted into pure sopping panic. "The journals weren't introduced into evidence. He never once asked me about—"

"He was protecting you. The statutes of limitations are up on most of what we did, but back then it could have ruined us."

Tom's hands dropped from the wheel to fall limp at his sides.

"That's why I need to talk to Adam," Nate said. "There was a note in his file that said something about his alibi not matching up with the rest of his story."

"What else was there?" Tom's voice was barely a whisper.

"I didn't have much time to look. I don't know if your dad followed up on the lead with Adam, but maybe he thought it'd be easier if everyone thought Lucy really had run away. If we talk to Adam, maybe we can figure out what he's hiding."

"You solve crimes now?" Tom had seemed close to hysteria, but was reeling himself in from the edge.

"I know, right? If only there was a taxpayer-funded organization meant to deal with things like this. We could even give them uniforms and badges to make it seem official."

Tom took the car out of park and backed the cruiser from its parking space. "If you harass him, he might press charges for the sucker punch you landed on him this morning. He told my dad he wanted you to stay away from him."

"It wasn't a sucker punch," Nate said, though that memory belonged to a part of himself that he didn't have access to.

Tom didn't respond, but he turned the car north onto the Strand.

The lake was swollen with rain, and the distant foothills were lost in veils of clouds. Nate watched the waters surge and recede against the shore. The mansions and their meticulously maintained grounds soon blocked his view. His body absorbed the bucking of the car as it churned through a stretch of inundated road while his mind pulled at strategies to get Adam to reveal whatever he was hiding. He hadn't fully unpacked this problem when Tom pulled into the short driveway of a small, wood-shingled ranch house. They were several blocks inland, not far from Grams's house on Bonaparte Street. It was a tidy home, but not much to look at. At a glance, Nate knew it wasn't right. A married lawyer with two children didn't live in a place like this.

"This isn't Decker's house."

"No."

"Whose is it?"

Tom activated the garage door and drove the cruiser inside. "Mine." He exited the car. "Welcome." He slammed the door shut.

Nate watched Tom disappear into the interior. He'd become unpredictable, his Tom. But Nate had no car, no phone, and no other options. He followed his friend inside.

The carcass of something that might have once been a couch lay along one wall of the narrow room. The carpeting was a noncommittal shade between brown and gray. Thrift store chairs and a low coffee table were dotted with books and bottles. A vacant dog bed sat in a corner.

If Nate had gone through a bachelor phase, his home might have looked similar. But at this stage in their lives, it pained him to remember that Tom had once wanted to be an architect.

"Looks comfortable."

Tom didn't bother replying. He'd already placed two mismatched glasses on the coffee table next to where he'd deposited his wallet and keys. His back was to Nate, but the squeak and pop of a liquor bottle explained itself. Nate wasn't interested in a drink, but he had to play nice until he understood why Tom had brought him here while murderers were loose and grandmothers were critically injured. He shrugged off his raincoat and folded it across an arm of the battered couch.

"To Lucy," Nate said after he accepted his glass. Bourbon. He took a sip and watched Tom drain his.

As Tom refilled his tumbler, an explosion of thunder rattled the windows, and the lights went out. The noises of the house wound down in a shuddering final breath.

Tom gulped his second glass without pausing. He'd barely finished swallowing when he began to speak.

"I killed her."

Nate frowned.

"You heard me."

"Cut it out."

"I'm serious."

"So am I."

"Look at me, Nate." In the dark room, Tom's face was nothing but shadow.

"I can't talk to you when you're like this." Nate didn't know this game, but he knew he didn't want to play. He placed his glass on the coffee table and stealthily grabbed Tom's keys while he was at it. If the Internet was still accessible, he'd try Googling Adam's address from Grams's computer. If he found Adam, he might have an easier time getting what he needed from him without the burden of Tom's chaperoning.

Nate was halfway to the garage when Tom surprised him with a body slam. They crashed into an end table, and a lamp tumbled to the carpet. Before Nate could regain his balance, Tom gripped him by the shoulders to shove him against the wall. A framed photo fell from a bookshelf and shattered across the floor.

"Look at me!" Tom screamed. Slicks of tears carved the hollows of his face. "I killed Lucy."

Part III

THUNDER

and

LIGHT

GRADUATION

—

VI

TOM TORE THROUGH the forest like a razor through flesh. Fast, straight, leaving a wake of pain.

The pain was his own.

A howl reverberated in his ears, though the only sound he made was the crash of his feet against the gnarled ground.

In the distance, Nate called for him, and for once Tom wouldn't answer. His friend's voice faded with every step. He couldn't bear to think about Nate, though it was impossible to think of anything else.

Had he really? *Had he really?*

Tom didn't know where he was running to until he got there: the Night Ship. It was two miles from the glade, but then it was in front of him. An island citadel silhouetted against the moonlit clouds.

The others had always been drawn to its creaking halls. They found solace in its stories and took comfort in the endless sigh of the lake against its pilings. Tom had never understood this. Maybe tonight he would.

He ran down the warped pier and didn't stop when he reached

the promenade. The long hall was void of all light, but he didn't slow. He felt as if there was nothing left to fear.

A finger of illumination pointed from the Night Ship down the promenade. Inside, Tom saw that one of the camp lanterns was lit.

"Johnny?" he called into shadows. "Owen?" He wanted to be by himself, but he didn't want to be alone. He had to run or stop or sleep or think or obliterate himself.

Tom climbed onto the scratched expanse of the bar and knocked over candlepins of bottles with a clumsy landing on the other side. They rolled and clanked as Tom groped at them. He squinted at their labels, looking for anything the sight of which didn't turn his stomach.

He found a fifth of triple sec, took a swig, and immediately ejected it through his mouth and nose. When he went to wipe his face, he remembered that he'd left his shirt back in the glade along with his shoes. He curled into himself on the ravaged floor. Against his ear, the wood trembled with the groans of the lake.

Footsteps tapped through the planks.

"Nate?" he asked. His voice was slurred with hope and fear. Using the knobs of drawers and cupboards as handholds, Tom hoisted himself into a position to see the dance floor.

A figure appeared just inside the doorway to the boardwalk. The kimono wrap draped over her shoulders made her shadow into that of a winged creature.

"Oh," Lucy said when she saw him. Disappointed but also relieved.

Lucy's face was streaked with makeup. Her tousled hair, wet and plastered against her neck. A mash of pulp that had once been a cluster of lilies hung above her ear. But she was still beautiful. She and Nate, they glowed with the same light.

"What are *you* doing here?" Tom asked. The words were petty and stupid, and he hated them and he hated himself for saying them.

Lucy lurched to the bar. The tumbler she held made a dull clank as she half-dropped it on the counter. She studied him for a moment before lighting a tiger's smile. "What'd he do to you?"

"Who?"

"Please. Look at you."

"Look at *yourself.*"

She made a sound like a laugh. "Fine. Look at *us.* Look what he did to us."

Tom squinted at her. His eyes didn't want anything in focus. "It's your fault," he said. "Messing around with Adam Decker."

"Yeah, it's my fault saying hello to an old friend starts a riot."

"He's not our friend."

"You're so"—she thought about it—*"loyal."* It wasn't a compliment.

"Don't you remember what Adam did to you?"

"What a dumb question. But that's the past, Tom. That life is over. All those insipid platitudes they vomited up at us today, but here's one you could actually use: Our futures begin now. Do you get it?" She looked at him, and he hated everything about her face.

"What about *you*?" Tom asked. "When Nate looks into the future, you think he sees you?"

"I know he does."

Her certainty enraged Tom not because it was delusional but because it wasn't.

"Wouldn't be so sure." He wanted to shatter the smug look on her face. He wanted to be the one who did the hurting, just this once. "Not after tonight. He was angry, Lucy. *Furious.* I've never seen him so mad."

"Poor Tom," she said, sighing. "You think things are going to be the same in the city, but I promise you they won't be. Dinner three nights a week—that's what he told you, isn't it? If you think that's going to last to Thanksgiving, you're dreaming."

"*I'm* dreaming?" Tom shouted. "Once he's in the city, he won't be able to spit without hitting a girl better looking than you. They'll be smarter and nicer, too. And you can bet their dads aren't in prison for murdering his entire family."

"He doesn't even *see* other girls."

He laughed at her, and it rang of pure scorn. He didn't know he'd carried such a sound inside of him. "The thing is that girls here are afraid of you, Luce. They'd never try anything with Nate. But in the city? Down there you'll be back to being nobody. Mountain trash. Those girls flush shit better than you every day."

The words were savage enough that even Lucy seemed taken aback.

"Did you see the way he looked at you when he was finished with Adam? The way he screamed for you?" From the way her face tightened, Tom thought she had. "You were running away from him, weren't you? That's why you didn't answer. I don't blame you. I'd run, too." Tom remembered that he *did* run, but he slapped the memory down before it could surface. "He's probably still looking for you. Just imagine what he'll do when he finds you. That's the *future* you're so excited about."

Lucy's lips turned white, and she whirled away from him. She stalked back through the doors to the boardwalk.

Tom followed her—and this, forever, was one of the mistakes that most haunted him. He should have declared victory and gone home. Instead, he joined her to look out over the black waters. To get in another jab? To forestall being alone for a few minutes more? He never settled on a reason that was good enough.

The coarse wood of the boardwalk was wet under his feet. The cloudburst had drawn the worst of the humidity from the air, but Tom still savored the feel of the wind against his skin. Lucy leaned against the railing, surveying the abyss of the lake. Tom joined her.

He wondered what she'd say next and how he'd answer. The Creature of Catastrophic Futures was a distant memory, and through the prism of this desperate bravery, anything seemed possible.

A shoal of clouds pulled aside to reveal the low moon.

"If we're lucky, he won't remember any of this tomorrow," Lucy said.

Her tone surprised him. Lucy was vicious and relentless, and Tom had expected her to try to reassert her superiority. But she sounded flattened. Defeated.

"Maybe you're right," she continued. "Maybe I shouldn't have gotten within thirty feet of Adam."

"Obviously." Tom wanted to rub Lucy's face in her mistake. He wanted her to feel as raw as he did, even if it was only for a night. But there was something unguarded about her that dulled the thrill of denting her confidence.

"A little innocent flirting." She shook her head. "And it *was* totally innocent. Because is it crazy for me to remind Nate that he's not the only thing in my life? That I'm an actual human person who exists even when he's not in the same room as me?" She rubbed her face, wrecking what remained of her makeup. "Do you know how exhausting it is to be perfect for him all the time? Don't you get tired?"

Lucy Bennett at her best was cruel and formidable, but the girl next to him wasn't either of those things. The Storm King saw pain as a zero-sum game, but Tom didn't think making Lucy feel worse about herself would make him feel any better. Vindictiveness for the sake of malice wasn't a thing he was built for. Maybe he and Lucy had more in common than he thought.

It was such a strange night.

In its sleep, the town along the shore was as dark as the forests that blanketed the mountains. The Lake was different in the night, just as it was different in a storm. New possibilities seemed to arise like the stars beyond the scrim of clouds. The future was ahead of them. In this unvisited place, maybe he and Lucy didn't have to be enemies.

"At least he's getting it out of his system," Tom said. "He can't get away with being so wild in the city."

"Try telling him what he can't do."

"You already did. No Thunder Runs. No Night Ship. No more revenge."

"He doesn't need it anymore. You should thank me. Everyone knows you hated the whole thing."

Drops pattered around them, but they were both already soaked. Light rain broke against glinting waves like sheets of static.

"He can be a lot," Tom said tentatively.

"Too much. He's too much all the time." Lucy drew something across the splintered railing with the pad of her index finger. It could have been a heart. It might have been a question mark.

She shivered and pulled her kimono wrap tight around her shoulders. Her arms were still bare. She moved closer to Tom, and it was shocking to feel her skin against his.

He couldn't remember the last time the two of them had been alone together. Her profile was softer in the moonlight. What appeared unassailable in the sober hours now looked fragile. She'd never let him close enough to see the craquelure of her true self.

Was this what Nate loved about her? Tom wondered. Was there something in the way she was flawed that made him feel whole? Did he think he was holding her together? Did they keep each other from shattering?

"You were angry in there," she said. "I've never seen you like that. Wouldn't have thought you had it in you."

"People are full of surprises."

"Nate would say that."

"I'm sorry, though—about what I said. I didn't mean—"

"Don't apologize." She turned around, leaning against the railing to face him. "You'll ruin it. We're all changing. We're growing up. That's a good thing."

"Maybe I don't want to change so much. I like things the way they are."

"You should be able to call someone on being a bitch when she's acting like one. You don't have to be Mister Nice Guy all the time. People love Nate because he does what he wants. He's himself, and no one else and nothing can stop him. Wouldn't it be nice to stop worrying about what people think and do what you want? Just once?"

She cupped Tom between his legs with one manicured hand, and the breath went out of him. Her fingers kneaded his shorts and Tom seemed to look down upon himself from a great height.

She grabbed his hand and placed it on her right breast.

He held it there loosely, as if moving even a fingertip might rupture it.

"Squeeze it. Feel it," she said.

He did. They were heavier than Emma's, her nipple thick and hard. Nerve endings from his palm to his brain caught fire and blazed away.

She moved his other hand onto her other breast. "I'm beautiful, Tom."

He knew this. It was undeniable.

She clenched him hard enough for him to jump. "Don't you want it?"

"No." His voice was only a breath louder than a whisper because he wasn't sure. Maybe he did.

"You should," she sighed into his ear.

Tom knew he had to pull away from her, but he couldn't. "Nate," he gasped. She was squeezing him so hard. "He would totally—"

"But this is all about Nate," she said.

He didn't understand.

She was close enough now that her lips grazed his ear. "Because being with me is the closest you'll ever get to being with him."

Tom took her words. He parsed and split and reassembled them into every meaning he could conjure. He stared at her smirking face. Her laughing eyes and her mocking lips. Hate soaked him like a plunge into ice water. He shuddered under the touch of this creature. This monster.

His hands were still on her breasts. Without thinking, he pushed her away with all of his strength.

She was through the railing and halfway to the water before either of them remembered to scream.

Fourteen

I called for her. I *screamed* for her, but she didn't answer. I ran down to the undercroft, opened the launch, and jumped in the water, but it was so dark I couldn't see my own hands. I swam and dove for as long as I could but I couldn't find her. I kept calling for her, but she must have hit her head against the pilings. I didn't mean to. I swear to God I didn't. But I know it doesn't matter what I meant."

Nate could not find words. The man in front of him looked like his Tom, but this didn't make sense, because how could his Tom have killed Lucy?

Tom took his gun from its holster. The room was dark, and the pistol was a wedge of obsidian.

"I tried to do it before." He looked at the gun cradled in his hand. "I thought about it so many times."

"Tom." All other words were still lost to him.

Tom dropped the weapon into Nate's hand. In his palm it felt heavy and cold and alive.

"Do it, Nate. That's why you came back here, wasn't it? To find out who killed Lucy and make them pay? The equations of pain have to be balanced. Murder makes it easy math."

Nate lagged behind the scene like thunder from distant lightning. He tried to see what Tom had seen. He tried to reconcile this with the countless ways in which he'd imagined their graduation night unrolling and with what he'd learned from the chief's files. When Tom's words filtered through the maelstrom of his mind in a way that he actually understood, he tossed the gun onto the couch like it was on fire. "I'm not going to kill you, Tom. Christ. What's the matter with you?"

"Dad must already have all the evidence somewhere in that closet. Jesus, maybe he's known this whole time!" Tom went to retrieve the gun. "You'd be doing me a favor. You don't know what it's been like, Nate. You can't imagine. And the equations of pain. You always said that—"

"Listen, Tom—"

"*You listen to me!*" Tom screamed. He threw himself into Nate, pushing him hard enough to send Nate's elbow through drywall. The bottle of bourbon shattered against the floor.

"Tom." Nate heard something dangerous in his voice. It was a tone that should have warned his friend away, but then it might have been exactly what Tom hoped to hear.

Tom threw a punch, and Nate caught it with his palm. He twisted his friend into a choke hold and they both fell backward onto the coffee table, snapping two of its legs. Books and empty beer bottles crashed with them to the carpet.

"Stop it, Tom."

Tom kicked at the air and sent the TV stand careening. The flat-screen tumbled and then broke against the floor. He jabbed backward with his elbows at Nate. The two of them struggled in a tangle on the shard-spangled floor, and it became hard to remember who was trying to hurt whom.

Tom had a few pounds on him, but Nate had strength and lever-age on his side. He pinned his friend's arms down and let him kick and writhe and yell.

Medea battered the windows as Tom slowly exhausted himself.

Even after his body went limp, Nate held him tight. The birdcage of Tom's chest heaved in his grip. "You didn't kill her," Nate said, now sure that Tom could hear him.

"I *did*," he panted. "I *told you*—"

"You said you couldn't find her. But someone hid her in the head-lands."

Tom hesitated. "Someone must have found her body along the shore and panicked. They hid her so no one would blame them. It doesn't matter how she got to the headlands. What matters is who killed her in the first place."

"She didn't drown, Tommy. She didn't hit her head. She was strangled." Nate loosened his grip and nudged Tom off him.

"Maybe I strangled her, too. Maybe I put my hands around her neck and squeezed right before I pushed her into the lake. I don't know. I was so goddamned mad, Nate, I could have done anything. And MEs can get things wrong. Especially if the remains have been in the wild for so many—"

"She was raped. Her underwear was torn and stained with blood and semen. Did you rape her, Tom? Did you brutalize her so badly that you broke both of her wrists? Would you remember something like that?"

"What? What are you talking about?"

"Someone raped her, strangled her, then hid her body in a place where she wouldn't be found for a long time. And that person wasn't you. It wasn't."

"You're lying."

"I'm not. Her postmortem report's in the locked closet in your dad's office. Read it yourself. Your birth date's the pass code."

They lay on the floor in silence for what felt like a long time. Thun-der shook the windows in their frames, and rain drummed their glass.

Tom's eyes were wet, his eyes wide, his forehead creased. This morning, Nate would never have guessed Tom could keep a secret like this for so many years. It must have festered inside him like a malignant growth. No wonder he'd lasted only a semester at NYU.

Tom finally broke the silence with a noise like he himself was being choked. His body started to shake, and he rolled into Nate's shoulder. He sobbed into Nate's suit and the filthy carpet.

For fourteen years, Tom had been punishing himself for something he hadn't done. He wept himself dry.

We are all strangers, Nate thought. *Even to ourselves.*

The walls glowed and dimmed. Through the windows, Nate watched Medea's layers spiral across the sky. The shadows around the room shifted and deepened. Nate thought about how he'd gotten here, onto this stained carpet with the wreckage of his best friend beside him.

It'd be easy to stay here and wait for the hurricane to pass. But the real storm that plagued the Lake wasn't the sort that would dissipate on its own. Taped windows and sandbagged doors wouldn't be enough to keep the ones who mattered to him safe.

"I've got to go, Tommy."

"Where?" Tom's voice was small and muffled by Nate's sleeve.

"Things to do."

"Adam Decker?"

"I guess."

"It wasn't him." Tom pulled his face away from Nate's suit jacket. "He lied to my dad about where he was. That's why his statement didn't check out. He was with Emma. He knew we were dating, and he didn't want to tell Dad she cheated on me."

"How do you know?"

"She told me before I left for school. It was a onetime thing. He was all messed up after the fight, and I guess she felt bad for him. She was drunk and used to have a crush on him."

"You're sure?" This wasn't at all what Nate wanted to hear.

"It wasn't Adam."

There would have been such pleasing symmetry to linking his old enemy to Lucy's murder. Finding out that Adam had lied in his police statements had given Nate direction, and now he was back to where he started. He got up, brushed the dirt, lint, and fragments of glass from his pants and jacket, and slid into his raincoat.

"Where're you going?"

"People to see, Tommy. Places to go." Secrets to find.

"I'll go with you." Tom started to get up.

"Not this time." Nate knew where he had to go, and he had to go there alone. He picked Tom's phone off the floor and tossed it to him. Its screen blinked with texts and missed calls. "The Lake needs you."

Tom sat amid the broken and sparkling ruins of his living room and stared up at him. Nate wondered what Tom saw when he looked at him. Did he see his friend, or did he see the Storm King? Did he see someone to love or someone to fear?

"I'll have my phone if you need me," Tom said.

"Okay." Nate didn't remind him that his own phone was dead. He stepped over the shattered coffee table and past the kitchen to the front door. With a turn of the door handle, the wind burst into the room. The rain had let up for now, but the sky was a fury of thunderheads. Branches tumbled across lawns, and dead leaves swarmed like locusts above fallen trees.

Tom had followed Nate to the door. Nate handed over the car keys he'd pocketed. In the storm light, Tom's eyes were bloodshot, his skin a patchwork of flush and pallor. But his voice was the same as it'd always been.

"Be careful," he said.

Fifteen

This was supposed to be the lull in the hurricane, but Medea still dismembered Nate's umbrella within minutes, pinwheeling its cap down the street like a tumbleweed. He shivered within the carapace of his raincoat as the storm lashed him.

Fallen trees, downed power lines, and the barrage of the gale made his trek to the water's edge twice its fair-weather length.

In her hospital in Gracefield, Grams was cut off.

Without his phone, Meg and Livvy were unreachable.

But shrunk in her casket, Lucy was less lost than she'd been. The fractures of their graduation night had shifted, and new gaps in its story were exposed. These would have to be delved into no matter where they took him. No matter what they revealed. The way out was the way through.

Tom's secret had unnerved Nate. Of everyone from the old days, he'd thought Tom was the one he could most count on.

What else had he gotten wrong?

The problem was that people were capable of anything. Horrors and virtues churned inside us, and to know which of these trumped the others at any moment would be to sense every texture of the future. Nate used to know this.

Translucent dapplings of purple and red petals covered the base of the Night Ship's barricade like fragments of a destroyed mosaic. The deluge had displaced husks of dead glow sticks from the children's shrine. They bobbed in troughs of water that swelled above an overflowing storm drain.

If Emma was with Adam back on graduation night, then Nate's old enemy had an alibi. The files in the chief's closet might hold clues to other suspects, but Nate would need Tom to go back there, and his friend was currently in no such condition.

This left only one place for Nate to look for the answers he needed.

His wingtips slipped and skidded as he scaled the barricade. The old wood was soft under his feet. More of the pier's planks had fallen away since Nate had last been there. The boardwalk was as buckled and gapped as a brawler's smile. The season had brought slick moss to its boards, so he took his time crossing it. He still didn't like the lake.

The froth of the gray water resembled fins and spines of creatures thrashing just below its surface. It was a longer walk than he remembered. The hurricane, his exhaustion, the events of the morning, and the way memories of the past bled into the present gave the world a hypnagogic quality. Nate imagined walking these broken planks across the decades. Into not only his own past, but the history of the Night Ship itself. Back to the bloody days of old Morton Strong. Back to the cruel heart of Just June's Century Room. Into whatever terror struck Lucy in her last moment. Walking to the Night Ship was to be caught in a purgatory between land and sea, history and future, suspicion and knowing, without ever getting an inch closer to home.

Then he was there, in front of the warped and broken door to the Night Ship's promenade.

The hall was a cacophony of dripping water, whispering drafts, and all the familiar echoes of the ruined place. The old pier's damp, rot-steeped air embraced Nate like he was its own wayward son. He hadn't been here since the day Lucy had vanished.

That morning, Tom had pulled Nate from the lake. Dragged him to the boat launch as if he were himself a drowned body. Every bit of energy Nate possessed had been spent diving and screaming for Lucy. Tom was able to heave him onto the launch's steps only when Nate had nothing left.

He remembered some things with intense clarity: the chill of the lake on his skin, the sway of the canoe beneath him, the look on Johnny's face when he first saw him.

After hauling Nate to the launch, Tom had made him wait in the boat as he loaded it up with the lanterns, sleeping bags, and coolers they'd kept at the pier. Dawn had fully broken by then, but light never reached the waters under the Night Ship. Nate stayed in the canoe, clutching the wet kimono wrap, staring at the ink-black surface of the lake, willing Lucy to emerge and knowing with absolute certainty that she would not.

Once Tom gathered their things, he paddled them back to the Vanhoutens' dock. He seated Nate in the gazebo while he woke Johnny. When the chief returned to pick them up, Tom spun a story about how they'd decided to search the shore with the canoe, just in case, and that's when they'd found the kimono wrap. The official account of the disappearance of Lucy Bennett began.

Knowing Tom's secret now, Nate marveled at how composed his friend had seemed. Tom thought he'd killed his best friend's girlfriend just hours earlier, and there he was, lying to everyone and covering his own tracks with the talent of Greystone Lake's villains of lore.

We are truly wonders.

The shrouded sky allowed a faint glow into the interior. Wreckage from the abandoned shops and cafés that flanked the promenade littered the place like grave markers. Nate expected it to feel strange to return here after so much time. He thought he might notice something different with his older eyes, but the promenade looked and smelled and felt the same. Impossibly so. Being there felt as familiar as if he'd walked this hall this morning and every morning that had preceded it. There was something immutable about this place. In the last age, when the world turned to ash, he could believe the Night Ship would endure, still groaning under the burden of its secrets.

But Nate revised this fantasy when he reached the sign with the galleon speeding for the harvest moon. The doors to the old nightclub were warped to the same spare width they'd always been stuck, but a spike of bloody light from the interior lanced the shadows of the hall.

Nate slipped inside. A lantern was lit on the corner of the bar, its glow muted by a scrim of red fabric. The dusty dance floor had been swept clean and was studded with neatly organized piles of gear. Coolers, cooking supplies, sleeping bags, books, and bottled water, their shadows casting totem silhouettes against the peeling crimson walls.

"Took you long enough."

A lean shadow separated itself from the threshold of the velvet-cloaked staircase.

"James." Of course these vandals had made the Night Ship their home. "Long time."

"Where's Pete?"

The missing boy. "I don't know," Nate answered.

"Did you kill Maura?" The thin young man paced the edge of the dance floor, his gaze never straying from Nate. Nate had known James as a boy, but not well. He and Lucy both had good reasons to keep their romantic and family lives separate. The odd light and broad shadows of the room gave the bones in the young man's face a delicate geometry.

"No."

James wheeled on him. "Lucy?"

"No." Nate had questions for James, too. Just the sight of the young man in this place made the thing inside of him wrench itself with blood hunger. Grams was in an ICU, and there was no question this boy was somehow responsible. But the circumstances required the finesse of a surgeon, not the black rage of the Storm King.

"She said you were a good liar."

"Lucy told you that?"

"She told us everything."

"I doubt it. You were what, five years old?"

James circled around the far end of the bar, careful to keep his distance from Nate. His face shone like a stoplight in the lantern's glow. Nate heard him open a cupboard or a drawer, and a moment later he dumped a thick stack of documents fastened with binder clips onto the scratched bar. The packets slid across the black wood like a deck of cards.

Nate approached the bar and picked up the first sheath of paper. As he did, James backed away. As though they were two magnets with the same polarity, an invisible barrier repelled the young man.

The pages of the document were filled with lines of strong, confident script. Nate flipped through enough of them to be sure. They were photocopies of Lucy's journal entries. From the heft of the packets strewn across the bar, Nate guessed these were the complete contents of the journals the chief had shown him this morning.

These journals were how James and the others had learned about the Storm King, the Thunder Runs, and all of Lucy's high school friends and enemies. This was how they'd made their list of suspects, and this was how their list of suspects became a list of targets.

"The chief gave you odd jobs at the station, and you thank him by ransacking the evidence room."

"They weren't *in* evidence. It was a cover-up from the start. The guy spent the last fourteen years trying to convince Mom that Lucy'd run away. Guess where he came up with that 'goodbye note' she left?" James jutted his chin at the pages spread across the scarred bar. "You know how it wasn't dated? That's because the chief trimmed the top of the page to get rid of it. Luce wrote it *over a year* before she disappeared. It's from right after that douchebag Decker emailed the whole planet those pics."

"How do you know?" Nate had to ask, though he believed it. That note had never felt right to him. Yesterday, he wouldn't have thought the chief capable of fabricating evidence, but now he knew better.

"The original's missing a page. Six notebooks filled, and only one torn-out page. Right between the entries for November thirtieth and December second. The tear matches the edge of the note. The chief didn't tell anyone he found the journals, then he read through them, found that note, and thought: Hey, here's a neat way to avoid investigating my son and his best friends for murder. He sold that whole runaway line of bullshit to Mom right up till those tourists found her body." James's voice rose with each sentence. "I worked at that place for months before I found them. Making their coffee, filing their transcripts." The Bennett family resemblance extended beyond coloring and cheekbones. The look on his face was pure loathing.

" 'Months'? It took me five minutes to find his secret stash of research, and that included breaking the pass code to the door it was locked behind."

"What, you want a round of applause?"

"Everything you know came from these?" Nate held up the sheath of paper.

"That packet's a copy of her last notebook. His notes said the rest were in her room, but the chief found that one right here. Read the last entry."

Lucy's script was larger in the packet's last pages. It listed with a drunken slant unbound by the ruled lines.

Sometimes I don't know if I can do it anymore and be everything he wants me to be all the time.

"Out loud."

Nate almost lunged for the boy then. He was no one's performing monkey and never had been. James was younger, but Nate had

always been fast. Catch James, and he'd find out everything the vandals knew. Catch James, and the game was over.

"Why are you smiling?" James asked.

A note of fear crept into the boy's voice. For now, this was enough
to sate the beast inside Nate. When he read the entry aloud it was an
act of magnanimity and not of submission.

*So am I using him, or is he using me? Is that what love is—two
people using each other? . . .*

*I could leave Nate, and no one would care because in the normal
world this happens all the time. No one would skewer me with dirty
looks from across the street or tell the twins what a legendary bitch
their sister is. I think I could be kind if I wanted to be. I think I could
be just about anything if I could just be free. . . .*

He didn't let his voice falter, though it wanted to.

*Nate didn't look at me while he hacked away at Adam, but he
did when he was finished. And Christ, his face. That way he smiles
like a wolf. All teeth. I've seen that look before, but he's never used it
on me. Not ever. It's different when those ice-cold eyes are on you. So
I ran. Because I know Nate isn't really there when he's like this. He's
something else, and whatever that thing is, it scares me. I think it
scares everyone. . . .*

The last words made him shiver.

Someone's coming.

Now that he finally knew what had happened to Lucy, they were
pure horror.

Someone's coming.

"I told you. We know everything," James said. If looks could
kill, the boy's snarl alone would have been dismembering.

"Everything. Right. Except for the one thing that actually matters." Nate tossed the packet back onto the bar with the others. He
dialed up the disgust. He had to, because despair was the only other
option. "So what's the plan? You terrorize everyone whose name
shows up in Lucy's journals and . . . what?"

"One of you killed her."

"Maybe. And?"

"And?" James spat out. Rage made his face ugly. "And you have to be punished!"

Nate wanted James to have a plan. He'd hoped that it was some masterful conspiracy hatched after fourteen years of plotting that had landed Grams an inch from death.

But James was no Storm King.

For the first time since Lucy's remains had been discovered, Nate contemplated a future in which he never found out who'd murdered her. James was right that the players she'd written about in her journals were the most likely suspects, but it could have been someone else. A total stranger. You only had to pick up a newspaper to know that in a universe that stacked chance upon chance, death could find you anywhere.

James still stared at him. Had he said something? Nate wondered. He saw the ivory-knuckled fury in the boy's fists and felt the furnace of his gaze. Lucy, Maura Jeffers, Grams, Pete Corso: The equations of pain were grotesquely out of balance. Of course James was angry.

Nate detected movement behind him, to both his left and right. Shadows skulked toward him across the scuffed floor. Medea and the gnashing of the furious lake must have covered their footsteps as they crept up from the undercroft or down from the Century Room.

Nate took a step back. The short kid built like a fireplug, the goth girl, the pale towheaded boy. This was the strange tribe from Lucy's funeral. As they neared the lantern's aura, Nate saw baseball bats, wooden planks, and pikes of rebar clutched in their young hands. In the blood-tinged light, the vandals' faces looked like slabs of meat in an abattoir.

"Not too close." James waved the others away as if Nate were a rabid beast. "Not till I say."

Nate reconsidered the young man. He *did* have a plan.

"What'd you do to Pete?" James asked again.

"I told you—"

"They were supposed to tag your house last night. Now Maura's dead and Pete's missing. We cruised Bonaparte Street this morning and what'd we see, Carlos?"

The stout boy took one cautious step into the perimeter of red light. He held the rebar toward Nate like an exorcist brandishing a cross. "Nothing?"

"That's right. Nothing. They never tagged your house, which means they never got by you. Which means you *did something to them.*"

The goth girl took a step closer, the scarlet glow of the lantern lighting the moon of her face like a Christmas ornament. The plank she carried was spiked with nails.

They were psyching themselves up to do something. Something Nate was certain to find unpleasant. They had the numbers and the weapons. At the moment it was only courage that they lacked, and James buttressed this with each word.

Would they beat him? Shatter his surgeon's hands? Kill him? In the halls of the Night Ship above the raging lake inside the livid hurricane, anything seemed possible.

Then Nate spotted her, loitering behind the others. Gone was the confident bartender who'd slipped him a pint the day before. This was an ashen vestige of that girl. One look and he knew what she'd done. A part of him had known all along.

"Hello again, Tara Jane."

"No one calls me that." She muttered the words to the floor. Guilt rang from her like the note from a struck bell.

"She's going to die, Tara." His eyes wanted to well, and he let them. Let these children see the Storm King cry and see if that got him anywhere.

"Who?" But she knew. She was different from her twin brother and older sister. She didn't have their marble faces and frosted armor.

"Wasn't she good to you, Tara? My grandmother?" It made sense that whoever set the fire at the pub had access to the place.

"Stop talking to her," James said.

"She gave you a job, didn't she? She gave you a chance when no one else would."

"She wasn't supposed to be there!" Her voice was pure anguish.

"Teej. *Shut up.*" James turned to face his sister.

Nate felt the current of the room shift. Some of the kids began to look unsure.

"There *is* a murderer here," Nate shouted. "But it's not me."

Menace had been gathering speed, but now doubt was ascendant. Nate used the confusion to go for the doors to the boardwalk. Not too fast, not too slow. Confident yet nonthreatening.

"The Union's gone, too, not that it matters," Nate said, as if they were in the middle of the conversation instead of at its end. "You already tore out the heart of that place."

The white-blond boy with the baseball bat stood in front of the doors, but Nate gave him a look that sent him scurrying.

"No one was supposed to get hurt!" Tara was crying now.

"*Teej,* for Chrissake."

Nate seized the opportunity to slip out the exit. The teens had the strength to stop him but still lacked the nerve. They weren't following him, either. This didn't surprise him. The Night Ship was its own universe with its own rules. Things that felt inevitable there might become unthinkable in the fresh air of the living world.

Still, he quickened his pace on the boardwalk along the northern side of the pier. This section of the pier had always gotten the worst of the weather, and the years had taken their toll. The wood creaked ominously underfoot, and Nate soon reached a stretch where an entire stride's worth of planks were missing.

He girded himself and jumped across the gap. The plank he landed on cracked in protest, but he was quick to keep moving.

The rain had picked up again, and the wind was a mounting scream through the Night Ship's spires. Across the savage waters, the headland's peaks were devoured by clouds.

James could still rally the others through the promenade to intercept Nate, so it was important for him to hurry. But then he saw something that rooted him to the warped wood.

There was a body in the lake. He saw the black cap of a head and the dark outlines of legs and arms tossed by the furious waters only a few dozen feet from him. His first thought was of Lucy—which was impossible—and his second thought was of Pete Corso. *The lake returns what it takes.*

Then Nate realized that the person in the water wasn't lifelessly bobbing. They were swimming. In the lake. In the middle of a hurricane. He watched the figure complete a half dozen strokes before he could believe his eyes. The body was slight, but there was something feminine in what he could see of the hips. Her limbs and head were dark because that was the color of the dry suit she wore as she cut an expert wake across the water toward a patch of shore close to the northern boundary of the town.

Back-plotting her trajectory led Nate to believe that the swimmer had exited the Night Ship through the boat launch in the undercroft.

Nate couldn't imagine anyone he knew swimming through such weather. There was no chance it was a member of James's crew.

This was someone else. Someone not in Lucy's journals or in the chief's files or on James's hit list. Someone new. Nate was sure of it.

It was reckless to run across the fragile boardwalk, but Nate did it anyway.

Sixteen

Medea kicked spindrifts of water at Nate as he darted along the shore.

Few of the Strand's homes were north of the Night Ship, but he ran through the backyard of every one of them as the headlands loomed in the gray distance. It was hard to track the swimmer through the curtains of rain and the whitecaps of the tempestuous lake. Just when he thought he'd lost her, a crooked arm of slick black broke the foaming surface.

The figure cut for the shore where the Strand turned from the waterline. Nate watched the swimmer emerge from the lake, her steps almost dainty as they negotiated the swell of surf and treacherous rocks. She shook off the lake's cold water with feline contortions.

His black raincoat and a tangle of frayed juniper hid him as she made her way across the beach. She followed the arc of the Strand as it swung from the water. This was the farthest edge of Greystone Lake. The mountains dominated the northern horizon, and woods grew thick where the residential streets ended. This was the route

Nate's father had driven them that day in April, before he took the turn that switchbacked into the sky.

The Tatum house, the site of their high school graduation party, was located deep along this landward stretch of the Strand. At first, that's where Nate thought the swimmer was going, to that place of so many last moments. But she struck out north long before the turnoff for the Tatums'.

He trailed the woman by a few hundred feet. It seemed like she was leading him into the wild, then he noticed the ghost of a gravel driveway pocked with puddles and broken with thickets of weeds. When he lost sight of her among the trees, he followed the curve of this faded path to reach a decrepit hovel of a place.

This forest abode made Tom's unkempt ranch house look like the Empire Hotel. It was a half step up from a shack: a single-floor construction more like that of a detached garage than a home. Bare patches marred the roof where shingles had migrated elsewhere. Its walls might have once been painted, though Nate could not guess at the color. The browns of rot and greens of growth shaded the house into the palette of the forest as smoothly as a bird's nest. Look at it from the corner of your eye and you could imagine it wasn't there.

He watched it for some minutes before understanding what he'd come here to do.

Nate's feet crunched against bristling undergrowth as he circled the house, but Medea's winds and rains drowned what noise he made. Borders of light glowed from the edges of the rags that covered the windows. There was a battered storm cellar entrance on the rear side of the structure. The handles of its hatch were bound with a rusted length of chain. This place was more than it appeared.

A house like this wasn't supposed to be in a tidy town like Greystone Lake. A swimmer like the one who rattled inside it had no place here. Not even a Daybreaker would be so committed an acolyte to those colorless waters. Who was she?

The question sent a shiver of hope up his spine.

He'd left Lucy's funeral little more than an hour ago, but was there a chance there'd been a mistake? Could the tests they'd used to identify the body have somehow been wrong? The odds of this were infinitesimal. But maybe it wasn't impossible. So little was *impossible*. Greystone Lake itself had taught Nate that.

The storm cellar's door was warped and splintered. Nate braced his foot against the hatch, then pulled and twisted one of its handles until it tore from the rotted wood. He tossed it aside and threw open the door. Medea devoured his every sound. The air that billowed from the entry smelled of incense and extinguished candles: church and street fairs, holidays and mysteries.

He descended into the cellar with only the wild sky's meager light to find his way. A short flight of steps brought him to what felt like an uneven floor of packed earth.

Nate stumbled against something and sensed objects stacked like columns in the dark. Medea's winds followed him through the hatch, bumping him from behind. A flock of papers danced around his feet, and the room's contents swayed in the gale.

He didn't get more than a few yards deeper into the basement when one of its many piles crashed across his path and sent another one tottering. Unless he wanted the room reduced to utter wreckage, Nate had to close the hatch.

As he backtracked to reseal the entrance, he glanced down at the steps. What he saw froze his hand in the searing air. One of the papers skirting his feet had wrapped itself around his shin—an envelope dyed a shade of red so dark it could be mistaken for black.

Somewhere deeper within the cellar came the rattle and creak of a warped door being opened. Light blazed into the claustrophobic space.

In a story worthy of the Lake, the burst of illumination would have been that of a lantern, as if they were in the seventeenth century and not the twenty-first. The woman holding that light would be none other than his lost Lucy.

But the shock of light came from a set of bare bulbs that studded the ceiling. And the person who'd flicked their switch was a woman as old as the mountains. She had a wiry plume of gray hair that stuck from her head like the tail of a diving whale. He hadn't recognized her under the cap of the dry suit, but that mess of hair was unmistakable. She was the same woman who'd accosted him on the street outside the Empire the night before. She was dressed in a garment that might once have been a bathrobe.

Nate wondered how much of his idiotic fantasy that Lucy was still alive could be blamed on the head trauma. Or was it just this place? This town and how its every street and structure was poisoned with futures that would never happen.

"You." The woman's voice was a rustle compared to the roar she'd leveled at him during their earlier encounter. Bewilderment stood where anger had been.

Now that the space was lit, Nate saw black-red envelopes scattered across the dirt floor. Dozens of them. Hundreds. Piles of clothes and books and papers and boxes clotted the tight cellar, and the black-red envelopes stood out like crime scene splatter.

"Where did you get this?" Nate waved the black-red envelope at her. As if he wasn't the one who'd just broken into her home. He still had his grandparents' invitation to the Night Ship's 1964 Independence Day party in his jacket pocket, and he pulled it out to compare the two. The envelopes were identical, their color was inimitable. Blood when it's starved for oxygen.

"It's mine!" She snatched the empty one from him and pawed at the others strewn across the floor.

"Who are you?" Nate asked.

"You're in *my* house." The woman looked up from the ground to squint at him. "Get out of here. Go back to where you came from."

Over the woman's shoulder, a piece of paper was taped to the cinder block wall.

Mama was supposed to kill us, but she didn't.
Mama was supposed to kill us, but she couldn't.
Mama was supposed to kill us, and she should have.

The woman followed Nate's gaze to the odd note and snatched it off the wall with the speed of a cracking whip. She crumpled it into a ball and glared at Nate. "Get out, or I'll call the police."

Nate squared his shoulders. The basement stank of fear, and it wasn't his. He recognized something familiar in the woman's face. Something beyond the knotted hair and leather countenance.

"Do I know you?"

The woman snorted. She trudged past him to close the exterior hatch. With Medea banished, the tight space became close and quiet.

The woman's presence tugged at something deep inside the archives of his mind. He flipped through faces in his head. She wasn't a teacher or a store owner or the grandmother of a childhood friend. "How do I know you?"

"Who says you do?"

"You knew me well enough to yell at me last night outside the Empire." Even then, Nate had sensed something when he'd looked at her.

"Kids never saw me. Even when I wanted them to. And I wasn't ever there except after hours." She picked at the floor, collecting the black-red envelopes and tsking at their every crease and blemish. "You did your clubs—yearbook and newspaper and model UN and what have you—but stopped with the sports after what happened to your arm. Never saw me save a half dozen times in four years. Even then you didn't see me. Didn't see any of us, I bet. The invisible people."

"You were a janitor at the high school."

The woman shot upright in shock, as if she'd forgotten that she'd been speaking aloud. She muttered something Nate didn't catch and continued her gathering.

"What's your name?"

"Names, names. Everyone asks for names. It isn't what you're called that matters, it's what you *do* that counts. Bea told me that herself."

"'Bea'?" Now Nate was the surprised one. "Beatrice McHale? My grandmother?"

The woman looked at him, and the folds of her face moved in a way that was impossible to read.

"Bea's a strong woman. Someone that strong can change the world. You could've changed the world, too, boy. And you have, haven't you? But for better or worse?"

"I'm an oncologic surgeon," Nate said. He didn't understand why this woman was talking about his grandmother any more than he understood this impulse to justify himself. "I help people every day."

"You didn't always," the woman said. "One bad thing grows upon another, doesn't it? How much pain did you plant those years ago? What will the harvest be?"

Nate remembered how the lady had berated him the night before. "What did you mean when you told me that I ruined everything?"

"Now that I see your eyes, I wonder about you all over again. Maybe I shouldn't have said that. Maybe it really is never too late to be good."

"What's your name?" he asked again.

"Been called all sorts of things. But the best name I've had is May. One of the two prettiest months." Her lips twinged into a smile that might once have been sweet.

"'May.'" The woman was so unkempt that it was hard to narrow her age. She might have been a sun-damaged sixty or a miraculously fit ninety. But the black-red envelopes around the room were the same ones the Night Ship had used to mail their invitations. "Like May and June. The Night Ship Girls. Are you telling me that you're Just June's sister?" To someone from the Lake, meeting Just June's sister was like stumbling upon a unicorn.

There was something else in the woman's smile now, and it helped Nate see the beauty hiding within her face.

"You're supposed to be dead. In all the stories they say that—"

"*'Stories.'*" The woman snorted again. "Here's a town where even adults believe in fairy tales."

Morton Strong, Just June, the Boy Who Fell. The Lake loved its myths. Nate knew from experience that you didn't want to be a character in one of them.

"My whole life is made of stories."

"But what *kind* of story?" She pointed to the far end of the basement. Her swim must have limbered her muscles, but her gait aged as they cooled. Her steps to the rear of the cellar were mincing.

The back wall was a mess of newspaper articles and photos and drawings. Here was the collage of obsessive insanity Nate had been prepared to find in the chief's closet. The lair of a TV serial killer or the walls of a crime procedural situation room. Lines of red string branched in radiating webs that sprang from a single point, rippling across the walls like a cat's cradle played among a nest of spiders.

The woman picked at the wind-thrown magazines and clothes while Nate inched closer to the point of origin to which all the strings and images could be traced.

The item in the center of the wall was so yellowed with age and so thickly covered with red string that he could barely make out the headline of the newspaper clipping.

SOLE SURVIVOR OF HEADLANDS ACCIDENT

Under and to the right of the headline, he could see the face of a boy from the top of his mouth to the shock of his dark hair. Nate felt the blood rush from his head. The cellar was cold, but he felt sweat prick across his arms.

"Why?" His breath became short as his chest tightened. "How?"

"Sit, Nate." The woman was again right beside him. "I'll tell you everything. Everything I can."

Nate's body acquired the gravity of a larger, denser world. He fell onto a pile of lumpy upholstery. "What is this?" he asked. He stared at his picture and the wall of paper and images and string as if it was an oncoming train.

"It's like you said, boy. A story. But to get to the end, you need to understand the beginning."

THE NIGHT SHIP
GIRLS

THE LAKE BROKE red and gold as the sky wept its sparks.

Fireworks launched from Blind Down Island cracked the summer night. This was the lake's magic hour. Its one time a year when every rainbow shade gleamed across its undulating skin.

The lake returns what it takes, yet did anyone but June notice that it never revealed anything of itself? Its waters were as vacant as a mirror, only reflecting the sights that dazzled above it. Armies of leviathans might assemble an inch below its surface, and the children who blazed its shore with sparklers and the revelers who pranced in their Night Ship silks would never see them coming.

"Boss needs a refill, Junebug."

Carl ran the kitchen. He had the gut of a circus strongman and a face like an exploded engine, but he was always good to June. The girls snickered at her and poked fun at May, but Carl was like an uncle to the twins. He was family, just like the Night Ship was home. Now they had to leave it all behind.

Strong was as particular about his beverages as he was about everything else. A special concoction of liquors, herbs, exotic fruits, and expensive vintages filled a silver punch bowl custom-made for his personal use. Old Morton entertained the VIPs in the Century Room. But no matter with whom he dined, this rich brew was rarely shared.

The Harlot Queen herself pranced up to her with the boss's empty bowl and dropped it next to where June was slicing strawberries for the baked Alaska platters. Garters barely concealed under a silk chemise, black heels half as high as the Night Ship's spires, an ostrich feather–plumed fascinator pinned to a froth of golden hair. "Don't get your filthy prints on it," Scarlet said. June had seen her papers and knew her real name was Doris. She'd loosed this little nugget to the most gossipy of the whores, and scarlet, too, had been the wench's rage.

She'd replaced June as Strong's second. She was as beautiful as June had been but hadn't an eighth the gray matter. June suspected old Strong was going soft in the noggin himself. Anyone could see Scarlet was a poor substitute, but while June had shared Strong's calculation and ruthlessness, Scarlet shared his bed.

She was sure Scarlet's whispers and pouts had much to do with the fact that the twins would soon have to light out for territories unknown.

The harlot cocked her head at June, daring her to say something smart. The girl had no concept of the game they played. She wouldn't have understood the rules if June had written them out then read them aloud. June cracked a smile as sweet as the meringue that baked nearby. She held it until Scarlet tossed her head and sauntered back through the doors that swung out to the dance floor.

Any one of the litany of humiliations June had recently sustained might have slumped her into melancholy, but she wasn't built for brooding. Instead she stoked the fire within her into an inferno.

Strong believed that turning the twins out on their behinds was a solution, but June intended for it to be just the beginning of his problems.

"Have you seen the women's dresses, June?" May bubbled into

the room all skips and smiles. Not done up like the whores, she wore the same black pencil skirt and crimson blouse as June. They were the Night Ship Girls, and this was their costume. Regardless of their being on the brink of exile, Strong enjoyed the idea of identicals walking around. Other than the filthy apron fastened to June, the only visible difference between them was that May had a smile where June kept a frown. May adored the Fourth, and Strong let her walk around with a tray of canapés for the guests. "There's this one the exact shade of Mama's favorite lipstick."

May mentioned Mama at the slightest provocation. It'd been five years since she'd sickened and died. It'd left a hole in both of them, but May filled hers with fond remembrances, while June dug hers deeper with regrets and recriminations. *If Strong had sent for the doctor sooner. If the air of the undercroft weren't so damp. If she'd noticed the blood Mama hid in her handkerchief when she coughed.*

"And you won't believe the sparklers and candles!"

"They're the same every year, May."

"But you *must* see them. They're the most beautiful things."

"I will, dearest."

"Do you think Uncle Morton will let us visit next July? It's like something out of *Cinderella* or *Sleeping Beauty,* isn't it? So magical, you'd think anything can happen."

"When the singing woodland creatures show up, find out how they are with a paring knife then send them in here."

"I'll help you, Juney."

"No, dearest. You'll get juice on your blouse, and then they won't want you on the floor." June didn't want May implicated in what happened next. "Listen." She cocked her head as if listening. "I think they're starting the finale—you don't want to miss that."

May's face broke into unfettered delight, and she kissed June on the cheek before scurrying back to the dance floor.

June hoisted Strong's silver bowl to the corner of the kitchen where she'd staged the array of bottles with which she'd already twice refilled the vessel. This batch would have some extra bite.

Carl supervised the baked Alaska as the sous chefs plated a pyramid of cream puffs. Even if they'd been paying attention to June, with her back to the rest of the kitchen no one could see what she was doing.

The cognacs first, followed by some bitters and a bottle of Dom Pérignon and a dash of Château Margaux. Bénédictine DOM and Sazerac Rye. Two sprigs of crushed rosemary, the juice of four blood oranges, paper-thin slices of star fruit.

A dollop of amber honey was next, but antifreeze was nearly as sweet. A can she'd hidden earlier sat in the cabinet at her feet. It was the size of a paint tin; she'd pried its lid open during the party preparations. When she brought it to the counter, the venomous green of the poison brimmed to its lip.

Morton Strong imbibed like others breathed. He had the tolerance of an oil rig worker, but a measure of antifreeze would set even him back a step or two. When Strong had dropped the bomb, he told June that she'd become an embarrassment. June would show him just what embarrassment looked like. A bout of unstoppable nausea among Greystone Lake's finest would do that and more. Strong had grown up in the stinking canyons of the Lower East Side. Among those teeming streets the currency that mattered most was that of respect. Respect won by fear. And no one feared an aging nightclub owner who couldn't hold his liquor.

This was just a taste of what was to come. June had been Strong's right hand for two decades, and she knew, both literally and figuratively, where a great many bodies were buried. She had the rest of Strong's life mapped out for him, and he wasn't going to like its destination.

"Boss's drink ready, Junebug?"

Carl's voice was closer than June expected. It startled her enough to drop the can into the punch bowl. The viscous slurry glossed the silver bowl in its noxious green. June retrieved the can as quickly as she could, but it was wet and slick. More than three-quarters of its contents had been added to the punch. Too much. Far, far too much.

"I still have to add the Courvoisier," June said. She mixed the sludge into the rest of the liquid to hide it, but knew she'd have to make it all over again.

"Sure it's fine as is, sweetness."

June barely had time to drape a dish towel over the can before he was alongside her.

"This deep in, he won't taste a thing anyway." Carl grabbed a handle of the bowl. "I'll have one of the girls take it to him."

"Should at least polish it up first," June said. "You know how he hates smudges."

"You're too good for all of us, Juney," Carl chuckled as he carried the punch bowl away from her. "I'll miss the pair of you, but it's our loss and the world's gain."

"I'll bring it out, Carl," June said. She hurried to catch him. She could stage a fall between here and the dance floor and use that as an excuse to make a fresh batch.

"Boss doesn't want a scullery troll like you with the guests." Scarlet had appeared at the kitchen's swinging doors. "And in that disgusting apron." The whore sneered at June as if she were carrion. As if she were worse than nothing.

"Maybe better to let Scarlet take it," Carl said. "The boss being so particular and all."

June could still stop the punch from making it to the dance floor. If finesse and sycophancy failed her, she could dispense with the pretense and knock the bowl out of Scarlet's hands.

"Any man with two eyes would be particular about *that* serving them," Scarlet said as she took the bowl from Carl.

June could have stopped everything right there, but she didn't. She let Scarlet disappear onto the floor with the gleaming bowl of poison. As the swinging doors shuddered to a close, June caught ever-diminishing glimpses of dancing sparklers and whirling silks. Howling brass and the buzz of conversations warbled and then were muted as the doors settled to a close.

"Taking five, Carl," June said. "Ask one of the boys to fetch May to our room?"

"Sure, June. And don't you listen to Scarlet. You know the type. Can't feel good herself without bringing others low."

"Water off a duck's back." She got on her tiptoes to give the man a peck on the cheek. She realized in that moment that she would not see him again. She wouldn't see any of this again. Allowing that silver bowl to leave her sight made this a certainty.

From the kitchen, she took the staff passage to the undercroft. Footfalls from the dance floor above beat a rhythm through the ceiling. Beneath the bandstand, the bass shook June's bones to the marrow.

Once in their room, June pulled two suitcases from the closet, then went for the loose plank in the wall next to May's bed. A fair amount of cash had flowed through the Night Ship in June's day, and she wasn't a dummy by a long shot: She'd skimmed her share. From the secret stash, Benjamin Franklin stared back at her in astounding multitudes.

She used a straight razor to slit the linings of the suitcases and fed the thousands into them as if they were satin piggy banks. The stacks sagged in uneven lumps. June loathed sloppiness, but she didn't have time for a more thorough job. A glance at the clock told her she'd left the kitchen over twenty minutes ago. Carl would cover for her, but eventually someone would come looking. But being discovered in mid-escape wasn't her biggest concern. Once that silver bowl had been sent on its way to Strong another kind of countdown had begun.

A few quick stitches resealed the suitcase linings, then she began emptying entire drawers into the bags.

"June, you're not even folding," May said from the doorway. "Mama would have folded first."

"Close the door, dearest. I have a surprise for you."

"A surprise?" May's face lit up like the lake at dawn.

"A trip. A vacation, just like we always talked about."

"To where?"

"Wherever you like."

"The city? Oh, or the islands? Or maybe California!"

"All those places. But we need to go tonight. We need to go now."

They'd have to keep moving. For a while, at least. But maybe forever. This was the path June had committed them to once she let that bowl leave the kitchen.

"In the middle of the party? How will we say goodbye?"

There was a noise upstairs. A scream that held a single note like the clear blast from a trumpet.

"We'll send them postcards. One for each place we go. Help me, now. Fetch our shoes. We can sort them later."

"Maybe we can go to the city first. I'd like to see Broadway, where Mama danced. They say you can see the lights for miles. I bet you can see them from the moon."

Upstairs, the music came to a halt like a crashing train. Now the screaming was impossible to miss. In the sound, June heard more than surprise and disgust. These were keening wails of terror.

May glanced toward the hall. "Someone's hurt." Her face was an amalgamation of uncertainty and concern.

"Stay here, dearest. Get the shoes. May. May!"

May disappeared down the hall.

June started after her, then remembered the suitcases packed with their clothes and lined with their life savings. She forced the bags shut and dragged them to the closet.

A tremendous crash shook the pier, and June couldn't imagine what had caused it. She locked the door to their room and ran down the passageway to the kitchen stairs. The screams were a roar, and she could hear now that they belonged to both women and men. Their cries reverberated through the planks even louder than had the band's music. Water poured in streams down the walls as if the pier had sunk and the lake now sat above it instead of below.

The kitchen was empty when she got there. Faucets ran into the sinks, and smoke billowed from the ovens. June had been in the undercroft for little more than half an hour, but in that time Armageddon had descended upon the Night Ship.

"May!" Panic threatened, but she forced it down. She was Just June. She was queen of this place. She was a terrifying creature to behold, and there was nothing she could not do.

She burst through the kitchen doors into the smoke and shouts of the nightclub.

Tabletops were pillars of flame that clawed for the ceiling. Blazing curtains wreathed the windows in fire. There were bodies, too. Crowds were packed as tight as herded animals at either end of the club. Three women and a man lay in the center of the dance floor vomiting onto the black planks as the bright curves of fish flapped around them like bacon on a skillet. June could only assume that Strong had shared his special punch after all.

A man and woman were stooped over an elderly gentleman in the throes of a seizure. Alone among the guests, this couple tried to help. They protected the convulsing man from the violence of his own limbs, while the rest of the guests tore at each other to get to the exits.

The sparklers and candle centerpieces must have toppled and begun the fires that triggered the panic. Apparently, in their frenzy to escape, the crowd had also destroyed the club's immense aquarium.

The stampede for the doors had left a trail of men and women trampled amid shattered glass and wrecked furniture. Legs were buckled at unreal angles and rib cages rendered concave.

Looking at their broken bodies, June's fear crested and then overwhelmed everything else. She screamed for her sister, but her voice was lost in the bedlam.

The Century Room had vanished in a tempest of smoke. The air was thick and biting, and the edges of things began to blur. June ran to search the faces of the fallen. Some were conscious and others were not. Some were familiar and others were strangers. May wasn't among them.

Like a levee overwhelmed by floodwater, something finally broke loose. The people pressing for the boardwalk exit burst from the suffocating space, taking with them some of the Night Ship's smoke and noise.

June tried to regain her internal balance. May was here. She would never leave without June, just as June would never leave without her. May was June's heart, and June had to find her. She must have gotten caught when the crowd bolted for the exits.

On the boardwalk, wind scattered the smoke across the lake as if it were fog. As if it signified a change in temperature and not absolute catastrophe. Across the water, celebrations continued at the Wharf. There, it was still Independence Day. It was little more than a mile away, but from where June stood, it might as well have been a portrait of a lost world.

There were bodies here too, some silent and skewered by broken windows and others wretchedly loud as they thrashed on the ground. Part of the boardwalk railing had given way, and the shouts of those who'd fallen into the cold water rose through the planks like the damned.

This was hell, and June was its architect.

She found May crumpled against the south railing. Her neck was turned in an impossible direction. She was examining a region of her back that should have required a mirror to see.

June didn't remember walking to May, but then there she was. She stepped outside her body as it curled against that of her twin. From above, the two of them looked as she imagined they had in the womb. Nested into each other like two halves of a single perfect thing.

"Dearest." June sobbed into May's forehead. She put her hands on either side of May's head, willing the pulse in her wrists into her sister's temples. In one of the Lake's stories, there would have been enough life left for May to utter a last sentence. One last word that June could dip in gold and carry around like a locket. But May's eyes were empty. Her twin was gone.

For the first time, June was alone.

June once believed that she could do anything, but in her first moment of solitude, she knew that she couldn't do this.

May was June's heart. No one can live without their heart.

She didn't think. The time for plots and schemes was over. These were relics of an era as dead as the sister she lay beside. With May gone, there was nothing left to plan for. There was only one last thing to do.

When the crowd had broken through the back windows, they'd taken a set of drapes with them. Many of the curtains from the other windows burned and charred, but these were still velvet and crimson as deep as blood. June found their cord and tied one end around her ankle and the other around a wrought iron bench that sat not far from the boardwalk's broken railing.

June was not physically strong, but she could summon the energy to push the iron bench through the gap in the railing. She could find the strength to do this one final thing.

"I'd do it all differently if I could." June kissed May on the forehead for the last time. She savored the jasmine scent of her sister's hair and the slender arch of her nose. June didn't know if there were worlds beyond this one. If there were, it seemed unlikely that their paths would lead to the same clearing. This was goodbye.

Behind June, a woman gasped. "Your sister." She knelt in front of May and rested two fingers against her neck and then concentrated with an intensity June found transfixing. This was the same lady who'd been helping the stricken people inside.

June had walked through the same room, cluttered with her own victims, and barely spared them a glance. May never would have done such a thing. No person with an ounce of humanity would. The first of the sirens sounded in the distance.

I'd do it all differently if I could.

"I'm so sorry. Such a gentle girl." She removed her fingers from May's neck.

June's vision cleared enough to realize that she knew this woman.

She was married to the owner of the pub in town, Union Points. Mrs. McHale. She was a severe-looking one. Yankee stock. A spine of steel and chips of glass for eyes. June had seen her at the grocery and at the docks. She'd never scorned the twins like most of the others in town. If they met, she'd nod and give them a polite "Good day," as if they were anyone else.

"I killed her." June realized she was sobbing again. Only an hour ago, such a display would have disgusted her, but that life was over. May was gone, and June would soon be fast on her heels. "I killed them all. It was an accident, but it was my fault. If I could do it all again, I'd do it better. I'd *be* better. I wouldn't hurt anyone. I'd be like May." She was aware of the woman's gaze trailing along the artery of curtain cord that fastened June's ankle to the leg of the wrought iron bench.

"So much loss tonight," Mrs. McHale said. "Little sense in adding to it."

"I can't." June moved closer to the bench. Like a wounded beast protecting her injury, June would defend the braid of velvet that tethered her to the future for which she'd set her sails. "I can't live without May."

June and Mrs. McHale gazed across the waters to the prelapsarian festivities at the Wharf. Concoctions were drunk by the gallon there, too, but they weren't laced with antifreeze. Their hangover would not consist of riots and fires and death.

The two of them were about the same age, June realized. But Mrs. McHale was a wife and mother. June was nothing. She wasn't Strong's right hand. She wasn't queen of the Night Ship. She wasn't even a sister anymore. The Night Ship Girls were gone.

They were quiet like that for long, still moments. There was sanctuary in this. The peace before the plunge.

"June can't live without May." Mrs. McHale spoke deliberately. Like each word was its own sentence. "But can May live without June?"

June didn't understand the woman. "She was *everything*."

"She wouldn't want you to die."

The sirens were louder now.

"The police will come for me. They'll lock me in a cell and there'll be no way out."

"They'd never put you in jail, dear. Everyone knows May wouldn't hurt a fly."

"Are you some kind of moron?" June wept. The woman didn't have stupid eyes, but what she said was nonsense. "I'm *June. She's* May."

"It isn't what you're called that matters; it's what you *do* that counts."

"She's dead because of me."

"She doesn't have to be dead. Not really." Mrs. McHale placed a finger to June's chest. "You can be May. You can live for her. Live it like you say you would if you could do it all again. Live it like she'd have wanted to."

"I'm June." Her voice had shrunk into a mewling thing. The world seemed to tilt.

"June's the dead one," Mrs. McHale said, shaking her head. The blue gems of her eyes lit through June like flames through wax paper. "You're the one who lived. You're May. And you're going to make up for it. You're going to make it matter." She began to unloop the dirty apron from June's neck. "It's never too late to be good."

June realized that for once she was being the slow one. Mrs. McHale was ten miles ahead, where the country was green and gentler than any June could fathom. She couldn't imagine it now, but maybe one day she would. Maybe one day she'd make up for the suffering she'd caused.

"I'm May." She tried the words out to see how they fit. "I'm May." She heard her new voice, layered with humility and wonder and maybe even the tiniest measure of hope. "I'm May."

And from then on, she was.

Seventeen

Y ou're Just June." Nate squinted at her. She might as well have confessed to being the Easter Bunny.

"It's only a name," the woman said. She waved her hands as if her identity did not utterly rewrite the history of the Lake. "May was as sweet as pie, and her head was about as soft. Had to depend on people's help for everything. I didn't know people could be so kind. And after everything June did to this town. So much suffering. And the pain, you know how it ripples?" She pointed to the walls lined with newspaper clippings and webbed with string.

"So, you're June pretending to be May," Nate said. "I think I'd know if May, the Night Ship Girl, worked as a janitor at my high school."

"It was a good job. Quiet at night. Nice to clean things up instead of making the mess."

Nate tried to picture Just June scrubbing the urinals in the boy's room.

"But they didn't call me May. We were born right there on the pier, though old Morton never wanted us born in the first place. Mama was supposed to kill us the second we came out, but she couldn't. She never even got us birth certificates. That's how much the Night Ship was our world. When we left it, we didn't exist. It was well and truly like the lives of May and June had been a dream. Your grandmother helped me. She helped so much. She's a woman people listen to. At the town hall, they filled out all the forms like I was an adult foundling. Got to choose my new name. A new name for a new life. I was Annabelle Strong. Annabelle, just like our mother. Annabelle, to remember, and Strong so as never to forget."

Nate didn't know what to believe. Still, he was sure that the black-red envelopes around the cellar had come from the Night Ship. And he could imagine Grams acting the way the woman claimed she had all those years ago.

"I followed you here from the Night Ship. I saw you swimming away from it. Why were you there?"

"I was following you. And I was watching the children." She shook her head. "Those poor children."

"'Poor children'? They're not victims." The smell of Grams's burned skin built in Nate's nose, and he fought the tears that surged alongside it. "They've been terrorizing the Lake."

"But that's what victims do here, isn't it? It's what I did when Old Morton tried to kick me out. You did it, too. You and your friends."

"Yeah, this is the part where I ask you why my face is in the middle of your wall of crazy. What does any of this have to do with me?"

The woman blinked her huge eyes at him. Nate knew from the stories that Just June was supposed to have green eyes. Even in the basement lighting, he could see that the woman's irises were the color of a tropical lagoon flecked with gold.

She grabbed his hand, and her old skin was like silk.

"Everything."

THE BOY WHO FELL

III

THE DEMON JUNE cannot be vanquished, but the lake quiets her. In its clear waters she forgets the screams from the Night Ship. When she pushes her pace she can almost unhear the grind of a sister's spine as her head lolls unanchored upon her neck.

June had found the waters intolerably cold, but May adored them. A lap around the lake's southern bulge helps her become the twin she's supposed to be.

All the Daybreakers search for something on their morning circuit: fitness, focus, solitude. She both erases and rewrites herself in the mirrored waters. She pursues the tenderness and generosity that will make her worthy of this second chance.

May's life is a simpler and smaller one than June's. Though the sweetest of creatures, she cannot hope to leave more than a faint mark on the world. She does her menial work humbly and gratefully, and she spreads kindness where she can. But June erupted a mountain of suffering onto the town along the shore. May's greatest efforts can only pick at this imbalance one pebble at time. After decades, she knows she's made only the feeblest of dents.

She swims the lake to become the better of the twins, but she also swims with the hope of discovering how a speck like herself can accomplish something that truly matters.

One day in April, the lake delivers her answer.

She first sees the thing as a flutter of shadow, as if the sun has blinked. The waters explode when it appears as a monolith not ten feet in front of her. The waves of its impact crash against her like a rebuke by the angriest of lovers.

It takes her a moment to understand that it's a car.

For an instant, fear takes her and she peers at the faultless sky. If one car decides to fly off the top of a cliff, surely others might follow its example. Then she remembers that she isn't entitled to be afraid anymore.

But it doesn't make sense. A car in the lake.

Only the trunk is visible from the surface, so she dives to get a better look. The water is blistered with air bubbles, and it's hard to see anything in detail. The front of the car is crushed. The windshield is a gaping mouth and the passenger-side door is crumpled like discarded paper.

A groan rises from the wreck as it lists toward her. The water churns as the car topples. She just manages to get out of the way as it crashes to the lake bed.

The passenger's side is now pressed against the bottom of the lake, and the entire vehicle is underwater. A stain like tannin clouds the water. It billows from the front of the car. She can taste it in her mouth. Blood.

The driver's door is also smashed. She tries to open it, but it's impossible. The explosions of air bubbles that had pocked the water have thinned to tendrils that streak like spider's silk. A child's hand bobs, delicate and still, through the glass of the rear door. The horror of the sight sends her back to the surface.

She takes gasping bites out of the spring day. She's afraid again, but this time it isn't for herself.

When she plunges back under the surface, she makes for the rear door, but finds its handle locked or jammed. She pounds her fist against the glass, to no result but dull thuds sounding through the deep like the beat of a weak heart. Flesh and bone will not be enough.

She feels around the lake bed for a rock. By the time she finds one, her lungs are already aflame, but every second she takes for herself is one stolen from the child trapped in the car. Through the glass, thin limbs float blue in the dim light. A burst of short dark hair sways weightless in the cold water.

A boy.

It takes her four tries to break the window. There's a moment of pure relief when the glass shatters into opacity like rimes of ice. But the window doesn't dislodge. No matter how hard she batters it, it doesn't budge.

The pain in her chest is insurmountable and she has no choice but to return to the surface. She pants into the bright sunshine. The day is perfect but corpses wait just below the lake's calm surface. Only the long shadow of the Night Ship tempers the flawless day.

June would accept that the boy in the car below is dead, but she isn't supposed to be June anymore. It would take every goon who ever worked the Century Room to drag May from this wreck.

One deep breath and she's back underwater. She grabs the luggage rack to anchor herself, and stomps against the cracked glass with the heels of both feet and all the strength she has. Again and again and again.

Finally, something gives way. She swims down to probe the window with her fingers. There's a small hole, a place where the glass has buckled. Using the rock, she resumes her assault on the weak point. The boy is out of time, but she isn't going fail him. She'll give him everything she has.

More hammering, until there's a hole big enough for her bony hand to fit through. She reaches into the car and unlocks the door.

June didn't believe in deities or prayers, but May had faith in a benevolent universe. She can feel May with her now, more than ever before. It's May who tries the handle.

The door opens as smooth as the lake on a windless day. She grabs for the boy, forgetting about his seatbelt. His head bobs indifferently against hers as she reaches across him, the strands of his thick young hair tickling her neck. When she unfastens the belt, she gathers him into her arms like he's her own son. Euphoria. Tears of unbounded joy.

After the agony of getting him out of the car, carrying him to the stone beach is easy. He's taller than she is, but hardly weighs a thing.

When her feet touch the beach with the boy in her arms she feels as if she's arrived on the shore of a new world where anything is possible.

It's only when she lays the boy on the rocks and looks into his vacant eyes that she remembers that he's dead.

His eyes are a shade of blue that is nearly iridescent. The eyes of a doll with a fanciful maker. The boy is dead, but his eyes are still bright. They are so bright that his skin seems transparent in comparison. His left arm is ruined, jagged like a shattered branch.

He's as dead as the others in the car.

But May wouldn't give up.

She pushes against his chest, using the CPR training she received when she first volunteered for the Red Cross. After compressions, she puts her lips against his and breathes her breath into his lungs. More compressions, more breaths. The exertions make her light-headed.

But May wouldn't give up.

Under her lips, the boy twitches. She pulls away from him as he ejects a geyser of water onto the bed of smooth stones.

He lies back, coughing, and it's like a switch is thrown. Color climbs his cheeks. Pupils constrict to pinpoints in the bright April sun. She thought they'd dazzled before, but now they glow. She's never seen a boy like this one.

Sirens sound from inland, and she knows not to be here when they arrive. May wouldn't need praise or newspaper photos or handshakes with the mayor. The Lake has forgotten May, and that's how May would want to keep it.

She rests a palm on the boy's head. He is not yet quite returned from where he's been. She'll watch from the water until she's sure he's safe.

She savors the feel of his thick hair in her fingers. They are bonded now, she knows. They are both on their second lives, and every good thing the boy grows up to accomplish will be more chips against the damage done by the demon June. He's the answer she's been waiting for.

"Make it count, my little miracle man," she whispers to him. She walks backward into the cold water. "Make it matter."

Eighteen

How Nate found himself free of the wrecked car and on that stony beach had always been a mystery. Finally learning the answer had to mean something. It had to change something.

The woman rolled up the right sleeve of her bathrobe. Strands of a half dozen scars wove the underside of her forearm. Nate understood she'd gotten these from reaching through the Passat's window to unlock the door and pull him from the lake's deadly embrace. He had a similar network of marks on his own ruined arm.

He clenched his hands into fists to keep them from trembling. The pain in his bad arm jolted up to his shoulder. All he could see was the glittering water. All he could feel was the lake licking his feet.

Things loosened inside him. Things for which there were no names.

"My brother." His voice sounded like rusted metal. He remembered Gabe's grip on his hand. He saw his brother's lips, opened in a perfect circle of terror as their car crashed through the guardrail.

"I didn't see him," the old woman said. "I've played it in my mind ten thousand times, and I didn't see him. The light was bad and when the car tipped, it—" Her voice was different than it had been. More textured, somehow. Her face was changed, too, as if somewhere in her story she'd changed roles.

"Why's my picture in the middle of this?" Nate pointed to the wall plastered with clippings and laced with string. He realized that he didn't want to talk about the accident or the lake or his lost family. He couldn't.

"Look at it," she said. "Go on."

The newspaper page detailing the car accident Nate had survived was yellowed after sixteen years. This was the part of the wall where the red string was thickest, centered from a nail pounded into his chest. One string linked Nate's photo to a clipping about the Deckers' house burning in the foothills so many years ago.

Nate followed this string onward to an article about the county arson investigators finding the cause of the fire suspicious. Charges weren't filed, but insurance money was never paid out for the house, which had been a total loss. From there the string continued. Though he was not implicated in the arson, Mr. Decker's reputation had been damaged, and he'd been unable to secure a loan to sustain his slumping businesses. His local retail chain had to file for bankruptcy, and two of its locations were sold off, causing thirty people to lose their jobs. Their names were listed on a page of legal paper. Notations were written alongside some of them: divorce, bankruptcy, depression.

"What is this?" Nate asked.

"Just look."

He chose another string. From his face, it connected with a photo of Tom posing in a soccer uniform. Either junior or senior year, Nate guessed. From there he followed it to a pencil-line drawing of a house with a tree collapsed against it. The string flowed from this image to an article about the high school's soccer coach being pulled over for a DUI. Next was a memo sent to the high school staff about the coach's termination.

The coach's last name of Corso. Tom's former soccer coach and also, surely, the father of Pete Corso, the missing teen. Nate had once directed a Thunder Run against him, which ended with a tree collapsing against his house.

"He'd been sober for ten years before that." The woman pointed to the drawing. Nate remembered that several windows had shattered, and part of the roof had sheared off. "The stress from the damage knocked him off the wagon. Lost his job. His marriage."

"You couldn't possibly know that," Nate said.

Pete Corso's photo was the next waypoint on the string. It was a smaller version of the one the chief had shown Nate that morning. Next to it was a sketch of the shattered window at the Union. Maura Jeffers's face appeared alongside Pete's. Nate had brought her father's business down with an insect infestation that had pushed the family finances past the breaking point. This was noted here, too, complete with a notice from the county declaring the infested building unfit for habitation.

The wall held a catalog of Nate's sins and what the woman judged to be their consequences. The documents and strings that covered the walls were a decades-long narrative in which victims became vandals and the vengeful became the punished. A story of anger and blowback. The saga of the Lake itself.

As Nate examined the wall, he saw suicides, high school dropouts, substance addiction, school suspensions, and dozens of other symptoms of misery. All the teens he'd seen in the Night Ship must have a story like Maura's and Pete's. Most of the events on this wall surely had more than a single cause. Still, Nate couldn't avoid the fact that the Storm King's malign reign had rippled far and wide. The red lines tracked soaring imbalances in the equations of pain.

If he'd drowned on that April day, the Lake would be a better place.

Bankruptcies and crumbling home lives led to unhappy children who grew up to be angry teens. And anger needed a target. Using the revelation of the Thunder Runs from Lucy's journals, James had weaponized these teens' fury against Nate, Nate's friends, and anyone else who could have played a role in Lucy's murder.

"You can't hold me responsible for all this."

"We're both responsible," the woman said. "I saved you. Everything you do, good or bad, is because of me." She pointed to a single string affixed to the nail set into Nate's photo. It was at the base of the nail, the first string that had been attached to it. It was different from all the others piled above it in that it was blue. That was that day in April, Nate understood. That was the day he'd been returned to begin his second life.

"I didn't ask to be saved." He thought of his family, strapped to their seats beneath the lake. That blade of a teen was still inside him, and he seethed at the idea that this woman thought she'd done him a favor. "Maybe pulling me out of that car was a mistake." He loathed the woman's judgment as much as he hated her certainty.

"I think about that all the time."

The thing inside him edged closer to anger.

"I'm not the one who poisoned a bowl of punch and started a riot and fire that killed a dozen people." He pointed at the collage. "So where's your wall of sins?"

The woman pointed to the blue string fixed to Nate's photo. She traced it with her finger diagonally across the wall, under clippings and images and notes. Nate saw where it met the warped ceiling.

"What do you think's upstairs?" she said. "More space there, but you'll pass me by soon enough. The new ones have been busy, and they're not finished." She turned back to him. Her face was still grim, but something around her mouth loosened. "I was very sorry to hear about Bea."

The sound of his grandmother's name gave him a powerful jolt. Indignation, despair, shame—he wasn't sure what he was feeling, but he knew that he didn't want to talk about it.

"I'm a surgeon," he said. He wasn't a bad man, and he wanted this woman to know it. "I save people's lives."

The woman stared at him, then shrugged.

"What do you *want* from me?" he shouted. "It's the past. It happened."

A slash of some gentler emotion broke across her face. "You're still just a boy, aren't you?" She reached out to touch the line of his jaw. Her skin was dry but smooth like the stones along the waterline. "It's never too late to be good."

Nineteen

It wasn't until he was back outside, rocked by arias of thunder, that Nate let the things that churned within him break loose.

It was pouring again. The forest shielded him from the worst of the wind, but its treetops shuddered at dangerous angles. The wail of their branches and hiss of their leaves united with the drumming of rain into a wash of noise that made the air itself feel alive. Through its buzz he heard whispers from the dead.

He'd relived his fractured memories of that April day uncounted times. Now he finally had the answer to his impossible survival. He should've welcomed the woman's story. Instead, he felt uncoiled. Inert.

He didn't know what to do.

A massive tree stood near the foot of the patchy gravel driveway. It reminded Nate of the elm in his grandmother's backyard. He fitted himself among the nooks of its gnarled roots and hunched his knees into his chest. Curled within his black raincoat and wedged against the tree's trunk, he felt protected from the storm. In this position he could imagine weathering anything.

Almost anything.

Once the woman explained the basement wall, he'd had to get out of there. A minute more and he'd have suffocated; he would have drowned. All his offenses laid out like a deck of cards. Every hand on display.

Did he have any secrets left? He'd plumbed the chasm at his core but knew he had yet to reach its darkest point. With so many lies folded in upon lies, anything could be there, waiting. It took a great actor to be a good liar, but to be a great actor you had to *believe* your performance was the truth. After wearing so many masks, could he even remember the shape of his real face?

Nate despised the woman for laying bare so many sins of his youth. He wasn't sure who she really was, but he believed her story about saving his life sixteen years ago. He should have thanked her; he should have wept into her filthy lap. Fairy godmothers did less for their charges than she'd done for him. But he wasn't thankful. He was bereft. She was, herself, clearly ambivalent on the subject.

And she wasn't the only one in town who thought he was a monster.

The compilation of suffering across the cellar wall was reductive, but the truth was inescapable. Nate and his friends had caused pain far worse than the wrongs they'd avenged. Those costs still mounted. In her ICU, Grams was paying for them right now. Maura Jeffers, Pete Corso—they'd all paid.

Nate had to check on Grams, but he didn't know if any of the phones at the house on Bonaparte Street would work without electricity. The police station would surely have a functional landline, but the idea of seeing Tom or the chief made Nate wish for Medea to sweep him up and whirl him to the farthest edge of her most distant band of cloud.

The worst kind of stranger was the one who used to be a friend, and this town was full of them.

Something in his side twitched. The dumb wedge of his phone gave a cadaveric spasm. He stood and tore open his coat. When he examined it, the device looked utterly lifeless, but Nate tapped its screen and put it to his ear.

"Hello?"

"Nate?"

"Meg." Hearing her voice was like the flash of the sun after a day spent deep underwater. "My phone got wet. I thought it was dead."

"I can barely hear you. It sounds like you're on Mars."

On Mars only the air and cold will kill you, he thought. She and Livvy were his tethers to the person he was supposed to be. By her voice, he marked how far from that path he'd drifted.

"Are you okay?" she asked. "What'd the doctor say? Did the funeral go all right?"

"Nothing's all right here. I shouldn't have come back. Or maybe I shouldn't have left. I don't know what to do."

"I can't hear you, honey. Can you hear me? I wanted to check on you and tell you Livvy's much better. The storm surge isn't as bad as they expected. We lost electricity for a couple hours, but it's back for the moment."

"The power here's gone. Barely after lunch and it's already dark. The sky's gray, and the town looks like it's been abandoned for a thousand years."

"I can't understand you, love, but your voice sounds strange."

"Grams is going to die, Meg. I can feel it. And it'll be my fault. I never told you why I didn't want to come back here. I think I even made myself forget some of it. I made mistakes, Meg. Bad ones. And now I'm paying for them. Everyone's paying for them."

"Love, I can't hear you."

"Tom thought—he thought he killed Lucy. But he didn't. Of course he didn't. Not Tom. But that's why he left NYU. He's been punishing himself about it for fourteen years. The secret's been eating him alive, and it isn't even true. How could Tom think he was a murderer? And how could he keep it a secret for so long? He didn't tell anyone, not even me. If he had, I'd have told him it was impossible."

"Honey—"

"But then I think, *is* it really impossible, Meg? How many things are *impossible*?" He thought of the things he'd done and the people he'd hurt. He saw the webs of red string lancing the basement wall plastered with his victims. "We're capable of anything, you know. We're liars and thieves and arsonists and murderers waiting for that moment when the universe compounds chance upon chance so that the only choices we have left are bad ones. I used to know this. I don't know how I ever forgot."

"What'd the doctor say about your head? Dammit, there's so much static I can't understand a thing you're saying. It must be your phone. Or the hurricane. I'll try the landline at Bea's house. I love you, Nate. We both do."

The connection terminated in a flush of noise that shuddered into silence.

"Meg? *Meg?*"

Nate pulled the phone from his ear, swiped it, pressed it, shook it, and stared at its black screen until he was sure she was gone.

Time passed. He wasn't sure how much.

He was cold and wet, and knew that he should get out of the storm. He forced himself from the splayed roots and into motion, walking along the shoulder of the Strand as it curved back to town.

Maybe the landline at Grams's house still worked. If it did, he'd call Meg back. He'd tell her everything. Even the worst things. He'd confess how he broke into a stranger's house and got into a fight with teens and almost strangled his best friend's father. He'd beg forgiveness for the way he'd let Grams get hurt and the Union destroyed and Johnny's leg shattered and Tommy's dog murdered. He didn't know how Maura and Pete fit into all this, but it was somehow part of the same thing. Meg would listen to him and be kind, because that's how you deal with a hysterical person over the phone.

Nate wouldn't really know how she took it until he saw her in person. If her eyes slid away from his, if her embrace shuddered with the slightest hint of hesitation, he wouldn't survive it.

Greystone Lake's roads were deserted, its houses dark. He wondered if this was what the end of the world would be like. Not devoured by fires or floods, but endless gray clouds a hundred miles thick swaddling the earth like a shroud. Shutting out the sun and cowing the besieged with unceasing volleys of thunder.

He broke inland before he needed to. He didn't want to walk past the barricade. He'd had enough of the Night Ship and the things it conjured.

There was a police barrier toppled at the base of the street, and Nate stepped right over it. Trees had fallen, power and telephone lines had collapsed, and debris was scattered across the road and lawns.

Storm damage was everywhere. Shingles fluttered from one house, and a tarp had been hastily draped over the windows of another. Shutters were torn loose, and retaining walls had crumbled.

One home situated on a corner stood out to Nate from the others. As he approached the intersection, he saw that a large side window was shattered. Not just the glass, but the grids as well. Sopping curtains flickered in the onslaught of the wind. This might not have troubled Nate but for the fact that this was Owen's house.

Owen hadn't made it to Lucy's funeral, so Nate had guessed he was either still with Johnny at the hospital, or handling whatever chaos Medea wreaked over at the Empire. Nate knew that Owen's father was dead and that his mother had suffered a stroke and was now an invalid. Mrs. Liffey had been a cruel woman and particularly brutal to her son, so it said a lot about Owen that he'd taken it upon himself to care for her. When Nate wondered what he might have done in Owen's position, he didn't like the answer.

Rain streamed from the daggers of glass that marked the Liffeys' broken window. There was certain to be water damage, and with Owen away it would only get worse. Nate assumed that a caregiver stayed with Mrs. Liffey while Owen was out, but perhaps Medea had tossed all normalcy to the wind and the incapacitated woman was temporarily alone.

If Nate had never done any good in this town, he could at least help in this tiny way.

The lawn was sopping. Water crested his shoes with each step.

Though he and the others had trashed the Liffeys' landscaping during Thunder Runs on more than one occasion, Nate had never been beyond their home's threshold. Mrs. Liffey had cherished her flowers, so Nate had come up with the idea of salting the gardens and lawns. They'd doused them with enough rock salt to poison the soil several inches deep. Even now, the grass was patchy, the shrubs bare and stunted.

If every decree of the Storm King rippled with ill consequences, he wondered what unexpected catastrophes that act of destruction had caused. Nate was in a mood where anything seemed plausible.

While the yard and flower beds were pitiable, the home itself was well cared for. It was a pretty Victorian with gray paint, black shutters, and white trim. Nate ascended the steps to the porch. The doorbell was useless without power, so he used the knocker.

No response.

He picked his way along the edge of the house. When he reached the broken window, he called into the dark interior. While he waited for an answer, it occurred to him that it wasn't clear how the window had broken. No tree had collapsed against it, and there was no trace of debris that might have struck it. A Klaxon sounded in his mind when he peered into the dim interior. A trail of muddy footsteps was smeared among the wet shards of glass.

Someone had broken into the house.

The legions of regrets fled his mind. He parsed the thousand sounds and smells of the hurricane and scanned every shadow of the room in front of him. There was danger here, and it required all of his focus.

Owen had said that the vandals hadn't hit him the night before, but maybe they'd been waiting for today. It seemed audacious to attack the place in daylight, but perhaps Medea had made them bold. Or maybe Nate's appearance and quick departure from the Night

Ship had enraged them enough do something reckless. Even now, they could be trashing Grams's house, but Nate subdued the reflex to run to Bonaparte Street. A house was just a house, and the one on Bonaparte Street was empty. But if Mrs. Liffey was alone here, she'd need him.

He climbed through the window and added his tracks to the ones that had been laid before him.

It was a tidy room with a fireplace, a corner of couches, wing-back chairs, and a large coffee table. Dentil molding lined the ceiling and floor, and expensive-looking wallpaper and bland art filled the space between. It was a room designed to be admired and not inhab-ited. This fit with what Nate knew about Mrs. Liffey. With her yoga-trim body, designer clothes, and pretty house, she was a woman who prized appearance above everything else. There was a collection of portraits of Mr. and Mrs. Liffey on the mantel, a handsome couple who looked plucked right from a J.Crew catalog. These were normal enough decorations, except that Owen wasn't in a single one of the photos. Nate wondered if in her ill health Mrs. Liffey could finally be proud of the man Owen had become.

The rug was soaked, and the slap of water followed him every-where he walked. The wooden floor was sure to be ruined, but storm damage was no longer his primary concern.

He crossed the glass-strewn floor as quietly as he could. Ham-mering away at the door and calling into the house would have alerted the vandals to his presence. If they were still here, then they already knew he was coming.

The mud tracks led to the dining room and then to the kitchen. He scanned the walls and counters for a landline to try, but the room's shadows were deep. He felt grit through the soles of his shoes and a suggestion of dirt spanned the kitchen tiles, but the dim light from the windows made it difficult to see anything in detail.

After probing drawers of cutlery, measuring cups, and napkins, his fingers finally grazed the grip of a small metal flashlight. He started to pan its light around the room when the spill of its beam caught a flash of color on the floor.

As he'd guessed, the tiles here had a coating of mud, but there was another color mingled in its brown: the unmistakable ocher of dried blood.

His pulse quickened, and the ache in his bad arm seemed to amplify. With the beam, he traced the mud and the blood to a closed door. The basement, he assumed. The blood across the floor was more than incidental: Someone had been seriously hurt.

A bang shook the house. Not thunder, a slammed door. Floorboards creaked and footsteps sounded.

They're still here. Nate grabbed an electric kettle off the counter, switched off the flashlight, and tried to sink into the kitchen's shadows.

The footsteps were even, unhurried, and getting closer.

A large figure appeared silhouetted against the dim light from the doorway.

"Nate?" Owen asked. "What are you doing here?"

"Jesus. I almost clocked you." Nate had never been so happy to see the big guy. "Someone broke into the house through the living room window."

"The window's broken? I didn't see—"

"There are tracks all over the place." Nate twisted the flashlight on and illuminated the filthy floor.

"God, is that—is that blood?" Owen asked.

"I think so. But keep it down because—"

"Oh, Christ, you think they're still here?" Owen dropped his voice to a whisper. "Like, right now?"

"I don't know. I just got here."

"Did you call the police? What about my mom! Do you think they have her?"

"I haven't seen her. My phone's dead. I was just looking for your landline."

"It's cordless, so it won't work without power. But I'll call from my cell." Owen put his satchel on the counter and began to rifle through it. "Christ. I can't believe this. I mean, seriously, what's next?"

The blood and mud stopped at the door, though there was something like a handprint on the frame, close to the knob. Nate painted the beam of light up the rest of the door and noticed a series of deadbolts and chains just below his eye level.

Sweat broke out at his temples, his body sensing something before his mind had time to catch up.

Why so many locks on a basement door?

One of Owen's huge arms closed around his neck.

Nate had time only to throw an elbow backward before he felt cloth over his face. An involuntary inhalation filled his mouth and nose with a sweet, faintly acetone smell that recalled his med school days.

Owen clutched him tight against his massive chest. Nate was enveloped, his arms pinned to his sides as if by steel. He stomped clumsily at his shins, but Owen's strength was absolute. A scream built in his head with each gasp into the chemical-soaked rag.

He heard a choking sound as his knees buckled. His vision spun down into stars, and the shadows of the room coalesced into black.

Twenty

Sleep was velvet, smooth and impenetrable. Like the Night Ship, it was a shade of red so dark it was only a step from black.

Bands of light resolved into overhead fluorescents. Nate's senses and self limped back to him, his thoughts numb and slow as if wading through icy water.

He was seated on a cold floor, his head propped against a post or column, the buzz of the lights interrupted only by a whisper like that of an oar cutting through the lake. He tried to move his legs, but his stomach mutinied at the idea. A foul, sweet taste coated his mouth. He was deeply aware of each breath he took.

The sensation of Owen's grip lingered around his neck and chest. He remembered the chemical-laden cloth and the trail of mud and blood, the high-security basement door.

Why so many locks on a basement door?

With exquisite care, Nate straightened his head. It felt like a planet perched on a twig. He noticed the walls first. They were covered with small black pyramidal shapes like the inside of an alien spaceship or the interior of a golf ball. Light disappeared into the strange material. His raincoat was gone, and he was dressed only in his sodden suit.

The basement felt impossibly vast, but Nate could tell that his vision wasn't right. There was a brightness to the far side of the room that seemed to rebound into infinity. Its glare hurt, as if his pupils were dilated. He wondered what Owen had drugged him with. Its burn in his throat made him think of a frog being prepared for a scalpel.

Shapes moved beyond the clarity of his sight—shifting blurs that struck him as both organic and mechanical. Something about them was very wrong. He could feel this in his arm and smell it in the air. There was a clotted animal stench so thick that it would take more than water and soap to purge. The strange whispering surged and ebbed from the bright end of the basement.

Nate's hands were bound behind what he was propped against. Whatever they were tied with felt narrow and had the slickness of plastic. He could twist his wrists within the ties, but couldn't begin to contemplate summoning the strength to break them. He didn't even know if he could stand.

A hiss hardly louder than the ring of the overhead lights came from his right. He moved his head toward it slowly. Flowers tracked the sun more quickly. His brain threatened to shatter against his skull as if its lobes were sculpted of blown glass only a molecule thick.

Another form was collapsed to his right. Long limbs splayed across the floor like a discarded plaything. *A man.* Nate squinted, trying to force his eyes to focus. *A boy.* Shaggy brown hair, wide dark eyes, a thin face crusted with blood and taut with terror. He was clothed in the same long raincoat he'd been wearing when Nate tackled him on Grams's lawn the night before.

Pete Corso. Alive after all.

Alive for now.

"Pete?" Nate spoke louder than he'd intended, and the whisper at the other end of the basement tapered to a hush.

"Thought you'd be out longer."

The bound boy's eyes snapped shut at the sound of Owen's voice.

Nate turned his head and watched one of the blurs solidify into Owen as the huge man approached. He'd changed clothes from what he'd been wearing before. Now he was shirtless and dressed in loose-fitting scrub pants.

"What'd you use?" Nate asked. His tongue felt three times its normal width, and he had to speak slowly. "Kind of rough around the edges."

"A little bleach, a dash of nail polish remover, and you've got yourself the makings of some halfway decent chloroform. Vet school wasn't a total waste of time, huh? I think I gave you enough to knock out an elephant. You're lucky you're not in a coma."

Nate didn't feel lucky. He was sure there was a reason why, across from him, Pete pretended to be unconscious. The lights flickered.

"I turned on the generator," Owen said. "Thing's worth its weight in gold."

"How's Johnny?" Nate didn't know what Owen had planned for him, but he suspected it was something worth delaying.

"Should be fine. The hospital says he's in surgery. Rehab's going to be a bitch, but what can you do? The Empire's a mess. You ever been in a room with two hundred annoyed tourists? How was the funeral?"

Heartbreaking, unmooring, devastating by every conceivable metric.

"Pretty much what you'd expect."

"Hmm," Owen said. He stretched his arm absentmindedly. Muscles from his abs to trapezius to forearm all flexed impressively. He was built more formidably than even Adam Decker had been in his prime. "Should've gone. I feel bad about that." He glanced briefly at Pete before turning back to Nate. "I'm sorry about all this. For what it's worth, I didn't see it coming, either. Though, I gotta say, I was surprised how easy it was." Something was specked across Owen's chest. White clumps clung to his skin like wet snow. "The Storm King himself. Taken down with a little kitchen sink knockout juice. Only human after all."

"You're not going to make me ask, are you?" Nate tilted his head to Pete Corso.

"Oh, jeez." Owen sat crossed-legged on the floor across from him. Close, but out of range from kicks and head butts. Owen wasn't taking any chances with Nate, only human or not. "These kids. We were never this bad. First they almost kill me by slicing my brake lines, then last night two of them break in. Caught them right here in the basement. I clocked this guy." He pointed to Pete. "The girl made it back to the kitchen, but it's not like I could let her leave."

"Maura Jeffers."

"That her name? I'd have asked the kid, but he's been out cold. Dosed him with the chloroform before I went out to help Johnny. Maybe I gave him too much."

"You killed her."

"Well, I didn't *mean* to. You know what it's like when it takes over. The anger. I was so goddamn angry. She was in my house. My own basement! Once she saw everything, she had to go no matter what."

"Why are you keeping Pete alive?"

"You know his name, too? How've you been in town for like, a day, and already know more than me? You're something else, Nate, I swear."

"I bet you know lots of things I don't know, Owen."

"Anyway, our boy—Pete?—he and his buddies are obviously the ones setting fires and destroying cars and breaking windows all over town. Since I've got him here, I want to know everything he knows. What are they after? What do they know? They're dangerous to us, Nate. All of us. They know what we did back then. And think of all the pain they're causing. Someone's got to put a stop to it. You re-member the equations of pain?"

No matter how much he wanted to, Nate could never forget that. If that wall in the woman's basement ensured anything, it was this.

"Somebody's got to keep them balanced. Just like you always said."

"We were kids, O. Stupid, selfish kids. We caused more pain than we avenged. We made things worse, not better."

"You don't mean that." Owen frowned at him.

"We should have stuck to video games and girls and keggers in the woods."

"No." Owen shook his head. He grabbed a fist of his own hair. "That's not what you're supposed to say." He stood and started pac-ing back and forth. The ferocious light from the fluorescents exiled every shadow from the room, and in their brightness, Nate noticed something on Owen's back. His vision was improving, but he wasn't sure what he was looking at. Smooth shapes rose from the man's skin as if it were embossed.

"Your back."

"Huh? Oh. Yeah." Owen ran a hand over the ridges that bubbled from his flank. He turned so that Nate could see the extent of the scarring. There were dozens of marks carved from his shoulders to his iliac crest. Twin tracks of close two-inch stripes like the gills of a strange fish. "Mom did that. One cut for every week I weighed over three hundred. She was always the worst, but at first even I didn't think she'd do it. But you always said there's no way to tell what people are capable of. Dad did *nothing,* of course. Actually, that's not true. He helped hold me down. But he paid for it. Mom pays a little more every day."

"You never told us."

"Did I have to? We were supposed to be friends. You should have *known.* You always knew when something happened to Johnny. You'd say, 'What happened, buddy? And who do we have to punish?'

It was the same with Tom and Lucy. It was like they were a part of you. You knew whenever Tom got a hangnail or Lucy had some girl roll her eyes at her in the locker room. But you never knew with me. You never even asked."

"We did Thunder Runs against your mom. We salted the lawn, we—"

"That was nothing, and you know it. You think some dead grass makes up for *this*?" He indicated his back.

"You should have called the police."

"Would that have made me feel better? Did all that hurt go away when they locked up Mr. Bennett for killing your family? Laws and prison sentences don't balance the equations, Nate. The pain, it has to be burned away. You know that."

Nate realized that the man in front of him was a monster of his own making. He'd had most of the pieces of the story, but hadn't seen how they fit together until now.

"Why'd you do it, Owen?"

"Dad had it coming. He *never* took my side. He let her get away with it, which makes him almost as bad. He had to go. I knew that'd be the only way I'd be able to deal with Mom."

"I'm not talking about your parents." Heat built in Nate's chest. It seared away the clouds in his vision and the lethargy of his limbs. "I'm talking about my girlfriend. I'm asking you why you murdered Lucy."

GRADUATION

VII

SOUND WAS STRANGE in the undercroft.

Owen listened, silent and still in the nook of one of its rooms. Some nights this was the only place he could sleep. The lake's sighs were like cradlesong. When he was here by himself, he could pretend he was not only safe, but powerful. Walking the dark and abandoned halls of the Night Ship he could imagine that this was his palace, and he was its Storm King.

He didn't spend every night here, but he spent many. It was the best way to avoid home. Nate and Lucy were often here in the small hours of the morning. He'd listen to them up on the dance floor. Peals of Lucy's laughter ricocheted around the warped halls. Owen was massive by any standard: many times larger than Just June had probably been, yet he was able to move within the hidden chutes and spaces of the walls to watch the lovers from the peepholes in the wood. He never told the others that he'd found the nightclub's legendary secret passages, and for this he was glad.

He'd watch Lucy's and Nate's perfect bodies in a tangle on the floor. They were on the ground but still somehow soaring. He'd hear what Nate told Lucy as their passion crescendoed. Sometimes, Owen wondered if they'd be so beautiful if he weren't there to witness it. On some mornings it was as if the three of them were equal parts of a single perfect thing.

Screams echoed through the halls tonight, but these weren't driven by pleasure.

Lucy had arrived some time ago, Tom more recently. They'd talked, which was strange because everyone knew they hated each other. Then they'd gone onto the boardwalk, but only Tom had returned. Owen watched from the peephole as Tom sprinted back inside, wailing for Lucy, rushing for the spiral staircase.

Owen followed the foot- and handholds back down to the undercroft. By the time he reached the lower floor, a series of clicks and bangs resonating through the floor told him that Tom had opened the Night Ship's boat launch. Lucy must be in the water.

He came to the Night Ship for all kinds of reasons, but tonight he'd come to think. Nate had been warning them for weeks that the Thunder Runs would come to an end, but Owen hadn't really understood what this meant until today. Nate was already gone in every way that mattered, and Tom was just behind him. Even without a diploma, how much longer before Johnny left, too?

His friends and the secret life they shared here were all Owen had. Without the Thunder Runs, the long desert of the summer stretched in front of him. Endless, stifling nights. Without the others, without the Storm King, he didn't know who he was or what his life would be like. He remembered how things had been before Nate ran into him that Halloween night. More than bleak, those days had been unbearable. He'd never told any of them, even Johnny, that when they'd collided with him in front of the barricade that night, he'd been wrestling with a decision of his own. He'd been wondering if he had the courage to trek to the Night Ship, take the long walk into the lake, and add his life to the silver water's tally.

The others all had their strengths. He wasn't close to being as handsome or smart as Nate. He wasn't one percent as rich as Johnny or as well-liked as Tom. All he was was fat. Fatter than anyone in town. His friends were what made him strong.

Tom's voice seemed to be coming through the floor planks now, which meant he was in the water. Tom had always been a worrier, but Owen couldn't place the pitch of terror in his voice.

Something had happened.

Tom's calls fractured into a low, irregular sound.

Risking a look down the hall toward the boat launch, Owen saw Tom on the floor in a puddle of water, his shoulders heaving with sobs in the lantern light. Lucy wasn't with him.

"Stupid," Tom said. He hit the side of his head with a closed fist—one, two, three times. "Stupid. Stupid. *Stupid*." The punches seemed to shake Tom loose of whatever spiraling descent he'd been locked within.

"Evidence." Owen heard him mutter. "Clean it up." Tom locked up the launch again, then hurried back to the staircase as he talked to himself. "She was here by herself when she fell. They'll say it was an accident. It *was* an accident."

Owen crouched in the dark as he listened to Tom scurry across the planks above him. A few months ago, they'd taken a stab at cleaning the mold from the great expanse of derelict kitchen. Owen guessed there were still cleaning supplies somewhere.

He imagined Tom upstairs, spraying and wiping and drying and fretting. Every few minutes a wail sounded from upstairs, lonely like the cry of a bird that was the last of its species.

Finally, the sounds ceased. When Owen was sure Tom had left, he took a lantern and reopened the boat launch. Nate never allowed them to take a light out on the water, but this was a special situation.

The lake returns what it takes. If Lucy had drowned, then maybe her body had floated to the surface. If Owen found her and hid her, he might be able to keep Tom from getting into trouble. It would be a secret just between the two of them. It'd be a bond unbreakable through the summer and all the way through college. It was the kind of thing that would tie them together for the rest of their lives. If he kept Tom's secret, Tom would help with the Thunder Runs. Nate would be gone, but Owen, Johnny, and Tom would be stronger than ever. Maybe they'd even be strong enough to get back at his mother in the way he really wanted to. Something that would hurt her for real. Something that would hurt her forever.

As he unlocked the boat launch, Owen felt truly happy for the first time in ages. Then the skirt of his lantern's light bounced off the lake's dark waters and illuminated the stiletto eyes of a soaked girl clinging to one of the pilings.

"I'm going to destroy him," Lucy said. "I don't care who his dad is." Her voice was hoarse and as flat as ice.

"Oh my God, Lucy!" Owen tried to keep the disappointment from his voice. So much for his friends. So much for the things he wanted. They slipped through his hands like water.

The launch creaked under his feet as he descended to help her out of the water. She sat on the launch shivering with cold and rage.

"I'm going to make him wish he was dead."

Owen listened to Lucy's expletive-laced summary of events. He'd already guessed at the generalities, and the details didn't much interest him. He nodded and gasped appropriately, but mostly he was wondering what to do next. He tried to think like Nate. He tried to imagine being the kind of person who knew exactly what he wanted and stopped at nothing to get it.

"First we'll call 911. The doctors will check me out and have everything on the record. The police will ask me for a statement, and I'll tell them everything. He hates himself so much he'll probably confess, the weak little shit."

Alarms sounded in Owen's head. If they did what Lucy said, it would pull them all apart, not bring them back together. "Nate wouldn't want us to turn on each other."

"Nate wouldn't want his best friend to nearly murder his girlfriend, either." Her clothes were soaked. The silky green thing she'd had on at the party was gone, and her white top was almost transparent.

"It must have been an accident. A misunderstanding."

Her body was slight but leanly muscled. He'd seen it before in more revealing circumstances than this, but never so close.

"Tom *almost killed me*. You think Nate's going to shrug that off?"

Owen tried to imagine a world in which Nate and Tom weren't best friends, and he didn't at all like the look of it.

"He'd want us to get along, to figure it out together."

She squinted at him. "He'd want *revenge*. That's why he burned down Adam Decker's house and started this whole thing. He burned it down because of me. I made him who he is, just like he made me. We created each other, and that's why he'll side with me no matter what."

Owen's head spun. He'd never been as quick as Nate or Lucy. They spoke in full paragraphs and recited doctrines of their own convoluted design, and it was usually all Owen could do to nod and pretend he kept up. But something Lucy said was wrong. It wedged itself into the gears of his brain until they could turn no further.

"You fell in love with Nate for burning down Adam's house?" Owen asked.

"That's what made us. All of us. Don't you remember? That's what made him the Storm King."

"But that was me," Owen said. "I'm the one who poured gas on the Deckers' house and lit it."

"I didn't—I mean—yeah, okay, you lit it. But the reason you were there was because of Nate. He's the reason for everything."

"But *I'm* the one who got your revenge on Adam Decker. It was *me*."

Lucy frowned at him for a moment. Her glare softened into blankness, and then she burst into laughter.

"Oh, Owen! You think I should have been with you this whole time? Instead of Nate?"

An image, unbidden but well-treasured, came to Owen of Lucy writhing in the dawn light of the dance floor. He felt himself flush. He spoke slowly, trying not to stutter. "I'm just saying that everyone thinks Nate has to be at the center of everything, but he doesn't."

"Jesus. Me and the Porker." Lucy's laugh glittered like a blade. "I mean, seriously?"

Owen shot a hand out to grab her wrist. It was a reflex, like a reptile's tongue plucking an insect out of the air.

"Don't call me that."

Her hand was a spindle in the meat of his palm.

"Watch yourself." Anger boiled across Lucy's face. She was a terrifying creature, but Owen saw the appeal. He witnessed it firsthand at least twice a week, bucking across the dance floor planks. She was like a challenge. A crucible. If you could have her, you could get anything.

Lucy tried to pull herself free of Owen, but she couldn't budge him.

"I'm not screwing around, Owen. Let me go. Let me go, or you'll be just as sorry as Tom will be." It was a threat, but fear was carved across her face.

Tom already thought he'd killed Lucy, and not a soul knew she was here. If she reported Tom to the police, Owen and his friends would be torn apart forever.

Instead of loosening his grip, he tightened it.

There was a snap and Lucy shrieked in pain. She came at him with her free hand. He caught it as if it had no more heft than paper. When she kicked at him, he pinned her underneath his bulk.

He held Lucy's arms against the warped dock and wedged her legs open with a knee. He could hold her entire upper body down with a single forearm. He choked off her scream with a fist gripped around her neck.

After so many years, Owen finally discovered where he fit. The others had brains or looks or money or loyalty, but Owen's potency was strength itself. He tore Lucy's clothes like they were tissue. He marveled at his power.

Lucy's face purpled in his grasp. The tendons of her neck stood out like ropes, just as they did when Nate was on top of her.

Owen held her down and squeezed. The lake surrounded them. He yanked down his shorts, and lake-chilled air kissed his bare skin. Lucy struggled like a flame caught in wind. Furious and desperate.

After a time she stilled.

That's when Owen knew that neither of them needed the Storm King anymore.

Twenty-one

A nd I really didn't need you anymore," Owen said. "Didn't need the others, either. For once they needed me."

Nate felt as if he'd fallen from a great height.

He imagined Lucy in the panic of her last breath: terrified and violated and disbelieving as her throat was crushed. Five fingers around one porcelain neck. It took a meager amount of pressure on the carotid artery to bring unconsciousness, and a bit more force to crush the trachea and fracture the hyoid. Even after so many lessons, Nate still found it astonishing how entire futures disintegrated because of such small things. A single hand and casual strength could destroy worlds.

"Tom didn't know I was keeping his secret for him, but I was. And Johnny doesn't know it, but I'm the one who finally got rid of his dad for him. That way, he'd get the Empire and everything else. He'd finally be his own man. And to be honest, I always thought me and Tom did you a favor with Lucy. She was insanely hot, but can you imagine being married to her? You've done so well, with your career and your family and everything. Things really worked out for you in the end, don't you think?"

That might have seemed true even as recently as yesterday, before Nate had stepped back onto this haunted shore. A wife he loved, a daughter he adored. He enjoyed an everyday happiness that anyone might envy. So, had things worked out for him?

"Yeah." It was true, but it was also terrible. He'd arrived at a fortunate destination, but reached it by a most treacherous route. Look at the ruin he'd left in his wake.

Owen grinned. Something about his face wasn't right. Before Nate could figure out what, the massive man lunged at him. One moment, Nate was watching his captor sitting cross-legged in front of him, and the next moment his face was knocked to an entirely new direction, his jaw blaring with pain from a backhanded slap. If he hadn't been tied into place, the blow would have sent him tumbling across the floor.

"Don't lie to me," Owen said. The joviality he'd kept up until now fell away. What remained was cold and razor-edged. "I know you, Nate. I killed your girlfriend. No one can forgive something like that. Especially not the Storm King."

The tang of his own blood seeped across Nate's tongue. He didn't know how he was going to get out of this basement alive.

"You know about these kids." Owen stooped next to Pete, and he used the dowels of his fingers to push open the boy's eyelids. Pete's irises were blank, but Nate saw what Owen didn't notice: The boy's right hand tightened into a fist. The kid was still feigning unconsciousness, and doing a remarkable job of it. Owen let the boy's head roll back against the post he was tied to. "What do they want?"

"They want you," Nate said.

"Me?"

"James Bennett's their leader. Lucy's brother. He has Lucy's journals. He used them to put together a list of people from the old days who might have killed her. That's how the vandals choose their targets."

"Why?"

"They're angry. Just like we were." The equations of pain. Agents of karmic justice. Whatever they told themselves, the Lake was a place where one bad thing grows upon another. And it's an action's ripples that matter, not its rationalization. Nate understood that now, too late for it to do any good.

"That's it? They don't have a plan?"

"I didn't think so at first. Now I'm not sure." Nate had to reconsider James's strategy. After fourteen years of silence, there had—finally—been developments in the mystery of Lucy's disappearance. This was due to the revelation of her remains, but also thanks to the chaos James and his friends had unleashed on the Lake in the wake of its discovery. Shake a tree hard enough, and something is bound to fall from its branches.

Owen snapped his fingers in front of Nate's face. "Care to share with the group?"

"They'll know it's you," Nate said. "The vandals have been able to hit so many places at once because they split into groups. James divvied up last night's targets among his crew, and Maura and Pete were paired up. James knows where they were supposed to go. They were supposed to spray-paint Grams's house, but I scared them off. James thought I'd killed Maura because Grams's house wasn't damaged. He assumed they never made it any further down their list. But Grams's wasn't the last place those two went. This was. Sooner or later, James and the others will come by and see that broken window, just like I did. They'll figure it out. I'd get out of here while you still can."

The whisper Nate had heard earlier from the bright end of the basement surfaced again, this time cresting into the threshold of intelligibility. *"No, you can't go, you'd never go, you'd never leave—"*

Nate squinted, and the dimensions of the room became clearer. It didn't expand into forever, as it had seemed when he first woke. That was just how his hazy brain had interpreted a large alcove with walls lined with floor-to-ceiling mirrors. With the unblinking ceiling fluorescents reflected endlessly against these mirrors, that section of the basement blazed. But something large and dark twitched near the center of this kaleidoscopic pocket. Nate's vision still wasn't perfect, but he saw this bulk reflected across the facets of the walls and echo into infinity.

Like the mirrored alcove it originated from, the wispy stream of words never seemed to end.

"He's a liar, always was, always will be—"

"What *is* that?" Nate found his own voice pared to a sliver of itself.

Owen slapped him again, this time with the porterhouse of his open palm.

When the pain arrived, it crashed like a breaking wave. The inside of his cheek felt shredded against his molars. Blood pooled behind his teeth. All he could think was that this was the hand that had squeezed the life from Lucy.

"You *are* a liar. You'll say anything to get out of here."

Nate spat a gob of blood onto the floor. One of his incisors felt loose. The man was as strong as he looked. He forced himself to focus on Owen and not the voice from the far end of the basement. "I can tell you what you want to hear, or I can tell you the truth."

"All right, Nate. Lay it on me." Including Mr. Liffey and Mr. Vanhouten, Owen was a murderer at least four times over, with two more victims bound in his basement. Any sane person would be unraveling in panic, but not Owen. Something burned in his eyes, but it wasn't fear.

"The truth is that you're screwed. Getting away with killing Lucy was pure luck. You've got no clue how much luck. The chief buried evidence because he'd been protecting Tom. Now there's another dead girl. They have Maura's body, and they'll find something that ties her to you."

"Doubt it. She was a mess, but I stripped her down, washed her up, first with soap and water, then with bleach. Trimmed her fingernails, scrubbed real well under them, burned her clothes." He brought his face closer to Nate's. "How do you know so much about the girl and the other kids?"

"People tell me all kinds of things. I've got one of those faces." Nate wasn't strong enough to break free of the ties that bound him, but if he positioned himself just right, and if he could get Owen to hit him again—

"You must have talked to them. At the funeral?"

"Look at the Porker, trying to use his little piggy brain." As insults went, it was a softball, but that didn't mean it didn't connect. Owen's upper chest and neck darkened into red splotches.

"You're trying to make me angry. Maybe you think I'm going to slip up and tell you something I shouldn't, but if you have a question all you gotta do is ask. Today, to you, I'm an open book." He smiled. *Because soon, what you know won't matter* is what his smile told Nate. *Soon all the things that you want and fear and love won't matter to anyone.*

"Did you have a thing for Lucy from the beginning?"

"Everyone did." He grinned at Nate.

"And then you told her how you felt." Nate shook his head. "That was brave of you, O. You must have known she'd turn you down. I mean, just imagine her with you." He chuckled as if holding this image in his mind evoked even a crumb of mirth. "The Princess and the Porker. There's a fairy tale to scare the kids away from refined sugar."

The flush on Owen's neck climbed to his face. Just for a moment Nate saw the boy Owen had been at the time of their graduation: a young man whose large size had made him an unmissable target during the most vulnerable years of his life, a shy boy who'd just sung the hottest girl in town the paean of his soul, only to have her laugh in his face.

The whisper sounded again from the other end of the basement.

"She didn't deserve you, that whore, that filthy girl, you are so much better, you are the most handsome—"

By now, Nate knew where the voice came from. A part of him had known since the first time he'd heard it. But that didn't mean he was ready to face it and all that it implied.

"Shut up!" Owen screamed, whirling to address the voice. His fury flared with terrifying suddenness. When he turned back to Nate, his teeth were bared like a wild animal's. But after a moment, this grimace twisted into a smile.

"I just remembered something about you, Nate. Pain's your kink, isn't it? So how do you hurt someone who likes it?"

Adam Decker had said essentially the same thing back in the lab junior year, right before battering Tom with a lacrosse stick.

Owen stood and walked to the bright end of the basement.

As Owen receded, Nate took in what he could of his surroundings. The room had no windows. From where he was bound he couldn't even see the stairs to the main floor. His dexterity had improved enough that he thought he could stand and maneuver around the post he was tied to, but that wouldn't do him any good as long as he remained flex-cuffed.

He wondered how long it would take people to figure out he was missing and how long from then it'd take for them to begin looking for him. *Too long.*

Owen returned behind a mass of something. As it rolled toward him, the edges of it quivered like the waterline.

"You remember Mom."

Nate had prepared himself for something terrible, but it still took him a moment to reconcile the silhouette in front of him with what he knew of the human form. As he'd guessed, the poor woman was the origin of the basement's whisper as well as its terrible smell.

You could call a person wizened in the grip of an illness a husk. Nate saw them in the hospital: ravaged patients reduced by their maladies to skin-cloaked skeletons. The woman being wheeled across the floor to him was the opposite of this. Bloated, swollen, obese: The images these words conjured weren't in the same hemisphere as the territory where Mrs. Liffey now resided. The bands of her desiccated lips twitched and puckered as they droned endless words.

Nate gauged her weight at somewhere between four and five hundred pounds. Piled onto a frame just over five feet tall, the effect was monstrous. Saddlebags of flesh slipped around the arms of her wheelchair and dangled past her knees. Her face was lost amid her billowing cheeks, her shorn head nearly submerged in the mountains that erupted from her scabbed neck. An assortment of stained blankets were clipped together to cover her, but the woman shivered as if she was freezing.

"A bad boy, a bad friend, the worse friend, poison, poison, poison—"

The last time Nate saw Mrs. Liffey she'd been lean and impeccably styled. Now, he couldn't even recognize her eyes, which were pocked like buttons from the pillow of her face. They were wet and drenched with animal panic.

"Owen." Nate's mouth had gone dry. He turned away from the woman. Looking at her felt like trampling whatever dignity she had left. Still, she whispered at him, hissing indictments and curses. He didn't know why her voice never seemed to rise above a scoured hush.

Owen crouched beside him and turned Nate's face so that it was again directed at Mrs. Liffey. "She loves being seen. Always checking her makeup in the car mirror, admiring her reflection in store windows. She could never get enough of herself. Now there's so much more to look at."

"What did you do?" A stroke could have left her wheelchair-bound, but that didn't explain the size of her.

"Let's show him, Mom." Owen padded back across the room.

To his right, Pete's eyes were wide and bright with horror at the sight of Mrs. Liffey. Nate shook his head at the boy. The kid's instincts were good: Playing dead might be the best way to stay alive. Pete closed his eyes but his shoulders quaked.

Owen padded back, with a brown grocery bag filled with something that crinkled as it shifted. "I know we just fed you, but you always have room for more, don't you? Greedy beast." He plucked a snack cake from the bag. An oblong tube of joyous yellow sponge filled with a core of impossibly white cream.

"Love them, yes, thank you, more, so hungry—" Mrs. Liffey

said, but as she spoke, her voice faded to a whimper, and the rate of her shaking accelerated. For the first time, Nate noticed that the cellar's floor was laid with clear plastic drop cloths like those used by painters.

"Remember how she used to call me the Porker?" Owen asked. "A pig still lives here, but it's not me." He unwrapped the cake and dangled it above her mouth. "Open wide, now. You know how."

She opened her mouth, and groaned with pantomimed pleasure as he forced the cake into her. He did this with another cake, and then a third and a fourth.

"All those years of starving yourself to look good, but this was all you wanted, wasn't it? Isn't it a relief to not care about what other people think?"

The woman said something, but her mouth was full and she began to gag. The mounds and rolls of her shook like a landscape caught in an earthquake.

A spray of mottled cream exploded from her mouth. Specks of it splattered over herself, the floor, and Owen. Nate now understood the viscous globs on Owen's chest.

"You know better than to fight it. Remember, you like the cheese puffs and the French fries and gallons of cola, but these are your favorite."

Owen grabbed a handful of Mrs. Liffey's forearm, and squeezed. Vibrations of agony resonated from the woman. Nate now saw how her skin was dented and swollen with bruises that ran the spectrum from black to yellow. Owen clamped his hand over his mother's nose to give her a choice between swallowing or suffocating.

"I'll tell you what I know," Nate said. He couldn't watch any more.

"I also give her pork rinds by the pound. You like that touch? You are what you eat, right?" Owen gave a sharp porcine squeal that made Nate jump.

"Stop it."

"But can't you see she likes it? Got to go all the way to the Walmart in Bright Mill to stock up on this garbage. Too many people around here know me, and they'd never believe I eat it myself. My body is a temple, isn't it, Mom?"

"So healthy, yes, perfect body, a perfect son, so lucky," Mrs. Liffey choked out, her eyes streaming.

"I'll tell you everything I know about the kids," Nate said.

"Maybe just a couple more."

"When the chief brought me to the station he started off by asking me about Lucy, then about Maura. He showed me Maura's picture. That's how I knew she was the one I tackled on Grams's lawn."

"What about James Bennett? How do you know he's their leader?" Owen withdrew the snack cake he was holding from Mrs. Liffey's mouth, but his other hand still pinched her nose.

"I talked to him in the Night Ship. He and his friends wanted a piece of me."

"They made the Night Ship their place, too?" Owen asked. He looked over his shoulder as if he could see the old pier through the basement's wall. "Haven't been there in ages."

"Lucy's journals were like an instruction manual for them. They changed up some things, but not that." The Night Ship was at the center of all their stories: Nate, Tom, Lucy, Owen, James. Even Just June. From a certain vantage, the Night Ship was the origin of every ripple—every red string that lashed across Just June's cellar wall. Would Nate carry so many regrets if the pier had never been built? Would he still be alive in the first place?

Despite the horror of his circumstances, Nate drifted while he considered this. He'd once stood on the Night Ship's dock bare-chested and entwined with a girl he loved. That dawn he'd looked upon the endless country of the future and found a golden design around which everything was connected. Around which nothing was ever lost.

Remembering this made his eyes swim. Through their liquid lens he saw Owen's face blank with concentration.

"Does the chief know that the girl, Maura, was one of the vandals?"

"He knows the only reason I could ID her in the first place was because I caught her and this guy"—Nate nodded toward Pete—"in the act. I told you, they're going to put it all together. There's no point in making it worse."

Owen smiled, and Nate wished he hadn't seen it. The man's smile was an abyss.

"Thanks, Nate. I know you like your secrets, but that sounded like the truth." He pulled away from his mother, and Nate got the feeling that he'd just made a fatal mistake. If he'd told Owen everything that he wanted to know, then Nate had just rendered himself useless. The huge man flexed his neck, then walked toward a nook of the basement that Nate couldn't see. As he receded, the thick welts of his scars ticked across his back like fleeting seconds.

"Owen, hold on. Where are you going?" But Owen's attention already appeared to be elsewhere. Nate backtracked through their conversation, trying to figure out what he'd missed. What had he told Owen that he shouldn't have?

Whatever was left of Mrs. Liffey shook and stared at Nate through glass eyes.

"So lucky, so lucky, so lucky—"

Owen was back a few moments later to thud two large red jugs in front of Nate.

"Memories, huh?" he said. He patted one of the gasoline containers. They looked like ten-gallon jugs: if filled, an absurd amount of weight for anyone not built like a minotaur. He toweled the cream and crumbs from his chest. "Let me ask you something."

"Okay."

"Did you ever wonder if *you* were the one who killed Lucy?"

"Of course not." But this was a lie. This was the secret Nate had long feared waited for him within the eye of the maelstrom that thundered inside him. Of the many dangers in stepping back into the forest of his past, none loomed larger than this. It was the cornerstone around which everything about him would rise or fall.

"But why? Before that note was found, you know that's what everyone was saying. They're saying it again now."

"I didn't think I killed her because *I didn't*." He didn't kill Lucy. Nate let himself feel this. He wasn't a murderer. No matter what, this was something he could hold on to.

"But *could* you have? That night Lucy let Adam Decker flirt with her, she was afraid enough of what you'd do that she ran out of the glade. Everyone saw it. And you were so messed up after all that partying. Don't tell me you remember every single thing that happened after you knocked Adam's teeth in."

"Everyone was messed up."

"But you're not like everyone else, are you? The Storm King thought rules were for other people. He thought he was better than everyone else. He thought he could get away with murder.

"Fourteen years later this guy comes back to town," Owen continued. "The day after he does, another girl washes up on the shore. Coincidence? Especially when he even admits to assaulting her earlier the night before? Then his grandmother's pub explodes with her in it. Whoever this guy thinks he is, whoever he's been pretending to be, goes out the window. He might say he's a doctor or a dad, but he's a monster."

"Come on, O."

"All those kids," Owen went on. He shook his head and bit his lips like he was talking via satellite to a morning show host. "All those poor, dead kids."

A knot tightened inside Nate. Three loops of fear tied with a through-strand of doubt.

"They never had a chance, really," Owen continued. "Once you set the Night Ship on fire there was nowhere for them to go." He tapped one of the red jugs with his feet. "Those poor innocents you had to make pay the price for your suffering. Because the pain doesn't disappear on its own, does it, Nate? It's got to be burned away."

Twenty-two

Nate understood his mistake.

He'd told Owen that the vandals used Lucy's journals as an instruction manual and that they met at the Night Ship. In the ferocity of Medea, they'd be at the abandoned pier as surely as Nate and his own friends' high school selves would have been there. Nate told Owen that the kids would expose him, and now the killer knew exactly where to find them.

"How about Pete here?" Nate felt the powerful impulse to keep Owen in conversation, as if he needed to buy time for something. For anything.

"You kill him too, obviously. Not sure exactly how yet." Owen smiled at the shag of Pete's hair. "In a perfect world, you'd get rid of him with the others, but you can't lug him all the way out there. Don't worry, though, we'll think of something good. You'll kill him today, right after you get back from setting fire to the Night Ship."

"But Pete's been missing since last night. Where's he been?"

"Grams's house, the Night Ship, somewhere in the headlands. Who can say?"

"You haven't thought this out." Framing Nate for the murders seemed like an impossible dream. But was it? So few things were truly impossible. "Why would I keep Pete bound up for hours and hours before killing him?"

"The same reason I did: You needed to find out about the other kids from him."

"Okay, so I kill him, then set the Night Ship on fire with the kids inside?"

"You set the fire first. You had to make sure Pete wasn't lying about where to find the others. Then you kill him. Then you kill yourself. You'll drown yourself in the lake, just like your family did. People will think it's poetic. A full-circle kind of thing."

"No one will buy it, Owen. Tom won't believe a single thing about it." Nate used to doze among the roots of an ancient tree and try to decrypt messages from the dead from the sibilation of its leaves. Now he tried to do the opposite. Through the walls of the basement and across the expanse of the steeping town, he willed the rain to tap his distress against the roof and windows of Tom's cruiser.

"Tom'll see that he got off lucky. Again." Owen slid his arms into a shirt. Nate was out of time.

"They're just kids, Owen. They're angry, scared." He'd never noticed how similar rage and fear were. More than cousins, they might be twins. Anger only looked like strength, but at least fear was honest. "Give them the mercy you didn't get." That's what Nate most wished for the furious boy he'd been. That he would have learned the bravery of compassion. "They don't know what they're doing."

"They hurt Grams and Johnny, and almost killed me when they cut my brakes. They're not innocent. If you were the guy you were in high school, you'd be begging to help me." He finished buttoning his shirt and heaved the gas jugs from the floor. "I usually chain Mom's chair up by the mirrors so she can admire herself. But I think I'll leave her here with you." He patted the stubble of the woman's scalp. "You've got an audience today, Mom. What a treat!"

The woman shuddered when Owen touched her. "*Thank you, yes, such a treat, such a nice thing—*"

"See you soon, Nate." Owen winked at him, and walked to where Nate assumed the stairs were.

Nate called after Owen but got no answer. It wouldn't have mattered anyway. Owen possessed the conviction of the anointed, just as Nate had in his youth. It was a blind certainty that cannot be surmounted.

He listened to the man's heavy ascent of the stairs capped by the dull thud of the basement door being closed. The stinking air of the room seemed to deaden all sounds. Nate couldn't hear the door being locked, but he was sure Owen engaged its every deadbolt and chain.

"You got a plan, right?" Pete asked as soon as Owen was gone. The boy's voice was splinters and creaks. His eyes were wet with terror. With Pete looking directly at him, Nate realized how astonishingly young the kid was. His forehead far outsized his jaw, as if his adult face was only half-inflated. "I know who you are. You look older than I thought."

"No one's looking their best today. Have you tried yelling for help?"

"For real? Yes. Like, a lot. Like, for hours once I was pretty sure he wasn't in the house anymore." Pete bounced his head in the direction of the spongy geometric material that layered the walls. "I think it's soundproofing. They've got something like it in the practice rooms at school. I guess he didn't want anyone to, you know"—he glanced at the woman in the wheelchair—"hear her."

"*Be good boys now, don't make him mad—*"

"Yeah, probably." Nate didn't know why Mrs. Liffey's voice seemed fixed at a whisper. The soundproofing suggested that it hadn't always been this way. "Mrs. Liffey?" Nate addressed the woman directly for the first time. Her eyes blinked wildly, her lips tasting the air as if nibbling a fruit. The smell that rolled off her made Nate's eyes water: rot layered with strata of sweat and waste. "Ma'am? How do we get out of here?"

"You don't want to make him mad—"

"Mrs. Liffey's left the building, bro."

Nate didn't know when the woman was supposed to have suffered her stroke. She'd probably never had a stroke in the first place. Owen might have been keeping her down here for years, trapped in a chair, doing God knows what to her. She was too heavy to move around on her own, and her mind didn't seem to be in any better shape than her body.

"No luck with the cuffs, I guess?" Nate asked Pete.

"They don't feel like much, but they're real strong. I thought if I got some sweat in there they'd loosen up, but nothing."

Nate yanked and hammered and pulled at the flex-cuffs but only tenderized the skin of his wrists. He tried to picture the ties. It was a single loop of plastic tucked into a locking mechanism to ensure a tight fit. He thought that if he could mess up the fastener, the band might loosen, but he couldn't get the angles to work. He ran his hands up and down the cylindrical post searching for some edge to worry against the plastic.

"He's going to kill us," Pete said.

"No, he isn't." But the kid was right. If they were still here when Owen returned, they were as good as dead.

"You think he'll burn us? Like the others?"

"No." Nate thought of the silver annihilation of the lake and shivered. "Do you have anything in your pockets?"

"I'm worried about them," Pete said. "My friends."

"That's why we've got to get out of here. Anything in your pockets? Keys, coins? Wouldn't turn down a box cutter." If Pete had something, Nate might be able to use his feet to drag it to himself by pulling at the plastic drop cloth beneath them.

"Keys are in my pocket, but I can't get them."

Nate watched the boy struggle and contort against the pipe he was tied to. Meanwhile, he continued working at his own cuffs. Pulling and releasing. Tensing then relaxing. Seconds or minutes ticked by. In their windowless basement, it was impossible to tell.

"I can't get them." Pete was out of breath. "You think he could really burn down the Night Ship? It's such a big place. And it's gotta be soaking out there, with the hurricane and everything?"

"Gas will make anything burn, and Owen knows the pier. He'll probably set it inside."

Nate thought that Owen would set the fire on the landward end of the pier, where the shops and cafés used to be, in order to block the kids' escape down the boardwalk to shore.

"They could swim for it," Pete said, uncertainly.

"Yeah, they could," Nate said. But that was easier said than done. Out that far, the lake was treacherous, and Medea had it hammering against the pier's pilings with more ferocity than usual. Just June, an expert Daybreaker, had braved the waters in a dry suit during a lull in the storm, but how would the uninitiated fare?

Nate was afraid it wouldn't matter, anyway. Owen was massive and powerful. He didn't need to rely on stealth and patience if he didn't want to. If he wanted, he could fall among the children like a wolf among poultry. He could be as brutal as he chose to be in order to prevent their escape, then make his exit and wait for the fire to scorch away the evidence.

Perhaps the old place had already gone down with all hands, the vicious waters alight with its reflected flames. Within the basement's soundproofed walls, they wouldn't hear town sirens going off or fire trucks wailing through the streets. Pete's friends might already be dead, and Owen could be on his way back here right now.

Nate slammed his cuffed hands against the pipe in a spasm of frustration. His fingers were tacky where they touched each other. A band of pain was seared around his left wrist. Struggling against his bindings must have torn his skin. The slickness of his blood gave his wrist more give within the plastic cuff, but not as much as he needed.

Mrs. Liffey's shaking had settled. Her eyes drooped, not open but not closed, either. The rims of her inflamed sclera glistened like veined crescent moons. Her mouth was still in constant motion, but Nate could no longer make out the words.

It was difficult for Nate to gather strength from the awkward angles of his arms. If only his hands had been in front of him instead of behind. If they'd been square against the small of his back and not looped around a wide support post.

But Nate had always been able to find strength when he needed it. He thought of Grams in her hospital bed. He thought of Lucy. He imagined her eyes bulging in her final moments, her cheeks purpling under the weight of Owen. Nate dug for anger, but all he found was anguish.

Maybe today was the day the lake finally claimed what had slipped from its grasp so many years ago.

Next to him, Pete was sniffling. Tears cut shining streaks down his face. The boy wasn't looking at Nate anymore. He wasn't looking at anything. Pete would die, too. So would the children in the Night Ship. When Nate thought of them gathered there, James and Tara and all the others, he tried not to think about what they'd done, but who they were. Kids with families and futures. Kids like Livvy. Kids just like he and Lucy and Tom and Johnny had been.

He leaned forward to press his left thumb against the curve of the post. As if in the clutches of a medieval torture device, he increased the pressure as he leaned forward millimeter by millimeter.

"Tell me what you planned to do to Owen after you broke in through the window upstairs," Nate said. He visualized the first carpometacarpal joint. He shifted to tweak the angles, clenched his teeth, and forced himself forward.

"Huh? Oh. We were going to mess with his water filter. Add a heap of red dye concentrate to it so all the taps would run red like blood."

The pain at the base of Nate's thumb grew from an ache to a

warning to an alarm. He felt things stretch in ways that they weren't meant to stretch.

"But then we saw . . . *her*," Pete said. "And he caught us. Then I think Maura made it upstairs, but he—he must have—"

Nate heaved all of his weight forward in a sudden lurch. He wasn't sure at first if the crunch that resulted was audible or the kind of sound that only resonated within the body it originated from, but as his peripheral vision went black, Pete stopped talking.

The pain was incandescent. Nate sweated limply against the floor and marveled at how many shades of agony there were. Easily as many as there were of anger and sadness. *But what about happiness?* he inquired of the plastic drop cloth. Eating out of containers with Grams at her little kitchen table. He, Tom, and Johnny casting from the dock on a summer morning. Meg's smile when he woke to find her looking at him. Livvy's tiny finger when she pointed at something she'd never seen before. For him happiness arrived in one flavor, but that never made it less sweet.

"Um, Mr. McHale? Are you, like, okay?"

"Call me Nate." His fingers quivered as he compressed them against his dislocated thumb. It was still a struggle as he slid his mangled hand out of the cuff. In his troubled years he'd dislocated this thumb twice before. He thought that maybe its history of trauma had made it easier to dislodge now. He thought that maybe the suffering you've already survived is sometimes the only thing that can keep you alive.

Nate was dimly aware of Pete swearing in awe as he got to his feet and cradled one hand in the other. It took a moment for him to find his balance. A wave of nausea hit him as he surveyed his askew digit. He attempted a clinical distance as he snapped it back into place. This time the adrenaline coursing through his system dulled the edge. If nothing else, the pain wiped aside most of the lingering effects of the chloroform.

"I'll look for something to cut you out."

"Don't leave me here!"

"I won't."

The walls of the mirrored alcove were angled like a department store fitting room. A post like the one Nate had been bound to was near its center. Chained to it in her wheelchair, Mrs. Liffey would have no option but to see from a dozen angles what had been done to her. A second alcove, next to the first, had a small kitchen with a refrigerator and sink. The corner across from the fridge was tiled and had a showerhead. If it was possible, it smelled worse here than it did anywhere else in the fetid basement. This must be where Owen sometimes hosed his mother down. A bin piled high with solid blankets was nearby.

Nate found a knife in a drawer. The blade was one step up from a letter opener, but he was able to use it to cut Pete's ties. The boy gasped as he clutched his arms to his chest and began rubbing the blood back into his hands. To get to his feet, he had to grapple his way up the post to which he'd been bound.

"I'm going to piss myself. I've had to go for, like, a day."

"There's a sink in the back."

"Do you think it's okay?"

"I won't tell."

As Pete staggered away, Nate bent to whisper into Mrs. Liffey's ear. "We're going to get you out of here." The woman seemed half asleep, but at least one word was still on her lips.

"*No, no, no—*"

Nate went up the steps to test the door to the main floor. It felt more substantial than the average interior door, and the locks and chains further reinforced it. Nate could hear them jangle as he battered his shoulder against it. Each jolt sent voltages of pain up his arm from his damaged thumb. It was back in its socket, but he must have torn something along the way.

Even if the steps hadn't offered such a poor vantage, Nate didn't think he'd be able to knock down the door.

He heard the rustle of Pete padding across the plastic-draped floor.

"Better?"

Pete's mouth twitched into the bud of a smile. It sat there for only a moment, but long enough for Nate to glimpse the boy underneath the terror. "What's the deal with the door?"

"It's solid, and there are a ton of locks on the other side."

An ax or sledge might get them through the door, but Nate doubted they'd find such tools down here. The basement was huge, but except for the kitchen with the shower, it was mostly empty.

"See if he left your phone—or Maura's—down here somewhere. Keep an eye out for anything we can use on that door. Weapons, too," Nate said. The dull knife he'd used to free Pete wouldn't be any use against Owen, but with the right weapon they might have a chance.

Pete looked at him in alarm. Nate didn't like the idea of having to fight Owen, either. The big guy had lost weight since their high school days, but he still had dozens of pounds on Nate, and it was all muscle.

They circled the basement in opposite directions. Far from the mirrored alcove and overhead lights, some nooks were almost entirely hidden by shadow. Under his palms, the soundproofing material fixed to the walls and most of the ceiling felt almost organic. He groped and probed and hoped, but didn't find anything useful.

"I'm sorry about the other night, you know?" Pete said when they both returned to the center of the room. "We were going to tag your grandma's house. I mean, nothing really bad, I guess, but we shouldn't have. So . . ." Pete trailed off and stared at his feet.

Nate waved away Pete's apology. It was hard to imagine he'd spent a moment worrying about graffiti or broken windows.

"There's nothing good down here," Pete said. "Nothing to even fight him with. I mean, there are a couple forks and things in the kitchen. But—"

"There're a lot of unhealthy-looking foods in the cabinets, and probably more in the fridge. See if you can skim off some fat and spread it on the drop cloth at the base of the stairs. Cream from those snack cakes could work, too," Nate said. "Maybe he'll lose his footing when he comes down and we can jump him from the sides."

Pete appeared to like this idea and hopped into action. At least it gave the kid something to do. Nate supposed that Owen might indeed slip on something greasy, but this wasn't the clumsy oaf Nate recalled from high school. Perhaps Owen had never really been like that in the first place. Nate remembered him only through the eyes of a raging, narcissistic teenager, and that boy had already been proved wrong about so much. He'd thought he could do as he pleased and not reap the slightest consequence.

While Pete tore through the kitchen, Nate returned to the mirrored alcove and kicked at the gleaming walls. He earned decades of bad luck before he knocked loose a long, glittering shard that he liked the look of. It might not do much to slow someone the size of Owen, but if Nate aimed for an artery or key tendon . . . It wasn't ideal, but it was something.

Nate took off his suit coat, bundled it around the base of the makeshift weapon, and rolled up his left sleeve. He traced the letters from the crook of his elbow to halfway up his forearm. Then he dug in with the tip of the shard. It was a clumsy blade for such work and Nate sliced as shallowly as he could, just into the dermis so that the lines and curves of the letters slowly filled with blood. The pain was noticeable but only a ghost of the torture reverberant from his torqued thumb.

When he was finished, he watched his final words weep crimson across the newborn skin on the underside of his forearm.

O'S BSMNT

A message written in flesh was one that could not be ignored. Owen might kill him and all the others, but he wouldn't get away with it. The lake returns what it takes, and if it drowned Nate, it would also deliver this last message for him.

Nate considered leaving more notes across the canvas of his body. He could tell Tom and the chief that Owen had killed Lucy, and Mr. Liffey and Mr. Vanhouten, too. He could apologize to Tom and Johnny for every way in which he'd poisoned their lives. He could pare missives of love to Meg and Livvy and Grams onto skin that might not have the time to scab, much less heal.

The burn of the cuts caught up to Nate, and he rolled his head upward with a grimace. When he did, he noticed that an edge of foam soundproofing material had come loose from where it met the ceiling. One corner of it dangled like an earmarked page. He walked to it and ripped it aside. He tore loose a panel six feet long and three feet high. When the last foot of the section fell away it revealed part of a window. A curtain of rain rippled down its glass.

The window was small: not more than a foot high. Nate's rib cage wouldn't fit through, but Pete was all height and no width. They'd break the window, clear aside all the glass, Nate would boost Pete up and through, then Pete would get help.

He should have been happy, but instead Nate cursed himself. He'd never in his life been in a basement without any windows. Even Just June's shack had them. Looking for them should have been the first thing he'd done. People depended on him, and he couldn't afford to make any more mistakes.

Nate set aside the shard, and wrapped his hand in his coat. He hammered his fist into the glass. If the children at the Night Ship were still alive, they had little time left.

Twenty-three

Night had taken the town along the shore.

The only light was the electricity that flickered among the ranges of Medea's clouds and a few generator-powered homes that struck out from the black like ships at sea. The storm's percussions of thunder and rain were so loud that Nate couldn't hear his own steps as he waded through the flooded streets running for Tom's house. They had to go to the Night Ship. They had to finally face the debts of their youth.

After clearing the narrow basement window of glass and lifting Pete through it and into the muck of a brimming flower bed, Nate had spent long minutes waiting for the boy to reenter the house and unlock the basement door. He and Pete hadn't known each other long, and their history before the basement was not encouraging. The teen might decide to leave Nate to Owen, and maybe Nate would deserve it.

"He'll come back," Nate told Mrs. Liffey as much as he told himself. "Then we'll all get out of here." Whatever future waited for

Mrs. Liffey beyond this stinking basement would be an improvement, though how much of one, Nate didn't know.

Though he'd been waiting for it, Nate was startled when noise came from the door to the kitchen. He crept to the side of the stairs, as the locks were disengaged, releasing a held breath only when he heard Pete call to him. He was lucky Owen had secured the basement only to keep people in and not keep them out.

"What about her?" Pete asked, pointing down the stairs.

"We won't be able to get her up the stairs on our own," Nate said. He turned back toward the wheelchair-bound woman. "We're getting some help, Mrs. Liffey. Don't worry. We'll get you somewhere safe."

She was fully awake again, and shaking so hard that at first Nate thought she might be having a seizure.

"He will kill you, he will kill us, he will kill everyone—"

"We'll be back," Nate promised. He climbed the last of the stairs and stepped back up into the kitchen.

"Start knocking on doors," he told Pete. There was no reason to whisper, but he did anyway. His limbs still carried extra weight from the chloroform, but this lightened with each breath of fresh air. "Get someone to call the police. Tell them about Owen and about the kids on the Night Ship. If the landlines and cells are down, have them drive you to the station."

"What if they don't believe me?" Pete asked as they reached the foyer.

Nate looked at the boy. Eyes bloodshot from crying, skin matted with pallor, his clothes and hair filthy with mud and soaked with rain. Words were only one kind of language, and Pete exuded a fluent dialect of pure distress. It was easy to forget that the Lake was· mostly just a normal town filled with normal people. If this boy appeared at their door, none of them would doubt the story he told.

They didn't have time to waste, but Nate found himself cupping the boy's chin in his hand as if Pete were his own son. "I'm sorry about what we did to your dad." A lifetime ago, Nate and his friends

had felled a tree against the Corsos' house. A DUI and job termination and divorce had followed. It was impossible to say how closely
these events were connected. Life grows one bad thing upon another.
But in a universe where small things could destroy whole worlds,
Nate and his friends had made people's lives worse and not better. "I
didn't know anything back then. If I could take it back, I would. I'd
take it all back." He wasn't thinking only of the Corsos or the Jeffers, but of Lucy and Tom and Johnny and even Owen. They'd
thought Nate was their friend, and he'd brought them nothing but
pain.

Pete pulled Nate's hand away. "Just save them, okay?" He wasn't
whispering anymore. "Save my friends."

Rivers of torn leaves lit by the flaring sky guided Nate's descent
to the shore. He abandoned the streets as soon as he could, cutting
through lawns and climbing fences to speed his way. His left hand
felt like it was the size of a catcher's mitt. It throbbed with his pulse
and screamed with each clench of his loose thumb.

Tom answered the door already dressed in his outdoor gear. His
friend's ramshackle house was in between Owen's place and the
Night Ship. Nate hadn't been sure if Tom would be home, but he was
so glad that he was.

"The hell happened to you?" Tom asked. He didn't look so great
himself.

"We have to go to the Night Ship." Nate was out of breath and
shaking from cold. How far and how long had he run through the
storm? How much farther must he go? Would he ever reach home?
"Owen, he's been—he's the one who—" How to even begin.

"I've been on Wharf duty since you left. I came back for a dry
uniform, but dispatch just called. They're sending me to Owen's.
Pete Corso turned up and he's been saying some crazy—"

"It's all true. But you can't go to the Liffeys'. We have to go to the
Night Ship."

"The—but why?"

"He's going to kill the kids. He's going to trap them in the Night Ship and then burn it all down."

"You gotta get out of the rain. You're shaking. Come on." He beckoned Nate into the house. "I'll get you some dry clothes and—*holy Christ*, what happened to your hand?"

"Please, Tommy. *Please.* He killed Lucy. He killed her while he raped her and hid her body in the headlands."

This seemed to get through to Tom. He threw his hood over his head and pushed past Nate, through the front door, and into the storm. Nate followed him to the treeless backyard where a sliver of the old pier could be spied through the dark silhouettes of neighboring homes and countless veils of rain.

An unmistakable orange glow wavered by the landward windows of the promenade.

They were already too late.

Twenty-four

The ragged shape of another downed oak blazed in the headlights.

Next to Nate, Tom swore as he stomped on the brakes. The tree was so massive that not even driving across adjacent lawns would have let them clear it. All routes to the Strand were blocked.

With the promenade already in flames, the only way to the Night Ship was through the old pier's boat launch, and they'd need one of Johnny's boats to get there. The Vanhouten mansion was no more than two blocks away, but every moment mattered.

They abandoned the car and scaled the tree's slick bark. Medea fought them through every step.

Tom had called the station from the cruiser as they tried to find a clear path to the shore. Another unit was already on its way to the Liffeys' house, and Tom alerted them to the blaze at the Night Ship. The dispatcher would summon the fire boat docked at the Wharf, but with the streets in the state they were in, there was no way to know when the Lake's volunteers would be able to scramble a crew.

Two fences and five lawns later, they reached the Strand within sight of the chimney pot arrays of the Vanhouten mansion.

They cut through the hedges and onto the slate walkway that flanked the veranda. Johnny would still be at the hospital, and the place looked as lifeless as the rest of the town.

Either Johnny or his father had commissioned the construction of a floating boat shed along one end of their dock. Two motored watercraft were moored there with an assembly of kayaks mounted at the shed's far end. The boats shuddered among their bumpers in the lake's onslaught. The structure's roof shielded them from the rain, but the waves surged over and between the planks at their feet.

"Owen must have taken the Scarab," Tom said. The shed had three berths and the center slip was empty. "I don't have a key to the Sundowners. We'll have to paddle."

Nate felt his friend's gaze on him as he turned to where the kayaks were stowed. They were sleek and shallow and as dark as the sky.

He gripped one end of the two-seater craft and tried not to think about the rolling topography of the lake. In the pantheon of such things, the lake wasn't a significant body of water, but Medea had whipped it into a frenzy of crested peaks. In more placid moods, these waters had twice swallowed Nate's life.

The craft bucked as they lowered it into the lake, as if the water itself grasped for it. Waves crested its sides to lick the cockpits' coaming, but its compartments were tight and designed for buoyancy. Nate forced himself to get in first.

"You don't have to go," he told Tom. The fiberglass sheath of the kayak grasped him like a shroud or a womb. He didn't know what they'd find at the Night Ship. The past was closed and only their futures could be unmade. Tom had to make his own choice.

Across the water, flames at the foot of the pier began to lash at the rain, but fire wasn't the only menace. A monster hunted children through its burning halls. The fairyland towers glistened in the growing light.

Something was ending.

Nate was ambushed by the thought of Meg and Livvy and how he might not see them again. He could hardly make sense of how they existed within the same reality as the Night Ship and this unceasing storm. But everything was connected. Good and bad. Past and future. Hurricanes and clear blue days. Stories and truth. Victims and villains. Every single thing was also something else. This was the universe's golden design. This was life itself.

When Nate looked up at Tom from the depths of the boat, he imagined that he could again be new and unblemished and unknowing. He could once more be the ten-year-old who'd fallen from a tree and had his two best friends reach in wordless unison to lift him back to his feet. The little boy who'd sat crooked between his mother's lap and a book, astonished to find an undiscovered world on every page.

Chances stacked upon chances had never permitted him to be a son while also a father, or a brother at the same time he was a husband, but maybe he could inhabit all these parts of himself at once.

Maybe he had to.

He didn't know if Tom would get into the kayak, because for a moment Nate wasn't sure he knew anything.

The craft lurched and then settled as Tom got in. They pushed off from the dock and slid their paddles among the whitecaps. The chaotic waters were nearly unnavigable. It was a constant dance to maintain their balance upon the lake's volatile surface, but the winds sent them north to the Night Ship as if that was where Medea wanted them to go.

They had many things to discuss in these last moments: What would they find on the old pier? How would they confront Owen? How could they save those kids with nothing but this two-seat kayak?

The storm sped them to the Night Ship, and before Nate broached these questions, the structure grew to encompass his entire field of view. The fire still seemed confined to the front of the promenade, though he couldn't guess how deeply it had chewed into the pier's interior. The derelict place was its own world, and from the outside it was impossible to know what happened within its warren of nooks and corridors. The children might already be dead, or they might not yet even know the Night Ship was burning.

"I should've known there was something wrong when you never went back to NYU after Christmas." It made Nate sick to think how little time he'd spent considering his best friend's sudden exit from New York, and he didn't know if he'd have another chance to apologize. *Poor Tom,* he might have thought in some stolen moment between performances of self-interest and acts of self-immolation, *too weak to hack it in the big city.* "I should've met up as often as I told you we would. I'm so sorry."

Unimpeded by branches and buildings, the weather on the skin of the lake was a physical mass of force and water. The rain was a constant fusillade, and Nate let blow after blow of it hammer his face.

"Lucy was my fault, no matter what Owen did," Tom finally said. "I never blamed you for any of it. If I said I did, I didn't mean it. If anything, you should blame me."

"You two wouldn't have even been here if it weren't for me. Your dad said I was poison, and he was right. I set your lives on fire." For the first time, Nate caught the scent of burning. "I was supposed to die with my family, Tom." He thought of the million dominoes of coincidence that must have fallen in just such a way to place Just June on that rim of shore at that very moment. "If I'd drowned with them, none of this would have happened. Lucy, you, Grams, Maura, Johnny, Owen, Mrs. Liffey—" This was only the top of the list. The wall in Just June's basement rippled all over the town along the shore.

They were nearly to the boat launch. With the double-handed push of the wind at their back, they had to use their paddles only as rudders. The launch was open, and a sleek blue vessel was tied up ahead of them: Nate guessed this was the boat Owen had appropriated from Johnny's shed. He grabbed the free mooring post and pulled them parallel with the ramp.

"That's not what it was like," Tom said. He stayed low to step from the kayak. "You don't remember the right things, Nate. You never did. It wasn't all rage and revenge. How could it be?" He fastened the mooring line and pulled Nate flush with the dock. "We were there for Johnny whenever things got bad with his dad. We tried to help Owen, too, even if he doesn't remember it that way. We were friends. How can you forget how much we laughed? We loved you."

It was Nate's turn to step onto the launch, and Tom gripped his arm to steady him.

"We still do."

Nate was still wiping at his face when they ascended into the undercroft. He knew that what they were headed into would require all his focus. He knew that he and Tom needed a plan for how to deal with Owen.

But the young screams that tore through the crying wind announced that the time for schemes and plots was over.

Twenty-five

The undercroft was dark, but Nate's feet remembered the way. The screams came from more than one person, and they pulled him to the spiral staircase, where he collided with a mass of something that sent him back onto his heels.

He felt a flood of warmth pour from his chin to his mouth. Tom's flashlight revealed a blockade of dressers and tables and chairs. Someone had barricaded this entrance to the upper floor.

"The kitchen," Tom whispered. The kitchen's staff service entrance was the only other route from the undercroft to the main level.

Wiping away the blood, Nate ran after the bounding beam of Tom's light. The hall here was narrow and its floors uneven. Just June and her sister, May, had once lived in one of the rooms that branched from this corridor.

Tom and his light disappeared around a corner, and Nate slowed to feel his way to the nook where he knew the service stairs were. Flecks of shedding paint cracked under his hands as he groped his way through several tight turns and caught up to his friend.

"It's blocked, too." Tom heaved all his weight at the door that led into the kitchen. Nate joined him in broadsiding the heavy wood with his shoulder. Every collision of his shoulder against the door rattled his brain and swelled his damaged hand to bursting. The door protested, but didn't budge. Something massive must be propped against it.

Tom counted off, and they crushed themselves into the door. There was a skin-rippling screech as the obstruction ground a quarter inch across the kitchen tile. Tom counted off again—and then again. Once they fought themselves through a few agonizing inches, they kicked and battered the door at its hinges. Finally they dislodged it and heaved it aside.

Now that they'd stopped making noise themselves, Nate realized that the screams from the nightclub had also ceased. Their sudden absence rang in his bones.

Tom climbed over the thing that had been blocking the door. When Nate followed, he saw the obstacle was a massive mid-century industrial oven.

Their single flashlight wasn't enough to illuminate the enormous kitchen. Dust and cobwebs shrouded rows of filthy counters. Shadows realigned with each twitch of the light and tendrils of smoke curled along the ceiling. The room smelled of both mold and campfires.

Nate hurried to the swinging door that opened into the cavern of the nightclub. "Ready?" he asked Tom. In the strange light, his friend's face was only half rendered. Beyond the door, the nightclub was alive with the moans of Medea and the pummeling of the lake. There was no way to know what was on the other side.

Tom nodded, then led the way with his flashlight. The swinging door was mercifully quiet as it opened into the vast, dark place. Rain thundered against the lofty windows as lightning flashed blue and gray through the trembling architecture of the sky. Smoke began to sting Nate's eyes.

The flashlight was a thimble of light in an ocean of black, but

Nate took in every detail the beam illuminated. The room had seemed orderly when he'd been here only hours ago, but chaos had since swept through. The space flashed with broken glass. Foodstuffs were scattered across the dance floor. Tables and chairs had been upended. The doors to the promenade were obstructed with a pile of furniture, just as the spiral stairs had been.

A cataclysm of electricity erupted above the foothills, capturing the lake and mountains in a daguerreotype of Medea's fury. When Nate blinked, a blue negative of the jagged bolts remained seared onto his eyes. An immense tree of light with a life span of only an instant. The thunder reached them two seconds later. The pier shuddered in its shock wave: an avalanche that obliterated everything else beneath it.

Nate walked into a displaced propane tank, sending it rolling before it came to rest against the husk of a broken lantern. Tom traced its passage with the light.

"He broke all the lanterns," Tom whispered.

Fear blossomed in the dark, and terror was every monster's ally. Where was Owen, Nate wondered. Where were the children? Why was it so quiet?

"There," Tom said. His flashlight illuminated a tangle of bright sleeping bags. They were twisted and abandoned in knots of blue and red. All except one. A boy was on his side in a puff of quilted down. A splash of scarlet doused his neck and shirt. His white-blond hair gleamed like a halo except where it was dark and clotted.

Nate pushed his way past Tom. He kneeled next to the boy and bent close enough to smell the peanut butter on his breath.

"He's breathing. Pulse steady." His airways were clear. "The blood's still coming." The wound looked as if it had been made by a blunt weapon. Nate hesitated to investigate too deeply, but it was possible the skull had been fractured. "Can you hand me the—"

The boy gasped, and the unexpected sound caused Tom to swear and leap backward.

"You're okay, buddy," Nate told the boy. Clothing was crumpled around the sleeping bags, and Nate folded a T-shirt and pressed it against the boy's head wound. "Glad you're awake. Can you tell me your name?"

"He hit me," the boy whispered. His enormous brown eyes glistened with terror. "He came from the walls. He came from—" Then he shuddered slightly, closed his eyes, and slumped his head onto his shoulder.

"Is he?" Tom asked. He panted like he was out of breath. "Is he—?"

"Still breathing, just unconscious," Nate said. "Can you shine that light here?" He had to stanch the bleeding.

"'He came from the walls'?" Tom said. "The hell does that mean?"

"You know the stories." Nate began tearing the shirt into strips. "They say Morton Strong had peepholes in the walls of the Century Room to spy on his customers. In the stories, there were ways for people to climb from the undercroft to the upper levels without ever being seen."

This morning, Just June had been little more than a story. Before her remains were found, Lucy herself had faded into the gauzy treatment of myth. In a decade, who could say what tales the town along the shore would trade about the Storm King and the day the Night Ship burned to its pilings in the rage of a hurricane?

Tom swept the room with the light as if it were the rotating pulse of a radar. "They must have been asleep when Owen got here," he said. "After he set the fire he comes back here and clocks this kid. The others run. Owen chases them, and with the exits blocked he knows there's nowhere else for them to go. We must have gotten here right when it kicked off. They probably all . . ." Tom trailed off and Nate became aware that his friend had stopped swiveling and fixed his light on a single spot.

"Jesus."

"What?" Nate had begun wrapping the strips of fabric around

the boy's head, fixing a wedge of cloth into place as a makeshift compressive bandage.

"By the kitchen," Tom said.

Nate finished dressing the wound and followed the beam of Tom's flashlight. It revealed a place near the entrance to the kitchen. But instead of the wall that should have been there, the beam lit an open hatch, a square door about three feet wide. Its borders were aligned with the natural contours of the room's wood paneling and a horizontal rail of molding that struck across that wall. They'd walked past it on their way from the kitchen without noticing it. Back in high school, he'd passed by that wall hundreds of times without imagining it was anything but what it appeared to be. The same could be said about Owen Liffey.

" 'He came from the walls,' " Tom said. He flashed the light back to the stricken child. "Is it okay to move him?"

"Safer than it is to leave him here." Furniture had been heavily stacked against the Night Ship's broad glass doors to the promenade, but a glow already dawned around its edges. The smell of burning was intensifying. "It'd be better to stabilize his neck, but we'll have to wing it."

"Take him down to the launch," Tom said. He spoke in his official, deputy tone.

"Where?" Nate used as guileless a voice as he had in his repertoire. *You're the boss* is the sentiment he wanted to convey. *Whatever you say, Tommy.*

"Put him in the Scarab. Even without the keys, going adrift is better than trying to swim for it with the current and the storm," Tom said. "I'll get the rest. There should be four of them, right? Tara, James, and the two others. That's everyone from the funeral accounted for. They've gotta be upstairs. Be ready to cut the line if Owen beats me back down."

"Then what'll you do?" Nate imagined his face as open as a child's. He'd scripted every possible twist in this conversation the moment he laid eyes on the injured boy. Now he just had to wait for his cues and remember his lines.

"The patrol boats and fire ship will be here eventually. The lake's dangerous, but some of this stuff will float."

"But what about the pilings? It's not the Atlantic, but one bad hit and—"

"There's no other way to do it." Tom said this in a way that told Nate that his thoughts had already moved on, up the spiral stairs to the Century Room to meet whatever awaited him there.

Nate nodded and turned back to the boy. He inspected the bandage to make sure it would hold. He handled the teen's skull as delicately as if it were a cracked egg.

"I bet you're a good doctor." Tom's voice was thick and just a whisper above the lashes of rain whipping the windows. "I bet you're a good dad."

When he was finished, Nate shoved his hands under the boy's frail body. He grunted with exertion as he hefted the skinny form. The kid couldn't weigh much more than a hundred pounds, but Nate knew he had to make it look good.

He started to favor his right hand, and let his right knee buckle under the new imbalance. All the while cradling the boy's head and keeping his cervical spine as straight as possible.

"He must only weigh, like—" Tom dove to catch Nate from toppling.

"My hand," Nate said. He made his thumb tremble as he raised it to the light. Even without the tremor it looked convincing. The base of the digit was a swell of flesh the color of roast beef and the size of a baseball. "Wait, maybe I can—" He tried to rearrange the boy over his right shoulder while trying to stabilize his head. It was impossible, of course, but he needed Tom to see that for himself.

It took Tom a moment, but he got there eventually. He swore under his breath. "Goddamnit." He pulled the boy out of Nate's grasp. "I'll be back in a minute. Stay here. Don't go upstairs without me."

Nate made sure the boy's head was as supported as it could be, then he pulled the flashlight from Tom's hand. "I'm just going to take a quick look at that hatchway."

"Hold up," Tom said. "Nate!"

But Nate didn't hesitate as he hurried back toward the kitchen and jammed his head into the strange space in the wall. He flicked the light up and down. It was a shaft of raw wood, ribbed with supports that could serve as a ladder. The base of the chute terminated in the undercroft, but the top of it appeared to go above the Century Room, perhaps all the way up to one of the Night Ship's decorative spires. Generations of cobwebs clotted with dust tensed and relaxed as if caught in a giant's breath. Had that been a leg? Nate adjusted the light to see straight up the shaft. Impossible to tell.

"Must've been a tight fit. He's built like a sasquatch." Tom was behind Nate, squatting on the floor and peering over his shoulder. In his arms, the boy was dramatically motionless. "I don't think we should split up."

"We've got to get this kid out of here, and you're the only one who can carry him. I'll wait for you and keep my eyes and ears open."

"I don't believe you'll stay put."

"Then you'd better hurry." He shoved the flashlight back into Tom's hand.

"Wait," Tom said. He maneuvered himself and the boy so that Nate could reach his sidearm.

"Keep the light and keep the gun," Nate said.

"If I can't be here, then I want you—"

A cascade of crashes quaked the pier. It wasn't thunder this time. It was shattering glass and screaming steel and splintering wood. The Night Ship was dying.

Tom was going to say something else, so Nate beat him to it. "The last time I shot a gun, all I had to do was spam the A button. If you weren't talking so much, you'd already be on your way back." He allowed a hint of the Storm King into his voice. "*Go,* Tom. And cradle his head."

Nate couldn't see Tom's face, but he didn't need to. He could have sketched it line for line. He held the kitchen door open, then helped support the boy as Tom scaled the oven that blocked the entrance to the undercroft. Before taking the service stairs, Tom turned back to him.

"Nate, I—"

"Christ, Tom, just *go*. Try to get back before the entire pier collapses."

He listened to his friend descend the dark stairs.

Nate didn't know what would be necessary to get the children off this pier alive, but he knew it would be unpleasant. The future branched in a hundred ways, and the doors at the end of those halls opened into pain. Tom already carried all the burdens he could bear. If he could, Nate wanted to spare him from whatever came next.

Young lives were in the balance, among them Lucy's own brother and sister. Nate had to save them. No matter what it cost, he had to save them.

He slid out of his wingtips and padded once more across the kitchen to the swinging doors. His night vision had always been good. The nightclub was etched in gray scale pushed to the darkest edge of its spectrum, but not quite black.

Gradations of shadow and memory's blueprints guided him to the spiral stairs draped in disintegrating velvet. As he ascended, he let his hand brush against the shreds of fabric. Decades ago, it'd been lush and deep and rich, but everything decays. Everything ends.

He reached the top of the staircase and walked across the balcony that overlooked the dance floor. The shapes of rotting banquettes and chaise lounges stood sentinel along the walls. A hallway beyond the balcony led to a series of rooms once used for a panoply of illegal activities. Chandelier light used to catch the silk of men's tuxedos as they threw dice and laughed with one another. Upon these scarred floors, women in lace and feathers danced in clouds of cigar smoke. They were ghosts, but now something worse haunted these halls.

Far from the great windows of the dance floor, the Century Room was impermeably dark. Nate would've been able to see just as clearly with his eyes closed. He tried to sort the storm sounds from all the other whispers of the place. The ticks and cracks of the nearing fire. The surge and release of the lake. Somewhere in there someone must be breathing. Somewhere underneath everything else were young hearts convulsing with fear.

Unless he was too late.

He took the central hall slowly, his socked feet making no more than a shush across the floor. He sensed more than saw the rooms he passed. They were silent, but that didn't mean they were empty. If Owen had been in the walls, then he could be anywhere.

The hall continued. Nate tried to remember if this passage had always gone so deep into the building. For the first time, he wondered how it was possible for such a vast structure to exist on a pier in the first place. Multiple levels, warrens of halls and rooms. An entire world somehow stood upon these century-old pilings.

When it happened, Nate's ears were more helpful than his eyes.

The crack of a planted foot. The hiss of fabric chafing against fabric. The whirr of something slicing through the air at tremendous speed.

Nate had time only to raise his arm to his face before the blow struck him. A baton or bat of some kind. He had a flash of standing in a lab, the sound of glass shattering, his body accepting the punishment of a lacrosse stick from the bulbs of his knees to the quiff of his head.

Another assault, but Nate's old skills resurfaced. Despite the dark, he caught the baton in his palms. Ignoring the alarms from his hurt thumb, he yanked his attacker toward him and torqued them both to the floor. The figure beneath him was too small to be Owen.

"James?"

"I *knew* it was you," James said. He writhed underneath Nate. Nate pulled the weapon from the boy's grip and tossed it away. It felt like the baseball bat he'd seen the kids with earlier.

"Where's Owen?"

"Get *off* me."

"Where're the others?"

"James?" A whisper came from nearby.

"Move the couch back and lock the goddamn door, Teej."

Nate's pupils imploded in a supernova of light.

"Teej!"

"James, he's not even wearing rain gear."

Nate felt dangerously vulnerable in the glare of the flashlight's beam. Like a spotlighted actor or a prisoner attempting a doomed escape.

"Look at him, James," Tara said. "Just look at him."

Nate still squinted against the light as the boy slowed his struggling.

"What happened to you?" she asked. Nate remembered that his face was smeared in blood from colliding with the pile of furniture obstructing the stairs from the undercroft.

"A lot. We have to get out of here. But turn off the light. He'll find us."

"We aren't going anywhere with you," James said.

They were about the same height, but Nate had no trouble pulling the young man up by his shirt collar. James sputtered as Nate dragged him through the doorway where Tara stood.

"It's *him!*" a boy screamed from the far corner of the room. Nate recognized him as the one who'd menaced him with rebar a few hours earlier. The boy backed away, into the pierced goth girl—the last of the four teens to account for.

The goth girl shushed him and draped her arms protectively around his shoulders. "Quiet, Carlos," she said.

"Shut the door," Nate told Tara. They didn't have time for this, but he also didn't have time to manhandle all four of them downstairs one by one. He had to convince them he wasn't their enemy. He felt where the bat had struck his arm. A contusion was blossoming along his ulna. Battered but not broken.

He could finally see Tara now that the full blaze of the flashlight wasn't in his eyes. She shrank from him, but Nate thought this was due more to guilt than fear.

"What's burning?" the goth girl asked. Medea's winds and the lake's lamentations filled the room with peaks and troughs of sound.

"Everything. There's a boat and a kayak down at the launch, and we don't have the keys for the Scarab, but—"

"Where's Pete?" Tara asked.

"Pete's fine. He's with the police right now."

"Oh, well, I guess everything's just *great,* then," James snarled, giving Nate a full dose of Bennett family venom. He yanked himself free of Nate's grip and stalked into the shadows at the opposite end of the room.

"What about Mikey?" the boy, Carlos, asked. He and the goth girl edged alongside Tara, closer to the light. "The man was hitting him and—"

"Mikey was hurt pretty badly," Nate said, assuming Mikey was the boy they'd found downstairs with the head wound. "Tommy— Deputy Buck—is taking him to one of the boats. We've got to get down there, too."

The room they were in was both long and wide. Tara's flashlight illuminated the patch of floor where everyone but James was huddled. What Nate could see of the walls bristled with curls of shredded paint. Dark striations stained the plaster below the paint like the thick arteries and spindly capillaries of a cardiovascular system, as if the Night Ship itself was alive.

"How did you get in here?" the goth girl asked. "We blocked all the ways in and made sure every window was boarded over."

"You barricaded *yourselves* in here?" Nate assumed it'd been Owen who'd clogged the exits and shifted the oven in order to keep the teens from escaping, though it was hard to imagine how even Owen could have done this all on his own so quickly.

The goth girl scowled at him. "This is our place."

For a moment, Nate was stupefied—then he remembered what

this pier used to mean to him. This was a place of his own, where he could be the truest version of himself. Or that had been the delusion. The problem was that the Night Ship was a trap masquerading as a haven.

"James said you weren't going to scare us out of our own home," Carlos said.

"And you're not going to," James said from the light's perimeter. Nate had tossed away his baseball bat, but James now picked up a stalk of metal that might have once been part of a floor lamp. The boy was so angry. His rage was as blinding as Nate's own had once been. "We aren't going to fall for your tricks. What're you trying to get us to do?"

"Owen's trying to kill us. Can't you smell the smoke? He set the Night Ship on fire. He clubbed Mikey. He killed Maura." Nate's shoulders dropped. Exhaustion took the steel from his spine. "He killed Lucy."

There was a moment of perfect silence in the room.

"And he's going to kill us next. We have to get down to the launch." Nate reopened the door to the room. "*Please.* Your hurt friend's down there. We don't have any more time."

Carlos and the goth girl looked back at James and then at Tara, and then at each other. Nate willed for them to move, and he could have dropped to his knees in relief when they did.

James took a step forward as if to stop them from leaving, though he didn't. His face was alabaster in the light, his jaw clenched like a vise. But his eyes, his eyes were raw with pain.

"You need to be quick, but you also need to be quiet," Nate said as the duo passed him and stepped into the hall. The path to the launch was currently clear, but he didn't know where Owen was. The pair didn't have a light, but these children were of the Night Ship. They'd find their way.

"He killed her," Tara said, as the sound of her friends' footfalls diminished. She didn't say this as if it were a question.

"You're lying," James said, but there was no conviction in his words. He looked at Tara. A tear glistened on the precipice of his chin.

"He—" Nate's throat constricted. A sound came from his mouth, but it wasn't a word.

"It's been Owen Liffey this whole time?" Tara asked.

Nate nodded because he didn't trust himself to speak.

"We couldn't see who came at us," she said. "We were all downstairs sleeping. Mikey started screaming. There was blood all over him, and then we saw this guy in a raincoat and hood. But it was only for a second. The man started breaking the lanterns and we all ran up here—" Her eyes were wide and liquid. She looked so much like Lucy. "We thought it was you."

It made sense that Owen would take out the lights. If the teens never saw him, they couldn't identify him. Even if some of them escaped the Night Ship, Owen could still try to scapegoat Nate for the rampage.

Nate kept forgetting that Owen was deranged, but not stupid.

"Owen Liffey killed Lucy," James muttered to himself. As if hearing this in his own voice would help him make sense of it. "Owen killed Lucy."

"I thought we blocked everything," Tara said. "What did we miss?"

"There are passages in the walls," Nate said. "Just like in the stories. We never found them, but I guess Owen did."

"Someone tried to get in here right after we wedged the couch against the door," Tara said. "He almost broke it down. It took all of us to hold it. Then he stopped, and when we didn't hear anything else for a while, James went out to take a look."

James looked furious again, but for once this anger wasn't directed at Nate.

"I don't know where he is," Nate said. "But the kitchen stairs are clear now. We can make it down there. If we see him he won't be able to stop all of us." If it came down to it, he'd waylay Owen long enough for the kids to escape.

"The Night Ship's burning." Tara turned to her brother. "We have to go."

James closed his eyes and then nodded, suddenly looking completely spent. The truth was hard, especially when it changed on you. He let the metal rod clatter to the floor, and took a few steps toward the door, then stopped and turned back to the shadows.

All at once, the dark behind James shifted.

Tara screamed. It was a banshee's wail, but it barely reached its full pitch before Owen had an arm as thick as a tree trunk wrapped around her brother's neck.

Twenty-six

Tara's scream didn't fade so much as end. Choked as her twin's breath was cut, as if the two of them shared the same thread of a windpipe.

In the circle of the flashlight's beam, Owen was a monolith of black behind James. He wore the same raincoat he used to wear on Thunder Runs. With its hood cowled over his face, he might have stepped from any kind of nightmare.

"Lower the light," Owen said. The calm of his voice was even more disturbing than the shade of purple ripening across James's face. The boy kicked at Owen's shins and jabbed elbows backward into the iron of the man's chest. He may as well have fought a mountain.

The beam stuttered as Tara obeyed.

The flashlight's new position illuminated the floor behind Owen, where Nate noticed a semi-digested rug in the swath of its light. A corner of it was curled against an open trapdoor that seemed designed to blend into the floor's hardwood. Another access to the hidden passages that connected to the hatchway by the dance floor.

"I guess I shouldn't be surprised, Nate." Owen cleared his throat. Nate's eyes began to weep from the smoke. His soft palate had acquired a harsh, thick texture.

"Let the kid breathe, Owen."

"Don't tell me you're on their side. These kids"—he shook James without a hint of exertion—"must have committed about fifty crimes in the last two weeks. Some of them felonies. Hell, don't forget that before the week's up they might even add murder to the list."

Nate batted aside a flash of his grandmother in the ICU, lanced by tubes and swaddled in gauze. Next to him, Tara shrank deeper into the dark.

"You've got to think this through." Nate's voice was even, but his mind raced. Both the baseball bat and the metal rod were out of reach. He'd never get to them before Owen snapped James's neck, which was the most present danger. Tommy would reach them soon, but perhaps not soon enough. Nate knew he'd have to talk his way out of this.

He tried to imagine the texture of Owen's mind. He knew what his old friend wanted; Nate just had to convince him that this was precisely the thing that he offered.

Smoke rippled across the ceiling, and their futures narrowed by the moment.

"Where are the other kids?" Owen asked. "I thought they were all up here."

"They're safe."

"Try again." Owen hefted James, and the boy's face darkened. His legs flailed like those of a child's toy.

"They're downstairs. But it doesn't matter, Owen, because—"

Owen took two gigantic strides toward Nate. When he did, Nate realized that he barely came up to the man's chin. Every cell in his body told him to run, but he buried this impulse in ice. He still had two children to save.

At Owen's approach, Tara backpedaled into the doorway, and Nate thought that it was this that had stopped Owen in his tracks.

"No, Tara. You don't want to leave," Owen said. "That would be very bad for your brother. Trust me on this one." Then to Nate, "They know too much. You know that."

"It doesn't matter what they know. It's what they *say* that counts," Nate said. He spoke in the voice of the Storm King. A blade of confidence polished with cunning. "They're not innocent. You said it yourself: They're in a world of trouble. We can use that, Owen."

Owen had maintained the upper hand during their last conversation, but that had been back in his own basement while Nate's senses had been dulled by homemade chloroform. Now, the razors of Nate's mind were sharpened by adrenaline. Now, they were in the Night Ship, which was *his* domain.

"It's too late for that." Owen shook his head, but Nate spied something in his eyes. Doubt? Hope? Whatever it was, it was something he could use.

"Of course it isn't too late." Nate sighed. For a few minutes he needed Owen to believe he was the Storm King again. "We both want each other's silence. So we can make a deal with them. We can still get out of this."

"I know you're trying to get into my head, Nate. What do you mean, a 'deal'?"

"We don't want to go to jail!" Tara said.

Nate glanced at her, a bit surprised. He couldn't have scripted that better.

Conflicting emotions clashed across Owen's face. Nate could imagine the gears of the man's mind spinning and grating. Remembering the past while trying to chart the future. Balancing who Nate was against what Owen had done. It boiled down to a single question: Was Nate his enemy or, even after everything that had happened, was there a chance that Nate might still be his friend?

The big guy loosened his grip enough for James to steal a single harrowing breath.

"We've got to show them that we can be trusted," Nate said.

"Then we come up with a story that works for everyone. That's how we'll do it."

"And we can?" Owen asked, frowning. Nate could see him trying to keep up, trying to anchor himself to something that was true. "We can—be trusted?"

"Of course!" Nate laughed, then winked at him.

It was a kind of magic, playing the puzzle box of another's mind to get a desired outcome. Not true magic so much as sleight of hand. A person could only be fooled if they didn't know where to look, and if they, deep down, wanted to believe the lie in the first place.

"Get the others, Tara," James choked out. "We've got to get our stories straight."

The Bennett twins, they were quick, Nate had to admit. Just like their older sister.

"Come with me, James," Tara said.

"No," Owen said. "He stays here."

Nate nodded. Like this was a hard-won concession and not another kind of trap.

Because he knew he'd just hooked Owen, and soon the man's mind would begin to work against him. Psychology was a wonderful tool if you knew how to use it. Owen thought he'd succeeded in holding on to James, whereas in actuality all he'd done was lose Tara. Soon, his cognitive dissonance would begin to use one poor decision to reinforce another. Soon, Nate's hook would work its way so deep that Owen would beg to be reeled in. Then they could get out of here.

"Hurry back," Nate told Tara. He turned away from Owen and stepped toward her. "The air up here's getting worse by the second." *Cast off,* Nate mouthed to her.

"Okay," Tara said, reading his lips. But she didn't go. Eyes swollen with tears, she glanced back at her twin.

"*Go,* Teej. It's already hard enough to breathe!" James croaked into Owen's sleeve. *I love you.* Nate watched the boy's eyes signal to Tara. *I love you, and I need you to be safe.*

Nate wished Lucy had lived to see these two grow up.

Tara placed the flashlight on the ground, so Nate didn't see her face as she left. He heard her sniffle and could imagine her tears, but they were all beginning to tear and drip and choke.

"So how's this going to work?" Owen asked. He still sounded unsure, but now he'd come too far and committed too much to afford doubt. This was a game of confidence, and he had already lost.

"First we have to get off this pier," Nate said. "The fire boat will be here soon, and we don't want them to find us. We can go to Johnny's house to regroup."

Nate had moved closer to the doorway during Tara's exit. The baseball bat was in the hallway, hidden from Owen's sight, but all Nate had to do was stoop to reach it.

"And then?" Owen was desperate to believe Nate. The Storm King always had a plan.

Then it all fell apart.

"And then you turn yourself in." Tom's voice came from over Nate's shoulder. "It's over, Owen."

"Tommy!" Owen sounded perplexed, but also somehow delighted. "Just like the old days! Too bad Johnny's on the disabled list. He always hated being left out."

"Pete Corso's with the police, O," Tom said.

Nate watched most of the doors to the future slam shut.

"The police?" Owen said, still not quite getting it. "You're police, Tommy, but you're my friend, too, aren't you?"

Owen was indeed doomed no matter what, but there was no advantage in him knowing it. Quite the opposite. Even a harmless animal would attack when cornered, and Owen was as far from harmless as Nate could imagine. Tom had ruined everything.

Nate had to come up with another way out.

"Did you hear me?" Tom asked. He had his gun out of its holster. It wasn't pointed at Owen, not yet. "The kid you've kept tied up since last night is with the cops. Officers are at your house. They're in your basement. They're with your mother. Do you understand?"

The last strands of the spell Nate had been weaving collapsed around them.

"You lied?" Owen blinked at Nate with the stupefied look of a child who'd just pulled Santa's beard to find their father's face underneath. "You were never going to help me."

"It's finished, Owen," Tom said. "There's no reason for this. Let the kid—" He cut himself off with a stutter of staccato coughs. Nate had covered his nose with his sleeve, but his head still rang from the fumes. They had to get out of here.

"No." Owen shook his head, the peak of his hood shifting from side to side. "We can still get out of this. We always get out of it." Heard often enough, even the most audacious lie sounded like the truth.

James's face darkened as he wheezed in the acrid air and Owen tightened his grip.

"Don't make it worse than it already is," Tom said.

Owen had the boy's slim neck in his titanic grasp. Tom had a gun. The Night Ship was burning. The room was filling with smoke. Nate had no weapon or leverage. They careened toward something terrible, and he was somehow only a passenger.

"We can still figure this out," Owen said. "What's another lie or two?" A quake of collapsing infrastructure shuddered across the pier. "Did Nate tell you how I covered for you, Tommy? Did he tell you how I saved you that night you pushed Lucy into the water?"

"I've got an idea," Nate said.

Owen laughed, or it began as a laugh. After a second it turned into a hacking cough, though he didn't loosen his grip on James, who was now lank in his arms.

"Hear me out," Nate said. "But first, we've got to go downstairs. That'll buy us a couple minutes before we die of smoke inhalation." The commands of the Storm King no longer held sway as they once did, but his logic was indisputable. If they stayed up here, they would die, and soon.

Nate walked from the room without waiting for a response. The key was to exit quickly and leave Owen too stunned to do anything but follow.

Once in the hall, he sprinted for the stairs. Flames still hadn't reached the threshold of the nightclub, but the air up here in the Century Room was poison. Nate's balance faltered and his vision narrowed as he took the spiral steps. He had to rely on his arms clutching the banister as he half-ran, half-fell down the gyre.

Black smoke now poured from the glass doors to the promenade. It rippled upward to the ceiling like whitewater captured in a long exposure. Beyond the furniture the children had piled in front of the exit, the glow from the fire had burgeoned to a noontime intensity.

Nate expected some negotiation between Tom and Owen as they choreographed their exit from the Century Room, but he knew he didn't have much time.

More collapses shuddered from the landward side of the pier. Their crashes were answered with blasts of thunder from Medea.

The tall, south-facing windows had been meticulously boarded. Nate hurried to one near the back of the club, in the seating area beyond the pedestal that held the husk of the shattered aquarium. Most of these planks had been in place back when Nate was in high school, but others were fresh additions. The slats looked as thick and formidable as a wall, but Nate knew this place. He knew the Night Ship was rotted from its spires down to its pilings. The wood was like clay under his fingers. Even with his injured hand, it didn't take long to rip out enough of the rusted nails to clear a section from the base of the window up to the height of his shoulders.

Only when he looked through the cracked pane during a blink of lightning did he realize the poor state of the boardwalk abutting this window. At least a third of the walkway flanking this side of the pier had fallen away. They'd have to be careful. Nate would risk braving the storm-pitched waters only as a last resort. The lake couldn't be trusted.

Barking coughs sounded from the stairs while a flashlight beam cut through the bank of smoke that deepened against the arced beams of the ceiling. Tom must have forced Owen down ahead of him. When the huge man appeared at the base of the stairs, he had James slung precariously over his shoulder.

Owen wasn't bearing the weight of the kid as easily as he had. The thickening air must have taken its toll on him. When he staggered from the stairs, Nate rushed to him with one palm raised in peace.

The big guy flinched when Nate helped him ease the boy to the floor. Then he took a few steps forward, bent over, and began coughing sludge up from his lungs. James was still unconscious, from either the smoke or Owen's choke hold. Nate made sure the boy's airways were clear and that he was breathing.

Owen retched in the dark, and Nate went to him. They weren't supposed to fight each other. The universe was ruthless and cruel in the way it stacked chance upon chance. *It* was the enemy, not other people: least of all your own friends. It was only with your friends that you had a chance. But these were the ideals of better people born to luckier lives.

From the flashlight's bounding beam, Nate knew that Tom was still on the floor above, but he'd reach them soon.

So many emotions churned inside of Nate. This place. This town. These people. They conjured so many things in him.

"You killed Lucy, but her death isn't all on you, O," Nate said. He wondered when was the last time Owen had received compassion. He wondered if anyone had ever told him that it's never too late to be good. He grabbed Owen's shoulder, as if they were friends again. Like they weren't both monsters. As if all the years of rot had been pared away and they were back in that very first storm when Owen was a chubby kid with sleepy eyes and Nate was little more than undead. "It's my fault, too. I see that now. And I'm sorry."

"You're sorry?" Owen was winded, still bent at the waist with his hands braced above his knees. He spat something thick onto the floor. "That doesn't change anything." His voice was a rasp almost lost beneath the pounding of rain and the crescendo of flames from the promenade. "You said you had an idea," he said. "A way to get us out of this."

"The other kids all got away, O. But I've still got to save this one. I can't let you stop me."

"Just tell me your idea," Owen wheezed.

"You're not going to like it." Nate dropped to his knee and plunged a fistful of rusted nails into the Achilles tendon of Owen's left leg. The man's scream sliced through the roar of the fire and the howl of the storm.

So few of the Lake's stories had heroes.

Nate scrambled to get James clear of the hulking man, but he wasn't fast enough. As Owen toppled, he grabbed Nate's ankle, sending him hard into the floor.

"Liar!" Owen roared. "Traitor! Still trying to play me like all your other puppets." He yanked Nate toward him. Nate pawed at the planks he sprawled across. He knew he had to stand, he had to get clear. But he couldn't.

"Pull a string and watch the Porker dance!" Owen made a sound that was somewhere between a cough and a howl. He pounded Nate in the ribs with the hammer of his fist, and it was like being hit by a car.

"You think I want your apologies?"

The pain in Nate's side was worse than muscular trauma. At least one rib was cracked. He tried to call for Tom, but he could do no more than gasp.

Owen tried and failed to get to his feet, swearing with the pain that must have come from using his ruined leg. One of the nails Nate had stabbed Owen with clattered to the floor. Four inches long, dripping black, and gnarled by decades of winters. There were six more where that came from.

"You know when I actually wanted something from you? When we were kids. When Mom cut a chunk out of me once a week. And where were you? Where was the Storm King?" He kneeled on Nate's spine and ground into the vertebrae. The pain was electric. Nate spasmed from his toes to his fingers. "But you *still* think you call the shots here. You're not a god, Nate. Here, I'll prove it to you." Owen grabbed a fistful of Nate's hair and pulled his head back. Pinned by Owen's weight, Nate's spine stretched and bent, and his brain couldn't tell him where all the agony came from.

If the wind would listen he'd speak it his love. He'd telegraph it from Medea's coils across the storm-ravaged miles to the New Jersey hills where the best pieces of himself resided.

The sound of the gunshot felt like it was enough to knock a person over. It pulsed through his ears as it rang through the nightclub's halls.

"Tommy!" Owen bellowed. Pain had ratcheted its pitch, but his voice had regained that same strange delight as before. He released Nate's hair and rolled off his back. Dropping back to the scarred floor, Nate was as still as a living creature could be. Each ragged breath sank him deeper into the planks.

"What took you so long?" Owen asked.

"Checked the other rooms," Tom said. "Had to make sure there wasn't anyone else up there."

Nate could feel his fingers as they probed the splinters of wood he lay on. He couldn't see his feet, but they seemed to move when he asked them to.

"You're a credit to your profession, you know that?"

Nate experimented with bringing his knees into his stomach. His right side screamed. Its protest was noted, its concerns respectfully deferred until some future time.

"He doesn't have a plan for us. Just another of his lies. So'd you think about what I said, Tom?" Owen asked. "I'm right, aren't I?"

Nate rolled onto his side to look at the pair. The slant of Tom's figure looked distressed, but he'd reached the dance floor in better shape than Owen. His flashlight was in one hand and his gun was in the other, pointed to the air into which Nate assumed it had been fired. He had a strip of cloth tied across his nose and mouth.

"Maybe."

"*Definitely.* This can all be traced back to him. It's all his fault, and he even knows it. He just told me as much." Though it must have been torture, the huge man pulled himself back into a standing position.

Nate also made the excruciating transition from his side to his feet. He'd hobbled Owen, but not disabled him. He had to get James out of here.

"You, me, Lucy, Grams, these kids. It all started with Nate. You know what the Storm King would say. All that suffering. All that pain. Someone's got to *pay* for it."

Nate would have given anything to see Tom's face.

"And the other kids, they don't know you pushed Lucy into the lake that night."

"It was an accident."

The glass door to the promenade shattered and the glare of flames filled the nightclub. Long shadows leapt and dove across the walls.

"You know that doesn't matter. You're part of the reason he lost Lucy, and the Storm King doesn't forgive."

Nate stooped to lift James from the floor. The teen was thin, but he was dead weight. Nate's vision went white when something in his side clicked out of place with the strain. When this pain decreased to a simmer, he began to drag James inch by inch toward the window from which he'd cleared the planks.

"We can still talk our way out of this. The kids'll listen to you," Owen told Tom. "It's like when we burned the Deckers' house back in high school. That fire bound us all together. Just like killing Lucy tied the two of us together. And that kind of makes up for all the bad stuff, doesn't it? When something good comes out of it?"

The smoke had fully erased the Century Room. Flames devoured the pile of furniture that had blocked the exit to the promenade.

"It's too late for him, Tom," Nate said. Talking was like lighting his throat on fire. "Come here and we'll get out of here together. I don't blame you for Lucy, and neither would she."

"You can't trust him," Owen said. "After everything he did to us? How can you believe a thing he says? Look at my leg, Tom. Look at what he did to me. You really think he'll do what's right for you instead of what's right for him?"

Nate was nearly to the window, but he felt the approaching inferno like hands on his back.

"He's getting away, Tom," Owen said. "He's got the kid, and he's got your future, too. You'll lose everything when it gets out. Your job, your family. What'll your dad say? If they don't put you in jail they'll run you out of town. Then where'll you go? With *him*? Just like in college, huh? He'll have you over for dinner three times a week, right?" Owen laughed. "But just imagine life without him, Tom."

Fingers closed around Nate's bicep. Nate turned, utterly relieved. The cloth across Tom's mouth was gone. But the look on his friend's face wiped clear Nate's smile and drained what remained of his strength.

"I can't do it, Nate," Tom said. "I just can't." The hand holding the gun came up.

"Imagine being free," Owen said.

Tom's face was anguish. "I'm sorry."

He hurled himself at Nate.

Upon impact, Nate and the boy he carried crashed through the window, landing hard on the boardwalk. Through the shattered glass, he saw Tom turn back to Owen and point his Glock at the dance floor. The rotted wood beneath Nate buckled.

Then Nate was in the air, falling through the broken boardwalk and into the bottomless mouth of the lake.

One moment he was suspended like a gull on the wind, then he was under the surface. The body slam of its cold was more painful than Owen's foot in his side. Up and down, air and water, alive and dead. Everything became uncertain in the dislocation of the collision. But his arm was still crooked around James's limp body, and the last bubbles of his breath pointed him back to the living world. With a grip on James's shirt, he kicked them both for the surface.

When he was within arm's reach of the air, the purgatory of the lake exploded into the most glorious of dawns. The waters burst into rippling mosaics of flame shadowed with the lacework fractals of waves.

Twenty-seven

Worlds perish in all kinds of ways. The Night Ship both burned and drowned.

A blast of heat singed Nate's lungs as he broke through the surface and gasped for breath. He pulled James's head clear of the water. There was too much noise to hear if the boy was breathing. Nate had to put his ear to the teen's mouth to make sure he was still with him.

Above the waterline, the lake was undone.

Rafts of flaming debris flared amid whitecaps like cities burning across the tundra. Medea scoured water, smoke, steam, ash, and sparks into gusts that blazed and seared and chilled.

Nate's back took the brunt of the impact as the current crushed them into one of the pilings. Above them, the floor of the undercroft gaped with an enormous hole rimmed with fire. There'd been an explosion, Nate understood. One of the tanks of propane the children had kept in the nightclub. He was certain Tom had shot it on purpose.

Tom.

Nate screamed for his friend as the lake whisked him through the rest of the pilings. Something within the nightclub collapsed, and it dislodged a large section of the pier's undergirding. Its plunge reared walls of water that again submerged Nate. This time it was harder to kick back to the surface.

He had his arm slung around James's neck in the same way Owen had, though with the opposite intention. The boy lagged behind him as Nate struggled to keep them both afloat. Around them, torrents of fire reached for the sky and were whipped by the hurricane. Not all the wreckage from the pier was aflame. Shingles from the roof bobbed like leaves across the water. The waves broke against massive sheaths of rotted woodwork.

When he regained his breath, Nate again called for Tom. The wind swept away his voice. He could barely hear himself.

He watched as the Night Ship's last spire collapsed into a galaxy of sparks. They curled like a nebula into the storm and then were extinguished. With the end of the pier unsealed by the explosion, the hurricane fed the blaze within the promenade, sending it to the landward side like a blowtorch. Where the waves weren't black, they were dipped in flame.

He didn't know if the children had taken both the kayak and the motorboat, but it didn't matter because he couldn't see either.

James's face fell below the waves again, and Nate fought to give him a better angle, but it was impossible. The water was too rough. The waves crashed into them without pause, and Nate was at the end of his strength.

The current had them, and he couldn't see the shore.

His legs should have burned from the exertion of keeping afloat, but the water was so cold they'd gone numb. Another wave threw the two of them back under, but this time Nate saw something: a light ahead of him, but also underwater, where no fire could burn. He held James above him as he dunked his head again to look. It didn't make sense. Twin columns of illumination sliced through the clean water like the headlights of a car.

A car in the lake, Nate thought.

Impossible.

But it wasn't impossible. He knew this better than anyone.

He struck out for the lights and the current urged him along. Perhaps this was where the lake had always wanted him to go. He swallowed its water by the mouthful as he tried to breathe and keep James afloat. He passed debris on the way, but none of it was significant or stable enough for him to steal even a moment's rest.

The lake drew them closer to its center, and Nate let it. The town along the shore became a memory. Had he lost his mind? Nate wondered. He tried to remember the exact effects of carbon monoxide intoxication.

They were far from what remained of the Night Ship, but close to where Nate thought he'd seen the headlights. He confirmed this by another sojourn under the surface. Instead of two, there was now only a single beam of light, and he didn't know if this was good or bad.

A raft of flotsam was ahead. It had none of the contours of Victorian style woodwork. It wasn't furniture or a fairyland tower. It had the beacon of a lit flashlight fastened around one wrist and the profile of Nate's best friend.

Tom floated face-up, rocked by the waves. Nate shook and screamed at him but got no response. He couldn't tell if he was breathing. The skin of his face was cold, but so was Nate's own.

With his swollen hands, Nate grabbed the collar of Tom's raincoat and dragged him along with James. For a few moments this seemed like a possible way to continue.

Away from the blaze and smoke of the Night Ship it was easier to see the shore.

Far ahead he could see the stony beach where he'd once been both saved and damned.

The beach loomed and then receded. The currents had carried him this far only to tease him. He kicked for the shore, but the lake pulled him and the others away from land and up to its northern bulge. Its waves pummeled his face and flooded his throat. Tom's head fell below the water and Nate tried to lift him, but then James began to sink.

No longer burning, his arms felt like stones. They pulled him down along with Tom, James, and their sopping clothes. Deep into the cold water where his dead had waited so long for him.

In the flares of the storm, Nate saw the dim spike of a person on the beach ahead. She stood among the stones, her coat whipping in the gale like the shrouds of a wraith.

Perhaps June wanted him safe, but the universe was an uncertain place. What kind of ripples would saving him cause this time, she might wonder. Would a third chance bring more blue string than red? Impossible to know. Dangerous to guess.

This time he'd have to save himself.

His lungs screamed and his breath grew shallow. Above him cannon flashes burst and sparked in volleys between thunderheads.

Nate realized that he was drowning.

He was drowning.

He understood that they weren't going to make it. He'd killed his best friend and his first love's little brother.

"I'm sorry, Meg." Another mouthful of lake forced its way into him. "Livvy." His voice was torn by the roar of the storm and crushed by the relentless slaps of the waves. "I'm sorry, Tommy."

Lightning strobed the shore. A last glimpse of a world lost to him. The air crashed like a giant pounding against the door of the sky.

"Do you hear it, Nate?"

Tommy.

Nate didn't know how powerfully he'd been anchored until he was freed. His burdens, his regrets, loosed like weights through the colorless waters.

His friend's hand tightened on his wrist.

"Do you hear the thunder?"

THE STORM KING

THE TALE CHANGES with the teller.

One day, twins named for the two prettiest months of the year were born to a woman who could not bring herself to kill them.

One day, a man drove his family along a road that switchbacked into the clouds then plunged them under the waves.

One day, a clapboard farmhouse in the foothills burned in a barrage of hail.

The Lake loves its stories. They are told and shared and treasured.

But they aren't the truth.

Details are embellished, characters dropped or added or made composite.

The rendering of emotion and action through words is an uncertain alchemy.

You see, you change a story just by telling it.

And sooner or later the bottle runs dry, the boat returns to its slip, or the fire burns to coals. Every story ends.

But life? Life has loose ends.

...

THE NIGHT SHIP was gone.

Weeks after Medea, they were still clearing its debris from the shores. Parts of the promenade's iron ribs still arced from its charred base, but it would all be gone soon. Some of the Lake's hurricane recovery funds had been earmarked for its demolition. Nate watched crews chip away at its carcass. The sound of their saws glided across the waters to the Wharf like the calls of birds.

"You should show Livvy the beach," Grams said.

"Good idea. We can skip stones." Nate had taken all of them to the stony beach the day before. He'd had to carry Grams there, but she weighed only of bones and sweaters. It was difficult to reach the nook along the shore, but it had saved his life twice.

Fall was thick among them now. The leaves and their color were falling away, preparing for the drop into winter. The sky was blue and held nothing more sinister than cumulus clouds. Sailboats sliced across the silver water for the lake's northern bulge. But Nate and his grandmother had eyes only for what remained of the Night Ship.

"I wonder if they'll forget," Grams said. Her mind was like a damaged record. Sometimes it caught on repeat. Sometimes it played verses and tracks out of sequence. But if you knew the score well enough, you could follow the tune.

"They won't." He believed this.

Nate heard Livvy's staccato run before he saw her. She barely slowed before barreling right up to Grams's wheelchair.

"Johnny says the Night Ship ghosts could be anywhere now!" Her face was red from the wind, and her eyes were bright with delight.

"What should we do?" Grams asked.

"Run! We run!" She sprinted down the boardwalk, startling a flock of gulls into flight.

"Having them for coffee's more my speed, dear," Grams said.

Sometimes she was like her old self.

Johnny hobbled toward them on his crutches.

"You have a real way with her," Nate told him. "Should the therapist send bills to the Empire or directly to your home address?"

"Tell her a story, I thought." Johnny was out of breath. He was terrible with the crutches. "Kids like stories, right? The ice cream was where I went wrong. Where does she put it all?"

They watched Livvy terrorize the birds, sending them fleeing from railings to benches and back again.

Beyond her, Tom and Meg leaned against the boardwalk's railing, watching the demolition to the north. Tom wasn't in his uniform. He'd never wear a uniform again.

The Night Ship's destruction was a cataclysm, but a fairly self-contained one. When that world ended, it took many of its sins with it. But there were still consequences.

Owen was gone. Both Pete Corso and Nate had heard him confess to the murders of Maura Jeffers, Mr. Liffey, Mr. Vanhouten, and Lucy. The man's imprisonment and torture of his own mother proved him capable of such crimes. The story had its monster, and the monster was dead.

In one small way, the Storm King had been right about the equations of pain. Nate's Thunder Runs and the recent spree of vandalism these had inspired had mostly canceled each other out. The vandals who'd been stalked by Owen as the Night Ship burned firmly believed that Nate and Tom had saved their lives. They were even. Mostly.

Tom had resigned from the police force as soon as he was released from the hospital. There'd been an internal investigation. Nate wasn't sure what arrangements were made or deals struck, but Tom's father retired from his longtime post as Greystone Lake's chief of police soon after. Nate didn't know how much of Tom's involvement in Lucy's death or the chief's tampering with evidence had come to light. In hard times, small towns make their own rules. What Nate did know was that Johnny had made substantial campaign contributions to several local politicians facing difficult elections next year.

The Lake loved its stories, but it enjoyed its secrets, too.

Nate's phone chimed, and he pulled it from his pocket.

JAMES: INSPECTION GUY SAYS OK FOR TUES

Tom was managing the contractors tasked with rebuilding the Union, with James and Tara assisting. There was structural damage to the building, and it'd be months before it reopened. When it did, the twins would help manage the place.

"You're a kind boy," Grams said. Sometimes she wasn't there at all, and other times she seemed to possess a kind of telepathy.

"Working on it."

Nate understood now that the Storm King's equations of pain were problems that could never be balanced. One side was always in deficit. Its math was designed for reciprocity, its stakes going ever exponential.

Nate's grandmother would never be whole in either mind or body. Tara hadn't meant to hurt Grams when she set fire to the Union, but she had. It gnawed at Nate. Every day it was like a blade in his gut. The unfathomable unfairness of chance.

He had so little practice with forgiveness. When Grams repeated herself, or forgot trips to the stony beach, or was stumped by Livvy's name, he had to remind himself that Grams wouldn't blame Tara, and that she wouldn't want Nate to, either.

She'd tell him that it was never too late to be good.

Because everyone is guilty of something.

Everyone deserves to be punished.

So where does it end? Because it had to end. It had to.

For her part, Tara knew this clemency wasn't easy for Nate. That's what made it worth so much. That's what made it matter.

Still running at full speed, Livvy leaped at Tom. He had a welted scar cupped like a hand from his jaw to his left ear, but it didn't scare her. His eyes went wide for a moment before their collision. When he caught Livvy, his face broke into the same pure smile he'd had as a boy.

A pod of Daybreakers cut through the waters to the south. Their dry suits were dark flecks against the vast mirror of the lake. Nate couldn't tell if June was among this group of swimmers, but wherever she was, he hoped that the ghosts that drove her to these cold waters haunted her less fiercely than they had. He believed that she'd be happy with the way he planned to live this third life.

Strong but also true. Tough and also kind. Not assembled, but whole.

But to start it right, he knew he had to start it clean.

He'd told Meg everything. After surviving what he had, telling her about the boy he'd once been and the things he'd done hadn't been as hard as he'd feared. The truth had changed things in subtle ways between them, just as it had changed Nate himself. But they were okay. They were good. And this gift exceeded every other stroke of fortune Nate had enjoyed, because he knew he'd spend his life trying to deserve it.

Meg kissed Livvy's head, and their hair mingled in the wind. With Tom, the three of them grinned at something as they made their way toward Nate, Johnny, and Grams.

The vicious boy Nate used to be had a lot of ideas about the future, but he couldn't have imagined an afternoon like this. A day when power wasn't confused with happiness or fear mistaken for love.

If he could, Nate would tell that boy that a life built on revenge and buttressed by rage is no kind of life at all. He'd tell him that mercy and strength could be the same thing. That no matter how dark things seem, good days are ahead of him. Really, he cannot imagine how good these days will be.

Meg, Tom, and Livvy reached Nate. A different kind of smile on each of their faces.

The lake returns what it takes.

It's a warning, but it's also a prayer.

Acknowledgments

THIS NOVEL WOULDN'T have been possible without Mark Tavani's clear-eyed vision and razor-sharp advice. I also owe a colossal debt of gratitude to Tracy Devine, who brought this book through its critical last drafts with great insight and devotion, even going so far as to take the manuscript with her on an enriching sojourn to France and Germany. It was a very lucky manuscript, and I'm a very lucky author to have had two such fine editors lend their talents to me.

An essential sounding board for tribulations both great and small, my agent, Elisabeth Weed, has been a source of unfaltering support for *The Storm King* since the days when this novel was little more than an image in my head of a broken boy walking down an abandoned pier.

I'm deeply indebted to Jane Fleming Fransson, Alessandra Lusardi, Robin Wasserman, and Sarah Landis for their heroic work through the course of many (many!) drafts. Their smart counsel and incisive notes were the keys to puzzling out many tricky moments within these chapters.

The guidance I received from Jennifer Hershey, Jenny Meyer, Jody Hotchkiss, Hanna Gibeau, Betsy Cowie, Dana Murphy, and Hallie Schaeffer was expert, essential, and enormously appreciated.

I owe special thanks to Mary-Kate Duffy, who was both a valuable set of eyes on these pages and an invaluable cheerleader every step of the way. Gigantic thanks, too, to Pat Gilhooly for being an excellent medical consultant, photographer, and mom.

Writing is a mental game and William Duffy, Kevin Duffy, Ann Marie Ricks, Fiona Duffy, Bridget Raines, Aaron Raines, Theresa Maul, Robert Maul, Carolyn Maul, Barbara Mulvee, Lynn Weingarten, Charlotte Hamilton, Ivy Koelliker, Phil Wood, Beth McCarty Wood, Susan Burns Halldorson, Chris Halldorson, Dan Poblocki, Katy Burfitt Rockwood, and Carla Francis all helped keep me in fighting shape. Thank you for your boundless enthusiasm and encouragement.

I'm also very grateful to the excellent and talented team at Ballantine, especially Gina Centrello, Kara Welsh, Kim Hovey, Susan Corcoran, Kristin Fassler, Greg Kubie, Quinne Rogers, Jessica Yung, Matt Schwartz, Vincent La Scala, Paolo Pepe, Carlos Beltrán, Michelle Daniel, Debbie Glasserman, Chuck Thompson, and Karen Richardson.

ABOUT THE AUTHOR

BRENDAN DUFFY is an editor and the author of *House of Echoes*. He lives in New York.

brendanduffybooks.com
Facebook.com/BrendanDuffyAuthor
Twitter: @Brendan_Duffy